A Second Chance

A Second Chance
Book Four
of the
Belanger Creek Ranch Series

By
Gloria Antypowich

A Second Chance

Copyright@ 2014 by Gloria Antypowich
Canadian Copyright Number:
Library and Archives Canada Cataloguing

ISBN
Softcover: 1512202932
E-book: 9781512202939

All rights reserved. No part of this book may be reproduced or transmitted in any form or by any means, electronic or mechanical, including photocopying, recording, or by any information storage and retrieval system, without permission in writing from the copyright owner.

This is a work of fiction. Names, characters, places and incidents either are the product of the author's imagination or are used fictitiously, and any resemblance to any actual persons, living or dead, events, or locales is entirely coincidental.

Published by Gloria Antypowich
Contemporary Fiction/Western Romance/Adult content

5 stars! Reviewed By Rabia Tanveer for Readers' Favorite

In A Second Chance by Gloria Antypowich, a mother has to make a decision. Either run away with her son or believe him when he says that the man they both love loves them back. Sarah Brite lived her life in fear of her violent husband. When the time came to choose between him and her son's safety, she chose her son. Together, they leave him and come to live at Belanger Creek Ranch. The peaceful community lives together like a family and finally Sarah finds time to actually breathe freely.

However, Grayson McNaughton has her on the edge. He is handsome, charming, and her son Taylor is getting closer to him every day. After many futile attempts at ignoring the attention, she finally gives in and lets herself be happy. Just when she gets comfortable, a revelation from Grayson's past makes her shudder. She wants to leave with Taylor, but he does not want to go. He believes Grayson and does not want to leave him behind. What will Sarah do? Should she listen to her son, or should she listen to her heart?

A Second Chance by Gloria Antypowich is an outstanding novel. Gloria did an amazing job. She showed a clear picture of really happens in the lives of single parents and how cautious they are in starting a new relationship. I really liked Taylor; where Sarah was over cautious, he was cool headed and believes Grayson the person, not his past. He is a really cool kid, and he will turn out to be an awesome man. I really enjoyed this book.

Note from the Reviewer to the Author:
I really enjoyed it. Although, I have not read the rest of the books, I'm looking forward to more from you with Grayson, Taylor and Sarah.

***
5 stars! Reviewed By Janelle Alex, Ph.D. for Readers' Favorite

A Second Chance is the fourth book in the Belanger Creek Ranch series authored by Gloria Antypowich, and this one has quite an interesting plot. A young woman, Sarah Brite, is on the run and hiding with her ten-year-old son, Taylor. The boy's father is a violent man and has already found Sarah and Taylor numerous times. With threats upon their lives, Sarah keeps her past a secret while working and living at Belanger Creek Ranch. That is until Grayson McNaughton finally encourages her to share her secret with him. He would love to build a romantic relationship with Sarah and be a father to Taylor, but he has his own deep, dark secret. When Sarah learns what that secret is, she pushes Grayson away. However, a freak accident on the ranch ends up bringing the two of them together again. Antypowich doesn't end the story there though. Instead, she continues on even after Grayson, Sarah and Taylor become a true family.

Gloria Antypowich writes with more in depth details than the average romance novel. You may find this style refreshing as it gives you more mundane details of the characters' lives or you may find it uninteresting. Also, there a slew of characters to keep track of in the Belanger Creek Ranch series; therefore it makes it easier if you read all the books in the series to avoid confusion. No matter, A Second Chance is quite enticing and sweetly romantic with an edge of suspense. To top it all off, Antypowich's main characters in A Second Chance are the epitome of second chances. Well done!
***
5 stars! Reviewed By Gisela Dixon for Readers' Favorite

A Second Chance (The Belanger Creek Ranch Series Book 4) by Gloria Antypowich is the fourth book in the Belanger

Creek Ranch romance series. This book takes place on Belanger Creek Ranch whose owners, Colt and Frank Thompson, were introduced to us in the first book in the series. However, one can read each of the books in this series independently of each other.

A Second Chance starts with an introduction to Sarah Brite and her young son, Taylor, both of whom are on the run and in hiding from Taylor's father. On the ranch, they meet Grayson McNaughton, who himself has some dark secrets in his past. Soon, Taylor grows to look upon Grayson as a father figure and becomes quite close to him. Sarah and Grayson are quietly attracted to each other as well until secrets from their past start coming out, casting a shadow on all of their lives. Can they ever become a family? Or will their past lives destroy their present? This novel has plenty of twists and turns and plenty of surprises in store until the last page.

A Second Chance (The Belanger Creek Ranch Series Book 4) is another well-thought out book with a solid plot written by Gloria Antypowich. I like the fact that this is not your typical boy-meets-girl book and the events and characters are real with real life problems and issues. I also liked the way in which the bond between Taylor and Grayson is portrayed. Overall, this is a good novel for a rainy day.

***

TABLE OF CONTENTS

OTHER BOOKS 10

DEDICATION 11

ACKNOWLEDGMENTS 13

CHAPTER ONE 15

CHAPTER TWO 20

CHAPTER THREE 25

CHAPTER FOUR 43

CHAPTER FIVE 54

CHAPTER SIX 60

CHAPTER SEVEN 69

CHAPTER EIGHT 79

CHAPTER NINE 84

CHAPTER TEN 94

CHAPTER ELEVEN 107

CHAPTER TWELVE 115

CHAPTER THIRTEEN 133

CHAPTER FOURTEEN 147

CHAPTER FIFTEEN 161

CHAPTER SIXTEEN 168

CHAPTER SEVENTEEN 181

CHAPTER EIGHTEEN 196

CHAPTER NINETEEN **218**

CHAPTER TWENTY **232**

CHAPTER TWENTY ONE **249**

CHAPTER TWENTY TWO **257**

CHAPTER TWENTY THREE **263**

ABOUT THE AUTHOR **270**

OTHER BOOKS

by Gloria Antypowich:

The Second Time Around, Book One of the Belanger Creek Ranch Series
Full Circle, Book Two, of the Belanger Creek Ranch Series
The Hand of Fate, Book Three, of the Belanger Creek Ranch Series

DEDICATION

This book is dedicated to the many people who struggle with the consequences of decisions that they have made. I think we have all done smaller things that we wish we could change; however, some choices are more monumental and have lifelong consequences. I believe *self-forgiveness* is first step to healing. Forgiveness can be sought in external ways, but until a person makes peace within, they are unable to truly accept any form of forgiveness and rebuild a life with the support of those who love them as they are.

Below are two quotes that resonated with me, as I watched the main characters in this book come to life.

The best kinds of people are the ones that come into your life, and make you see the sun where you once saw clouds. The people that believe in you so much, you start to believe in you too: the people that love you, simply for being you. The once in a lifetime kind of people. (Unknown quotes)

Family isn't always blood. It's the people in your life who want you in theirs. The ones who accept you for who you are: the ones who would do anything to see you smile, and who love you no matter what. – (Unknown)

My second dedication is to *Chuck*, a quiet, caring, kind individual that my son and daughter-in-law knew many years before I started to work on *A Second Chance*. I had never met him: however, I knew where he lived, so I looked up his phone number through Canada 411 and cold-called him. I introduced myself and told him why I was calling, and when I asked him if he would be willing to talk to me, he didn't hesitate.

Even though his situation was quite different from that of the character in this book, it was similar in the way that both circumstances were accidental, and their personalities were of the same nature. He gave me insight into the emotional repercussions of being responsible for a traumatic event. I found him to be an exceptional individual: warm, friendly, genuine, open, and honest. I have a special spot in my heart for him.

ACKNOWLEDGMENTS

I want to express heartfelt appreciation to the following people who read and reread this manuscript, edited it and seeing it through fresh eyes, have made unbiased suggestions: Monicka Gregory, Sharron Hynes, Darlene Bell, Diane Maureen Pleasance, Cathy Hoy, and Donna Wassenaar Rezansoff. There were times when I struggled; this project would have been much more difficult without your support. You are all very special to me.

Monicka Gregory is a Social Media maven. She is the owner Bizz~Linkzz Social Media Services. She also has a successful web page of her own; Kids Goals at **http://kidsgoals.com/** When my original editor became ill, I contracted Monicka to edit this book. She is honest, diligent and insightful and I am very pleased with the work she did.

Sharron Hynes is a long-time friend, who is very creative in her own right. She designs and sells beautiful all-occasion cards and business cards. She is a musician and singer. She and her husband, Mel, sing and play with their band the Kootenay Legends. Their CD's are enjoyed by many people around the world.

I also want to say a big Thank You to Steve Caresser and the team at ePrintedBooks- (**http://eprintedbooks.com/**) Steve

Caresser and I have worked together before, and I appreciate the quality of work that he produces. It is a pleasure to work with him again. ePintedBbooks offers a wide range of author services, as well as a virtual bookstore. Steve is also the author of five books. I have read the Sacred Crow, What Every Married Woman Needs, and Five Gallon Bucket. He has produced several audible poems and he is in the process creating "The Whole World News" Reality is what you make it. Steve and Jason Skinner are the newscasters for this production.

Laura Wright LaRoche, at LLPix Designs, (**http://llpix.com/**) designed the covers for the Belanger Creek Ranch Series. She was a pleasure to work with. I'm convinced she can do anything—that she has magic in her fingers! I also discovered that Laura is an author and her creative imagination shines in that field too. I have read both Black Woods and Black Woods Revealed. They have touch of paranormal, along with mystery and horror. I thoroughly enjoyed them and the image of the "beast" lingered with me for days! Broken Soul is on my Kindle, waiting to be read. Her books are available on Amazon.com.

I also want to thank Jen Blood for evaluating the four book series in the first draft. She gave me terrific input, suggestions, and encouragement. Since then, she has established a successful editing service (**http://jenblood.net/adian-enterprises/**) and has become a bestselling author. It was a once in a lifetime opportunity for me and I would never be so fortunate now. (I cannot claim that she is a close friend) I am a big fan of her writing, and I have read all of the books in the Erin Solomon Pentalogy. Look for them on Amazon!

And last, but not least, my husband Lloyd Antypowich, a prolific author who has published six books at this time: A Hunting We Did Go, From Moccasins to Cowboy Boots, Horns and Hair of the High Country, A Chip off the Old Block, Louisiana Man and Grasshopper McLain and Gotleep the Frog); also my children and their spouses, my grandchildren and the great-grandchildren that I'm blessed to have—I love you all. I appreciate the times you have encouraged me, ragged on me for spending too many hours sitting at the computer and asked when the books were going to be published –after two years, you must have wondered if it would ever happen!

CHAPTER ONE

It was Christmas Day. Sara Brite stood at the livingroom window and looked down over the buildings and corrals that were the heart of Belanger Creek Ranch. Coming here was the best thing that had happened for her and her son, Taylor, in recent years. The area was rural and not a place where the father of her son would be apt to find them. Of course, she would never let her guard down. She'd always remain aware and alert, ready to move at the slightest hint of danger. Duncan Talbot had resources and he'd tracked her down before. If that happened, and *if* they managed to get away again, she and Taylor would immediately disappear, slipping under the radar, just as they had done before.

The ranch 'family' was close-knit, and they looked out for their own. She and Taylor had been invited to the Bate's place for Christmas dinner, along with the rest of the 'family.' Brad and Shauna Lee Johnson and their two children would have come from Swift Current. Frank and Colt Thompson and the twins, as well as Ellie and Ollie Crampton, had left the ranch the day before, and drove to the farm at Cantaur to begin celebrating with all of the 'family' on Christmas Eve. Everyone was excited about Christina and Tim Bates new twins, but Taylor didn't care much for babies.

He said they just cried and puked and messed their diapers. He had wanted to hang out at the ranch and help Grayson McNaughton do chores. Sarah appreciated the invitation, but she was reluctant to allow herself to get very close to anyone, so making the decision to stay home hadn't been difficult.

She smiled when she saw her son go flying down the steep driveway on his plastic snow saucer. She watched him swerve around the ranch hand. The man jumped aside as Taylor narrowly missed him.

Her gaze settled on Grayson. He was a nice man; attractive, unassuming, gentle, soft-spoken, and kind hearted. But.... She frowned as she acknowledged that he was the biggest threat to her peace of mind at Belanger Creek Ranch.

***

Taylor Brite loved the feel of the wind on his face as he flew down the steep driveway. He swerved the well-worn plastic snow-saucer around Grayson McNaughton, spraying him with the dry, crystalline snow. Grayson jumped aside, and Taylor laughed with glee.

Grayson was really cool. In Taylor's mind, he was the best friend he had; even better than Sam and Selena, the Thompson twins, who were a year younger than he was.

Sam was OK. He was laid back and fun; but Selena was bossy and very competitive. She always wanted to win, and she pouted when she didn't. Sometimes he was tempted to push her down and wash her face with snow, but he knew he couldn't do that. He'd be in big trouble all around, if he did.

When Grayson reached the bottom of the hill, he tipped Taylor off the saucer and rubbed his ears against his head. "You little devil you. You tried to run me over, didn't you?"

Taylor was laughing when he protested. "No. I was just trying to see how close I could get."

Grayson rolled him around in the snow and then reached out to take his hand and pull him to his feet. "I'm going start the snow machine. I'll pull you behind on your saucer if you want me to. Do you think your mom would like to come along?"

Taylor was jumping up and down. "That'll be fun. I'll go get her." He turned. "Where are we going?" he asked, as he started to run up the hill to the house.

"We'll go across the road."

Sarah Brite was still watching from the big window in the living room at the main ranch house. Taylor had blossomed during the year and a half since they'd come to the ranch. A day didn't go by when she wasn't thankful that Colt Thompson had hired her. Although she remained alert and ready to act for Taylor's safety, she felt safer on the ranch, than she had since she'd worked for the Harahan's in Toronto. The only thing that shadowed her peace was Taylor's attachment to Grayson; for her son's sake, she knew it was a relationship that she shouldn't have allowed to develop.

She smiled as she watched Grayson roughhousing with her son. She saw them exchange friendly banter, then watched Taylor start running up the hill. He was out of breath, but grinning from ear to ear, when he came in.

"Hey, Mom! Grayson wants to know if you'd like to go for a ride on the snow machine. He's going to go across the road into the pasture, and he's going to pull me behind on the saucer."

She frowned. In recent months, she had grown very aware of Grayson as a man, and he hadn't hidden the fact that he liked her. She hadn't encouraged his tentative advances because she didn't want to get involved with anyone. She knew how uncertain the future could be.

"Aww mom, come on. Have some fun for a change. All you do is work."

"Taylor... you know why I do what I do."

He looked crestfallen. "We're safe mom. Nobody will find us way out here."

"Taylor! Not another word about that. We can't get too comfortable."

His smile disappeared. "I know. But it's Christmas. Won't you come out for a ride? For me?" he added pathetically.

She sighed. *He knows how to push my buttons.* "Oh...alright, I'll pull on a warm pair of pants and my winter coat. Just give me a minute."

The smile reappeared and his eyes twinkled again. *It takes so little to make him happy.*

He fidgeted while he waited impatiently. When Sarah followed him outside, he persuaded her to sit on the snow saucer with him and they sped down the hill.

Grayson was surprised when he saw the sparkle in her eyes and the color in her cheeks. Most of the time, Sarah looked like she was carrying the weight of the world on her shoulders. He often wondered what her story was. Why was she on her own with ten-year-old Taylor?

He watched Taylor lean back and shove her off the saucer.

"You rascal," she gasped. "I'll get you for doing that."

Taylor landed on top of her and pushed her down in the snow. It feathered into her dark hair and snuck over her collar.

"Taylor," she squealed. "You're getting snow down my neck."

"If I let you get up, will you promise not to come after me?"

She shook her head and struggled to push him off.

"No? Then I guess I can't let you up."

"Taylor. I'm your mom. You have to listen to me."

"Sorry; I've got to look after myself."

Grayson started to laugh. "Do you want some help, Sarah?"

Taylor lifted his head and looked at him in disbelief. "You trait…"

"Got you," Sarah cried as she threw him down and pushed him into the snow, burying him as he had her.

Grayson grinned as he listened to Taylor giggle while he thrashed around in the softness, struggling to get out from underneath his mother.

When Sarah finally let him up, he turned onto his hands and knees and crawled away from her. Then, he stood up. He pulled off his gloves and began to shake snow out of his hair. He ran his hands along his collar, under his coat and up his back, around the waistband of his snow pants and finally digging tiny balls of it out of the fabric around his wrists. "You're mean."

"Hey! You started this, remember?"

He grinned good-naturedly and grabbed the saucer, giving his mother a hip-check as he walked by her.

Grayson smiled as he walked to the back of the snow machine. He knotted a light nylon rope to the hitch and tied it to Taylor's snow saucer. "Have you ever done this before?"

Taylor shook his head.

"What? Where did you grow up?"

Taylor laughed nervously and looked at his mom.

"We didn't have snow machines," she said flatly.

Ouch, that hit a nerve, he thought. He turned to the boy. "Okay, first of all, you have to wear this helmet." He tossed one that he had hung on the snowmobile handlebar to him. "When I start to pull, let the rope tighten. Then you'll have to hold on and try to steer the saucer, but if it starts to tip or flip, let go. You don't want to get dragged. I'll keep an eye out for you." He looked at Sarah. "Your mom will too."

Grayson handed Sarah the second helmet that was on the seat behind him. While Taylor settled on the saucer, Grayson sat on the snow machine seat. He motioned for her to get on behind him. She tried to sit back, ramrod stiff. He turned to look over his shoulder. "Have you ever done this before?"

She shook her head.

"Put your arms around my waist and hang on. You'll need to move with me as we ride or you'll throw the machine off balance."

She felt conflicted, and it showed.

He winked. "Come on Sarah. It's just a ride. I'm not going to get any crazy ideas."

She blushed. "I wasn't thinking that."

He smirked, even though he almost felt sorry for her. "No? What were you thinking?"

"Just…"

"Aww mom, just put your arms around him so we can get moving. You'll fall off if you don't, and I'll run right over you."

"You would, too," she muttered as she slid her arms around Grayson's waist.

He didn't go too fast, keeping an eye on Taylor. Sarah gradually relaxed and rested against his back. Her mind spun off, remembering another life when she had ridden with her arms wrapped around another man.

CHAPTER TWO

Fourteen years earlier, she had eyed Duncan Talbot with distaste when he'd swaggered into the corner store where she worked. *A bad ass biker.* He was everything she'd been warned about when he came through the door; leathers, chains, tattoos, a scarf tied backward over his head, eyes hidden behind sunglasses. *Degenerate.* Her dad's summation of him rang in her ears.

He'd shopped for smokes and beer, further confirming that opinion of men like him.

Duncan Talbot was in many ways a degenerate, just as her dad had declared him to be. He was twenty-five years older than her, but he was a charming degenerate, and he came back repeatedly throughout the next year. In the end, he wore down Sarah's resistance. She had fallen for him, and despite her mother's tears and her father's outrage, she had hopped on behind him on his bike and sped away. She had threaded her arms around his waist and rested herself against his back, moving in unison with him as they rode through the curves and passed in the traffic.

Sarah was jolted from her memories when Taylor yelped. Grayson uttered a curse and turned the machine around. She became alert immediately and turned to see what had happened. The saucer had flipped and was bouncing crazily behind the snow machine. Taylor had rolled off. As she watched, he rose up on his knees and shook off the snow. He was wearing a happy grin.

A wave of love flooded through her. His father may have been a useless, violent, degenerate, but their folly had produced the most precious thing in her life. While she feared and detested everything about his biological father, Taylor was the one thing she cherished more than anything.

She watched as Grayson helped him get straightened out and settled on the snow saucer again. *He's good with Taylor. Duncan would never have been like that. He didn't want a child and he had no patience with the inconvenience of having one.*

She stood up to let Grayson ease himself onto the seat in front of her and then settled down behind him. She slid her arms around his waist, conscious of their position, and more acutely aware of him as a man than she wanted to be.

He eased the machine forward until the rope tightened and then he accelerated. As he became more confident, Taylor wove crisscross paths behind the machine, whooping with glee as the snow saucer briefly became airborne on occasion, then dipped down to catch the snow and whipped across the other way. Sarah's heart filled with happiness when she turned her head and saw her son's exuberant, smiling face. *Coming here has been the best thing that could have happened. I don't know when I've ever seen him so uninhibited. He's always been so serious and careful.* She swallowed hard.

Grayson slowed the machine and stopped. He looked up at the sky, noting the position of the sun. "I think it's time to head back to the ranch. It's about two-thirty."

"How do you know that?" Taylor asked.

"See where the sun is?"

Taylor looked toward the hills in the west. "Yeah, it's just above the trees."

"In a couple of hours it will be dusk, so we'd better head in and do the chores for the night."

When they got back to the ranch, Grayson drove up to the house. He let Sarah get off and she walked to her apartment. He helped Taylor unhook the snow saucer and then they both got back on the machine and rode down to the barnyard. Taylor wrapped his arms around Grayson's chest and hugged him. Grayson's heart lifted with happiness. It felt good to be hugged so freely.

Later, the three of them sat around the table, chatting as they enjoyed the Christmas feast that Sarah had made. Minutes before Taylor had come to ask her to go with them on the snow machine ride, she had put the turkey in the oven. She had prepared the vegetables earlier too, so she only had to cook them when she got back. Taylor heaped his plate with turkey and mashed potatoes and gravy and corn casserole. He wolfed it down and went back for seconds. Grayson looked at Sarah and chuckled. "This guy's got a hollow leg."

She nodded. "It must be from all that fresh air."

Taylor was grinning from ear to ear. "Come on you guys. I had a great day; I don't know when I've *ever* had so much fun." He pushed away his plate. "What's for dessert, mom?"

Sarah looked at him with disbelief. "Dessert? Are you serious?"

He rubbed his stomach and then felt down his leg. "I'm pretty sure I have room…right here in my hollow leg." He looked at Grayson and smiled.

Sarah shook her head. "Why don't we have dessert later? Maybe we could play a game, or watch a movie and give all that food time to settle. Would that be alright with you, Grayson?"

Taylor was up in a shot and pulling on Grayson's arm. "Please stay. We could watch a movie. The Thompsons lent us some good ones."

Grayson messed his hair and looked at Sarah. "That sounds like a nice way to spend the evening." Sarah nodded and asked him if he'd like a drink. He thought for a moment and said, "I'll make my own after I help you clean up the kitchen."

Taylor hurried into the living room and picked out three movies while Grayson helped Sarah clear the table and made his own drink. Sarah poured herself a glass of red wine. Taylor was leaning against the doorway, waiting impatiently for them. "Which movie do you want to watch, Grayson?"

Grayson studied the three Taylor had lain out. He winked at Sarah as he rubbed his chin thoughtfully. "They all look interesting, son. You pick one and we'll watch it."

A flush stole over the boy's face. "You called me *son.*"

Grayson shot a look at Sarah. She bit her lip and looked away. He didn't miss the glisten of tears in her eyes.

"Hey Taylor, if you'd been my son I'd be proud of you." He

hugged him. "Now let's watch a movie." He knelt by the DVD player and let the boy slide the disc into the empty slot. Then he handed the remote to the youngster and taking his other hand, lead him back to the couch. Taylor sat in the middle, with the two adults on either side. Sarah noticed that he rested his head against Grayson's shoulder and eventually the man lifted his arm to drape it around her son's shoulders, letting the child's dark head rest against his chest.

A knot of anxiety rose in Sarah's chest. Grayson was a great guy and he'd make a wonderful father, but he wasn't Taylors. She squeezed her eyes shut. *Why couldn't he have felt that way about Colt?* She sighed with resignation. *Colt is Sam and Sarah's dad. Taylor wants one of his own, so it's easy to see why he's drawn to Grayson.*

She felt Grayson's hand touch her shoulder. Her eyes flew open and she met his questioning look. Their gaze held for a moment, and then she looked away. Taylor reached out, took each of their hands in his, and leaned against the back of the couch. "Sitting here like this is nice isn't it? It's just like we're a family."

Sarah squeezed his hand. "Taylor, Grayson is a wonderful friend, but you are going to embarrass him if you keep saying things like that."

Taylor leaned over and looked into Grayson's face. "Am I embarrassing you, Grayson?"

"I'm not embarrassed, Taylor. But, you have to realize that for us to be a family, your mom and I would have to have a different relationship than we have. When you say things like that, you are putting us in an uncomfortable spot. We're friends and I like your mom a lot, but we're not...well, we're not like a mother and father."

"But you could be. Then we'd be a family, wouldn't we?"

Sarah placed her hand over his mouth. "Enough! *I'm embarrassed now.*"

Taylor pushed her hand away. "But mom, Grayson's said he likes you a lot, and he's nothing like Duncan. We aren't afraid of him. He isn't mean and he wouldn't hurt us." He looked at her earnestly. "He'd be like Mr. Thompson. He'd take care of us...."

"Taylor Brite! That's enough." She jumped up. "I'm sorry you had to listen to all that Grayson."

Grayson stood to face her. "Sarah." He reached out and touched her arm. "Please don't apologize. Taylor is a great kid; as I said

before, under different circumstances I'd be honored to be his dad."
Sarah looked at Taylor. "I think it's time for you to go to bed."
"Aww, Mom. It's Christmas. And we haven't had dessert yet."
"Taylor…I mean now! Grayson and I are going to have a talk."
"About him becoming my dad?"
"No, about why he cannot become your dad."

CHAPTER THREE

Taylor's disappointment was obvious when he ejected the disc and stood up. He threaded his arms around Grayson's waist. "Thanks for the best Christmas ever! Don't listen to mom when she tells you that you can't be my dad. I'd love it if we were a family."

Grayson rubbed his head. "This was the most special Christmas I've had in ten years, Taylor, and people are what make my Christmas special. I'll see you tomorrow."

Taylor hugged his mom and gave her a peck on the cheek. "I love you Mom." He gave her a cheeky grin. "And I know everything is going to be okay."

After he had gone to his room and shut the door, she turned toward Grayson. She felt awkward because of her embarrassment, and she couldn't quite look into his eyes. "Uhmm...would you like another drink?"

"Are you having one?"

"Yes. I think I will. I need to help you understand Taylor and me...where we come from, what our life has been like and what it will be in the future."

"Okay. I'll make my own drink. Can I pour you a glass of wine?"

She nodded, walked over to sit at the table. She watched him as he mixed his drink, and then poured her a glass of wine. He carried them to the table and she sighed deeply as he put the glass in front of her. He walked back to the island, collected the bottle of rye, a can of coke and the wine and brought them to the table with him. "I think we might need these."

Sarah laugh was strangled. "You must be clairvoyant."

He touched his glass to hers, his expression serious. "Alright, Sarah Brite; tell me why you are carrying the weight of the world on your shoulders."

Her head snapped up, her expression one of quick denial.

Grayson held up his hand. "You initiated this talk, Sarah. I recognized that you were hiding something when you first came here."

Sarah's mouth dropped. "Wh..a.. t do y..ou mean?" she sputtered

He reached out and touched her arm gently. "Even after a year and a half, you're still always on guard. You're careful about how much you tell about your past, and so is Taylor. You've schooled him well. If he lets anything slip, one look from you and he covers it up and changes the topic.

"You're constantly checking to see where he is. I'll bet the two of you could find each other and disappear in a shot if the right situation came up. I'd say you've rehearsed it, practiced it, and possibly even done it. Today is the first time I've seen you relax and lose that haunted look for a few minutes."

Sarah rested her elbows on the table and entwined her fingers, resting her forehead against them, her thumbs pressing against her temples. Tears slipped down her cheeks.

Grayson moved to the chair beside her, putting his arm around her shoulders. "Sarah, tell me what's going on. If you are in danger, if someone is looking for you and Taylor, we need to know so we can protect you. In the city, you can slip away and get lost in the crowd. Here in the country, you might be harder to find, but it could be harder to get away too."

Sarah began to sob. "I'm so tired of looking over my shoulder, and it's not fair to Taylor."

Grayson pulled her head against his shoulder and let her relieve her tension. Finally, she snuffled and heaved a big sigh, then pushed away and sat up. "I'm sorry about that."

"Don't be. I think you needed to let all that go."

"I can't say I *feel* better right now, but it was a release. If I ever really let go, I couldn't stop."

He pushed her glass of wine in front of her again. "Have a drink and then we'll talk."

Sarah sipped at first, and then took a long drink. When she sat the glass on the table, Grayson refilled it and then moved back to the chair at the end of the table, so they were facing each other.

Sarah reached out and twirled the stem of her glass with her fingers. "When I finished high school, I was a typical teenager. My dad was old fashioned in his thinking and his attitude really grated on me. To him everyone, who didn't see life through the same prism as he did, was just a useless, degenerate. That was his favorite word. In his mind, every teenager's brain was fried by drugs; they drank themselves into oblivion and partied endlessly. They were just bone lazy and didn't want to work and they would steal the good folk blind.

"His plan was for me to remain at home and help mom. I would look after my younger brothers and sisters, do housework, work in the garden and help in the office where she did the books for his logging operation, just like I had all through my adolescent and teenage years.

"But I was ready to get out and spread my wings. I wanted to live a normal life, outside the four walls that had confined me through all of my growing up years. So against his will, I got a job at the corner store in town. It was a minimum wage, dead-ender, but I felt so free, I felt like I could fly." She looked into his eyes with appeal. "Can you understand that?"

He nodded.

"I went home once in a while, but dad was so critical and disapproving, it spoiled the visit. Mom and the younger kids were happy to see me. My older brothers kidded and joked with me, but dad just heaped guilt on me every chance he got, pointing out how heavy mom's workload was. He mocked my minimum wage and asked me what park bench I was sleeping on, or how comfortable the local YWCA digs were. Then he'd remind me that my room was still there." She shook her head sadly. "He never did get it…he never understood how controlling he was and how he drove me away from him, and the home where everyone else that I loved lived. I needed freedom to breathe and grow.

"I worked at the corner store for a year. I wanted to be a teacher, but on my wage, I couldn't save any money to go to university, so I just went to work day after day like a rat on a treadmill. Shortly after I started working there, Duncan Talbot came into the store. He pulled up next to the sidewalk on a big Gold Wing. He had a black silk scarf tied backward around his head, wore sunglasses, and was covered with tattoos and leather. When he came swaggering through the door, I could hear my dad's derisive description ringing in my ears. *Degenerate!* I have to admit, he didn't fit my idea of a stand-up guy either. The average logger or millworker around town didn't look anything like him.

"He had stopped to buy a package of cigarettes, but he was scoping out the territory too, though I was too innocent to know it then. He was a lot older than me, but he flirted a bit and I flirted back. I thought he was just passing through.

"He wanted to know where the parties were around town or where everyone hung out. It was a Monday night and as far as I knew, there wouldn't be much happening again until the weekend when all the bush monkeys came back to town. The weekend would be a blur of activity and then they'd all head back out to work. The guys that worked at the mill just carried on with their shifts. If they happened to have the weekend off, they'd join in. If not they'd just get together in small groups, often at someone's home.

"He left and I never expected to see him again, but he came back on the weekend. Then he started coming in a few times during the week. I got to know him better and he seemed like he might not be such a bad guy, so when he asked me out for dinner I went. On my day off, we started traveling on his bike to other small towns.

"I introduced him to my older brothers. Brian is easy-going and willing to accept anyone. Al is more like dad and he picked up on the age difference right away. I didn't take Duncan to meet Mom and Dad until he asked me to move to Montreal with him. Of course, mom was shell-shocked. Brian and Al had mentioned him, but she couldn't believe I was moving to Montreal with him...for God's sake *Montreal?* That was so far away and they didn't even speak English there!

"Of course, Dad blew his stack and he ranted on and on. What was I thinking? Well, as usual I wasn't thinking! What did I know about this degenerate? He was old enough to be my dad. Look at all those tattoos, and... Jesus Christ, did he have pierced ears? Didn't I remember anything that he'd tried to teach me? What did Duncan do to make a living? He'd bet his bottom dollar he was a drug dealer.

"Mom was crying and dad was steaming when we left. His parting shot was to let me know that if I left with that degenerate, I was making my own bed and I had to lie in it. The door would be slammed in my face if I ever dared to come back. In defiance, I yelled back, telling him I would never darken his doorstep again... and I haven't."

Grayson finished his drink, shaking his head as he placed the glass on the table. "Sarah, people say things they don't really mean when they feel they're losing their grip on the situation. If you'd gone back..."

"I couldn't eat that much crow." She looked away. "Especially, when it turned out that he was right for the most part, but at the time I was desperate to get out of The Pas, and all I could see was a wonderful future ahead. Duncan had recently settled in Montreal. Two months before he asked me to move in with him, he'd bought a fancy condo in a well-respected part of the city. He showed me pictures. The condo was beautifully furnished, a dream home for a country bumpkin like me. When he wasn't a biker, he cleaned up nicely and wore expensive clothes. Now I realize that I was his trophy 'wife', dressed to kill and dripping with expensive jewelry. He drove an expensive car; we went to expensive restaurants and parties and mingled with high profile people."

"Are you...were you...did you actually get married to him?"

She shook her head. "No, I just assumed he'd marry me in time. Other than the few people I met on a superficial basis when we went out, I had no idea about his life. And I knew nothing about his work, or where he went when he was out of town. When I said I wanted to become a teacher, he was agreeable and paid my tuition. When he was home, we were like a husband and wife. I was getting my education and when he was away, I had time for myself. It seemed ideal.

"I found out I was pregnant early in my second year at university. I was thrilled. It was hard to tell how Duncan felt. He wasn't as excited as I thought he'd be. When Taylor was born, he wouldn't let me record him as the father."

Grayson shook his head. "I can't imagine a man not wanting to claim his child."

"He insisted on a paternity test. I was shocked because I knew he was the only one who could be Taylor's dad. He said he didn't believe he could father a child because he had a very low sperm count."

Grayson reached out and covered her hand. "That had to be hard for you."

"It hurt that he'd doubted my fidelity. Taylor was born the first week in June and our life totally changed. Duncan stayed out overnight more often. When he was home, he lashed out at me. At first, he'd say scathing things. Then he started to slap me around. I was constantly off balance because I never knew what to expect. Would he be civil, would he simply ignore me or would he hit me?

"One Friday night he pushed me around and in the scuffle he dislocated my shoulder. The pain was excruciating. He wouldn't take me to the hospital because the bruises would have raised too many questions. He brought in a 'private' doctor who put my shoulder back in after he gave me a sedative.

"I think I woke up before they thought I would, and I heard them talking in the hallway. When the doctor warned Duncan to be more careful, he said that he was tired of me anyway. He should have dumped me months before.

"The doctor laughed and said there was a good market for women like me in South America. Duncan said he wished it was that easy; having the kid was an additional problem. I heard them talking about a shipment that was coming in. The doctor asked him if I had any idea about what he was doing. Duncan snorted and said I was just a country hick and I didn't question anything. The doctor warned him to be careful because if I ever found out, he'd have to make sure I couldn't talk. That scared me half to death."

"Jesus, Sarah...."

She nodded. "My world had been ripped to pieces. Duncan Talbot wanted to get rid of me and I had no doubt that he was involved in the drug trade. It was hard not to react, but I didn't dare."

"You had to be absolutely terrified."

She squeezed her eyes shut and hung her head. "If I hadn't been so naïve, I would have wondered about that possibility earlier. I never really understood what his job was. He usually dressed in a suit, so I thought he was going to 'work,' I just didn't know what kind of work. When I look back, I have to admit that I didn't want to see it. I didn't want to acknowledge that my dad had been right about him from the beginning.

"I knew I had to make a move soon. Every day, I could only hope he wouldn't come home and tell me we were going to South America...or anywhere else for that matter. Every day I considered my options and thought about what I could do. Duncan had been very generous during our first months together, and true to my roots, I had saved a few thousand dollars. It was a start. It would help us travel and find a place to rent somewhere, but I knew we'd be desolate in no time and that frightened me.

"One night, about a week after he'd dislocated my shoulder, Duncan hadn't come home by midnight. It had become a regular occurrence and usually meant that he'd be out all night. I wrapped Taylor in his blankets and put him in the stroller. I put the bag that I'd packed for him in it, as well as the one I had put together for myself. I filled my pockets with all the good jewelry he had given me. Then I put on my raincoat and zipped it closed, pulled the hood up over my head and slipped out the door of the condo. I knew the surveillance cameras would record my movements and the time I left, but it couldn't be helped. The opportunity had presented itself and I had to take it."

Grayson realized he was holding his breath. He exhaled and turned his empty glass. "So, did you get away without any problem?"

Sarah looked exhausted. "Have you any idea how frightening it was to be in a big city like that and not know where I was going or what I was doing?"

"I can only imagine. It must have been terrifying."

"I had no idea who I could trust. He undoubtedly would try to track me down. He'd check the taxi companies and find out where I went. If I took a bus or the train, even if I flew, he could trace me. If I walked down the street, I could be noticed, especially if I was pushing a stroller. If I walked down a back alley, I could get mugged. Taylor and I could both be killed."

"What did you do?"

"I walked down the street. There were trees along the sidewalk and I stayed in the shadows. Fortunately, it was quiet and I didn't meet anyone. I went two blocks. Then I turned the corner and went two more blocks. Thank god, Taylor was sleeping. I looked around and there wasn't any traffic moving, so I crossed the street and walked for another few blocks. I could tell by the lights in the distance that I was moving closer to a commercial area. I crossed the street again and just kept walking toward it. I'd turned off the GPS tracking on my cell phone before I'd left the condo, so he couldn't easily find out where we were. I was tempted to use it to call a taxi, but I knew he could check the records right away, so I hoped I'd find a pay phone. It was three in the morning by then, and I was emotionally and physically exhausted.

"By three-thirty, I had reached a main thoroughfare. I didn't want to walk down the brightly lit street, so I decided to go down the back alley and peek between the buildings. My heart was pounding in my throat. I saw a bus stop about a block away. There was a bench there and nearby there was a payphone, so I decided to chance it. When I'd almost reached the phone, a bus pulled in. My heart almost stopped. Then, I realized it might be the answer to my problem.

"There was only one passenger and he was sleeping, so I fished in my purse for the fare and we got on. I rode it until we got into an area that I'd never seen before. I decided to get off in front of an old hotel right next to a stop. I stood on the street and watched the bus pull away. It was almost five o'clock. I went into the hotel. It was old, but it looked clean. The man at the desk was half-asleep, but he took my money and didn't ask any questions. I took Taylor up the stairs to the room and prayed he would sleep for a few more hours. I needed to figure out where I was and decide what my next plan of action would be. If I was really lucky, I might have until noon, or even that evening before Duncan realized I was gone. Then I suspected all hell would break loose and I'd be hiding in earnest."

She took a sip from her glass of wine.

"I found an information package in the room. It included the bus and train schedules. I decided to take the Megabus to Toronto. I put Taylor back in his stroller and left. The guy at the desk was asleep, so he didn't even see us. I called for a taxi from the payphone outside and asked the driver to take us to the station at Rue St. Antoine. After he let us out on the street, I put Taylor back in the stroller. Then I took the battery out of my phone and dropped them both through the grid covered water drain along the curb. There was no way for Duncan to contact me then. When I bought the tickets, I paid cash and held my breath while I gave them phony names for both of us. No one asked any questions, so I tagged the stroller to be stored underneath and carried Taylor onto the bus. The bus left at eight thirty that morning and we were in Toronto by mid-afternoon.

"I found a motel in the suburbs and we stayed there for a while. It was older and quiet, a bit out of the way. I needed to rest. I had to rethink my life and come up with some idea about how I was going to protect Taylor and myself. I was scared to death because I was certain that Duncan would use his contacts to track us down. I knew that if he ever found us, we wouldn't get away.

"Living in the city offered anonymity, but I needed to make money, and I couldn't consider leaving Taylor with anyone. I watched the classifieds for a few weeks and one day I saw an ad for a companion that looked promising. I called the number and arranged to meet the people. They lived in a beautiful home in an older area of the city. The name of the woman who needed assistance was Julie Harahan. She'd been injured in an accident years before and was in a wheelchair. Although she managed very well, she needed a companion; a housekeeper, cook and someone to help her with the things she couldn't do herself.

"Her husband, Ryan, was an engineer who worked in a mine in northern Russia. He was gone for three months at a time, and then came home for a month and left again. The three of us made an immediate connection and Julie fell in love with Taylor. They had no children of their own, and the idea of having a happy, smiling baby in the house sealed the deal. The fact that I didn't have a driver's license surprised them, but Julie had a handicap converted van and she drove wherever she needed to go, so it wasn't a major obstacle.

"The job was an answer to my prayers. The pay was reasonable and it provided board and room for Taylor and me. I was able to relax for the first time since the night I'd heard Duncan and the doctor talking.

"I realized that I could attract trouble for them by being there, and it bothered me. After I'd worked there for six months, I decided to tell them everything the next time Ryan came home." She smiled weakly. "And I did. I even admitted to being a stubborn, pig-headed teenager who wouldn't listen to my parents."

Grayson grinned. "You were stubborn, you still are. But in fairness to you, it sounds like your dad was out of touch with things, Sarah."

"It was his reality, and unfortunately it bit me in the ass."

Grayson chuckled. "So how did the Harahan's take it when you told them what had happened?"

"I was afraid they might ask me to leave, but instead they were protective. They both thought we were pretty safe there. The neighborhood was made up of older people, so it wasn't likely that Duncan's kind would be cruising around and come into contact with me. Ryan had installed alarms on the house and garage and perimeters of the yard when they'd bought the place several years earlier.

"I never went out by myself anyway; not that I couldn't have, I was just too afraid. Ryan also set up a joint bank account, for himself and me. He used his grandmother's name to give me signing authority."

"What?"

"I know. Crazy…but he brought the paperwork home and we filled everything out using his grandma's name. He took me to the bank and introduced me as his sister and I signed everything as if I was her. "

Grayson shook his head. "So as far as the bank knew, you were his sister, but you were using his grandmother's name. Wow—talk about confusing."

She nodded. "As I said—crazy, but it made me very hard to trace. He also got a credit card and an Interact card. Most of my wages went into the account and gradually he took all of the pieces of jewelry that Duncan had given me and pawned them in different places when he traveled. He'd put the money into the account, and it added up. Later it gave me a safety net when I needed it."

Her eyes met his and he saw the fear and tiredness in them. "I worked at their place for four years. Then one morning, when I went out to get the morning paper, there was a package sitting on the step, addressed to me. I took it inside; it wasn't until I had the brown paper wrapping half torn away, that I realized there were no stamps or postal markings so it hadn't come in the mail. Furthermore, I never got mail, as I'd completely dropped off the grid."

Tears filled her eyes. "I knew that he'd found me. I started to shake and my heart pounded so hard, I thought I was going to faint. I was crying when Julie came into the room. She finished opening the package. Julie is a real lady, but she swore like a lumberjack when she got that package open. It contained a sharp knife and a note for me. It's engraved in my mind.

"Did you really think you could give me the slip? You made a big mistake when you ran out on me. No one gets away with that. For now, we'll play the game of cat and mouse, babe. Keep looking

over your shoulder, cause you'll never know when it's going to happen, but know this—IT WILL and it'll happen when you least expect it. I never wanted the kid, but he is mine. I'll probably let you raise him until he's old enough to be of use to me. But then again, I might get tired of toying with you and decide to put an end to this. If I do, rest assured, I'll do away with him first and make sure that you watch."

Sarah was sobbing. Grayson stood up and moved over to the chair beside her. He slid his arm around her and pulled against him so that her head rested against his chest, then stroked her hair gently, letting her cry. "What did you do, Sarah?"

"I wanted to take Taylor and run, but Julie convinced me not to. She begged me to wait until Ryan came home, so we could all decide what to do. When I calmed down and thought about it, I realized she was right. The note was a taunt, meant to terrify me and send me running. I'd be much more vulnerable if I left, than I was there behind the Harahan's alarmed doors. I'd be leaving Julie there alone and I knew that I couldn't do that. I loved her as much as she loved Taylor and me. Ryan was going to be home in six weeks, so I stayed.

"Julie put the knife and the note in the safe, and we carried on with life. A month later, there was an envelope on the step for me. Inside, there was a picture of Taylor and me in the backyard and another note. It said *Keep looking over your shoulder babe. The time is near.*

"Julie was afraid too. There was no doubt that he was there, watching us. Once again, I wanted to just disappear, taking Taylor with me, but I couldn't. I wondered if we would even survive two more weeks until Ryan came home, but then what? Julie put the envelope and its contents in the safe with the first package.

"We counted down the days. It wasn't much of a homecoming for Ryan. The entire evening was focused on the threats, and how we should handle everything. Ryan decided to involve the police. He had a couple of close friends in the department and one of them worked undercover. He phoned them the next day and told them what had happened.

"Sergeant Maxham came over the same day. We showed him the packages that had shown up on the doorstep and I told him about my past with Duncan; including what I'd heard Duncan and the doctor say.

"After they talked a while, it was decided that the police would make a presence in the area by going house to house, asking if anyone had noticed any unusual vehicles or different people walking around on the sidewalk or in the back alley. Besides that, they would randomly patrol the streets in a ten block radius so no one would know for sure when they would be there.

"Charlie Adcock came by a day later. He was an undercover member of the Drug Squad. He logged in on Ryan's laptop and showed me a bunch of mug shots of guys they were interested in. Half way through, I spotted Duncan Talbot. When I pointed him out, Charlie nodded and told me that I needed to be careful. They suspected he was involved in violent crimes; that he would have people killed at will, and wouldn't be above doing it himself. Charlie thought that I would be a personal score that Duncan would want to settle himself. He wasn't used to being thwarted.

"That day he and Ryan spent most of the day in the back yard, drinking beer and hunkering down like old buddies. They were very visible the next day too, and later they drove off in Charlie's Hummer. They went to Ryan's bank and then to a department store where Ryan bought a set of luggage. When they came back to the house, Ryan made a big deal about putting the Hummer in the garage.

"When they came into the house, Charlie and Ryan explained what they had been doing while they were out. Charlie had contacted another undercover agent that he'd worked with in the past. He'd asked him to him to meet Suzanne Cunningham and her four-year-old son, at the Halifax airport early the next morning. He explained that he was asking as a favor for a special friend of his, and we were coming in on a private jet. He gave him all the specs, assuring him he'd have clearance to meet us at the plane on the runway.

"Bert Chambers also agreed to drive us to a small resort near Peggy's Cove about thirty miles away. He said he'd help us get settled in a cabin that had been reserved for Suzanne there. Charlie and Ryan impressed upon me how important it was to maintain my identity as Suzanne Cunningham and Ryan gave me a cell phone registered in her name. He'd made arrangements for the monthly payments to automatically come out of our joint account and he assured me that, even though the Interact card was under his grandmother's name, it would work anywhere, so I would be alright. He advised me to withdraw money from a bank machine or ATM as

I needed it, and pay cash for everything."

Grayson nodded. "No paper trail with cash."

"That evening, Ryan barbecued steak in the backyard and we ate out there. Ryan surprised Julie with the luggage and announced that they were going to fly to Vancouver for a week. When she protested and asked about Taylor and me, Ryan said we would look after the house while they were gone. They put on a convincing show for the small camera the guys had detected when they studied the picture of Taylor and me and realized that it had been taken by a surveillance camera mounted near the perimeter of the yard.

"Later that evening, we put all of Taylor's things in one of Julie's old suitcases, along with most of his toys. I packed everything I had in another one. We went into the garage. There were a lot of tears as we hugged and said goodbye. Then Taylor and I curled up in the very back of the Hummer and covered up with blankets. Our luggage was put on the floor in the back seat. Charlie backed the vehicle out of the garage, once we were settled, and pulled up in front of the house to wait.

When Ryan stepped out of the back door, he pulled it shut, and then, as if it was an afterthought, he opened it and called me by name, reminding me to set the alarm, adding that they wouldn't be long."

Grayson picked up the bottle of wine and topped up her glass. "They paid meticulous attention to every detail," he said as he set it back down.

"They did. Charlie drove us to a small airport out of town, and he put Taylor and me on a private jet that belonged to a business associate of Ryan. Everything went smoothly and by mid-morning, we were settled in our new home. It was small but cozy, and the McNeils, who owned the resort, were really friendly. They knew Charlie well, but I'm very sure he never had told them anything about Taylor and me. They loved Taylor and the two other members of the staff doted on him too. Eventually, I worked around the resort for minimum wage. We were there for three years."

"Did he find you there?"

"I didn't see him, but one morning, at about four-thirty, the owner knocked on our cabin door. I was shocked when I opened it and found him there. He stepped inside without waiting for me to invite him in and shut the door quickly. Then he apologized, and said that he had to talk to me.

"A man on a Harley had come cruising into the resort the evening before and asked a lot of questions. Mr. McNeil didn't like the guy, so he brushed him off: afterward, the more he'd thought about it, he wondered if the biker had been fishing for information about the baby and me. Following his gut instinct, he'd phoned Charlie in the middle of the night and told him what had happened. Charlie was alarmed. He told him to take us to his cabin near the lighthouse, and hide us there until he could talk to Ryan and make other arrangements.

"One look at my face was all it took to convince him that I was terrified. I quickly packed a light bag for us. He took it, and I carried Taylor to the pickup. He told me to crouch down, so no one could see us when he drove through town and turned toward Halifax. After he had traveled several kilometers, he took a side road and backtracked, snaking through back trails, until we came to a broken down cabin nestled in the trees. I looked at it curiously, until he shut off the motor and calmly said, 'This is it.'

"I was confused. I asked *what* it was.

"He said we were at Charlie's cabin. When I asked if he was serious, he grinned and told me that was the old cabin. The new place was behind it, through the trees by a lake. It had running water, solar power for the lights, propane for cooking, and a fridge. He assured me I'd be safe there until other arrangements were made for us. He carried our suitcases through the trees to the cabin. His wife had boxed up some food for us so we wouldn't go hungry. Then he left, cautioning me not to let anyone see me if they came around. He said he'd be back as soon as he heard from Charlie."

She was crying again. "I felt so helpless and vulnerable."

He held her against his chest, feeling every bit as helpless as she must have felt then. He couldn't imagine the anxiety she had experienced.

She sat up and looked at him, shaking her head. "Charlie called Ryan's friend and reminded him of the trip he'd made to Halifax three years earlier when he'd used his jet to fly Taylor and me there. The guy had remembered, because even though he was Ryan's friend and he trusted him, he said the whole thing felt off. Charlie gave him a very brief explanation and told him we were in trouble again. He asked if he would fly him to Halifax. The guy welcomed the chance to get out, so they were in the air in a couple of hours.

"Charlie rented a truck and arrived at the cabin mid-afternoon.

When I heard the vehicle, I freaked out and we ran deep into the bush. He put two and two together and realized what had happened. He stood on the deck and called me, telling me who he was and that he owned the cabin. I was so relieved to see him; I threw myself into his arms and hugged him."

"How could Duncan have found you?"

"Charlie and I went over and over that. The only thing we could come up with was that when I registered Taylor in the home schooling program I had to provide his birth information. I'd stayed off the grid until then, but I ordered the DVD courses so he'd have the lessons, even if we found ourselves in a place where we didn't have the internet."

She shook her head in frustration and looked at him imploringly. "But Grayson, he has to have an education. I want him to graduate in a recognized program, so he can go on and have a decent future. That poor child has lived his whole life under such deplorable circumstances. We live in a free country, but because of his father, I have taught him to live in fear. We never make any deep friendships, I'm forever looking over my shoulder, alert and suspicious of almost everyone and ready to pack up and move at a moment's notice. It's not right to do that to a child, but I don't know how else to protect him.

"If it weren't for Julie and Ryan, I'm certain I'd have collapsed years ago. Their love and support have kept me going. I never get to talk to them, but every once in a while I find an unexpected extra amount in my account. It's their way of assuring me that they still are watching out for us. I appreciate it so much, but there are times when I get so tired of being on the run and feeling afraid. Sometimes I just need a hug, and I need to be able to talk about how I feel."

He pulled her against him as they sat side by side. "Sarah, I'm here any time."

She nodded. "I can't believe I'm telling you all this. I'm putting you in danger too, just by being here, by letting you know all this. He will find us again, and he won't care who he hurts as long as he punishes me and eventually gets rid of me."

"He is not God, Sarah. He'll make a mistake one day and get caught. Where did you go after you left the resort?"

"Charlie took us back to Ryan and Julie's place. We flew back on Air Canada. He booked the flights; when I insisted that I'd pay for them, he told me he traveled a lot and he had air miles to burn, so he used them. Julie was excited to see us. Of course, she had another companion by then, and it felt strange for me to just visit.

"I tried to keep Taylor on track with his lessons, but that was really difficult. He was distracted by the sudden move from the resort, and the weirdness of the two of us staying in Charlie's cabin. Children sense things we often don't realize; things they don't know how to express. He was seven by then and he started voicing his concerns and asking questions. While we were at Charlie's cabin, I gave him a sanitized version of what was happening."

"How did he react?"

She frowned. "He didn't really know how to act. He wanted to protect me. But that's one of the things that is so wrong about the way I've raised him."

"Sarah; you've done the best you could. How could you fight something like that, all by yourself?"

"I've kept the two of us in a protective bubble. Truthfully, until we came here to the ranch, Taylor had no idea about what a family was; a mother, a father, other children or friendships. I don't know if you remember, but the first weekend after we arrived, it was Christina and Tim's wedding. Do you realize he'd never been in such a big group of people before, and certainly not without being glued to my side? They were all strangers. I asked him later how he felt about it."

"I remember he was pretty quiet and kept to himself most of the time. What did he say to you?"

"He didn't know how to act. He felt out of place, almost afraid. I was busy helping and although I was constantly checking on him mentally, I wasn't afraid so I wasn't seeking him out. He must have felt like I'd abandoned him."

"How did you end up coming here?"

"When Ryan came home, he and Charlie met with Charlie's boss. After I'd first identified Duncan's mug shot, Charlie had told Ryan that the drug squad had been watching him. They knew he was involved with the trade, but he was careful. He'd built a wide network among the *respectable* elite in major cities across Canada. He's a chameleon and when he was a high roller he associated with the top end of society, but he also was known to get on his Harley and explore the rural areas, looking for any small niche to get a hold in. That was what he was doing when he met me at the corner store.

"Truthfully, if they hadn't been watching him, Charlie probably wouldn't have gotten involved, despite how strong his friendship with Ryan was. Anyway, while we're not in the witness protection program, they gave us new identities; that included a new SIN and birth certificate. We became Sara and Taylor Brite. Ryan closed our joint account and put the money in a new account that they'd set up under my new identity in Regina. They gave me a new Interact card and a credit card. Ryan, bless his heart, provided me with a new cell phone and this time he paid the contract in full.

"Julie and Ryan had friends in Swan River, Manitoba. It's a smaller, out of the way town and I felt it could be a good place for Taylor and me to start over. We brought Taylor in on the conversation, and later he and I talked when we were alone. Taylor would like to have stayed at Julie and Ryan's; he liked them and he felt safe there. But, when I explained that we had to start over and it would be different this time, he just shrugged and said OK.

"We rented an apartment and lived there for almost a year. I met Julie Regeer and we became friends. Taylor hung out with her kids, but he was never really free with them. The economy was tight and I could only find part-time work at the restaurant. When Christina phoned Julie and told her about the job with Colt and Frank, I felt good about it.

"When we drove out here, Taylor was more excited than I'd ever seen him about anything. Things clicked between all of us, and suddenly my son found himself living in a healthy family environment. He's home schooled by Ellie, and I know enough about her to be confident that she does a great job. It's the best thing that's ever happened to us, but..."

"But?"

"Grayson, you're not blind or insensitive, you have to know that Taylor is bonding with you. He sees you as a father figure. And god only knows he deserves one; he needs one. But it will kill him if..."

"Sarah, don't do this."

"I can't just sit back and let him get hurt again. When Duncan finds us, we're going to have to run again."

He stood up, pulled her to her feet, then placed a hand on each shoulder and looked deep into her eyes. "Sarah, Taylor is ten years old. I hate to tell you this, but he's going to start resenting you if you keep trying to push him back into that protective bubble you've created. Every year his personal feelings are going to get stronger and just as you resented your dad, he will come to resent you."

Tears started to run down her cheeks. "I know that, but what can I do?"

Grayson's arms enfolded her as he pulled her against him and rested his chin on her head. "Sarah, let's talk to Colt and Frank when they come home. This scumbag has controlled you with fear for far too long. He's not invincible. It's time somebody stood up to him." He took her hand. "You're as wound up as a ten-day clock. Let's sit down. Maybe if we watch something mindless, you'll relax a bit."

He led her to the couch in the living room and turned on the TV. Sarah rested her head against his shoulder and stared aimlessly at the old western he'd selected.

In the early morning hours, Taylor came to the living room to see why the TV was on. His eyes widened in surprise when he saw his mom on the couch, snuggled in the curve of his best friends arm, with her head nestled against Grayson's chest as they slept. He giggled as he headed back to bed. *He's going to be my dad.*

CHAPTER FOUR

The Thompson and the Crampton families arrived back at the ranch late in the afternoon on the twenty-sixth. Everyone was tired, so they went to bed. The next morning Grayson and Colt met at the barn and did chores. When they were finished, Grayson asked Colt if they could have coffee at the ranch house, adding that he and Sarah had something to talk to him about.

Colt grinned. "Have I been missing something? I haven't noticed any hanky panky going on between you two. Now Taylor is another thing. That kid adores you, but Sarah? I never noticed that so much. I must be slipping!"

Grayson gave him a light shove. "I imagine I could do a lot worse, but that's not what we need to talk about."

When they got to the house, Colt and Grayson stripped off their winter coats and boots and went into the kitchen. "Fran?" Colt called.

"Just a minute," she answered from the laundry room.

"We're ready for coffee and some of Sarah's shortbread cookies." Colt checked the coffee pot and found it empty. He whistled as he made a fresh pot. Grayson took four cups from the cupboard and got the cream out of the fridge. Colt was putting cookies on a plate when Frank and Sarah came into the kitchen.

Grayson's eyes met Sarah's. He walked over and put his arm around her shoulder. "I told Colt we have something to talk to him and Frank about."

She groaned. "Grayson…."

He tipped her head back and looked into her eyes. "There's no point in waiting."

Colt grinned and quirked an eyebrow as he looked at Frank.

Sarah cringed. "I didn't tell you to do this…"

"I know you didn't, but you can't keep trying to handle everything on your own."

Her eyes shone with unshed tears, as Grayson led her to a chair. He began to sit down, and then looked at her. "Do you want a glass of wine or a shot of rye?"

"It's only ten o'clock in the morning," she protested.

"Well, I thought you might want a shot of courage." She shook her head and smiled feebly.

They all sat down, sipped their coffee, and ate the cookies. Finally, Colt looked at Grayson. "Alright, what's the story?"

Sarah closed her eyes and spanned her hand across her forehead. Grayson nudged her. "Do you want me to give them the basic outline?"

She shook her head, but Grayson started to speak and recounted the story she had shared with him the night before. Tears were running down her cheeks when he finished, and he reached out and covered her hand with his. "Did I miss anything?"

"No." Her voice was almost a whisper. "You have a very good recall."

Colt released his breath in a loud whoosh. "Damnit, Sarah, no wonder you're so jumpy."

Frank twirled a spoon in her fingers. "This is the twenty-first century isn't it? How does a creep like that stay on the loose?"

Grayson's expression was serious when he spoke. "For one thing, no one has openly confronted him. He's operated beneath the radar by controlling Sarah with threats and fear. He's careful. He sent her packages, but he never signed anything or left fingerprints. He is playing a war of nerves, slowly wearing her down. He's the kind who will wait as long as it takes, but when he gets the chance he'll strike and we all needed to be aware that he's out there. That's why I insisted that she tell you. With our support, she can relax and live a normal life and Taylor can be a normal kid."

Sarah hadn't realized how much relief sharing her story would bring. She felt safer; protected. In the coming days, she laughed more freely; there was a spring in her step that had been missing before. Frank smiled as she listened to her singing while she folded laundry.

During the week, Ellie came to the ranch house and taught Taylor and the twins, using the home school curriculum that they'd followed since they'd started school. On Friday nights and the weekends, the children went out and worked on the ranch with the adults. After feeding and chores were done, Frank often spent time with the kids, showing them how to use their lariats to rope the horns she had stuck into a bale.

Sam became very adept with the rope; Selena didn't have the inborn talent that her brother seemed to possess, but she worked hard and was determined to master it. Taylor was an eager pupil too and he often slipped out after school and practiced while Grayson watched him.

January slipped by quickly. The weather was mild and after the morning chores were done, Grayson often took the snow machine for a ride in the afternoon. He noticed the change in Sarah, the lightness in her step, the sparkle in her eye. One day he asked her if she'd like to go with him. She looked at Frank, torn because she felt she should be working.

Frank smiled. "Everything's under control here. Go for a ride, it'll do you good to get some fresh air."

They rode across the highway, into the field where Grayson had taken her and Taylor on Christmas day. He powered up a draw in the coulees and pulled around at the top so they could look across at the fields toward the buildings. He shut off the motor and they got off and stretched their legs. He watched her as she stood there in the brilliance of the sun, watching it play across the snow crystals in the field below. "You're happier these days."

She smiled. "They say confession is good for the soul. I should have thanked you before now."

"No need to thank me." He kicked the snow with the toe of his heavy boot and looked out toward the ranch. "We all have our secrets, Sarah. Some of them are bigger than others. But yours was so painful, the burden of it was too big to carry alone. I'm proud of how well you've done."

"Thanks." She turned to face him, then took a couple of steps to put her arms around him and looked into his eyes. "Grayson McNaughton." She swallowed hard. "I'm sure you saved my sanity when you told Frank and Colt about my living nightmare. And for certain, you are the best thing that has ever happened to my son."

He hugged her back and rubbed his nose against hers. "So I can be Taylor's daddy now?"

She pushed him away. "I didn't quite say that. But I don't mind that he looks to you as a father figure, now. He needs one and you're good for him." She turned away and looked out over the ravine. "Have you ever been married?"

"No." His voice was brusque.

"Why? You're such a nice guy and you are so good with the kids, you should have had at least two or three of your own."

"At one time I thought I would, but life happened. Marriage and kids didn't."

"What are you...a one woman man? Did you get your heart broken?"

"No. It wasn't anything like that."

She looked at him with sharpened interest. "You're not giving up anything are you; the man who pried my life story out of me."

"I didn't pry it out of you."

"No, I guess you didn't, but you didn't hesitate to tell it to Colt and Frank."

"I did it for you and Taylor's safety." He got on the snow machine and started it. "Time to head home I think. Get on behind me, girl. It's a long walk to the house."

February came in cold and blustery. One evening Tim heard a knock on the bunkhouse door. He was sprawled on the couch watching a hockey game; rather than get up to answer, he yelled, "Come in." He was shocked to see Taylor when the door opened. He sat up quickly, sudden fear pounding in his chest. "Is something wrong?"

Taylor shook the fresh snow out of his hair. "Yeah, it's really cold out there."

"What are you doing here?" He looked at his watch pointedly. "It's way past your bedtime. Does your mom know you're here? It's practically a blizzard out there."

Taylor walked across the floor, his boots dropping chunks of snow out of the grooves in the soles, his coat shedding snow and water as he moved. When he sat down, Grayson could feel the excitement vibrating off him. "Everything's cool. I just wanted to talk to you without mom knowing."

Grayson frowned. "What's bothering you?"

"Well, it's Valentine's Day next week. I've been saving every penny I make and I counted my money tonight. I have one hundred dollars. I wondered if you'd drive us into Maple Creek so I could take you guys out to dinner."

Grayson breathed a sigh of relief. He wrapped his arms around the boy and hugged him close. "You had me worried, son. I thought something serious had happened. I don't know if you realize it, but your mom told me about your father and how you guys have been running from him. For a moment, I thought he'd found you again." His arms tightened as he dropped a kiss on Taylor's wet hair.

Taylor reveled in the moment. His mom hugged him all the time, but Grayson's arms were so strong, his shoulders so thick; he soaked up the feel of it, like the desert sands absorb water. Then Grayson's words sunk in. He pushed back and looked at him. "She told you?"

"Yes, on Christmas night after she sent you to bed."

"I found the two of you sleeping on the couch the next morning."

Grayson put a headlock on him and teasingly rubbed his ears. "You know there's nothing going on between us, you young jack. Your mom loves you so much she would do anything to protect you. She has been carrying an unbearable load and while I almost had to break her arm to get her to start talking, once she did she spilled it all. She cried a lot, and she was exhausted when she was done, so I got her to sit on the couch with me and relax for a few moments. We fell asleep. It was totally innocent.

"When Colt and Frank got back, I pushed her into telling them—well actually I told them, but she was there when I did it. The two of you are not going to run anymore, Taylor. We are going to stand as a family, and if it comes down to it, we will take that bastard on."

Tears filled Taylor's eyes. "I don't remember him you know. I just know mom is really scared of him, and I remember when we hid in a cabin back in the bush and a man named Charlie came to get us and took us back to a place where we'd lived before. I really liked those people and I wanted to stay there, but Charlie and Mr. Ryan said it was too dangerous. Mr. Ryan took us to Swan River. I didn't like it there; it was boring and mom was afraid to let me go anywhere in case that bad man would find us again. I'm happy we came here. I love the ranch, and I love you." His thin arms slid around Grayson's waist and he rested his head against him for a moment.

Grayson put his hand on the boy's head. "So, you want to buy your mom dinner for Valentine's Day?"

Taylor stepped back, nodding. His eyes met Grayson's with sincerity. "And you. I want to take both of you out for dinner."

Grayson smiled at him. "I appreciate that, Taylor. I would tell you that you don't need to buy my dinner, but I know you want to. I'll be honored to drive us to Maple Creek for dinner on Valentine's Day."

Taylor beamed. "Thanks. I knew I could count on you."

Grayson grinned and gave him a gentle nudge. "You'd better get back to the house. Your mom will be freaking out."

"Naw…she thinks I'm asleep. She said good night to me at eight thirty, and she went to bed too."

"Taylor! You know what you've done is wrong."

Taylor grinned as he opened the door. "I know, but nobody got hurt."

Grayson walked to the door and watched as Taylor ran up the hill to the house. When he was satisfied that the boy had arrived safely, he went inside. Thoughts of Taylor and Sarah preoccupied his mind. Sarah had fought so valiantly to protect him, but no matter how hard she had tried, she hadn't been able to fill his need for a father figure in his life.

He thought about his own childhood. His parents loved and connected with their two sons. Lee McNaughton had played hockey and baseball with them, and took them fishing and hiking. He'd given them values and sound advice and they'd always known he would be there for them. His brother, Jon, was the oldest. He went to university and became an architect. Today he was well known for his achievements and owned a respected company in Toronto.

Grayson had followed in his father's footsteps, and became a veterinarian. Growing up, he'd been the one who brought home the hurt dog, the stray cat. He'd rescued a baby owl and nurtured it until it was full grown. At that point, his parents had insisted he set it free and when he had, it had hung around in the maple trees for weeks, swooping down to greet Taylor when he came home from school.

He'd always loved animals and spent his spare time, Saturdays and summer holidays at the veterinary clinic with his dad. He'd helped stitch small animals and in his teenage years had assisted his dad with major surgeries. When he left for vet school, he had a solid understanding of veterinary procedures. Eight years later, he had finished his undergraduate work and gotten his DVM. He had a world of opportunity at his feet, but he went back to Elliott Lake to work in his father's clinic. He'd dreamed of taking it over one day; buying his dad out, getting married and raising the kind of family he'd grown up in. He was twenty-eight and full of dreams.

His lips twisted with derision. He stood up, turned off the TV and went to bed, but sleep evaded him. His inglorious fall to disgrace haunted him as the past played over and over again, like a broken record. It was strange how a moment in time could reshape your whole world. "Yes, Sarah. Everyone has their secrets," he whispered, bunching the pillow under his head one more time.

February fourteenth turned out to be a clear, cloudless day and that night the temperature fell quickly. Sarah tried to convince Taylor and Grayson to go for dinner another evening, but Grayson read the disappointment in the boy's eyes and insisted that they go. They listened to music on the satellite radio as they drove to town. Grayson sang along, and before long, Sarah joined in. They laughed and shared little things about their childhoods.

Grayson told them about ice fishing with his dad; Sarah reminisced about the fun she had riding a sleigh down a hill with her younger brothers and sisters. Grayson talked about how supportive his parents had been; Sarah revealed that her father had controlled their family, deciding how all of them would live within it. She admitted that she had rebelled. They discussed the pros and cons of her choices. She blamed herself for letting her stubbornness get her involved with a man like Duncan.

Taylor had listened thoughtfully to both of them, but when she berated herself about living with Duncan he looked at her and said, "But mom, if you hadn't done what you did, I wouldn't be here."

Sarah's eyes widened, her mouth sagged open. "Oh Taylor," she whispered as she put her arms around him. "You are so right; you are the most precious thing in my life. I've never been sorry that I had you; only that I put you in so much danger."

Frank had helped Taylor make reservations and he told Grayson which restaurant to go to. When they pulled into the parking lot, Taylor squirmed in his seat, excited and filled with anticipation. Frank had assured him that it was a very nice place and he was bursting with pride. When they got out of the truck, he took his mother's hand, and then reached for Grayson's, and they walked into the restaurant looking like a happy family.

Taylor stepped up and told the hostess they had a reservation. Grayson helped Sarah take off her coat and laid it over the back of the booth. Taylor waited for her to slide in, and then sat beside her, leaving Grayson to sit across from them. He looked at his mom. "You look really pretty in that dress." He looked at Grayson. "Doesn't she?"

Grayson looked at Sarah and smiled. "She does. I don't think I've ever seen her dressed up before."

"Well, it isn't every day that my son takes me out for dinner."

Taylor insisted that they each have a drink, and he'd figured in the price of the Valentines special for each of them. Sarah looked at him with pride. "How did you learn to handle money so well?"

"I've seen how you do things mom, and you've had to be really careful with your money. I told Frank how much I'd saved, and I told her that I wanted everyone to have a drink and a nice dinner. She phoned the restaurant for me and let me talk to a lady who told me the things we could order. We put the phone on speaker, so Frank could listen too. We wrote down the prices and then Frank and I discussed what I had enough money for and I decided what we'd have. It was fun!"

Sarah looked across the table at Grayson. She caught him looking at her in a way that sent a tingle through her. He realized he'd been caught and noted the blush that rose up her neck and flushed into her cheeks. He winked at her, hoping to relax her unease. "I was just thinking how pretty your mom really does look tonight, and wondering how I could be so lucky to find myself included in the company of the greatest kid in the world and his beautiful, courageous mother."

Sarah looked away quickly. Then her eyes came back to his. "You have more than earned your place here, Grayson. You have done so much for both of us; I can't imagine where we'd be without you. Taylor's relationship with you has given him the assurance and stability that I couldn't provide. You are the single best thing that has happened in his life."

"Possibly, but it would be next to you."

She laughed. "I'm his mother; he happened to me. You happened to him."

"And you mom," Taylor added.

The next day Taylor was bursting with pride when he told Frank how well everything had gone the night before. "We were just like a family, the way you and Colt and Sam and Selena are," he concluded before he headed to the classroom.

Frank looked at Sarah, who shrugged her shoulders. "I know, but what do I do about it? He worships Grayson. Grayson thinks the world of him. They're good for each other. But ...if push came to shove?" She shook her head. "I hate to take my chances on who he'd chose."

Frank snorted. "That's total nonsense. There's no doubt he'd choose you."

"He probably would, but not without a sliver of resentment that would eventually take root and grow enough to damage what we share."

"How do you feel about Grayson?"

"How do I feel? He's a nice guy. He's kind and considerate of me and he loves Taylor. He's come from a normal background...you know a family where people do things together and show affection. His parents encouraged him and his brother to do what they choose to do, not what they had mapped out for their son's lives." She shook her head. "He has a far better idea of how to live as a family than I do. I grew up with a father who acted like a member of the Gestapo. I was rebellious and when I defied him and left, he told me I could never come back, and I haven't.

"Instead, I got myself in a mess. No kid should grow up without friends because his mother is afraid the wrong person will see him. No kid should grow up in a constant atmosphere of fear, knowing that mom might pack up and move you somewhere strange at the drop of a hat. Coming here has given him the most normal life he has known. He has the twins to play with, he sees how a family relates by the example you guys live, Ollie and Ellie are like grandparents and Grayson fills the void that a father should have."

Frank nodded. "You know what Taylor wants, don't you?"

Sarah stared at her, lost for words.

"That little boy wants you two to make his world complete."

Sarah shook her head. "No...no, we're not like that."

"Can you really be so blind? Or are you just so filled with denial that you can't see what's happening."

"Frank, I...I will never marry anyone until I know Duncan Talbot is dead or in jail for the rest of his life."

"You're not married to him."

"No! Thank God."

"Then why does he have this hold on you?"

"I'd die if he hurt Grayson..." Her eyes grew big and she clapped her hand over her mouth.

Frank stepped to her side. She put a hand on each shoulder and looked into Sarah's eyes. "Remember that. Don't push him away. I suspect he needs someone in his life too. Maybe he's been waiting for you and Taylor."

Sarah turned and went into the porch. She put on her boots, a heavy winter jacket, and snow pants, and went outside to wander through the snow along the walking path that led to the ridge above the house, where the blades of the wind generators sliced through the air, producing the electricity that powered the ranch house. The morning was clear and cold. The sun was bright and glinted on the crystals in the snow. She sat down at the base of one of the generators and wrapped her arms across her chest in an effort to ward off the chill as she looked out over the ranch below.

Ollie was running the tractor, dropping round bales in the feeders. Colt was exercising a young horse in the round pen. Then she saw Grayson walk across the barnyard, carrying two five-gallon pails. She watched him move with ease through the corral gates and dump the grain in the wooden troughs. She watched as he went back to the bin, noticing how trim and athletic he was as he swung himself up over the corral planks, foregoing the need to open the gates. In a few minutes, he came back with another two pails and worked his way through the gates to the next corral and the next wooden trough.

She thought about how she had caught him looking at her in the restaurant the night before and smiled. *Could it happen?* The cold had seeped through her heavy clothing and the chill drove her to her feet. Her teeth chattered as she hurried back to the house. She took off her boots, coat and snow pants in the porch and went into the kitchen. She decided to bake homemade bread and cinnamon buns. Work was always her escape.

During the last week of February, calving started. Colt, Frank,

Grayson, and Ollie took turns working in the corrals, checking for cows that were delivering and assisting when necessary. By the first week in March, the rate of calves being born each day had leveled out at the highest numbers and the crew was very busy. Each calf was tagged, had its navel swabbed and was given an A, D, & E injection, as well as one of Selenium. Every three hours, one of the team members made the rounds through the corrals at night too.

One night Colt did the two o'clock shift. He found four cows in the process of delivering, but one that had given birth earlier that evening, was lying on the hay with a uterine prolapse. His first instinct was to run up the hill for Frank, but she had taken the previous shift and he knew that she was tired. He decided to wake Grayson and get him to help, hoping that between them they would be able to put the uterus back inside the cow.

Grayson was on his feet immediately when Colt said the word *prolapse*. He told Colt to fill the electric kettle on the counter and plug it in. He dressed quickly and headed for the vet room, telling Colt to pour the hot water into the aluminum bucket on the counter and grab a sheet of gauze from the drawer below it.

He was collecting the instruments he needed when Colt reached the barn. He went to the fridge and grabbed a bottle of Lidocaine and one of penicillin. They hurried to the corral and Colt led the way to the cow who was grunting with discomfort, still trying to force the weight of the swollen organ out of her body.

As Colt watched his movements, he recognized that Grayson knew exactly what he was doing and he wondered why he hadn't noticed it before. As he thought about it, he realized that in the four years Grayson had worked there, they had always called on Frank to do the serious veterinary work.

Grayson made a quick assessment of the situation, and then set to work. Colt watched in fascination as he handled the task with knowledge and skill. In an hour, he was finished. He shook his head and looked at Colt. "I can't guarantee she'll make it. She'd been down for a while before you found her. It was a bad one."

"You handled that like a pro. Is there something I don't know here?"

CHAPTER FIVE

Grayson gathered up his instruments and put them in the vet box. "I'll take these to the bunkhouse and clean them up."

"You didn't answer me, Grayson. Is there something I don't know about you? Watching you work here, I would swear you are as well trained as Frank."

Grayson headed to the barn. Colt frowned as he followed, swinging the aluminum pail by the bale. He leaned against the vet room door watching Grayson put away the medicine. Finally, Grayson turned and faced him. "Look Colt, just give it a rest."

"That's not how I'm built, man."

Grayson muttered a curse, then met Colts penetrating look. "I *am* a vet…and a damn good one."

Colt nodded. "What are you doing here?"

Grayson heaved a heavy sigh. "Have you finished checking for calves?"

"No, when I found that cow I came right to the bunkhouse."

"Alright, I'll go work through the herd with you. When we are done, we can go to my cabin and I'll fill you in. But I'd better put these instruments in the sink first."

Colt went to the corral and Grayson followed him five minutes later. It took them an hour to check all the pens. Everything was quiet so they went back to the bunkhouse and Grayson made a pot of coffee. He looked at Colt soberly. "You asked why I'm here. Two years before I came here, I was charged with Aggravated Assault."

"You were what?" Colt's voice was shocked.

"I hit a guy and when he went down, he hit his head on the edge of a sharp rock. It was one of those fluke things; you probably couldn't do it again if you tried. He didn't die, but he'll never be the same."

Grayson was tense as he watched Colt, who looked at the floor for what seemed an eternity before he finally looked up. "How many times did you hit him?"

Grayson ran a hand through his hair. "Just once."

"That's all?"

"I'm not a fighter, Colt. Hell, I've always been the biggest chicken-shit pacifist you could ever meet, but he was so damned crude, I just couldn't let it go. I reacted without thinking and I'm sure he didn't expect me to take a swing at him or he'd have been all over me before I had a chance."

He picked up two cups and brought them to the table. "I'm sick about what happened; I don't think I'll ever be able to put it behind me. No one deserves what happened to him, but he was a crude mouthed bully, and he was used to pushing everyone around and getting away with it."

"Were you convicted?"

"No; I have my dad to thank for that. At first, I couldn't see beyond what I'd done. I'd ruined a man's life; I'd ruined his family's dreams. I couldn't see a future for myself; in fact, I didn't feel like I deserved one. I just wanted to plead guilty and disappear. But Dad hired a damned good lawyer.

"The guy I hit was a *Hixon* and his family wanted to destroy me. They wanted their day in court; they wanted to prove to everyone what a terrible a person I was, and show that my actions had robbed their son of an illustrious future. It was revenge for their loss.

"The judicial system is painfully slow and it took almost a year to get into court. My lawyer asked for the case to be moved to a different jurisdiction because things got pretty ugly in town, and he felt that the jury would be tainted. George Hixon was the mayor, and they were a well-known family in the community. A lot of people took sides with them. Needless to say, they were really upset when they heard the verdict. They filed an appeal immediately."

"Where was the trial held?"

"Sudbury. The Hixon family were really upset about that because they were counting on local support. Some of their friends came, but a lot of the others who wouldn't have been brave enough to ignore the trial in Elliott Lake, were a no-show in Sudbury. But...that wasn't the underlying reason for the verdict. There were witnesses who saw, and heard, everything that happened that night. I believe that is what convinced the jury that a conviction on the charge of aggravated assault wasn't merited."

Colt nodded.

"The Hixons wanted me to go to Kingston Penitentiary for fifteen years. They were furious about the verdict and filed an appeal immediately, but my lawyer had crossed all his t's and dotted all the i's, leaving no room for an appeal."

Grayson poured coffee and sat down. "Look, I know I should have told you all this when I came, but this job was perfect for me and I was afraid I wouldn't get it if I laid everything on the table then. Being charged with something like this wasn't easy. Living with what I've done is even worse. But if you want me to leave, I'll pack up and go."

Colt was startled. "Good God man, no! The thought never occurred to me. You've been here for four years and you're a perfect fit. You've become a member of the family. I'm just surprised by all this."

Grayson let out a tense breath. "I can understand that and I appreciate your attitude. I promise you, I am no threat to you or your family...or anyone else for that matter."

Colt shook his head. "I'm beginning to feel like this ranch is a sanctuary for people on the run."

"I'm not running from anyone but myself, Colt."

"I didn't mean that. But now I have you and Sarah here."

Grayson nodded. "I feel sorry for Sarah. She's living with a time bomb, never knowing if or when it might explode. The ranch is off the beaten track, so it makes her feel safer, but that guy has tracked her down repeatedly, so she's still looking over her shoulder. It isn't fair to her or Taylor."

A knock on the door interrupted the conversation. Colt looked at his watch and shook his head. It was five in the morning. He got up and opened the door.

Frank stood there, hair sleep tangled, her face concerned. "What's going on? You let me sleep in."

"Come in. When I came out at two this morning, one of the cows had prolapsed."

"Is she alright? You should have come and got me," she protested.

"Everything is fine. Grayson did a great job of putting everything back in place. He knows what he's doing."

Frank smiled. "I noticed that from the start. He really understands the animals and just seems to know what to do. He's a natural."

Colt and Grayson looked at each other, then Grayson took a deep breath. "There's something I should tell you, Frank."

She looked at him quizzically. "What's that?"

"I'm a vet."

She stared at him, not comprehending his words momentarily. "What do you mean...?"

"I'm a trained vet."

"But...what are you doing here?"

Colt put his arm around her shoulder. "Remember when you came here, hon? It's ironic, but your positions are similar in some ways. You were escaping your past; so is Grayson."

She laid her head against Colt's shoulder and smiled. "Well, look how it worked out for me. I got married and started a new life."

Grayson shook his head. "I don't see getting married in the cards for me, but I am building a new life."

"There's always Sarah," Frank said with a smile.

"I'd be honored to marry someone like her, but I doubt if she'd want to take on my past. I need to tell you the truth, Frank. Colt and I just went through it all."

Frank listened with concern as Grayson filled her in. When he was finished, she stepped forward and hugged him. Then she stood back and put her hands on his shoulders, and looked into his clear blue eyes. "We have to live with the consequences of our actions, Grayson. You know the Hixon family will never forgive, but you have to forgive yourself or you'll never be free. As for us here at the ranch, who are we to make judgments based on what happened in the past? To us, you are one of the family; a gentle, kind and caring man and an excellent worker."

Tears shimmered in Grayson's eyes. "Thank you, Frank. I'm

glad you both know the truth now. It takes a big load off my shoulders. I don't know what I'd have done if you'd told me to leave."

Frank's hands slid down his arms to clasp his fingers. "Grayson, you were charged but you weren't convicted. Those are two different things. And even if you had been convicted, in the four years you've been here, you have proven yourself to us. You have nothing to worry about."

Grayson cleared his throat. "I guess I need to tell Sarah."

Frank nodded. "If you are serious about wanting to build a relationship with her, you have to tell her the truth."

"Is it dishonest of me to not want to tell the kids?"

Colt and Frank's eyes met. Frank shook her head. "I don't think it's necessary. They all think the world of you, and they might find it hard to deal with figuring out how their hero could have found himself in that position."

"Thanks again Frank. It would be hard to see the disillusionment in their faces."

Colts look was sympathetic. "Do you still have a good relationship with your family?"

"Yes, but this whole thing has been very hard on them emotionally and socially. You don't hurt the mayor's son without repercussions, especially when they are one of the oldest, most respected families in the area. Every time mom sees Mrs. Hixon pushing Dillon in a wheelchair, it's got to be hard to face. Dad has taken abuse because of my actions too. My brother lives in his own world and his peers and friends in Toronto probably don't even know I exist, so he avoids the embarrassment."

Frank looked at him curiously. "Have you kept up your license?"

"Yeah. I actually went back to work with dad, but I couldn't do it. It was too hard, staying and working in that town. I don't know if I'll ever practice again, but I've kept it up."

"I'm glad to hear that. Getting your training is intense work. It would be a shame to let it slip away."

Colt looked at his watch again. "It's time to do another check. Grayson, you need to get some sleep. Fran and I will go through the corrals and then I'll catch some shut eye. Ollie and Fran can cover the next few hours."

Over the next week, Grayson's mind was filled with turmoil.

Telling Colt and Frank the truth had lifted a heavy weight of anxiety from his shoulders. Their response to his revelation had been an even greater relief. They hadn't denounced him; they had accepted him as he was.

After the trial he'd still been so filled with guilt and regret that he couldn't have acknowledged acceptance if it had been offered; he'd withdrawn into himself, shutting the world out, certain that everyone despised him; in truth many of them had. When he couldn't bear the tension anymore, he'd left town, convinced that everyone would be better off without him around. He'd stayed in touch with his parents by phoning them three or four times a year, but other than that, the ranch had become his cocoon of safety. During the past four years, he'd learned to care for everyone who lived there; they had become his family.

Now the compassion of that family had stirred hope in him. The adulation of ten-year-old Taylor warmed his desolate heart. Sarah's fierce protectiveness and unconditional love for her son filled Grayson with longing. Would she accept him with the same benevolence that the Thompsons had? He knew he had to tell her his secret soon. If she was shocked and shunned him, he'd have to leave. He couldn't bear to see the pain in Taylor's eyes. He couldn't bear to see the disillusionment and betrayal in Sarah's.

Every day Taylor came to the barn or the bunkhouse to see him. Each night Grayson laid in bed, thinking about the child who had become so special to him, the boy who openly showed his affection for him, and unabashedly spoke of his desire for him to be his father. His stomach burned as he thought about what could happen when Sarah knew the truth about him. He often buried his face in the pillow and let his tears silently flow. Regret was his companion when he finally fell asleep; regret for the action he'd taken in a moment in time and the lasting effect it had made in his life.

CHAPTER SIX

Sarah threw in the last load of laundry and went to the kitchen to start preparing supper. The house was quiet. Frank was taking a nap; calving had taken its toll on everyone's sleep. Ellie and the children were still in the schoolroom. Colt was at the corrals, working among the cattle with Grayson and Ollie.

She smiled when she thought about Grayson. She hadn't seen him all week and she realized that she missed him. Taylor had gone to see him every day. He loved to go to the corrals and help Grayson with whatever he was doing. If he was working with a new calf, Taylor would hand him the tag and the applicator, ready for him to use. And he'd talked about holding bottles of A, D & E and Selenium for Grayson and handing them to him when so he could fill a needle and inject the newborn calves. If the calf needed dehorning, Taylor was there to give Grayson a helping hand. Grayson had warned him never to get the dehorning paste on himself and Taylor took him seriously. If a calf had scours, Taylor would help Grayson catch it and give it scour pills. He'd come home more than once with stories of cows who'd threatened them, trying to protect their calves. *You always keep the calf between you and the cow when you're working on it, mom. Grayson says she'll never run over her calf to get to you. She'll snort and bellow and paw the dirt trying to scare you away; she even blew slobber on Grayson's shirt, but she didn't hit him and knock him over.*

She'd died a thousand deaths, afraid that her son would be hurt, but Colt had assured her that Grayson always put Taylor's safety before his own. In her heart, she knew that Grayson would protect him, and Taylor was totally involved in the new world that Grayson was sharing with him. She had done everything she could do to help Taylor grow into an emotionally healthy child, but the man he admired so much was meeting the one need she could not fill.

She hadn't realized how much he'd wanted and needed a man in his life, until he'd turned to Grayson. At first, it had alarmed her, but now it warmed her heart to see the way that they had bonded. Grayson was the kind of man she would have chosen to be her son's father. He was kind, considerate, thoughtful and respectful of everyone. In her heart, she knew he would never be involved in violence and criminal behavior, the way Duncan Talbot had been.

She noticed her heart was beating faster as she rinsed the potatoes and put them in a pot with water. Grayson's face filled her thoughts; his clear blue eyes, his heartwarming smile that exposed the dimple in his left cheek. The lock of blonde hair that tended to fall forward on his forehead, and his tempting defined lips that had hovered close to hers more than once, uncertain and cautious. She ran her tongue along her lips, imagining his touch, shivering with the reality of her thoughts. *I could fall in love with that man. What did Frank say? Maybe he's been waiting for Taylor and me.*

When class was over for the day, Taylor, Sam, Selena, and Ellie came to the kitchen for their daily after school snack. Taylor drank his hot chocolate quickly and gobbled down a cookie. Then he hurried to the porch and put on his heavy coat and boots. "I'm going down to the barn to see what Grayson's doing, mom."

"If you want to, you can invite him up to our place for dessert tonight."

"Whoopee. I'll do that. I hope he's not too tired to come."

Later that evening Grayson knocked on the door at Sarah's apartment. Taylor beat her to the door. "Hi Grayson," he greeted him. "Come in. Mom's got hot chocolate for us and some cake."

Grayson took off his coat and hung it on a coat hook. Then he turned and grabbed Taylor, pulling him under his arm and ruffling his hair affectionately. He smiled as his eyes met Sarah's. "Hi there, stranger, I've missed seeing you. Thanks for inviting me up."

Sarah blushed softly. "It's nice to see you, too. You guys have been so busy with calving, but its Friday night so I thought Taylor could stay up later and we could spend part of the evening together."

Grayson walked over and slid his arm around her waist, pulling her against his side. "That sounds cozy. It beats looking at the walls in the bunkhouse."

"Do you guys want to sit here at the table or should we sit on the couch and watch a bit of TV?"

"Let's watch TV. I can sit between you two like we did at Christmas. I like that; it feels like we're family."

Sarah and Grayson smiled as they looked at each other over his head. "Let's go then. After we've watched for a couple of hours, I want you to go to bed, Taylor." Grayson look became serious. "I have something private that I need to talk to your mom about."

Taylor couldn't hide his grin. "Let me guess. Are you going to ask her to marry you, so you can really be my dad?"

Sarah's face flushed red. "Taylor! People need more reasons to get married than that."

Grayson hugged his shoulder. "No, Taylor. That's not what I want to talk to your mom about. This is something else entirely."

Taylor fidgeted as he sat between his two favorite people. His mind was teeming with possibilities and he couldn't concentrate on the TV program. Finally, he yawned and said he thought he'd go to bed. Grayson looked at him sternly. "I don't want you standing at the door and trying to listen to your mother and I talking, Taylor."

Taylor looked sheepish. "I won't. Call me when you're finished and let me know."

Grayson's eyes suddenly glistened with emotion. "This is a very serious talk son. You may not like what happens after we have it."

"Naw, she likes you."

Sarah, shaken by the sadness in Grayson's eyes, felt her chest tighten. Grayson walked Taylor to his room and gave him a hug goodnight, then closed the door and came back to Sarah. "Can we sit in the kitchen, Sarah?"

Sarah nodded and followed him. He walked to the table, pulled out a chair for her, and sat down across from her. He tapped his fingers on the table, glanced at a picture on the wall, cleared his throat and looked at Sarah intensely. "Do you remember the night we sat here before?"

Moisture gathered in her eyes. She nodded.

"You told me your secret."

Dread flooded through Sarah as she nodded.

"God," he said softly as he rubbed his hand across his mouth. "I wish I didn't have to tell you this, but I've been living with a secret too."

Sarah's eyes were frightened. She twisted her hands together as she stared at him. "Are you married? Do you have a family?"

"No. It's nothing like that." He ran his hand nervously through his hair, his look was pleading. "God, how do I tell you this?" He swallowed hard. "Six years ago I hit a man. He fell and hit his head on the sharp edge of a rock. It caused brain damage. I was charged with Aggravated Assault."

The color drained out of Sarah's face. "No," she gasped, jumping up from the table. "What have I done?" she cried. "How could you do this? You encouraged Taylor, he loves you...but you are a common criminal just like his father."

Grayson stood up and reached out to her. "No, Sarah. What happened was a freak accident. I am not..."

Sarah turned away from him. "Damn you. I let my guard down. Things were going so good here. I began to trust you...have feelings for you, dreams of a future. The ranch is the best thing that ever happened to Taylor. He thinks you are perfect. How am I going to tell him he has to stay away from you? He's going to be devastated, but I can't let him be influenced by someone like you...we're going to have to leave."

Grayson pulled her into his arms. His tears mixed with hers. "No, Sarah. You can't do that. I'll leave."

"He's going to resent me no matter what happens. He won't want to stay on the ranch without you." She pushed away from him. "Damn you," she cried as her hand flashed up and slapped his face. "I wish we'd never met you! Get out of here."

Grayson stumbled to the door, grabbing his coat on the way. Sarah ran to her bedroom and fell on the bed, sobbing inconsolably. Taylor lay in bed, listening to her distressed cries. His heart twisted with fear. *What had happened?*

He waited for half an hour. Then he couldn't stand not knowing what was wrong. He got out of bed and went to his mother's bedroom door. He pushed it open and tiptoed inside. Sarah lay on the bed, her sobs accompanied by pitiful moans. He sat down beside her.

"Mom," he whispered fearfully. "What is wrong?"

"Oh honey, I'm so sorry."

"About what mom?"

"Grayson…he's not who we think he is. He's…he's …I know how much you love him, but he's a violent man. You…you can't hang out with him anymore. We're going to have to move again. I can't let you…"

"No!" Taylor's cry was a wail. "I don't want to move again. And Grayson is *not* a bad man, he's like my Dad, and I know he loves me. He loves you too; you're just too stupid to see it. I'm not moving away from Grayson."

"Taylor, I'm your mother. You'll listen to me."

Taylor's look became set and stubborn. "I am not moving again and… I'm not leaving Grayson. You're wrong about him. I know it!"

Sarah jumped off the bed, grabbed Taylor by the shoulders, and shook him. "He hurt a man Taylor. The police charged him for hitting a man and hurting him so bad that he has brain damage. He is not a good man for you to be with. What if he got mad again? What if he hurt you?"

"He'd never hurt me. He looks after me and teaches me things."

Sarah's tear reddened eyes flashed with anger. "Yes, he does! And how long will it be until he teaches you to fight?"

"You are so…so par'noid mom. Sometimes I wonder if my other dad ever really did chase us or if you just got scared and ran all the time."

Sarah shrieked "Taylor! You don't know what you're saying. Your father is a violent, evil man and he will never quit looking for us. How can you say that to me? Is this what you've learned from Grayson?"

"Listen to yourself, mom. You know something, I've never seen him."

"If you had seen your father, I would be dead and God only knows what would have happened to you," she yelled.

"That's what you say. How do I know what he's like? You're telling me Grayson is a bad man, and I know that isn't true. He would *never* hurt me."

"Go back to your room, young man."

Taylor ran through the door and slammed it behind him. Sarah sat on the edge of the bed, her heart pounding, her stomach rolling. Suddenly she lurched into the bathroom and vomited into the toilet.

Taylor grabbed his coat and slammed out of the apartment. He ran down the hill to the bunkhouse. He didn't even knock, but just walked in. Grayson was sitting at the table. His eyes were red, his face streaked with tears. His shoulders sagged with dejection and he was nursing a drink in his hand. A bottle of rye sat on the table in front of him and there were two empty cans of Pepsi lying beside it, but five more sat behind the bottle, waiting to be used.

When Taylor came in, Grayson took one look at his ravaged face and stood up. He reached out and pulled the boy into his arms, holding him close. "I'm sorry Taylor."

Taylor clung to him like a lifeline. "I know you're not a bad man. I love you, Grayson, and I know you love me. I trust you. Mom's crazy."

Grayson shook his head. "Taylor, your mom has spent her whole life trying to protect you. She'd do anything for you."

"No, she wouldn't. She says I can't see you anymore," he sobbed. "She says we have to move again. I don't want to move again, and I want to be with you."

"Taylor, you won't have to move. I'll leave."

"NO!" Taylor screamed. "NO, No, no! I don't want to stay here without you."

A knock on the door startled both of them. Before Grayson answered, Colt pushed the door open. "What's going on in here?" He looked at the two of them, taking in the tears and the anguished faces. His eyes focused on Grayson. "Son of a bitch!" he cursed. He slammed the door shut and stood shaking his head. "I guess you told Sarah."

Grayson nodded. "I had to Colt. If things were different..." He shrugged. "I probably wouldn't have, but it wasn't fair not to when Taylor and I are so close. And I kind of hoped...I thought maybe she was beginning to...you know..." He sighed. "But there's no chance of that now. As soon as I told her I'd been charged with Aggravated Assault, she lost it. I can't blame her. She wants to protect Taylor. She just sees me as another violent criminal now."

"She doesn't want me to be around Grayson anymore." Colt could hear Taylor's heartbreaking. "She said we will have to move again. I don't want to move again. And I'm not going to stay away from Grayson. He's like my dad...like you are to Sam and Selena. I told her I'm not moving again and I'm not letting her make me stay away from Grayson. She's so par'noid, sometimes I wonder if she just imagined all that stuff about my other dad."

"You are dead wrong about that Taylor. I checked into your father. I know some people in the police force and they put me in touch with a guy who works undercover. He has helped you both and he has nothing but praise for your mom. She has good reason to be afraid. Your father is a dangerous man. He's involved in drugs but he's smart, and they haven't managed to catch him yet. Everything your mother told us is true. You owe her a lot. She has made keeping you safe her life's work."

Taylor looked subdued, and then he began to sob. "I want Grayson to be my dad. He feels like my dad. He said he'd go away so mom doesn't want to move, but I don't want him to go. I want to be where he is."

Colt and Grayson looked at each other. "I don't think anybody has to leave. Did you tell her everything, Grayson?"

"I didn't get beyond telling her that I was charged. She assumed the worst and blew her stack. In a way, I can't blame her, Colt. She trusted me with her son. It's just one more letdown."

"Look, I'll take a quick look at the cows and see if anything is happening out there. Then I'll go up and get Fran and we'll go over and talk to Sarah. Once she gets the full picture, I'm sure she'll see things differently." He stepped toward the door. "I'll stop on my way back to the house and take you with me Taylor. After Fran and I talk to your mom, you need to apologize for some of the things you said to her tonight."

He looked pointedly at Grayson. "Don't go doing anything stupid. You're not going anywhere. We want you right here on the ranch. We'll work all this out. No one is going to leave."

***

Frank knocked on Sarah's door. She and Colt waited, but there was no answer, so she knocked again. When there was still no answer, she looked at Colt. "I'll go in and check on her. Colt nodded and opened the door. He waited while Frank tiptoed into the bed room. As she approached the bed, Sarah uncurled from the fetal position and looked at her. Her face was blotchy, her eyes swollen from tears. "Frank," she whispered, dissolving in tears again.

Frank sat on the bed beside her, taking her hand and pulling her into her arms. She ran her hand down her head, caressing her hair. "Everything is going to be alright, hon."

Sarah shook her head. "Taylor hates me, but I can't let him hang around with a man who is so violent." She sobbed. "How could I have been so wrong? I trusted him, I was beginning to have feelings for him, and I'd begun to dream again."

"Shhh. Sarah, your first instincts about Grayson were right. He is a good man."

Sarah pulled away. She shook her head. "How can you say that? They charged him with Aggravated Assault. That's not the kind of man I want my son to look up too."

"Do you trust Colt and me?"

Sarah nodded.

"Do you think we would let a dangerous man work here? We have children too."

"But he told me…"

"He told us too."

"How can you let someone like that stay?"

"You mean a man who made a mistake? A man burdened with guilt and remorse. He could have lied and hidden the truth from you… from us? A man who needs the isolation of this place as much as you do, but is prepared to leave so you won't feel you have to? You mean that kind of a man, Sarah?"

Sarah's anger surfaced. "He hit a man and went to jail for it. How long will it be before he's teaching my son to fight?"

"He'd never do that. And he didn't go to jail, he wasn't convicted."

"But he said…"

"You didn't give him a chance to finish telling you what happened. You just assumed he was convicted. Let him tell you all the facts, before you make such a harsh judgment. Do it for your son; Taylor is totally devastated. Do it for the man who loves that child more than many fathers love their own kids. Do it for the man who loves you and your son so much, he's offered to leave so you won't feel you have to go."

Colt appeared at the door. "She's right Sarah; Grayson is in as bad a shape as you are right now. It's killing him, knowing that he's lost your trust and created a rift between you and Taylor. He said he would leave, and Taylor was hysterical. He doesn't want to lose Grayson. I told him no one was leaving, that we will all work this out together."

"You're not going to guilt me into changing my mind."

"We're not trying to guilt you into anything. We just don't want you to do something you will regret later, Sarah."

CHAPTER SEVEN

Taylor eased past Colt, into his mother's bedroom. He looked at her tear-ravaged face and shifted on his feet awkwardly. "Mom, I'm sorry for saying you were par'noid and the things I said about him... about my father and that I'd never seen him, and I thought you were imagining things. Grayson got after me and told me you were protecting me, and Colt said he checked out my father and he says he's a really dangerous man. So I was wrong about that and I'm really sorry."

Frank stepped away from the bed to make room for Sarah to reach out to her son. He stepped into her arms and hugged her. "Everything I've ever done, was to keep you safe, Taylor. You mean more to me than my own life."

"I know that mom, I really do. But you are wrong about Grayson. He would never hurt me or you."

"Taylor, you're thinking with your heart because you want a father and you have bonded with Grayson. I've got to see beyond that. I've made my own mistakes by thinking with my heart and my wants. I have to be wise enough to protect you from making the same mistakes I did."

Taylor pulled away. "I'm not going to let you take Grayson

away from me, mom. He says he'll leave, but if he goes, I'll…I'll run away and find him."

Sarah gasped.

Colt stepped in and put his arm around Taylors's shoulder. "Taylor, nobody is leaving. Everyone is overwrought right now. Go to bed and try to sleep. In the morning, we'll work through this."

"She's not going to do this to us again," Taylor cried.

"Go to bed, Taylor."

Taylor stormed out of the room. Colt turned to Sarah. "Try to go to sleep. We'll talk in the morning." He reached for Frank's hand, led her out of the room, shut off the light and closed the door behind him.

The next morning Colt and Frank were up early. They were sitting at the table having coffee, when they heard the porch door open and Taylor came into the kitchen. He looked exhausted.

Colt pulled out a chair and motioned for him to sit down. Frank reached out and laid her hand over his. "You didn't get much sleep, eh?"

He shook his head. "I'm so mad about everything. I love mom, but I don't want to have to choose between her and Grayson. I wish he'd never told her what happened."

"He was being honest, Taylor. It took a lot of courage for him to do that. He knew it might upset your mom, but he couldn't deceive her about his past, especially when you and he have such a close relationship."

"So he did something wrong once, but he's not like that now."

Colt's face filled with compassion. "Taylor, I believe that is true or he wouldn't still be here. He made a mistake in the heat of the moment and something terrible happened. It was an accident and his actions were not typical of his character. I know that, because after he had told us what had happened, I checked him out with the police." He touched Taylor's shoulder. "But you have to be careful about who you trust. Really liking someone is not reason enough to trust them unconditionally. Your mother knows that better than most people do. She learned the hard way and she doesn't want it to happen to you."

"But she won't even listen."

Frank squeezed his hand. "Someday, when you are grown up and have children of your own, you will understand how protective being a parent makes you. Your mom's trust has been broken. She's been afraid for both of you for so long; she is always on high alert and anything that makes her nervous or suspicious makes her ready to run."

Taylor bit his lip. "I don't want to run anymore."

Colt squeezed his shoulder. "Once your mom has gotten some rest, I'm sure she will calm down. Then I will have a talk with her and see if we can't work this out to everyone's benefit." Colt put his coffee cup aside and stood up. "Do you want to come to the barnyard with me? I have to check for new calves."

Taylor hesitated. "I can say Hi to Grayson, can't I?"

"We have to respect your mother's wishes. I don't think you should visit him in the bunkhouse, but if you go to the corrals with me and he's out there working, I don't think it will do any harm for you to say hello and help him with the chores."

Taylor stood up and went to the porch to put his coat and boots on. He pulled on his toque and went outside with Colt. When they reached the barn, Grayson was already out checking the cows, looking for new calves. Taylor gave Colt a pleading look and then darted across the pen to his side. He nervously stuck his hands in his pocket, and then looked up at him beseechingly. "Hi," he said softly.

Grayson gave him a tired smile and touched his head. "Hi, Buddy." Grayson's face was drawn and gray. His eyes were bloodshot, his demeanor sad. It bothered Taylor to see how distressed his friend looked; he wanted to throw his arms around him and give him a hug, but he resisted the impulse. Instead, he said, "Colt says everything will be okay."

Grayson nodded and silently handed Taylor the ear tagger. He reached into his pocket and took out some tags, handing them to Taylor as they moved side by side to find the next calf.

When the chores were finished, Colt told Grayson to get some rest. He assured him that he was going to talk with Sarah later, and he was certain that they would work things out. "I doubt that she will trust you a lot, but I'm pretty sure that she will accept you working with Taylor. It may take a while before you'll be able to take him fishing or horseback riding, but I'm going to remind her that Fran and I, and Ollie and Ellie, will all keep an eye on you guys and make sure nothing unhealthy is going on. You and Taylor can still spend time together while you work. That's better than being cut off completely, and it's better than either one of you leaving the ranch."

Grayson nodded and turned toward the bunkhouse.

Colt and Taylor went back to the house for breakfast. Sarah and Frank were sitting at the table, having a cup of coffee. Sarah looked as exhausted and disconsolate as Grayson had. Her eyes met Taylors imploringly. She could read the unhappiness in his face. "Come here?" she said softly, opening her arms to him. He walked toward her hesitantly, and when he hugged her, she could feel how torn he was.

Frank had breakfast ready. She called Selena and Sam from the family room and they all sat down to eat. When they were finished, Colt told Taylor and the twins to go into the family room. Then he suggested that he and Sarah go to his office.

He filled Sarah in about the conditions that led up to Grayson's arrest. He also told her about the guilt that Grayson carried over the damage he had done to the victim and explained why he had sought anonymity on the ranch.

Sarah was adamant, insisting that she did not trust Grayson's influence on Taylor.

Colt looked at her and sighed. "Sarah, do you remember why you left home?"

She looked at him defiantly. "That has nothing to do with this."

"I suggest you give that some thought. You told me that you resented the way your dad controlled everyone's life."

"I did, but what has that got to do with this."

"Sarah, Taylor is very attached to Grayson. Be careful, or you will make feel the same way about you. Grayson fills a place in his life that you never can. He desperately wants a father, a man's influence. The relationship they share fills needs for both of them. You can force Grayson out of Taylor's life, but you can't force him out of your son's heart. As much as he loves you, he will resent you if you do."

She closed her eyes. "He already does," she whispered.

"Sarah, when you told us about your past, I followed up on your story. I contacted a friend of mine in the police force who happened to know Bert Chambers, the undercover cop that helped you. I spoke to him and he told me what you'd been through, and what Taylor's father was all about.

"When Grayson told me about his past, he was so honest, so full of pain and guilt that I believed him. But…I'm not a fool. I'm a man with a family to protect too, so I contacted Bert Chambers again and asked him to check out Grayson's story. I also told him how attached

Taylor was to him. He reported back, and Grayson's story checks out. He also said that the local police got the impression that Grayson is a very kind, gentle man, who normally would have walked away from the situation."

"Woulda, coulda, shoulda," Sarah spat. "My point is that he didn't walk away that time. How do we know there won't be a repeat performance?"

Colt groaned with exasperation. "Well Sarah, it's your decision to make. Grayson has worked here for four years and he's been nothing but a model employee, so I'm not going to let him leave. You are more than welcome to stay and you are as safe here as you could be anywhere. On top of that you and Taylor have the support of everyone who lives here...including Grayson. I think you need to weigh the pros and cons. You can force Taylor to go with you, but you know how he is going to react. If you choose to stay, you can minimize the amount of time that Taylor spends with Grayson.

"There is always one or more of us working with Grayson and we'll keep an eye on them. Taylor can come out and work around the ranch when Grayson is working, but you can stop him from visiting him at the bunkhouse, or doing fun things with him, like going fishing. Taylor won't be happy, but he will accept it better than if you force him to move again. He will still have contact with the man he idolizes and I know Grayson will respect your demands. He wouldn't do anything to cause your son more pain."

"So what you are suggesting, is that we stay here and Taylor be allowed to work with Grayson, so he won't feel like I've been unreasonable and taken away his best friend. And the rest of the crew will make sure Grayson doesn't have a chance to teach my son how to fight, or anything else I wouldn't approve of. And you actually believe Grayson is such a terrific person; he will never try to turn Taylor against me? I haven't been running for the past nine years because I'm stupid, Colt. You are trying to put a guilt trip on me so I'll see things your way."

Colt pushed his chair back and stood up.

"You told me you were stubborn and wouldn't listen to your parents when you ran away with Duncan Talbot. Well, you are still the most goddamned stubborn woman I have ever met! You seem to be willing to cut off your nose to spite your face. Think hard before you decide to move again, Sarah. And most of all think of where you could go and have an extra five pair of eyes looking out for you and

Taylor, watching for anything unusual that could be a threat."

Colt walked out of the office and left her sitting in the chair. Sarah wiped away her tears and stood up. After making her way outside, she went to her apartment and lay on the bed in her room.

Her gut was knotted, roiling with anxiety. *No one understands where I'm coming from. I'm the one who has struggled to keep us safe. I've had to make the decisions and be on the alert for anything that could harm us. Everyone thinks Grayson is beyond reproach, even though he has resorted to violence and been charged, but the fact remains that is who he is.*

She turned over and looked at the ceiling. *I have to really think about this before I make any decisions. Taylor is getting older and he isn't willing to accept that I know what's best for him. Grayson is the first man he has bonded with, and he will fight me and resent me if I take him away from Grayson.*

She watched the shadow of the curtains flutter on the ceiling. *Colt is right about the ranch being a safe haven and that everyone will watch out for us.* She sighed. *Maybe I am just stubborn. If I compromise and stay here, Taylor can still see Grayson when he works with him, but I can limit the amount of time they spend together one on one. That will lessen the influence he has over Taylor. Maybe with time, Taylor will outgrow his infatuation with him.*

She drifted with her thoughts, exhaustion overtaking her as she fell asleep.

Sarah slept until early afternoon. Frank and Colt were in the family room, visiting with Ollie and Ellie. They had told them about Grayson's past and Sarah's concern about his relationship with her son. There were mixed feelings about her reaction.

Ellie had summed up all their thoughts. "I can understand her feelings, but she'll make things worse if she lets her fear overcome reason. She's done a fine job of raising Taylor. He's a great kid and he's smart, but I see his desire to have a man in his life when he talks in class. He's attached himself to Grayson."

Frank shook her head. "Why couldn't he have looked to Colt? He's here; he works with the kids. He has included Taylor in our lives."

"Colt is Sam and Sarah's dad. I think Taylor wants someone he feels is his own. Grayson doesn't have children, so he has nobody else to divide his affection and attention for Taylor with. They reached out to each other; I think Grayson needs Taylor as much as he needs him. Taylor wanted to see Sarah and Grayson get together so he'd have a family. I've heard him refer to himself as *Gray's son.*"

Frank nodded. "I know Grayson was interested in Sarah, and I saw her changing toward him. I encouraged her to think about it. But now...I'm sure that possibility is dead in the water."

They looked up when Sarah came into the room. Her smile was strained. "Good morning; I guess it's actually afternoon. I'm sorry I slept in."

Frank stood up. "No problem. You needed to do that. Do you want some coffee, or something to eat?"

Sarah shook her head. "Where is Taylor?"

"He's with the twins. They're practicing their roping skills." Colt stood up and held up his hand to forestall any protest. "They are down at the barn, but I asked Grayson not to hang out with them in respect for your feelings. He said he'd already decided that he didn't want to aggravate the situation. He's taken a few days off and he went home to see his parents. He is so exhausted and emotional that I didn't want him to leave today. In my opinion, he shouldn't be driving, but he said he needed to go.

"He has given me his word that he'll be back by next weekend, and I'm holding him to it. I don't want to lose him; unless of course he decides to go back to practice veterinary medicine with his dad. Then I'd have to accept it, because he should be using his training, not wasting it working here as a ranch hand."

Colt could tell that Sarah seemed to have missed everything he'd said except that Taylor was at the barn with the twins, and Grayson wasn't there. She hadn't reacted to anything else, just turned when he'd finished speaking and walked into the porch. He heard her go out the door and watched as she walked down the hill toward the barn.

He shook his head. "She is so stressed; she's pretty much out of it. I wonder if she's decided what she's going to do. Maybe that's why she wanted to see Taylor."

Frank put her hand on his shoulder. "You've done all you could, Colt, it's in her hands now."

***

Taylor tensed when he saw his mother coming to the barnyard. He loved her, but right now he felt angry. He knew he was just a kid and he'd probably have to do what she wanted, but he was full of anxiety and resentment. He didn't want to be forced to make a choice, and in reality he knew he didn't really have one, but he couldn't imagine his life without Grayson.

He didn't go to meet her. Instead, he focused his attention on the cow horns that they were trying to rope. Sarah didn't miss his attitude and her chest tightened. She stood and waited until he made his throw. He missed the horns and his frustration was obvious in his body language.

"Taylor," she said softly. He didn't respond, but instead concentrated on coiling his lariat. She grimaced, pain filling her heart. "Taylor," she said firmly.

He slowly turned toward her. She read his feelings clearly.

She swallowed hard. "I want you to come for a walk with me, we have to talk."

He walked to the tack room reluctantly and hung up his rope. Logically Sarah had expected that he would feel this way, but in her heart she had hoped he would be willing to accept whatever she decided.

Her thoughts were painful. *What's the surprise? He is my son. He's like me.* She sighed. *Even at his age, I resented dad forcing us to do what he wanted. I thought of running away so many times, but I had mom and the other kids, and I didn't want to leave them. But as soon as I graduated, I was out of there.* She swallowed hard, thankful she had made the decision to stay. *He won't like the conditions, but he won't run away like I did.*

When he shut the door to the tack room, he faced her, his arms hanging dejectedly at his side, his eyes filled with pain, refusing to meet hers.

She reached out to him, taking his arm. "Let's go for a walk, Taylor. I've thought about this a lot and I've decided to stay here."

"But Grayson is gone." The words were bitter.

She frowned, recalling Colt's words. "He'll only be away for a week. He's promised Colt he'll come back. Apparently he went to see his parents."

Tears filled Taylor's eyes and spilled down his cheeks. Sarah stepped forward and pulled him into her arms, holding him close. Gradually he relaxed and slid his arms around her waist, resting his head against breasts.

Tears ran down her cheeks as she let him sob. Gradually his

painful cries subsided and he calmed. Then he hugged her and whispered in ragged tones, "I love you mom…but I love him too. Thank you for staying."

"There are some ground rules, Taylor."

He stood back and looked at her with red-rimmed, tear washed eyes. "Like what?"

"Let's walk, okay?"

He nodded and let her take his hand to lead him up the road. She was silent for a few moments.

"Taylor, there is a lot you don't know about my life, or remember about our life."

He shrugged his shoulders, but nodded.

"I realize how much you care about Grayson. If I decided to leave, I'm certain you would resent me: and I don't want that to happen. So, while it's still against my better judgment and it's based solely on your happiness, I have made the decision to stay. I have experienced things in life that you don't understand. Those experiences still make me very uneasy about Grayson. If a person commits a violent act, there must be violence in that person, and I don't want you to learn that."

Taylor shook his head. "He's not like that mom."

"We'll see in time, but for now, you can go to the barn and work with him when another adult is present. You can still see him and talk to him, but I don't want you going down to the bunkhouse, or the two of you going riding or driving to town."

"Mom…"

"Taylor. I have compromised; now you have to give some too. Colt and I talked this morning and he suggested this as a solution. He was confident that Grayson will honor my conditions, and I expect you to. Living here is a good thing for us in many ways, and I took everything else into consideration before I came to this decision. I know you really care about Grayson, and it wouldn't be fair to leave and cut him right out of your life, but I have protected you since you were born. I'm not going to stop now."

Taylor kicked rocks down the road. He turned and looked with longing toward the bunkhouse and tears welled in his eyes.

"Are you willing to live by the rules?" Sarah's words were firm.

"What choice do I have? If I don't, I'll never see him again."

"Alright, let's go back to the house. I want you with me, when I tell the rest of them what I've decided."

"Can't I go back to the barn?"
"Yes, after we talk to Colt and Frank. Ellie and Ollie are there too, so everyone will hear it from us."

CHAPTER EIGHT

When they reached the house, Colt, Frank, Ellie and Ollie had moved into the kitchen and were sitting at the table drinking coffee. Their conversation stopped when Sarah and Taylor walked in. The tension between mother and son was obvious, and an uncomfortable feeling filled the room. Taylor stood slightly behind her, head down, eyes focused on the floor.

Colt's stomach clenched when Sarah looked at him and cleared her throat to speak. "I've given a lot of thought to what you said this morning and I've decided we will stay here at the ranch. All my instincts are fighting this decision, but I've lived on high alert for the past ten years. As you pointed out, it is probably the safest place we can be and I know how much Grayson means to Taylor. I realize how much leaving here would hurt him, and I know it would damage our relationship. So Colt I trust you, and I am following your suggestion."

She reached for Taylor's hand and tugged him to her side. "I have told Taylor he can still work around the barnyard with Grayson, but I don't want him going down to the bunkhouse and spending hours alone with him. He isn't allowed to go off the ranch with Grayson; no fishing or running into town." She looked at the four sitting around the table. "I know that Taylor has come to look at Grayson as his dad because he is longing for a male figure in his life. But, Grayson is *not* his dad; he is his friend. Friends are really important and special, but eventually each person grows and makes their own life.

"I know you all believe that Grayson is a great guy, and I have to admit that I haven't seen him act in a way that proves he's not, but he obviously has a streak of violence in him or he wouldn't have hit that man. I have lived with too much viciousness in my life already; I have run from place to place trying to stay ahead of it. Taylor was too young to understand what it was like to find threatening notes and packages on the doorstep, when I'd done everything I could to keep us invisible. They don't give you a new identity because you are stubborn and paranoid; it is so you can disappear. I was only able to live a somewhat *'normal'* life for three years, before Duncan found us again." She swallowed hard. "I haven't been able to give Taylor an ideal way of life. But I've done the best I could, and now I don't want him to be influenced by someone else's violence. It's going to take longer to convince me that Grayson is the upstanding citizen you all think he is. I was beginning to trust him, and then I found out that he has been deceiving all of us, concealing his past. To me, that's ironic, since he was quick to reveal my situation to all of you."

She ran a hand through her hair. "I appreciate all of you; I care about you. I hope you will honor my wishes and my trust. My life has been rudderless since we left the Harahan's in Toronto. After being there for four years, I felt we were safe. They loved us and treated us like family, but then it became obvious that they couldn't protect us anymore…in fact, we could be endangering them.

"I need a home and friends, but I still need to protect my son. Taylor isn't happy with the compromise, but one day I hope he'll realize how hard this is for me."

Colt stood up and walked over to Sarah. He put an arm around her shoulder, then reached out and pulled Taylor into the embrace. "I'm happy you've made this decision, Sarah. I can appreciate your reservations and your fears, but I will stake my honor on Grayson. He will never do anything detrimental to Taylor, or you, for that matter. He is a kind, conscientious man who is drowning in regret and guilt over what his action precipitated. He could have stayed and worked with his dad, but he hasn't been able to forgive himself and he couldn't face the people in the community, knowing he had ruined a man's life. The reports I received showed that the victim was a known bully who came from an influential family in Elliot Lake. He was also spoilt as a child and that gave him an overbearing sense of entitlement that he carried with him into manhood."

He hugged Taylor. "Someday you will realize how lucky you were to have a mother who cares as much as yours does. This will all work out. Grayson will be happy to know you are going to stay."

Taylor nodded then looked up Colt. "Can I go to the barn now?"

"You'll have to ask your mom about that."

Taylor looked at his mom, who gave him a nod. He whirled away from Colt and out the door. Sarah sighed deeply and shook her head.

Frank was at her side. "Would you like something to eat, Sarah? I don't think you've had anything yet today."

Sarah nodded and sat down at the table with them. Ellie reached out and touched her arm. "Being a parent isn't easy. Sometimes it's thankless, but one day Taylor will appreciate how much you've cared. I'm glad you didn't try to cut Grayson right out of his life. In the classroom, I see how attached he is to him and I think it would have had lasting repercussions. He's not happy right now because he cherished those alone times with Grayson, but I'm sure Grayson will support your decision and help Taylor make the best of it."

Sarah rested her elbows on the table and buried her face in her hands. "God," she groaned. "You're all so convinced that he is such a paragon, and I'm totally wrong."

Ellie rubbed her arm. "No Sarah, you're a concerned mother. Who could judge you for that?"

"Well for one, my son."

After Sarah had eaten the sandwich Frank made for her, she excused herself and went to her apartment. She was emotionally and physically exhausted. She laid down on her bed and fell asleep. When she woke up at midnight, she checked Taylor's room and found him sound asleep. She went back to bed and slid back into a deep, healing oblivion.

***

Grayson returned to the ranch as he'd promised. Colt felt a sense of relief when he saw him drive in. He wouldn't have been surprised if he'd decided to go elsewhere, and it signaled to him the sincerity and honesty of the man. He hurried down to meet him when he parked his pickup by the bunkhouse.

"Glad to see you back here, man. How was the drive?"

"It's a long trip and I'm glad to be home."

"Home; I'm glad to hear you say that. How did your visit go?"

"Mom and Dad were glad to see me. Dad tried to persuade me to come back to the clinic, but I just can't imagine being there now. I'm happy to be back. Are Taylor and Sarah still here?"

"Yes, but she has some stipulations."

Grayson hesitated then asked, "What are they?"

"Taylor can come down and work around here with you, but she doesn't want him to visit you in the bunkhouse and he can't go off the ranch with you; no more trips to town, and no fishing."

Grayson looked frustrated, and then shrugged his shoulder. "Well…I guess I have to accept that. I screwed up and it will follow me forever," he said sadly.

"She's been through a lot, Grayson. She's stubborn and determined, but she considered his feelings, and the safety that living here provides. In a way, I think she's afraid of losing control of the situation too. Taylor is old enough to have an opinion of his own and he hasn't accepted her decisions without question, like he did before. He was very open about how he felt, and she realized she could alienate him and seriously damage their relationship if she didn't consider his wishes. Taylor isn't happy about the conditions. I told Sarah that you'd help him see that it isn't all that bad, because you'll still get to spend time together." Colt nudged him in the ribs. "I think you can find a lot of nails to pound around the corrals and other things that he can help you with close to home."

"Well, I'll make sure I stay out of her hair. I'll keep a low profile and stay away from the house. Pretty soon I'll be riding on the range, so I'll be gone most of the time anyway."

"Sorry guy, but that's probably the wisest thing to do for a while. I'm sure Sarah will see things differently given time. She got spooked when she heard what had happened and let's be honest, Taylor is the center of her world, and she's been the center of his. When he met you that equation shifted and I'm sure there've been times when she's felt pushed aside in favor of you. It has to have been a bit threatening for her."

"I tried to include her, Colt."

"I know."

"I even began to think we could be the family that Taylor

wanted. I care for her."

"You were making progress. Fran and I both saw a change in her."

"*Were,* is the operative word. I can't erase my past, the damage is done."

Their thoughts were interrupted by a yell. They looked up to see Taylor running down the hill from the house. His eyes were shining, his face beaming with joy. He ran to Grayson and threw his arms around him. "You're home! I've missed you so much."

Grayson hugged the boy, his heart filling with love. "I missed you too." He pulled back. "Maybe we shouldn't do this," he said cautiously.

Taylor took a step away, his face still glowing with happiness. "Why, because of mom's rules?"

Colt put a hand on his shoulder. "Remember, I gave her my word, Taylor."

"I know, but I told her I wanted to come down and say hello."

"Was she upset?"

"Well, she reminded me of what she had said, but she said I could go."

Sarah's eyes filled with tears as she stood at the big window in the living room. She watched her son throw himself into Grayson's arms, and she saw the way he hugged him back. *Please don't hurt my son, Grayson, because I'm just going to have to let go and trust you. He's not my little boy anymore. I can't give him what he needs right now, but you can*

She wiped the tears away as they spilled down her cheeks. *He hasn't hugged me like that for months.*

CHAPTER NINE

The weeks slipped away. Grayson avoided coming to the house; Taylor went out to do chores every afternoon after school. Sarah knew he was doing it to see Grayson, but he didn't go to the bunkhouse any more, and he never asked to go to town with Grayson. He spent every evening at the ranch house watching TV or movies with the twins after dinner, and then he came home and went to bed early.

On the weekends, he would get up early and go out with Colt and Frank to do chores. He never mentioned Grayson, but she often seen them together in the corrals. Even from the distance, she could see the happy spring in Taylors step, and their body language expressed the mutual enjoyment that they shared.

Sarah's heart ached. Taylor seldom smiled at her these days and he never made a move to hug her. He carefully complied with her wishes, but she knew he was doing it so he wouldn't rock the boat and make her upset. He was simply assuring that she had no reason to further restrict the time he could spend with Grayson. She was reaping the cold dregs of appeasement; Grayson was enjoying the warmth of acceptance.

One afternoon Frank came in a found her crying. "Sarah, what's wrong."

"Nothing."

"Sarah, you're not crying over nothing. Tell me what is wrong."

Suddenly Sarah found herself pouring out her fears and her feeling that she had lost Taylor."

Frank rubbed her thumb across the back of her hand. "Sarah, it's really just a symptom of his age. Believe me, if anything threatened you, he'd be there in a shot. He's reached that stage where boys are almost embarrassed to show affection for their mother. Sam is the same way."

"But he beams when he's with Grayson."

"Sweetie, you've always been there, and deep down he knows you always will be. His relationship with Grayson is new and right now Taylor is gorging on it, filling a hunger that's been there for ten years. He is learning to relate to a man. He enjoys the things they do together. It's exhilarating to him…like having a crush on his first girlfriend will be when that happens. He knows you don't approve of Grayson, so he's caught in the middle. He's probably afraid to say anything about what they do because he doesn't want to upset you. I'll bet he told you all about the exciting things they had done before you found out about Grayson's past."

Sarah nodded. "He did. He was so full of excitement."

"He's torn between the two of you right now. I'm sure he just wishes things could be like they used to be."

***

Easter Sunday fell on the twentieth of April. The 'family' had all come for the weekend; Shauna Lee and Brad Johnson, along with their children, Patch and Leanne, as well as Christina and Tim Bates, and the twins Shay and Zaira. They had become as closely knit as many genetic families, sharing their joys, fears, times of despair, and times of celebration.

Late Saturday afternoon Grayson sat in his bunkhouse, nursing the pain of being excluded from the celebration, but determined to abide by Sarah's rules. Colt had told him to come up to the house and had cursed when he reminded him of why he couldn't. "You are as much a part of this family as everyone else is," Colt had declared. "You've been with us for every occasion during the past four years. Sarah will just have to get over it."

But Grayson had shaken his head. "I have to abide by the rules, for Taylors sake."

Colt had stormed out, slamming the door after he growled, "Fuck her rules. How do you think Taylor feels, knowing you are down here by yourself?"

Grayson looked at his watch. It was only four o'clock in the afternoon; he had a long night ahead of him. He poured himself a stiff drink, lifted it to his lips and sipped, then set it back down on the table. He ran his hands over his face, pushing them back through his hair. Then he pushed the glass aside, stood up, and walked to his bed. His heart filled with pain and regret. He knew drinking wouldn't solve his problems; it would only numb his grief temporarily. Tears welled in his eyes. "If only," he groaned. "But I did and I can't change that." Grief was like a constricting band around his chest. He sighed, trying to release it.

"If only Sarah could have felt compassion and seen me as I am, instead of through her fear. If only I didn't love Taylor so much." A deep sob escaped him. "It would have been better if I had been Dillon. I wouldn't have had to live with all this guilt and misery." Tears ran down his cheeks, oozing down his chin and along his neck to be absorbed by his shirt. Gradually he found the oblivion of sleep.

At five-thirty, there was a timid knock at his door, but he didn't hear it. Sarah shivered in the evening chill and knocked again, louder this time. When she got no answer, she pushed open the door and peeked inside. Evening had fallen, and it was dark in the cabin. When she stepped inside, she could tell the fire had gone out because the room was chilly. In the last light of day that streamed through the window, she could see a drink sitting on the table. She looked toward the bed and could make out Grayson's form curled up on top of it. She could hear his soft breathing, so she stepped toward the bed and leaned down to touch him. Her hand touched his shoulder and he startled awake.

He squinted, trying to understand what he was seeing. "Sarah? What's wrong? Has something happened to Taylor?" His voice filled with fear as he heaved himself upright, bumping into her before she had a chance to step back. She reached out her hand, touching his chest as she steadied herself. She noted that it was damp before she regained her footing.

"Nothing's wrong with Taylor."

He ran his hand through his hair. "Then why are you here?"

"I...I came to ask you to come to up to the house tonight. Everyone else is there and you should be too. I mean, you should join all of us for the whole weekend."

His voice was ragged. "Did Colt tell you to come down here?"

Sarah looked startled. "No." Her expression was sad. "I just know it isn't right to shut you out."

Grayson looked at her numbly. She was stunned when she saw tears fill his eyes. He covered his face with his hands and deep ragged sobs shook his body. Sarah's heart twisted. She remembered the dampness on his shirt and instantly knew that he had been crying before he'd fallen asleep.

She sat down beside him and wrapped her arms around him. He resisted at first, then leaned into her and sobbed out his regrets, his grief, and his pain. The next thing Sarah knew her own tears mingled with his. She held him, as she would have Taylor, wanting to ease his pain and knowing that she was part of the cause of it. Without thinking, she kissed him on the temple, whispering "I'm sorry Grayson. I'm so sorry." She moved one hand up to run her fingers through his hair and cradle the back of his head against her. Suddenly she saw him through Taylor's eyes, through Colt and Frank's eyes. *I've been so stubborn, and judgemental and unforgiving.* Her proud heart melted as she nuzzled her face against the side of his. *This man, this big kind, capable man is crying like a child because of it. Even though I've hurt him so, he still has lived by my rules to protect Taylor.*

Grayson's sobs gradually subsided and he became fully aware of Sarah's comforting arms around him, her fragrant smell, and her hand cradling the back of his head, as she held him to her tear-drenched breast. He pushed away, embarrassed at his emotional outburst. "I'm so sorry about that," he rasped in a ragged, emotion-filled voice.

She shook her head and reached out to cradle his face with her soft hands, her tear filled gaze locking with his. "No…I'm the one who's sorry, Grayson. I've been so wrong. I only thought of myself and my own fears." Her voice was thick with emotion. "As if I haven't made plenty of mistakes; who was I to judge you so harshly." She groaned and settled her lips on his. Her hands played through his hair, then pulled him deeper into the kiss. They both lost themselves in it, both hungry for comfort, for forgiveness. When they came up for breath, Sarah caressed his face, wiping away the remnants of his tears. "Can you forgive me?" she whispered.

His hands reached up to cradle her face, his thumbs wiping

away the last of her tears. "Forgive you? I haven't been able to forgive myself. What do I have to forgive you for?" He closed his eyes and squeezed them tight. Then he opened them wide and looked at her. "Are you really here, or am I hallucinating?"

"I'm here, and you just heard me admit how wrong I've been."

He leaned forward tentatively and kissed her lips. They kissed again, but not with the same desperation as before. This time they shared a brief, gentler, healing moment. Then he pulled away and said, "I'm embarrassed. Men are not supposed to cry and sob like children."

She touched a finger to his lips. "That is such a pile of crap. Men, woman and children; we all need to release our pain. The real shame is when we deny it and shove it down inside." She smiled gently and ran her fingers across his cheek. "We'd better do what we can to repair the damage and go up to the house. No one needs to know that we've had private, personal meltdowns. Can I turn on the light?"

He nodded as he stood up. "I'd better put some wood in the stove and find a dry shirt. Do whatever you need to do; wash your face, comb your hair." He grinned ruefully, looking at her creased blouse. "I don't think I can help you with your clothes."

"I'll walk up the hill with you and slip over to my apartment while you go inside. I can repair the damages before I show up. The cool air will help to clear our eyes."

It only took Grayson a few moments to put wood in the stove, empty his drink in the sink, and change his shirt. Then they went outside and walked up the hill in companionable silence. When they reached the door, Sarah moved to take the walkway around the back of the house to her apartment. Grayson followed her around the corner of the house. "Sarah," he said softly. As she turned to look at him, he put his hands on her shoulders and looked into her eyes. "Thank you for giving me a second chance. I swear on my life, I'd never do anything to hurt you or Taylor. I promise you won't regret this." He swallowed hard and stepped away to disappear around the corner. Tears shimmered in her eyes as she waited, listening until he opened the door. After she heard it shut, she hurried to the apartment.

Fifteen minutes later, she went back to the ranch house to join the crowd. Taylor saw her immediately, as if he had been waiting for her. He hurried to intercept her with a worried look creasing his brow. "Mom...mom I need to talk to you."

Sarah slid her arm around her son's shoulder. "What's up?"

"I just need to tell you-- Grayson came up for supper. I was surprised when he came in." His eyes were pleading. "Mom, please don't make a fuss. I know this isn't part of the rules, but everyone else was so happy to see him. Please, just let it go this one time. I'll stay away from him; just let him visit with everyone tonight."

Sarah kissed Taylor's hair. "You know, it's Easter. It's time for forgiveness and love. Maybe I'll forget about all those rules from now on. Spend as much time with Grayson as you want. I know it makes you both happy."

Taylor just stared at her for a moment. His look morphed from uncertainty to incredulity. "Really?" Sarah nodded. He threw his arms around her and hugged her like he hadn't in months. He dashed away a tear, and whispered, "Thanks, Mom."

Her heart warmed as she watched him fly across the room. He didn't go to Grayson immediately; instead, he stopped and talked with Colt, and then exchanged a playful punch with Ollie. He poked Sam in the rib with his sock foot and they laughed at each other. Then he moved to Grayson's side and Sarah's heart ached when she saw the look that passed between them. She sighed as she watched Grayson slide his arm around her son's waist. Taylor looked at her, as if to make sure it was alright, and when she smiled he relaxed against Grayson. Sarah's eyes shifted from her sons to the older man's, whose gaze met hers openly, shining with gratitude and happiness.

Sarah went into the kitchen area and joined the women who were putting the finishing touches on dinner. She joined Frank at the island and helped her make salad. When they were done, Frank looked across the room where Taylor sat glued to Grayson. She looked at Sarah. "Are you OK with that?" she asked, nodding her head in their direction.

Sarah smiled. "Yes, it's Easter time and Grayson's been a part of this family for the past four years. He should be here, and to be honest when I see how happy they are together, I'm rethinking my rules. All the rest of you trust him, maybe I'm the one who is wrong. I've certainly been wrong before."

Frank squeezed her shoulder. "I'm glad you are rethinking things. Grayson made a chivalrous mistake and he has paid the price in spades. The worst part is he hasn't forgiven himself, so in many ways he actually is imprisoned. It's very sad."

Sarah nodded. "It has to be tormenting for him."

Later, after dinner and when all the kids were in bed, Frank went into the laundry room and brought out seven medium sized woven baskets, a large bag containing coloured Easter grass and another loaded with Easter treats and put them on the island.

Sarah smiled when she started emptying the bags. "When I was a kid we used to boil chicken eggs and then we'd dip them in food coloring and paint them. It was fun, although to be honest, I don't really like boiled eggs to this day. I use to see those fancy, chocolate eggs in the stores and drool over them, but dad thought it was all nonsense and mom made do with what she had. She'd hide the eggs around the yard and we'd have an egg hunt early in the morning before we went to church."

Frank smiled. "I was an only child, so I got spoiled. Every year the Easter Bunny left a beautiful basket full of colored grass like this stuff, and all kinds of Easter eggs and candies for me. Usually, there was a small stuffed animal as well, or as I got older mom would put in a delicate necklace or a bracelet. Unfortunately, for her, I never was the girly-girl she probably dreamed of having. I was the son dad would never have, and he took me everywhere with him, just like he would have taken a boy. I knew more about horses and cows and working around the barn than I ever knew about cooking and wearing frilly dresses."

Sarah set out the baskets and then opened bags of colored Easter grass. She smiled as she let it slide through her fingers. "I love this stuff; it's so pretty." She took handfuls of the three different colors and nestled them in each basket. Her expression became thoughtful. "My poor son: there were times when I could not afford to do the Easter thing for him. When we stayed at the Harahan's, Julie made sure he was spoiled, and she'd make up wonderful baskets for him. When we were in Nova Scotia, the McNeils made a fuss over him too, but there have been a few times when I just couldn't have done it on my own. Now, he'll go on the search for the baskets tomorrow and he'll enjoy the candy, but he's outgrown the childhood wonder. I'm sure he knows there's no Easter Bunny."

Frank laid her hand on Sarah's. "Don't beat yourself up, Sarah. You did the best you could, and all kids grow up. I've known for years that there is no Easter Bunny and no Santa Clause—but I still love to put out the baskets for Easter—and I still like the idea of

Santa Clause. It's all fun."

Sarah sprinkled a handful of large colorful marshmallow eggs in each basket, and Frank added some foil-wrapped chocolate eggs, and jellybeans.

Sarah laughed. "Frank, do you know what a sugar rush those kids are going to get?"

Frank grinned as she nestled a large chocolate bunny into the other sweets in each basket and sprinkled a bit more Easter grass over everything. "I know—thank goodness the Easter Bunny only comes once a year." She stood back and viewed their handwork. "I think we should put a name on each basket and we'll put Shay and Zaira's up here on the lawn, because they're too young to have any idea what this is all about, and they sure as heck can't eat the candy. Christina and Brad will have to find their baskets, but it will make for great pictures and create special memories when they're older. We did that with the twins." She went back into the laundry room and returned with some tags and curly ribbon. Let's make a tag for each basket. Shauna Lee and Brad will have fun helping Patch and LeAnne find their baskets around the barn. And we can put Patch, Serena and Taylor's down around the corrals and bale stacks. We'll go down with them and I want to get pictures of all of them. Grayson will be in there like a dirty shirt helping Taylor find his."

"He will, and Taylor will love it."

Frank reached out and hugged Sarah. "I'm so glad you've relented. It means so much to the two of them, and I'm sure it has to be a bit of a relief for you too."

Sarah sighed. "Please don't mention this to anyone, but I went down to the bunkhouse to ask him to come up to the house. I knew shutting Grayson out wasn't fair to him or anyone else. When I got there, I knocked on the door twice, but he didn't answer. I pushed it open and stepped inside." She swallowed hard. "I was shocked at what I saw." She shook her head and her eyes shimmered with tears. "He was curled up on the bed like a child in pain, and when I went to shake his shoulder I felt dampness in his shirt." She placed her hands over her eyes. "Wh.. when he sat up I knew he'd been crying. It's not something I'll forget easily." She lowered her hands and looked Frank in the eye. "Suddenly I realized what my fear and stubbornness was doing; how much I was hurting him, and how much I'd been hurting Taylor. I had to admit that I'd been wrong and give it up. Everyone else trusts him; I guess I have to give it a try too. We talked and he was so humble, so forgiving, I was totally undone. He cried again and I cried with him. We agreed not to talk about this, but I'm sharing it with you so you will understand where I'm coming from."

Frank kissed her cheek. "You're a great mother and a wonderful person, Sarah. I'm proud to have you and your son as part of our family."

Colt, Brad, and Grayson came into the kitchen from the family room. Colt stretched. "Well, the game is over and they lost again. I think it's time to go to bed."

Grayson stopped to look at the baskets on the island. "They look great girls. When are you putting them out?" He ran his fingers over the tag that was for Taylor and smiled softly.

"Sarah and I will go out early in the morning before everyone gets up." Frank looked at Sarah for confirmation. Sarah nodded in agreement. "We'll put a couple around the barn, and the ones for the older three kids will go out around the bale stacks and the corrals. I want to get pictures of everyone looking for and finding their baskets."

"It sounds like fun." Grayson chuckled, and then said, "When I was young, my parents used to put out baskets for us. One thing, I loved, was the huge big chocolate covered eggs filled with marshmallow. They were about four or five inches long and they had a row of white or yellow icing thingy's shaped like small Hersey kisses lengthways along the middle of the egg. They'd have other bits of icing thingy's on the face of the egg and sometimes there was writing with icing."

Frank laughed. "I remember those. They were so good; I loved the marshmallow filling. I haven't seen them in years. When my kids were little, I looked for them—I would have gotten a couple for me too, they were so good. For a while, they came out with something that looked similar, but they were hollow like those big bunnies in the baskets are. I was so disappointed, because the marshmallow inside was what made those big eggs my favorite Easter candy."

Grayson looked at Sarah. "Are you headed to your apartment now?"

Sarah nodded. "I think so. What time do you want to put the baskets out in the morning, Frank?"

Frank yawned and laid her head against Colt's shoulder. "We'll have a cup of coffee at six and then we'll head out. It won't take long and the kids won't be up until seven-thirty or so."

Grayson yawned too. "I'll be up for chores, so I'll see you both then." He turned to Sarah. "I'll walk you to your door."

Sarah's eyes met his. "I'm okay."

"Let me do it, just to show my appreciation. I've enjoyed tonight more than you can know."

"It's not necessary Grayson. I'm a big girl."

"I'm well aware of that, but I'd like to do it."

She shrugged and walked to the porch, reaching for her jacket. Grayson was quick to take it and hold it for her to put it on. She felt his fingers brush her neck as he lifted her hair over the collar.

They walked to her apartment in silence. At the door, Sarah turned to look at him. His eyes were solemn as he reached around her to open it. Sarah's eyes strayed to his lips, and she remembered their kiss. Part of her wanted him to claim her mouth again and a tightening grew in her groin. Part of her was indignant, daring him to take advantage of their truce.

Grayson pushed the door open and stepped back for her to enter. "Goodnight Sarah," he said softly. "I'll see you in the morning."

Sarah's emotions were conflicted. Part of her was relieved, and part of her longed for his touch, for the feel of his lips. She listened to the click of the door as it closed the sound of his footsteps on the walkway. Thoughtful, she peeked in to check on Taylor, and then went to her bedroom. Her encounters with Grayson McNaughton that day played through her mind, and her heart stirred with longing for the way they had been before he'd told her about his past.

CHAPTER TEN

Frank was drinking coffee when Sarah arrived at the house the next morning. To her surprise, Grayson was there too.

Frank wore a cheery morning smile. "I called Grayson and told him to come up for coffee. He can help us take the baskets down to the barn."

Sarah poured herself a cup of coffee and walked to the table, taking a chair across from Grayson. "Aren't we putting two of them up here?"

"Yes, but it's safer if we carry one in each hand. There are a lot of goodies in those baskets. We don't want to upset our masterpieces! Besides, I'm sure Grayson gets tired of having coffee by himself every morning."

Sarah shot a look at Grayson, and then turned back to Frank. "It's not as cold out as it has been some mornings."

Grayson's gaze focused on her when he spoke. "Spring is on its way and I'm looking forward to it. The shorter days have made the time drag. I can only watch so much TV and I start to get bored."

Frank nodded. "It's like eating too much candy—you get sick of it."

Sarah laughed. "Do you think the kids will get sick of it today?"

Grayson grinned. "Not likely. Besides they are going to have to share; my fingers are going to be reaching in those baskets too."

Sarah chuckled. "Do you think we should make one for him? We could hide it in the grain bin."

Grayson's eyes sparkled as he looked across the table at her. "I'm a tad bit old for an Easter basket... unless it contains kisses." He quirked an eyebrow. "Candy ones."

Sarah blushed. She wished she hadn't but she did, and Frank didn't miss the bi-play between them. She grinned as she stood up. "Okay guys, I think it's time we get moving. I'll take Shay and Zaira's baskets out and nestle them in a couple of the shrubs on the lawn. It'll just take me a few minutes and then we can head down to the barnyard with the others."

Sarah got up and headed for the porch. Grayson followed her and held her coat as she pushed her arms into the sleeves. Neither spoke. She turned to go back into the kitchen while he put on his coat. She brought two baskets and set them on the bench. Then she went back to get two more and did the same thing. Before she turned to go for the last one, she looked at Grayson and found his gaze fastened on her.

"What?" she asked.

"Nothing, I was just watching you."

"Why?"

He shrugged. "Because I like looking at you."

She blushed again. "Grayson..."

"You'd better get the other basket. Frank will be here any second."

As she turned, she heard Frank stomping her feet on the steps and then the door swung open. She spied the baskets on the bench and smiled. "Good, we're ready to go."

When Sarah came back with the last basket, she handed it to Grayson. She looked at the tag, and then took it back. "You can't take that one; it's Taylors and you'll be helping him look for his."

He snatched it back from her. "You can't hide it either; you'll be helping him look for it too." He looked at the ones on the bench. "Frank can't hide Sam and Selenas either, so she can take Taylors and Leanne's." He gave Sarah a mischievous grin, and she felt herself blush again. "You can take Sam and Patches and I'll take Selena's; that way no one will know where their kid's baskets are hidden. Fair?"

Frank laughed. "Speaking of kids, you two are acting like a couple of them. But yes, Grayson; I agree that your idea is fair, now lets go. It's six-forty five, and we're running out of time."

They walked down to the barn and each went their separate ways, looking for places to hide the baskets. At some point, the three of them passed each other in the bale stacks. When Grayson met Sarah, he stood in front of her, refusing to let her go by. His blue eyes focused on hers and he leaned toward her. Her lids fluttered shut, and colour rose in her cheeks as she waited, anticipating the touch of his lips on hers. He kissed her forehead instead. "See you later," he said softly, as he stepped aside, and moved on. Disappointment flooded through her.

When they finished hiding the baskets, Grayson went to do the chores and Frank and Sarah went to the house to make breakfast. Colt, Tim, and Brad were sitting at the table drinking coffee. No one else had rolled out of bed and made it to the kitchen yet, so Sarah and Frank joined them for a quick cup before they started cooking.

"So did you play Easter Bunny and get all the goodies put out?" Colt asked.

Frank grinned. "We did. Grayson helped us. He's doing chores now."

Colt looked at Sarah and smiled. "I appreciate you bending the rules, Sarah."

Frank smiled and touched her shoulder. "I think she's decided to throw them out altogether, Colt."

Colt looked at Sarah with surprise. "Is that right, Sarah—no strings attached?"

Sarah nodded.

Colt whistled softly, then stood up and walked to her side. He took her hand and pulled her to her feet, enveloping her in his embrace. "I'm so proud of you Sarah. I know it couldn't have been easy an easy choice for you, but you have no idea how hard this whole thing has been on Grayson. Then there is Taylor; he'll be in seventh heaven now that he doesn't have to hide his feelings. You've made the right decision and I guarantee you will never regret it." He gave her an extra squeeze and rocked her gently before he let her go. There was moisture in his eyes as he said, "You've just made my day, girl." He turned and went back to nurse his cup of coffee.

The rest of the crew had appeared before the waffles were made and the bacon and sausage was cooked. Sleepy eyed children trickled out of the bedrooms, caffeine deprived adults headed for the coffee pot. Grayson, Ollie and Ellie, and Christina, Tim and the twins came to the ranch house.

Tim and his family had been spending the weekend at Ellie and Ollie's, and Ollie was enjoying a new dimension in his relationship with Tim. They had been friends before, but discovering that he was actually his biological son had completed Ollie's life. He now had two grandchildren who bore his genes, and he was bursting with joy. He still loved all the other children in 'the family' who called him Grandpa, but Shay and Zaira were extra special. He couldn't hold them often enough, or long enough, and as he studied their tiny faces, he saw nothing but perfection.

Suddenly the kitchen transformed into a place filled with noise; talking, laughter and activity. Frank looked at Sarah and smiled. "Bedlam has arrived! Let's cook the eggs and get this show on the road. I'll fry some, if you'll scramble a pan full. I'll ask Shauna Lee to set the table and Ellie will make the orange juice."

In half an hour, everyone was seated at the table digging into the breakfast feast, and twenty minutes later, everyone was relaxed and replete. Brad lifted his glass of orange juice in a toast. "To Frank and Sarah, who spent all that time making a wonderful breakfast, only to watch it be inhaled in a few short moments; we appreciate it girls." He looked around the table. "Guys, I think we should pitch in and clean up. The girls deserve a rest." There were nods of agreement and the men began clearing the table and heading to the cooking area. Taylor elected to help them, sticking close to Grayson.

The women moved into the family room, taking their coffee with them. Selena and Sam were dressed for the day and eager to get on with the Easter basket hunt. LeAnne and Patch needed some coaching from Shauna Lee. Ellie and Christina passed Shay and Zaira to Frank and Sarah, who admired them and cuddled them. Frank reminisced about her early days of motherhood with twins and asked Christina how she was doing now. Christina smiled and said she didn't know how she would cope with without Tim's help; having twins was very demanding in the early stages, but they were all doing their best, knowing it would get easier. Sarah remained silent, unwilling to share her experiences. *Will our life ever be normal?* she wondered.

By eleven o'clock, the sun was shining and Selena and Sam were becoming insistent about starting the Easter egg hunt. Finally,

Frank stood up. "Okay kids, I guess it's time to check and see *if* the Easter Bunny stopped here last night. Let's move into the kitchen and get everyone moving."

When they gathered in the kitchen, Selena took her characteristic, determined stance. "Mom says we need to check and see *if* the Easter Bunny came by last night." She giggled as if she didn't consider that a possibility.

Everyone looked at each other around the room, and then Colt stood up. "I'll check the mail box by the porch door. We'll see if he's left a note, like he has other years." Colt went to the porch and opened the door, then stepped out and lifted the lid of the small box attached to the wall by the porch door. It had been put there for people to leave messages if they stopped by and no one was home. Colt reached in and pulled out a sheet of paper. He appeared to read it as he stepped back inside. He was shaking his head as he stepped through the kitchen door. "Well guys…he left a note, but I think he'd run out of eggs by the time he got here."

"Dad, we all know the Easter Bunny is just a story. Mom makes those baskets."

Frank's look was one of shock, as her eyes shot to Patch and LeAnne. They showed no reaction, probably because at their age they were too young to grasp the concept. She gave Selena a stern look. "Young lady, you need to think about what you say. Just because you think that, it doesn't mean that the other children do."

Selena met her look unrepentantly. "But it's the truth mom. The Easter Bunny is just a fairy tale."

Frank shook her head. The child was right, how could she deny it. "You are too smart for your own good Selena."

Colt interrupted the awkward moment and handed the sheet of paper to Sarah. "Will you read this Sarah?"

Sarah smiled as she read the sheet, which she already knew by heart as she had typed it up on her computer, printed it off and put it in the box. She cleared her throat and glanced at the sheet. Then she looked at Colt and smiled. "Selena, I think your dad was teasing you. This note says that the Easter Bunny left seven baskets—each one has a tag with one of your names on it. The note says that the baskets for Zaira and Shay are hidden on the lawn because they are too young to go looking in places that are more difficult.

"It appears that he hid Patch and LeAnn's baskets down around the barn, and it says here that their mommy and daddy should help them look for them."

She squinted as she looked at the page. "The Easter bunny must have been tired. I can hardly read this...I think it says that Sam, Selena and Taylor will find their baskets around the bale stacks and the corrals. Your names are on your basket, so if you find someone else's you should give them a *hint* about where they can find it. And Selena and Sam, the Easter Bunny wants your mom and dad to go with you." She looked at Taylor and smiled. "And Taylor; I am instructed to go with you too, but the Easter Bunny says that Grayson is supposed to go with us."

Taylor's smile was dazzling as he turned to look at Grayson. Their gaze met and held. Then Taylor walked across the floor and hugged his mother, hard. "I love you mom." Then he whispered, *I heard you printing that note this morning. I peeked at it, but I won't tell anyone.*

She ruffled his hair and hugged him back. "I want you to be happy hon," she said softly. He nodded.

Frank clapped her hands. "Okay everyone, let's go hunting. And moms and dads don't forget to take your cameras!"

Everyone headed for the porch to get their coats. As the crowd thinned out, Taylor leaned around the corner. "Come on mom."

"I'm just making hot chocolate in the crock pot. I'll come as soon as I'm done. You go ahead with Grayson."

"Mommm," he groaned.

"Go. I'll be there before you know it."

"Okay...but don't take too long. I want you to be there too." He turned and hurried out the door to meet Grayson and they walked down the hill. Sarah finished making hot chocolate in the six-quart slow cooker and set it on medium. Then she put on her coat and boots and grabbed her camera. When she stepped outside, she met Tim on his way inside with Shay and Zaira's baskets. Sounds carried clearly on the morning air and she could hear the kids shouting and laughing. She hurried down the hill and when she reached the corral, Taylor spotted her. "We're over here mom!"

Sarah looked around and decided to crawl over the corral fence and walk across the pen to the far side. Taylor was watching, a wide smile on his fence. A couple of calves ran frolicking and jumping in front of her. She smiled as she watched them.

Suddenly Taylors face turned to dismay and he screamed, "Mom, mom...watch that cow! You're between her and her calf.

MOM! MOM!!" He started climbing over the fence.

Grayson bailed over the fence right behind him, running to catch Taylor. "No Taylor! No!"

Everything happened at once. Confused, Sarah stopped in mid-step, staring at the commotion. Then something plowed into her back, driving her to the ground, rolling and pounding her repeatedly. She could hear an animal snorting as it punished her body, but she had no defense, no chance to get up. It kept ramming its head into her, and dimly she found herself wondering if it would ever quit.

Then she could hear the sound of repeated thuds near her. Grayson's voice sounded frantic as he yelled and cursed somewhere nearby. Dimly she heard Colt's familiar whistle signal for the dogs. Barking joined the cacophonous confusion. Suddenly the pounding punishment stopped. She lay there, stunned. *Can I move?* She wondered. *Am I broken in pieces?*

Grayson was touching her, gently pulling away the remains of her jacket. "Sarah, can you hear me?" He caressed her face. "Sarah, you have to be okay," he groaned as he slid his hand over her face, brushing away the mud. "Taylor needs you." He stifled a sob. "*I need you,*" he whispered.

Taylor was kneeling by her, sobbing as he plead with her. "Mom, I'm scared. There's blood all over." His words turned into a wail. "Mom, you have to be okay."

Colt and Brad's voice were what she heard next. "Ellie's gone to call the ambulance. Move out of the way guys, we need to get her on the stretcher."

She could hear Grayson trying to comfort her son. "Taylor, she'll be alright. We'll get her to the hospital and they'll know what to do."

Sarah heard Brad telling the men how to place their hands under her, supporting her neck to protect her in case there was spinal damage. Taylor was crying and she wanted to open her eyes but she just couldn't do it. As the four men and Frank and Shauna Lee, placed their hands under her body and lifted her onto the stretcher, she fought to the surface, pushing away the heaviness that enveloped her.

"Look!--her eyelids," Frank cried. "They are twitching. She's trying to open them. Just give her a moment before you move the stretcher guys."

Slowly Sarah's eyes opened, and she struggled to focus. Her

crusted lips formed one word. "Taylor?" It was barely a whisper, but everyone seen her lips move.

Grayson was crouched beside her. He touched her cheek. "He's here Sarah. Take your time." His hand folded around hers and she drew strength from him.

She sighed, hitching her breath as she felt the pain in her ribs. She groaned, and Grayson leaned close to her soiled face and hair. "It's going to be okay, Sarah. You've been banged up, you might have a broken rib, but you'll heal. If you can hear me, squeeze my hand, OK?"

She tried hard; everything was happening so slowly. Finally, her hand contracted slightly on his hand and he kissed it. "You're doing great. You'll be fine."

In the distance, she heard Colt say, "Ellie called the ambulance. They'll be here in a few minutes. I think it's better than trying to move her in the truck."

Sarah's eyes fluttered. *I feel like I've been run over by a tank—everything is starting to hurt.* Gradually her eyes opened and then suddenly she was *there,* fully conscious. Grayson was crouching beside her as he held her hand, and her eyes met his. "Taylor?" she whispered.

Grayson looked at Taylor. "Come here, son."

Taylor was there instantly, crouching on the other side. He threw his arms around her prone body. "I'm right here mom." Sarah groaned as the pain in her ribs knifed through her. Taylor pulled away, his eyes filling with tears. "I'm sorry…I didn't mean to hurt you."

Sarah gave a ghost of a smile. "I know" she whispered. "My ribs hurt. Sorry."

Grayson squeezed her hand. "The ambulance will be here pretty soon. It's safer to move you that way." His fingers brushed along her brow gently. "We don't want to take any chances. She really roughed you up and we don't want to aggravate anything."

Her eyes filled with tears. "I know. Thanks."

Sarah drifted in a cloud of pain and shock.

In a few minutes, they heard the ominous wail of the ambulance siren as it neared the ranch. Brad ran to the quad that sat in the barnyard and sped up to the driveway and out to the road to make sure that the ambulance didn't go past the ranch. Within moments, he led it back into the barnyard.

The two EMT's on board, John Phillips, and Tony Amber, got out. They collected their equipment and hurried to the corral. They monitored Sarah's vitals, fitted her with a cervical collar and immobilized her spine, made a physical assessment of her body, testing her reflexes and pain reactions. Then they moved the stretcher to the ambulance.

Grayson searched Johns face. "How does it look?"

"I can't say."

"Just give me a hint. That boy over there is her son."

John sighed and started putting some of his equipment away, murmuring as he worked. "If nothing unexpected turns up, I'd say she should be fine, but I can't guarantee that. We don't know if there are internal problems."

Grayson felt a load lift off his shoulders. "Tony, can her son and I ride in the ambulance with you guys."

"There isn't room for two of you. John will ride in the back with the patient. There's only one seat in front."

"Look—let her son squeeze in the back with her. I'll ride up here." Tony was shaking his head. "Well then let him ride up front and I'll follow in my truck."

"Don't put me in a bad spot, man. He's an emotional child. He'd be a hindrance if something took a turn for the worse. Follow us and he'll get there when we do."

Grayson turned to Taylor. "Come with me." He reached for the boy's hand and led him to the truck by the bunkhouse. "We're going to follow the ambulance to the hospital."

The rest of the 'family' were silent as they watched the ambulance, followed by Grayson's truck, go down the drive and turn onto the highway. Colt sighed and looked at Frank. "What do we do now? It seems wrong to keep looking for Easter baskets. I am.... That damned cow." He turned and looked at the animals that were standing quietly in the back of the pen.

Frank reached out and touched his arm. "The cow was just doing what animals instinctively do. She didn't understand that Sarah meant no harm to her calf. Having all of us down here probably stirred up unrest in the herd, and I certainly never thought anything of it when Sarah cut through the pen."

Ollie nodded. "Neither did I. But cows with young calves can be unpredictable. Once they get focused on a target, they don't back down willingly. Grayson hit her with that fence post over and over and it didn't even begin to register. It's a good thing you thought about the dogs, Colt. They got her attention and diverted her focus away from Sarah. Other than that, she might have killed her."

Shauna Lee sucked in her breath raggedly. "Let's hope she has no internal injuries."

"I'm certain she has some broken ribs. Hopefully, it didn't puncture a lung. Even at that I think she'll really have to be careful about getting pneumonia." Colt walked over and picked up the post that Grayson had used to batter the crazed cow. "This damned thing was almost ready to break. Look at the cracks and splinters in it." He shook his head, remembering the desperation with which Grayson had pounded the animal, as he tried to avert its attention from Sarah.

All the children were gathered around. Frank's look was serious. "You guys all need to remember what happened here. Don't walk into the corrals if you aren't with an adult, and even then, always be aware of what's happening around you. Later in the year, when the calves are bigger and the mothers are more relaxed it's not so dangerous. But right now, when the calves are new, they can be very protective and if one of the cows thought you might want to hurt her calf, and she decided to take a run at you, you wouldn't have a chance. You saw what happened to Sarah."

Colt nodded and said "And you know kids, it's the same with the bulls. I know you like to sit outside the corral fences and watch them fight, but remember if one of them decided to go after you it would be game over. We like our animals; we pet some of them, but we need to remember that they are still animals. Under the right circumstances, they can turn from being friendly to being mean, quickly. And in most cases you'll be the loser." He looked at Sam. "Just like when you play with the old dog and when he's tired of you mauling him and playing with his ears or tugging on his tail, he'll growl at you and get up and move away. If you don't quit, he'll growl again and snap. If you persist, he'll probably bite you—and you'd have it coming."

Sam looked away, knowing his dad was right. His mom had told him many times that old Sparky loved him, but he was old and tired and didn't want to play for very long; some days he didn't want to play at all.

Brad looked at Patch and ruffled his hair. "I think we should head up to the house." Everyone looked very subdued. Baskets and candies didn't seem important in light of all that had happened.

Sam reached out and took Frank's hand. He pushed close against her and laid his head against her hip. She bent down and looked into his face. Tears that were threatening suddenly spilled over and ran down his cheeks. "Mommy, do you think Sarah will be okay? That cow really hurt her. I feel so bad for Taylor." She crouched down and pulled him into her arms and he started to sob. "I don't know wh.. what I… I'd do it that happened to you, mom."

Frank hugged her son close. "Mommy works with the cows all the time, honey. I'm not saying that couldn't happen to me, but I know to watch for things like that. Sarah doesn't work in the pens with the animals and she didn't think about what could happen. She was thinking about helping Taylor find his Easter Basket."

Sam's arms threaded around her neck and she held him close for a moment. Then she stood up and took his hand. She looked across at Selena, who was watching soberly. "Are you okay, sweetie?"

Selena nodded and reached for Colt's hand. "That was scary. I hope Sarah is okay." She blinked back a tear. "I feel sorry for Taylor." She turned to walk away, tugging on her Dad's hand. "And Grayson, too; you know, Dad, I think he likes Sarah a lot." She looked up at Colt. "The way you like Mom."

Shauna Lee sighed. "Out of the mouths of babes," she said softly.

The group walked up the hill to the house. As they made their way into the porch, they could smell hot chocolate. Frank's eyes filled with moisture. "Sarah made hot chocolate in the crock pot before she came outside."

Colt sighed. He turned and walked toward the office. "I'm going to phone the hospital and see how she is doing."

Shauna Lee and Frank ladled out cups of hot chocolate for everyone. Each person took one and found a place around the big table. When Colt came back, he picked up his cup and leaned against the island. "Well, I talked to Grayson. The initial diagnosis is two cracked ribs, lots of bruising all over her body and superficial cuts on the back of her head. The head bleeds a lot so it looks really bad. They're doing more definitive tests right now, to make sure there are no internal problems. She's going to hurt big time for a while, but if the first impressions are right, she got off lucky. I'm sure we owe a lot of that too Grayson's dogged determination. He was like a man obsessed."

"Or a man in love," Shauna Lee replied.

Colt closed his eyes. "I think you may be right, but...I guess time will tell where that goes."

As the day turned into late afternoon, the shock of the morning wore off. Colt and Brad went out to find the rest of the Easter baskets, and everyone shared the goodies. Frank, Shauna Lee, and Christina played cards at one end of the table and the kids played with their coloring books at the other end. The guys went into the family room and watched TV. The smell of the Easter ham wafted tantalizingly in the air. Frank got up and put the vegetables on to cook that she and Sarah had prepped the day before.

Colt came into the kitchen and caught her in an embrace, as she stood at the island nibbling on raw veggies. "I love you," he whispered.

She leaned back and smiled as she looked into his eyes. "I love you too. When you see something like what happened this morning, it makes you appreciate what you have even more."

"That is true." He sniffed as he released her. "Supper smells great. How long will it be until it's ready?"

"I just put the vegetables on. It'll be an hour or so."

"I'm going to phone Grayson again and find out what's happening." Minutes later, he came back into the room with a smile on his face. "Grayson said they've ruled out any internal injuries." He shook his head. "It's hard to believe, but they are going to give her painkillers and an antibiotic and send her home. They should be leaving in half an hour."

Frank frowned. "I guess that's how the medical system works, but you'd think they would have kept her in overnight at least. Can you imagine how much she pain she'll be in the first week or so—not just the broken ribs, but all the bruising. It would be nice if they could have knocked her out for a week until everything started healing."

Shauna Lee clasped her hands together and leaned her chin on them. "I understand what you mean, but in honesty it's best if she gets mobile as soon as possible. And I'm certain they'll warn her about the possible complication of pneumonia with the broken ribs."

Frank nodded. "You're right. I just wish I could wave a wand and take the hurt away."

Colt leaned against the island countertop. "She's going to have a tough time knowing Taylor will be working out there with Grayson, too. She's always been afraid that he would get hurt and after this it's going to be hard to push those fears aside. He loves being out there; not just because he's working with Grayson, but because he learns quickly and has an affinity for the animals."

Frank walked over and stood behind her husband, leaning against him, placing an arm around him, with her head hooked over his shoulder. "We'll just have to do everything we can to help her through this. That's what family is all about."

He rested his head against her cheek. "You're right."

CHAPTER ELEVEN

Grayson shifted on the chair by Sarah's bed in the emergency room. It had been a long, heart wrenchingly emotional day, and he was wrung out. He looked at Sarah, who was lying with her eyes closed. Then he shifted his gaze to Taylor, who had stationed himself on the other side of the bed near her head. *Poor kid, he's exhausted,* he thought. *He hasn't slept since we came to the hospital, even though he's fighting to keep his eyes open.* He got up and walked around the bed, motioned for Taylor to stand up, then sat down and pulled the boy onto his lap. It was awkward because Taylor had grown a lot the past few months. Grayson shifted, and cradled the boy in his arms. His heart filled with love as Taylors dark head rested against his chest. "We're both lucky; she's going to be okay son. She's going to look pretty beat up for a while and she's going to hurt a lot, but we'll look after her and in the end she'll be alright."

Taylor nodded in agreement. Then his eyelids fluttered shut and he gave into the seduction of sleep. Grayson studied the contused face of the woman on the bed. Fortunately, the cow hadn't struck her face, but the ice and stones amongst the half frozen dirt in the corral had taken their toll, as she had been battered from behind. His eyes lingered on the discoloring that was starting to show. He shifted his free arm and reached out to take her hand. His fingers caressed hers, then squeezed her hand gently and held it. He felt her hand shift and turn to intertwine her fingers with his. Tears filled his eyes. *Oh, Sarah. God help me, I love you. I hope in time you'll love me back. I was afraid I'd never get to tell you how I feel after this morning, but I will as soon as I can. I don't care if you throw it back in my face, I have to tell you.* He tightened his fingers around hers.

Her caked, swollen lips tried to speak. Finally, she managed to croak out the words she wanted to say. "Thank you for looking after my son, Grayson."

He loosened their entwined fingers and grasped her hand. "I'll be here for both of you, Sarah. You're going to hurt for a while, but you will get better. I promise you that."

A tear trickled out of the corner of her eye and across her cheek and seeped into her hairline. He wanted to brush it away, but he knew he would wake Taylor if he moved. He squeezed her hand again. "Sarah, please don't cry," he said softly. "I want to wipe away your tears, but Taylor is asleep on my lap and if I do he will wake up."

More tears seeped down her cheeks, but she squeezed his hand again and whispered "You are such a kind man."

Tears filmed in Grayson's eyes, but he willed them away. "We'll be going home tonight, Sarah. We just have to wait for the doctor to discharge you and give you prescriptions for the medications you'll need. I'll stay at your place tonight to make sure that you are as comfortable as possible." He squeezed her hand gently again. "You are going to need pain meds for a while, but everyone will help you and I'll be there as much as I can. You're going to be back to your old self in a few weeks."

She tightened her grip on his hand and turned to look at him. "Not quite my old self. I'll be less judgmental and more forgiving. I can't tell you how sorry I am for how I acted." Tears flooded down her cheeks now.

"It's all forgotten now, Sarah."

"How can you be so generous?"

"He stroked her hand gently. "Because I…"

Doctor Elkins stepped into the room at that moment. "Alright, Sarah, I'm going to leave a couple of prescriptions at the desk for you. One is a painkiller; you are going to need those for a few days until your ribs and the tissue under the bruising start to heal. I'm giving you an antibiotic too. It's precautionary; those cracked ribs are making it hard for you to breathe properly and we want to avoid complications if possible." He touched her shoulder and smiled. "You've been lucky today, even if it may not seem that way right now." He looked across at Grayson and smiled. "I can see you are in good hands, so I'll have the nurse give you another shot. This will dull your pain for your trip home; in fact it should ensure a good sleep tonight."

Grayson cleared his throat. "Doctor, can she go home in hospital pajamas and a house coat. Her clothes are torn and dirty. We didn't stop to get clothes for her…"

"I'll tell the nurse." He smiled. "We won't send her home naked."

"I'll bring them back tomorrow," Grayson assured him.

The doctor chuckled as he ducked out of the cubicle. A few moments later, a nurse appeared with a set of hospital pajamas, a house coat, and a blanket fresh out of the warmer for Sarah. She motioned for Grayson and Taylor to leave the room. First, she administered a shot in Sarah's hip, and then helped her get dressed. Then the nurse told her she would get a wheelchair to take her out to the truck.

Moments later, she arrived with the wheelchair and helped Sarah into it, and then wheeled her to the ER desk to pick up the prescriptions. Grayson and Taylor hovered by their side.

Grayson took the prescription sheet and reached for the handles of the chair. "I'll take her to the truck."

The nurse smiled. "No, I'll do that; it's hospital policy. If you could park your vehicle right next to the sidewalk, it would make it easier."

Grayson nodded and hurried to move the truck. When he parked it, the nurse pushed the wheelchair out onto the sidewalk. Taylor was reaching to open the truck door, as Grayson scrambled out and ran around to their side, to help Sarah get up and onto the seat.

Sarah's face scrunched with discomfort, but she thanked them and the nurse smiled. "I can see you're in good hands. You'll be fine, Sarah." She closed the door and turned away as Grayson grabbed Taylors's hand and led him around to the driver's side. He helped him slide into the middle next to his mom, and then swung himself up under the steering wheel.

His eyes met Sarah's. "You just have to hang in there a bit longer. We have to stop at the pharmacy. It'll take a few minutes to fill the prescriptions and then we'll head home and get you into bed."

She nodded and looked out the window. Grayson drove to the pharmacy and went inside. He returned in a few moments and got in the truck. "It will be about fifteen minutes before we can pick them up." He nudged Taylor. "Are you hungry? It's been a long time since breakfast. We could run over to Subway and get something to go."

Taylor sat up straight and smiled. "I'm starved. Is it alright with you if we go, mom?"

Sarah nodded.

Grayson reached across behind Taylor and touched her shoulder. "Do you want anything?" Sarah shook her head. "Not even coffee or a bottle of water?"

"I should drink some water; maybe... I think I'd like a cup of coffee too." She leaned to rub her cheek against his hand as it rested on her shoulder. "Thanks."

He caressed her cheek with his thumb. "We're going to look after you," he said softly. Then he started the truck and headed toward Subway. He and Taylor went into the fast food restaurant and appeared a few minutes later with two Beef and Cheese Buns, two coffees, a bottle of water and a bottle of apple juice.

Grayson let Taylor slide in and gave him a bun and the apple juice. He put his bun and a cup of coffee on the dash, and then went around to the passenger door. He opened it carefully and handed Sara her cup of coffee, then tucked the bottle of water on the seat between mother and son, where she could reach it. She smiled wearily and thanked him as he shut the door. He started the truck and drove back to the pharmacy, collected the prescriptions and they were on their way home.

When they arrived at the ranch, everyone was anxious to see Sarah. Their hearts were full of love, but as in many situations like that, words were only tokens. Sarah stood for a moment, looking tired and forlorn. Then Grayson intervened. "I think Sarah needs to rest. Taylor and I will take her to the apartment and get her into bed. Her body is going to need a few days to recuperate."

Frank stepped forward, laying a hand on his arm. "Ellie and I will look after her."

Grayson's look pierced her. He shook his head. "No, Frank;

Taylor and I are going to look after Sarah. I'm going to stay at the apartment, and between us we will make sure she is alright. If we run into something we can't handle, I'll be the first to give you a call."

Frank's frown spoke louder than words. Grayson's eyes met her unflinchingly. "I hope you can understand that I need to do this. There is no impropriety here; I just *have* to be there." He turned to Sarah and took her hand, leading her to the walkway beside the ranch house to her apartment. Taylor followed them.

Silence hung heavily among 'the family.' Finally, Frank said, "Wow...I didn't see that one coming."

Shauna Lee looked taken aback. "That was pretty intense."

Colt smiled crookedly. "I think Grayson is pretty shaken up about what happened. We all know how he feels about Taylor. He's very protective; I'd say he's staking his claim with Sarah." He rubbed his chin thoughtfully. "I hope she doesn't hurt him again."

"Well, he knows what can happen. I guess he thinks it's worth taking the risk." Ollie turned toward the door. "I think we'd better let them settle their own affairs and keep our noses out of it."

Everyone trailed in through the porch door. They dispersed throughout the house; some sat around the kitchen table, others wandered into the family room to see what was on TV. The children settled on the floor with their toys.

Frank looked at Shauna Lee. "I could use a glass of wine, how about you."

Shauna Lee nodded and got up to help herself. "Do you want something Ellie? Would you like a drink Christina?"

Christina nodded. "I'll have a glass of wine too."

Ellie grinned. "I'll fix myself a rum and coke."

Frank lifted her glass toward Ellie. "Here's to the real woman amongst us! I seldom drink the hard stuff, I prefer my wine."

Ellie laughed. "I learned to have a drink with my first husband from the time we got married. We'd sit down every evening and have one drink, just to relax after a day of work. That habit has stayed with me, and now Ollie usually joins me. There is the odd time he's not in the mood and if he isn't that's alright, I'll still have mine."

Frank grinned. "You never know what happens behind closed doors. Ellie, I had no idea that you did that. I always imagine you cooking supper, bustling around tidying up the house, playing cards with Ollie, planning the next day's school lesson. I never thought of you having a drink every evening."

"It's good for the soul and the mind and the nerves. I look forward to that half hour when I sit and slowly sip it. It's my time, and if I share it with Ollie, that's even better."

They sat at the table and each took a few sips. Shauna Lee shook her head. "I'm still in shock over today's events. The fact that it's Easter Sunday has been almost lost in the trauma of what happened to Sarah this morning. I didn't realize that a cow could be so brutal. I'm certain she could have killed her if Grayson and Colt hadn't been there. It all happened so fast."

"It did happen quickly and people have been badly injured in that kind of situation; but what happened this morning doesn't make the cow a bad animal; in reality she is the kind of cow you want to have when they are out on pasture or the range. She would fight a wolf or a coyote the same way. She'd even take on a bear or a cougar, even though she could get badly hurt, but she'd fight to protect her calf.

"Unfortunately none of us were paying attention. We just didn't think when we saw Sarah start to cut across through the corral. The cattle are used to us, but she was a stranger and they notice things like that. That cow would have done the same thing to Karma or the ranch dogs. Our dogs are quick on their feet and they are trained to go for the heel, but we don't usually allow them into the corral when there are small calves around."

Christina shuddered. "I don't think I'll ever forget seeing that cow take her down. I'm just thankful she isn't hurt worse than she is. My kids are not going anywhere near the corrals."

Frank nodded in sympathy. "And honestly, they shouldn't go in the corrals when the cows are in there; especially not when they have small calves. In the fall, that same cow wouldn't look twice at Christina. It's more likely that the calf would run over her if it felt cornered and she was in its way. That actually happened to me when I was trying to push one down the alleyway into the chute. The alley narrows as it comes toward the chute and the calf panicked and turned. It was getting out of there and I was in its way. It knocked me ass over tea-kettle and went right over me. I got a bruise or two, but nothing serious. I'm certainly more cautious and try to protect myself now. If I'd have just flattened myself against the planks and given it room to go, it would have run right past me. The fact is cows are animals. They don't think the way we do; they work on instinct and survival."

Ellie twirled her glass on the table. "It was interesting to see how Grayson took over tonight."

Frank stared into the red liquid in her glass. "Yeah, that took me by surprise too. Up until this weekend, he's been pussy footing around her, trying to live by her rules. Then, she apparently went to the bunkhouse and asked him to come up and join us. His heart's been on his sleeve all weekend, but I didn't notice Sarah turning to mush. I mean, she was civil but not falling all over him."

Shauna Lee frowned. "What was going on there? Why was he pussy footing around and living by her rules?"

"Grayson has a past that threw Sarah for a loop."

"He's such a mellow guy, what was so bad."

"He made a mistake when he was young. He hit a guy who was being a jerk, and in one of those freaky ways that things sometimes happen, that the guy fell and hit his head on the edge of a rock and it caused brain damage. He was a big-wigs son, and they pushed for jail time. Grayson was charged with aggravated assault and but he wasn't convicted. He is actually a veterinarian and he'd planned to work with his dad in his practice, but when you hit the mayor's kid and he becomes an even bigger idiot than he was before, influential people and small town gossips don't let it die. The sad thing is he has never forgiven himself for what happened, and he came to work here to get away from his past."

Ellie shook her head sadly. "Sarah could not get beyond the violence of the act. They had been getting close, but when he told her about his past, all she could see was her need to protect Taylor. She was ready to pull up stakes and leave, but Taylor really loves Grayson and he turned against her."

Shauna Lee gasped. "Oh no! What a difficult situation for all three of them."

"Finally, Colt had a long talk with her and convinced her to stay, but she had rules. Taylor could see him when they were working in the corrals, but he was no longer allowed to hang out with him at the bunkhouse, or go to town with him or go fishing or anything else. Grayson lived by those rules to the letter and so did Taylor. It was sad, because Taylor has really bonded with Grayson. He wants a father, and I guess, in a way, for Grayson he's the son he's resigned to never have. They had to be so careful, they were almost like clandestine lovers."

Christina looked thoughtful. "I know it seems like Sarah over reacted, but none of us know what it's really been like for her. I can't imagine living the way she has, always on the alert, ready to run and fearing for your life. She's like that cow was this morning; she'd take on anything to protect her son."

Frank nodded. "That's true. I was pleased when Grayson come up here for the weekend, because he would have stayed away, if she hadn't gone down to talk to him. Whatever happened between them, she decided to throw out all the rules, which is good news for everyone."

Ellie nodded. "And there was warmth between them, even if as you say 'she wasn't turning to mush.' I noticed the looks that passed between them."

Christina chuckled. "If Tim and I could end up falling in love, there's still hope for Grayson and Sarah."

Frank sat up straight. "Speaking of you two falling in love; you just had an anniversary didn't you? You got married here on Easter weekend two years ago. And look at you now, you have twins!"

Christina smiled as she looked across the table at Shauna Lee. "Thanks to our angel."

"Oh, I'm no angel," Shauna Lee said with a chuckle. "But I love seeing you with those twins."

CHAPTER TWELVE

Grayson found himself hovering over Sarah, checking on her every few moments. In spite of the heavy medication she'd been given at the hospital, she'd been dozing fitfully. After a couple of hours, she looked up at him and smiled through her cracked lips, then lifted her hand toward him. He moved to her side to take it and leaned toward her, softly asking "What do you want Sarah?"

"A drink of water, please."

Grayson hurried from the room and Taylor tiptoed inside. "Are you okay mom?"

Sarah nodded. "I'll be alright. It's just going to take time, hon."

"Are you hurting a lot?"

"Right now nothing is hurting very much because the doctor gave me so much pain killer. But I'm sure it will hurt later. Fortunately, it'll heal with time and I'll be fine."

Grayson came back with a glass of water. "I looked for a straw but I couldn't find one."

She smiled wanly and reached to take the glass, wincing as her ribs protested, in spite of the medication.

Grayson protested. "Let me help you Sarah. That's what I'm here for." He positioned the glass by her lips.

She nodded, and then sipped greedily. "Thanks, I didn't realize how thirsty I was." She smiled again and took his hand. "Uhmm…will…will you help me get out of the bed. I need to go to the washroom."

"Sure thing." He extended his arm, bending it at the elbow so she could get a good grasp on it. "Just grab hold with your opposite hand so it won't put so much strain on your broken ribs, and I'll help you."

Sarah grunted as she grabbed his arm and allowed him to pull her up. He carefully helped her swing her legs over the edge of the bed, then rested his hands on her shoulders. "Do you think you can stand on your own?"

She grimaced and closed her eyes momentarily, then looked at him pleadingly. "Will you help me slide my feet down to the floor and let me get my balance. I'm sure I'll be alright then."

Grayson helped her off the bed, and gave a steadying hand when her feet touched the floor. She trembled, but caught her balance and smiled at him as she squeezed his arm. Her eyes met his. "Thank You." She took a tentative step, then another, until she felt certain that she could walk, and then she headed for the bathroom. Taylor's hands reached toward her, hovering in front of him as he watched her move. He desperately wanted to help. Grayson walked beside her, ready to steady her at the least hint of a wobble.

When she made it to the bathroom door, she smiled up at Grayson and said, "I can take it from here."

He nodded. "I'll wait here, just in case you have a problem. When you come out, I'll help you get back into the bed."

Taylor and Grayson stood guard outside the bathroom door, each feeling helpless and wanting to do more. Grayson smiled at the boy. "Are you hungry, hollow leg?"

Taylor rubbed his tummy and grinned. "I am; how about you?"

"Yeah, I am too. That's why I mentioned it. We'll ask your mom if she wants anything. Maybe they can rustle something up for us at the house."

"I'll bet there's some left over ham and fresh buns. I can run over and get some."

"Just wait and see if your mom wants anything before you go."

The bathroom door opened and Sarah looked at them. She had washed her face. That hadn't taken away the bruises, but it made her look fresher. She rested her hand on the doorframe to steady herself.

"I feel so weak, I can't believe it. Will you walk with me and help me get into bed, Grayson?"

He reached for her hand, and then tucked her into the circle of his arm. "Let's go. Taylor and I were just saying we are hungry. Are you? It might be good for you to eat something anyway. It's been a long time since breakfast."

After he helped her up onto the bed and swung her legs on the mattress, she lay back and gave a long tired sigh. "I don't feel like eating, but I probably should."

"I'll run to the house and see what they can give us," Taylor exclaimed. "Grayson and I thought a bun and ham would be good."

"Sarah smiled at him. "That sounds fine." She looked at Grayson. "Would you make some hot chocolate? Everything is in the kitchen."

He nodded. "I'll do it right away. If you need anything, just holler for me."

She closed her eyes and smiled as he left the room. *He is so considerate,* she thought.

Half an hour later, Taylor and Colt appeared with three plates of food. Taylor opened the door and stood back to let the older man in first. "Hey Grayson, we've got supper for all of us. Colt helped bring it over."

Grayson came out of the Sarah's bedroom. "Thanks." He took the two tinfoil covered plates that Colt held out to him. He sniffed. "This smells good! I didn't realize how hungry I was, but we haven't eaten much today." As he put them on the table, he said, "I just took Sarah a cup of hot chocolate." He nodded toward the bedroom. "Do you want to go in and talk to her while I get a knife and fork for her. She's still feeling a bit weak, but she is doing better. Getting some food in her will help. All those meds, with no food, is not the best combination."

Colt slipped off his boots and walked to the bedroom door. Sarah turned her bruised face to look at him. "Hey, girl, your new makeup is colorful."

Sarah smiled wanly. "I know. I look like I'm made up for Halloween."

He walked over, took her hand and smiled sympathetically. "Well, in a few weeks you'll be right back to your beautiful self." He squeezed her hand. "What happened this morning gave us all a real scare."

Sarah groaned. "I know. I just didn't realize…"

"None of us did until it was too late. I'm thankful that Grayson got to you so quickly."

"I am too. He's been amazing all day."

Just then, Grayson came in the door. "Sarah, do you think you could sit at the kitchen table and eat?"

She grimaced, and then nodded. "I guess the sooner I start moving around, the better." Her eyes held Grayson's. "Will you help me get on my feet again?"

Colt watched as Grayson moved to her side and helped her sit up. He stepped back, as Sarah let Grayson help her slide off the bed and plant her feet on the floor. Then they both walked beside her to the door. Colt preceded her and Grayson supported her with a reassuring hand at her back as she walked into the kitchen.

Taylor was grinning from ear to ear when he pulled out a chair for her. "Sit here mom. I hope you're hungry; supper looks great." He watched her closely as she sat down, and then threw his arms around her shoulders. "I'm so happy to see you walking. I was so afraid this morning…"

Sarah touched his cheek. "I know. I was too. But I'll be okay. Both you and Grayson have been so wonderful." Her eyes met Grayson and she reached out to touch his hand as it rested on the table. "I think I'm hungry…in fact, I know I am." She looked at Colt. "Please thank Frank for the food. This is wonderful." She picked up her fork and moved around some of the food.

Colt shifted on his feet and then walked to the door. "We'll see you tomorrow. And remember, we're all here for you if you need anything."

"I know that Colt, and if I need extra help, I'll be sure to ask for it. But as you can see, I'm in good hands with these two guys, and I'm sure I'll get better and better every day. I'm just going to be sore for a while."

"That's to be expected. Take as long as you need to heal." Colt nodded as he opened the door. "We'll see all of you tomorrow."

Grayson nodded back at him, as he stepped out the door. The three of them sat down at the table and enjoyed the meal. Taylor snuck a look at his mother and then one at Grayson. *This is like being a family,* he thought. Happiness shone in his eyes. *Maybe there is still a chance that my dream will come true.*

When Colt stepped into the house, Frank and Shauna Lee were

full of concern and questions about Sarah. "She'll be okay. Grayson is helping her get in and out of the bed. He stays close to her, making sure she stays steady on her feet, but he's not all over her. He asked her if she wanted to get up and eat supper at the table, and she decided she would." He grinned as he took off his hat. "To be honest, Taylor is as happy as a clam and Grayson and Sarah seem to be so comfortable with each other, I felt like an intruder."

Shauna Lee's eyes met Frank's with a question. Frank sighed. "Well, maybe they'll work through their problems. Something definitely changed between them on Friday night, and the incident with Sarah and the cow certainly proved where Grayson's heart is. For Taylor's sake, I hope they work everything out."

***

Grayson, Sarah, and Taylor ate in companionable silence. When Sarah had eaten as much as she wanted Taylor eyed her plate. "Are you finished, mom?"

"I think so."

"Can I eat the rest?"

She grinned and nodded. "You've got to fill that hollow leg, eh?"

Taylor grinned with glee as he took her plate and started eating. "I love this ham and the scalloped potatoes."

"Everything was good, but I'm full." She shifted on her chair. "My butt is getting tired. This chair is kind of hard. I think maybe I should go back to bed."

Grayson was on his feet immediately. "Okay, let me help you."

Taylor smiled as he forked the remains of Sarah's dinner into his mouth and watched Grayson help his mother to the washroom. His heart felt like it would burst. He knew his mom was going to be alright; in fact he knew everything was going to be alright. Grayson belonged with them, and in time, he knew his mother would see that too.

Grayson waited while Sarah went into the bathroom and washed her face and hands and brushed her teeth. When she came out, he followed her into the bedroom and helped her get into bed. He adjusted her pillows, making sure she was comfortable. Then he gave her the medication the doctor had prescribed for her.

As he turned out the light on her night table, she spoke softly. "Thank you, Grayson."

His look held hers. "You mean a lot to me Sarah. I didn't even understand how much, until I saw that cow take you down and I realized I could lose you."

A tear slipped down her cheek. "I know." She looked away. "I need time Grayson. I care for you too, but I've been afraid for so many years. It's not a simple thing to put away."

He clasped her hand, interlacing her fingers with his. "I'm not going anywhere, and I'm not going to let you go anywhere either. I'll give you all the time you need to accept that you are safe with me, but I'm not letting you go again. I love you Sarah Brite, and I love that son of yours. We are meant to be a family." He leaned over and lightly kissed her on the lips. "I'll bed down on the couch. If you need anything, just call. I'm a light sleeper so I'll hear you."

She watched him leave the room, closing the door, but leaving it open a crack so he would hear her if she called. She thought about him as the medication drew her into the oblivion of sleep. *He does love me,* she thought. *He's shown me in so many ways. But what if Duncan ever found us here? One more person would be a risk.*

Taylor had finished eating and gathered up the dishes when Grayson came back into the kitchen.

"Good job Taylor. If we do this together, we can have these dishes cleaned up in no time." They worked as a team and the few dishes, glasses, and cutlery were ready to send back to the ranch house. Grayson ruffled the boy's hair and smiled. "It's been a long day, young man. I think it's time we hit the sack. I'll sleep here on the couch. Where would I find a blanket?"

"You can sleep with me."

Grayson looked into his earnest eyes. "I appreciate the offer, but you're not used to sharing your bed."

"Sometimes I sleep with Mom."

"Yeah, but I'm not used to sleeping with anyone else. I probably wouldn't get a good sleep if I crawled in with you and then you won't either."

"Come on. I'd like to sleep with you."

Grayson hugged Taylor, knowing how much the boy wanted to feel close to him. "Not now, son. You need sleep and I have to go to work early tomorrow morning. Besides that, if your mom needs something during the night I will hear her call if I'm in here."

Taylor hugged the man he thought of as his best friend. "Alright," he said reluctantly. "What time do you have to get up?"

"I'll make coffee and then I'll head to the barn around five or five-thirty. If your mom wakes up before I get done with the chores, ask her if she wants a cup of coffee. I should be back by seven-thirty. I'll make breakfast for the three of us then."

Taylor got a down-filled quilt from the hall closet and gave it to Grayson. "I'll give you one of my pillows. I never use it. It's just there to make the bed look nice when I make it." He hurried down the hall and came back with a pillow. "Here," he said as he tossed it on the couch. Then he turned away and started down the hall. Suddenly he stopped, spun around and ran back, with the awkward gait of a long legged ten-year-old. He threw his arms around Grayson's waist and hugged him tight. "I love you," he blurted, and then whirled away and ran to his bedroom.

Grayson's eyes misted over as he reached for the king sized quilt, folded it in half and laid it on the couch. He shucked off his jeans and his shirt and crawled inside, pulling it around him, thankful for its generous size. He lay there thinking about the child in the bedroom down the hall. *He has no idea how hard it was to say no to him. I'd love to feel him curled up with his back against my chest, my arm around him, absorbing his warmth. But this isn't the time to do that. It wouldn't be fair to him, to me or his mother. Until I win Sarah over, until she accepts me and fully trusts me, I can't treat him like my own. Soon he will be too old for cuddling.*

Grayson sighed as he tried to settle and find comfort on the couch. He pushed his head into the pillow and could smell the scent of Taylor. His mind wandered to Sarah and the horror of the mornings events. He played over in his mind when he'd heard Taylor scream to warn her, and how he'd instinctively pulled him back and told him to stay. Everything was a blur in his mind. He couldn't remember where he'd found the fence post or running across the corral to beat the cow off as it pummeled Sarah. Only one thing was clear in his mind, the fear that he could lose Sarah. He'd fought with all his might to beat off the cow, almost unaware that Colt had called the dogs, which had eventually distracted the cow's attention. His heart still squeezed when he recalled the sight of her, laying there, her jacket almost ripped off, her top torn, mud in her hair, on her face; so still and broken looking. He swallowed a sob that wanted to escape. *It's over now, and I'll help her get better and I'll never let anyone or anything hurt her again,* he vowed.

Sarah slept through the night and to his surprise, once Grayson got past his thoughts, he did too. He woke up at five the next morning. He pushed the quilt away and sat up. The house was silent. He pulled on his clothes and went to the washroom. Before he returned to the kitchen, he peeked into Taylor's room and saw him sprawled across the bed. *He's definitely not used to sleeping with anyone else,* he mused as he moved down the hallway, stopping to look into Sarah's room. Her face was turned away from him, but he could tell that she hadn't moved much. He moved quietly as he went into the room to check on her. As he reached the far side of the bed, he could see her breathing softly, lips slightly parted. He fought the urge to reach out and touch her, knowing that it would probably disturb her sleep. He quietly left the room and went back to the kitchen where he set the coffee pot up to brew. Then he put on his coat and went out to do chores.

When he got to the barn, everything was quiet. He was filling pails of grain when Colt entered the door of the feed bin. "So, how did everything go last night?"

Grayson hefted one more pail, then looked at his boss and smiled. "Everything went well. Sarah slept all night; at least I didn't hear her moving around and I'm a pretty light sleeper. Taylor wanted me to sleep with him, but I told him I'm not used to sleeping with anybody else, so I bedded down on the couch. They were both sound asleep when I woke up at five o'clock. I put on the coffee and headed down here."

"That's good. Sarah's ribs are going to be pretty tender for the next four or five weeks."

"Yeah, the doctor cautioned her about that. He gave her stronger pain meds for the first week. Then he said to cut back to Tylenol 3's. She'll be alright. She just has to accept that she has to take it easy for the next few weeks."

"It could take as long as late summer before she is completely healed."

"If I know Sarah, she'll be up and around as soon as she can. As long as she's careful, I think that is good for her. I'll stay overnight at the apartment until she can get out of bed without any trouble. Right now getting up is hard for her and we have a system that works."

Colt bent over to pick up two pails. When he straightened, he looked Grayson in the eye. "Are you going to be alright by the time she is. I see where you are headed, my friend. I don't want to see you get hurt again."

"Well boss, you know this isn't my first go around with Sarah. When I watched that cow knocking her around yesterday, all I could think of was that I might lose her." He bent over to pick up two of the pails. As he straightened, his eyes met Colt's. "I'm going to do everything I can to win her over. If I don't succeed, at least I'll know I gave it my best shot."

Colt watched him walk out the door ahead of him. He followed him into the corrals and they went about doing the chores. At seven-thirty, they both headed up to the ranch house.

"Are you coming in for breakfast, or are you going to Sarah's?"

Grayson shook his head. "I'll go to the apartment and make breakfast. I'm sure they'll be awake by now."

Colt smiled and went into the ranch house while Grayson continued on to the apartment. When he opened the door, he could smell coffee and he could hear Sarah and Taylor's voices. He slipped off his boots and coat and hurried to Sarah's bedroom door. Taylor was leaning against the bed, talking to his mom while she sipped a cup of coffee.

Sarah immediately noticed when he entered the door. Her gaze met his and held, as he walked across the room.

He smiled. "Hi, guys." He nodded at Taylor. "I see you brought your mom a cup of coffee." He ruffled Taylor's hair. "How are you this morning, beautiful lady?"

Sarah smiled wanly. "Is my new color pallet that obvious already?"

"You are always a beautiful lady, Sarah." He leaned over and examined the bruises on her face. He briefly touched her cheek. "You're going to be a bit colorful in a couple of spots for a week or so, but it will fade away." He stood back, fighting back the urge to drop a kiss on her lips. "Do you want to get up? Maybe go to the bathroom? I looked in before I went out to do chores, but you were asleep."

Her eyes were dark with appreciation. "I should go to the bathroom. The coffee is starting to work its way through."

Grayson helped her sit up and swing her legs over the edge of the bed. She reached out and squeezed his hand. "I hope you know how much I appreciate you."

He leaned forward and brushed her forehead with his lips. His voice was thick with emotion. "I will never be able to forget what happened yesterday, Sarah. Now, I'll be here to do anything for you, to help you heal and get better."

Tears shimmered in her eyes. "It happened so fast. I just remember wondering when it would end."

"She was totally focused on you. It was a good thing Colt thought to call the dogs, because she was not too bothered by my efforts."

She slid her hands up his arms, stopping to squeeze his biceps. "But you did everything you could. Now, will you help me slide down to the floor so I can stand up? Nature is calling."

He grinned as he helped her stand up, and then watched protectively as she made her way to the bathroom.

He turned to look at Taylor. "What do you want for breakfast, big guy?"

"Pancakes, eggs, and bacon."

"All right, let's get at it. You can give me a hand." Taylor was eager to help and when Sarah came out of the bathroom, they were in the kitchen, laughing and talking while they worked together. Grayson had mixed a batch of pancakes and was starting to ladle spoonfuls onto the electric griddle. Taylor was laying bacon strips in the frying pan. She stopped to watch them, thinking how perfectly they meshed.

Grayson looked up to meet her gaze. "Hey, you're quick." He smiled as his eyes roamed over her face. "Do you want another cup of coffee?"

"I'd love one," she said as she walked slowly to a chair at the table. Grayson poured one and brought it to her, setting it on the table in front of her. "By the way you're moving I'd say you are pretty sore today."

"Yes, my muscles are protesting, but that's to be expected. It'll take a bit of time to work out the soreness." She sipped her coffee. "It looks like you two are having fun."

Taylor laughed. "You should have seen him making pancakes, mom. He missed the side of the bowl and splashed flour all over the counter and when he added the milk, he spilled it down the front of the cupboard."

Grayson tugged on the boy's ear. "That's because you were harassing me, you rascal."

Taylor giggled.

Sarah's heart warmed as she witnessed the bond they shared. *I just have to say the word and this would be our life. I know Grayson loves me, and I really care about him, but I'm just not ready to make that commitment yet.*

Grayson flipped pancakes and Taylor turned strips of bacon in the pan. When he was finished, Grayson told him to lay the pieces on a folded piece of paper towel to drain away the fat. Then, while Taylor set the table, Grayson cooked eggs. In minutes, they all sat down around the table and ate.

It was warm and companionable, something Sarah had not experienced since they'd left Julie and Ryan's place. She looked across the table at her son and then to Grayson. *But this is even different than it was with them. This is intimate.* Lost in thought, she toyed with what remained of her pancake with her fork.

She was brought back to the present when she felt Grayson's touch on her arm. "Is everything alright, Sarah?"

She looked up to find both of her companions looking at her. "Oh...yes, everything is fine. I was just thinking."

Grayson smiled. "They must have been deep thoughts. You were a long way off."

"Ah-ha...a penny for your thoughts, what were you thinking about mom? How nice it is for the three of us to sit around the table like this?"

Sarah flushed. "You have a one-track mind, Taylor. Life isn't as simple as you'd like to think. There are a lot of other things to consider, besides the fact that you want that to happen."

Grayson looked at Taylor. "Give your mom a break, kid. She's just been run over by a cow. It's not fair to pick on when she hurting and vulnerable."

"But..."

Grayson gave him a stern look. "Enough is enough. No one can snap their finger and make love happen. We are doing just fine now. I don't want to hear you ragging on your mom about this again." His heart ached to see the disappointment in the boy's eyes. He reached out and laid a gentle hand on his arm. "It's time to clean up the dishes and I have to get back to work."

He turned to Sarah and swallowed hard when he saw the look on her face. It was clear that she was fighting with her own emotions. Regret? Guilt? Sadness? He stood up and put his hand on her shoulder, massaging it gently. "What do you want to do this morning Sarah?" He smiled, his look holding hers. "Probably I should have asked what you feel like you can do this morning. Do you want to go back to bed, or can we make you comfortable on the couch and give you the remote for the TV?"

She nodded. "Lying in bed gets tiresome. I'm not an invalid, I'm just really sore."

"How are the ribs doing?"

She swallowed and looked away. "They hurt—a lot. I know that's to be expected. I'd like to walk around but sometimes the pain is so sharp it's breathtaking."

Grayson was shaking his head. "You have to give them a chance to knit before you do too much. In the long run, it will be better. We can put pillows around you to get you comfortable on the couch or in the big chair. You could snuggle under the afghan and watch TV if you want, or sleep a bit. I could bring my laptop up for you to use if you'd like that."

She stood up. He could see the pain in her eyes and he knew it wasn't from her physical injuries. He cradled her face in his hands and dropped a soft kiss on her lips. "Don't worry," he whispered. "Everything will work out."

Tears filled her eyes. "Your kindness and understanding is harder to take than Taylor's constant pressure. I can get mad at him, but how do I fight you?"

He steered her toward the couch. "Which is it: the couch or the chair?"

She looked at both. "I think the chair. It's big and it will support me."

"I'm going to be gone for at least three hours. If you needed to go to the bathroom, could you get out of the chair?"

"Let me try."

She cringed as she settled into the big comfortable recliner. "It feels good."

"But can you get out of it?"

Twice, she tried to push herself put and out of it. The expression on her face made it obvious that it was too difficult.

"This isn't going to work." Grayson turned and called to Taylor. "Let's see if you can help your mom get up out of this chair."

Taylor was at their side immediately. "What do I have to do?"

"Just take both of her hands and gently help her up on to her feet."

"I can do that," Taylor said with a grin. He reached out and took Sarah's hands in his and gently tugged until she was off the seat, then stepped back to help her get onto her feet. "See, I knew I could do it."

Sarah smiled and rumpled his hair. "Thanks, son."

"That solves our problem. For the next few days, you'll stay in so you can help your mom if she needs it."

Taylors's face fell. "But, I'm going to go out and help you."

"It's all right; I'll sit on the couch."

Grayson raised his hand to stop her. "No. Taylor can come out with me later on." He gave Taylor a stern look. "I don't want to see you sulking about this. Just remind yourself of all the times your mom has looked after you. Now it's your turn to help her. Go finish up the dishes and I'll get her settled and give her the painkillers she needs."

"Sheesh," Taylor breathed out as he turned away, going back to the kitchen.

Grayson positioned Sarah in the chair, and then disappeared into the bedroom for her pills. Taylor finished the dishes and then walked dejectedly to his bedroom, shutting the door behind him with exaggerated firmness. Grayson looked toward the closed door with a scowl when he came back. He didn't comment as he handed her a glass of water. After she had swallowed her meds, she reached out to him. "I'll be alright. He was counting on going with you. Just let him go."

Grayson shook his head. "No. That's not right." He leaned over and looked into her eyes. "Taylor wants me to be part of this family; he wants me to be his dad." He placed his lips gently on hers. Then he stood back. "If I were his father right now, I would never let him get away with acting this way, and you shouldn't accept it either. You're doing him a disservice if you do. He has to learn that he has responsibilities too and helping you now is what is expected of him. There will be lots of time for him to work outside with me."

She looked down at her hands. "I guess I've been a little overprotective and maybe I've spoilt him a bit. I didn't mean too. I've always felt so guilty about the life I've forced him into."

Grayson put his finger across her lips. "You've been a damn fine mother and he's a good kid. I'm proud of you both, but right now he needs to learn this lesson. I'll go have a man to man talk with him before I leave. You have to promise me you will not give in on this. We have to be on the same page, right?" He reached down and tipped up her chin, forcing her to look at him. "Are we together on this?"

She nodded and tears glistened in her eyes. "I just hate it when he's angry with me."

"Everything will be alright, I promise."

"Why are you so...so good to me? I can't give you what you want."

He wiped away her tears. "That doesn't change how I feel about you. I'm willing to take this slow and give you as much time as you need. The three of us will be together eventually. I'm very determined about this. Now I'll go have a chat with Taylor and then I have to go to work. I'll be back at lunch time."

Grayson made sure she had the TV remote, and then he went into Taylor's bedroom. She held her breath, wondering what he was telling her son, but there were no raised voices, no sounds of anger. Ten minutes later Grayson came out of the room leaving the door open. She heard him suggesting that Taylor could make a simple lunch for the three of them, and Taylor happily said he would.

Taylor came out a few minutes after Grayson left and asked her if she needed anything. She said no, and suggested they watch a movie together. He sat at the end of the couch near her chair and they watched a movie that he chose. When the clock showed eleven-forty-five, he asked her what he could make for lunch. She suggested he open two cans of soup and make sandwiches with the leftover pork roast that was in a container in the fridge. She watched with pride as he read the directions on the soup cans and added the correct amounts of liquid. Then she watched him slice the meat, put mayonnaise and lettuce on the buttered bread and top it with the slices of meat before he added the top slice of bread. He carefully cut each sandwich in half and placed it on a small plate. Then he asked her if he should make fresh coffee and she told him how to do it. By the time Grayson came in for lunch, the table was set and everything was ready.

Grayson didn't make a big fuss about what Taylor had done. He accepted it as a normal occurrence. Sarah was disappointed that he hadn't praised her son, but when they had finished eating, he looked at Taylor and smiled. Then he told him lunch was very good, in the same manner he would have complimented Sarah or Frank or even Colt. Taylor glowed with praise and nonchalantly said "Thank you," in the same way she would have.

Sarah looked at the both of them thoughtfully, realizing that

Grayson had treated her son like an adult and he had responded in kind. *Grayson McNaughton, I don't know how you got so smart, but you are the best thing that could have happened to my son...and me. But I am very afraid we may not be the best thing that could happen to you. I wish I could just give in and accept what you offer us. But what if?....* A threatening picture of *Duncan* crowded into her musing. No, she couldn't put anyone else at risk, especially not Grayson.

Grayson came in to check on them at three-thirty. Mother and son were playing a game of cards. He asked Taylor if he'd like to come out to do the evening chores with him. Taylor looked at Sarah first for her consent, and then jumped at the chance to go.

Grayson smiled as he watched Taylor scramble to get into his chore clothes. Then he turned to Sarah. "Is there anything else you need? Have you been up to go to the washroom?"

"Taylor helped me get up about fifteen minutes ago. He's been so good."

Grayson smiled. "He's a great kid." He looked toward the entry where Taylor was pulling on his jacket and stuffing his feet into his chore boots. "I asked Frank to make supper for us too. She'll bring it over at around four-thirty and she'll probably visit for a few minutes then. I told her you might appreciate some female company."

"Thanks. I appreciate that."

Later that afternoon, Frank arrived at the door with dinner for the three of them. She put everything in the oven to keep it warm, and then quickly set the table as she chatted with Sarah. When she was finished, she came and sat down beside her. "How are you doing, Sarah?"

"All things considered, I'm pretty good. I'm sore all over and my ribs hurt."

"Grayson said you have one fractured and two badly bruised?"

"That's what they said at the hospital. The bruised ones will heal faster, but the fractured one will be tender for a few months. But I'm lucky it didn't actually break. It could have punctured my lung or done more damage."

Frank closed her eyes and covered her face as if to block out the memory. "I'll never get that scene out of my mind. Because we work with the cattle all the time, we know that can happen but we are aware and avoid the danger."

Sarah's eyes filled with tears. "I just didn't think about it at the time. I was totally focused on getting to Taylor and Grayson and it made sense to cut through the pen, instead of walking all the way around. But in hindsight, I remember Taylor telling me many times, that Grayson always told him not to get between a cow and her calf. I made the mistake, but I can guarantee I'll never do it again."

"This has been a sobering lesson to all of us. No one thought about the danger. We were all caught up in the excitement of the moment." Frank sighed as she touched Sarah's hand. "Can I comb your hair for you or maybe help you shower tomorrow. Did they tape you?"

"Apparently they don't do that anymore."

Frank frowned. "I wonder why. It would give your ribs more stability and make it easier for you to move with less discomfort. How is your breathing? Are you having any signs of congestion?"

"No. I'm fine that way."

"I'm going to check online tonight and see what they say about taping the ribs. I know they always used to do that. I'll help you shower tomorrow afternoon. I'd come earlier, but I gather that Grayson and Taylor have the mornings covered." She smiled.

Sarah looked at her curiously. "I have no idea what he said to Taylor, but it was very effective. Taylor was willingly attentive to me and he made lunch without any protest."

Frank's smile was enigmatic. "He didn't say much, but from what he told me, I think he just talked to your son like he was an adult and he was proud of the way he responded. When he stopped by to ask me if I'd make enough supper for the three of you tonight, he told me Taylor made lunch and did a good job of it, but he thought making supper might be too much ask of him. And I'm happy to make supper for you guys every night, for as long as it takes for you to be well and healthy again."

Sarah's smile was grateful. "Do you think you could comb my hair? I'm sure Grayson would do it if I asked him, but it feels kind of...maybe it's too intimate for me now."

Frank looked at her thoughtfully. "I hope you realize how much that man loves you Sarah. He was so devastated..."

"I know Frank. But I'm so afraid..."

"Where is your hair brush?"

"It's in the bathroom."

Frank went to get the brush. Her expression was concerned when she came back. She made no comment as she started to brush

Sarah's hair. It was matted and tangled and it took all of her attention to work through it. When she was finished, she stood in front of her and looked her over. "Much better," she declared. She chewed on her bottom lip as she looked into Sarah's eyes, then she knelt beside her chair. "Sarah if you weren't afraid, would you want to be with Grayson? Not because he loves your kid, but because you care for him?"

"How do I separate everything, Frank? Is it fair to expose him to the damage Duncan will wield when he finds us?"

Frank took her hands and held them. "If there were no Duncan, could you care for Grayson? Not because of how hard he fought to save you on Sunday, not because he and your son love each other, not because he's staying here and looking after you because he loves you: how do you feel about Grayson as a man?"

"I've been too afraid to feel anything for years, Frank." Tears ran down her cheeks. "But could I imagine life with him, do I like it when he kisses me…?"

Frank's eyes flickered. "He kisses you?"

"He just gives me a brush on the lips or the cheek or the forehead; nothing passionate. But yes, and I do like the feel of his body, strong and hard against mine when he hugs me. The strength in his arms makes me feel secure. Am I tempted? Of course, I am. But there is so much more to consider."

"Please don't break his heart again, Sarah."

"I've told him I can't give him what he wants."

"He'll wait for you, you know. Don't let your fear rob you both. Duncan What-ever-his-name-is is not invincible. He has never had to face the Thompson clan."

"Frank, if Colt were to be killed defending me and Taylor, how would you feel then?"

"I'd hunt him down and take care of him. Sarah, he's played mind games with you whenever he's caught up to you, but did he ever have the guts to step out in the open in front of a witness? He knew he had you running scared, and he hunted you like a wolf hunts a moose. He just doggedly stayed on you, wearing you down. He'd probably have acted if he'd gotten you alone, but from what I remember you saying, he never openly approached you in front of anyone else. And you are never alone here; there is always someone else around." She glanced at her watch and stood up. "I have to go back to the house and feed my crew. Grayson and Taylor will be here any moment. I'll come over early tomorrow afternoon to help you shower and wash your hair. And please think about what I said about you and Grayson."

That evening after supper, the three of them sat around and watched TV. Then Grayson helped her out of the chair and let her go to the washroom before he helped her get into bed. He softly kissed her on the lips and said goodnight, then sent Taylor to bed and he bedded down on the couch for the night.

CHAPTER THIRTEEN

Frank stepped into the house at one-thirty in the afternoon, the next day, ready to help Sarah shower and wash her hair. "I went online and looked up how to treat fractured and bruised ribs. I discovered that they usually do nothing now, other than tell you to take it easy and rest, but I also found a site that showed how to tape the ribs. I brought some tape, in case you want to give it a try. I'm a vet, not a medical doctor, but if I was in your position, I would want them taped. I think it will support the area and make it less painful. It seems to me that the main reason, they have quit taping, is because they worry about respiratory problems, but you don't seem to have a tendency for that. I don't want to force my idea on you, but if you are interested, I'll do it for you."

"Let's get me in the shower and wash my hair first. Then I'll decide."

Frank set the temperature and helped her take off her clothing, and then motioned for her to step in under the stream of water. Suddenly she looked dismayed, and then laughed. "Sarah I'm not going to be able to help you unless I get in there with you. These small walk-in showers don't work like the good old tub."

Sarah clutched her right side and chuckled. "Just get in here and help me. Moving around like this hurts."

Frank slipped out of her clothes and stepped into the shower to help Sarah wash her back and arms and the left side of her body. "Sorry," she said with a giggle. "Colt, and Tim and Brad will rib us unmercifully if they ever find out that we've been naked in the shower together. But I don't know how else to do this."

Sarah smiled, even as she grimaced as she pulled her right arm against her ribs to protect herself. "What happens in the shower stays in the shower: we won't tell them. Let's shampoo my hair. It feels good to be clean, even if it does hurt."

When Frank was finished, they stepped out of the shower and she dried Sarah's hair and body. Sarah tried to put on her own underwear, but it was painful to bend and maneuver so Frank helped her.

"What do you think, Sarah? Do you want to try having me tape your ribs or are you exhausted?"

"I think you should do it. No matter how I move, these ribs hurt and it's not just a pain, it's breathtaking. I don't want to be totally dependent on everyone all the time. If taping gives stability, maybe they'll have a better chance of healing quicker."

"It's the choice I'd make. I downloaded a piece from the internet and it gives pretty clear instructions. As I said, I'm a vet, not a M.D. but I have a basic understanding of what I'm doing. We'll just have to keep an eye on your breathing."

Frank slipped out of the room to get the bag that she'd brought tape, scissors and the instructions in. When she came back, Sarah looked at her with embarrassment. "I guess there are no secrets between us now. I can't remember when anyone has seen me nude, in the shower." She looked in the mirror. "And on top of that, I've got some pretty interesting colors starting to show."

"Sarah, I never even thought of you in those terms. You're my friend, and I'm sure you'd do the same thing for me." Then she gently touched her right side. "Now, show me where you hurt—which ribs are damaged?

Sarah showed her the general area just below her right breast and Frank felt the ribs, noting Sarah's reaction. Then she cut three strips of tape and starting at Sarah's sternum, wrapped the tape along each painful rib, around her back, past her spine in each case. On each side of the affected ribs, she placed strips to stabilize the rib movement. When she was finished, she said, "Now, try to take a slow deep breath and see what happens."

Sarah breathed carefully. "It still hurts, but it does feel stronger."

"The big thing is you have to keep taking deep breaths. That's one of the worries about taping because the tape could be tight enough that would stop you from breathing deeply."

"No, that's not a problem. Maybe I'm just being a sissy, but it hurts to move and breath."

"Fractured ribs are painful. You need to keep taking your meds and that will help with the pain."

Sarah nodded. "I am. Grayson sees to that."

Frank held up a pair of flannel pajamas she had snagged from the dresser in Sarah's room. "Are these okay?"

Sarah nodded and Frank helped her put them on. Then she used the hair dryer to style Sarah's hair. When she was finished, she looked at her friend in the mirror. "Look at you. You're almost back to your normal beautiful self. Just a minute," she reached for a bottle of cologne. "You have to smell pretty too." She stood back and looked at her. "Poor Grayson, I'll bet he'll have interesting dreams tonight."

Sarah blushed. "That's not fair."

"Sometimes life doesn't seem fair. Let's get you back into your chair. This morning I made a big pot of beef stew in the slow cooker, and I'm going to make baking powder biscuits to go with it. So I'll see you in a couple of hours with supper."

"Frank thanks for everything; getting in the shower with me, taping me up, doing my hair and the meals. I owe you so much."

"You owe me nothing, girlfriend. Just make sure you get better, and please, think about what I told you about being safe here. That Duncan character wouldn't stand a chance with us redneck cowboys!"

Sarah blushed, and Frank grabbed her jacket and dashed out the door.

Two hours later Grayson and Taylor came in, bringing with them a casserole dish full of beef stew and a dozen biscuits.

"Hi Mom," Taylor shouted. "Frank sent supper with us. Gosh, this smells good."

Sarah wanted to get up and go to meet them at the door, but when she tried to move, a sharp stab of pain stopped her. Grayson saw her grimace. "Don't rush things Sarah," he said softly. "We can handle this. I'll put the food in the oven, and then we'll wash up and set the table."

Taylor headed for the bathroom, and Grayson washed his hands in the kitchen sink. While he dried them on the hand towel that hung on the oven door handle, he looked her over. He smiled, but he didn't comment. Instead, he set the table and pulled out her chair. Then he walked over and reached out his hands to take hers. His expression was soft. He gently helped her to her feet. Instead of releasing her, he pulled her close and inhaled her scent. "Uhmmm…you smell nice. You look nice too."

She looked up at him and smiled. "Thank you. I appreciate that you noticed."

"I notice everything about you Sarah." He lifted her hair off her shoulders, threading his fingers through it. Smiling, he dropped his hand away and said, "Let's go to the table and have supper."

As Sarah got settled at the table, Taylor came charging into the kitchen. Grayson smiled at him. "Where were you, hot shot? You must have done a good job of washing those hands. I set the table and got your mom up to the table before you came back."

Taylor flashed a guilty grin. "I changed my jeans. I got pretty dirty this afternoon."

Sarah looked at him curiously. "What were you doing?"

"Sam and Serena and I were playing rodeo with the yearlings in the corral. I got dumped in the mud a couple of times. Colt let us ride Frank's old roping horse and it really knows what it's supposed to do."

"You roped off the horse?"

Grayson saw her look of alarm. "It's nothing to worry about Sarah. Ollie, Colt, and I were with them. If they're going to be team ropers, they have to graduate from the horns on the bale sometime."

Taylor's eyes were shining and his grin exploded across his face. "Yeah mom, it was really fun. I only caught a horn twice, but I beat Selena." He laughed as his eyes met Grayson's. "She didn't like that. Sam got one four times; he's really good with a lariat. It was really exciting and if we keep practicing, we might be able to team rope in the rodeo someday. Frank used to do that, and Colt rode bulls. He let us try on the calves this afternoon."

Sarah's eyes narrowed. "Is that what you were doing when you got dumped in the mud?"

Taylor looked away. "Yeah…it's okay, mom. I didn't get hurt when I fell off, but I grabbed the rope and the calf ran and pulled me through the mud." He looked at Grayson for backup. "Honest, Grayson was running right there with me, trying to grab the rope. Colt headed it off with Smokie and he caught it. It was okay. I have to toughen up mom. I'm old enough to enter the junior steer riding events in some places now."

Grayson realized it was time to do some damage control because he could sense Sarah's protective instincts coming to the surface. "Sarah, it was no big deal. Colt picked up a protective vest and a helmet for the twins last year, and the three of them took turns wearing the gear. There are a few young yearlings that were born after the cows were turned out on the range. They didn't get dehorned or castrated last fall and they're not very big so Colt will keep them at the ranch when he puts the cows out on the lease. There are two younger bulls that we'll castrate in a couple of weeks, and he thought the kids would have fun fooling around on them." He put his hand on her shoulder. "You know I will always protect Taylor and Colt sure isn't going to put the twins at risk."

Sarah sighed and looked away.

"Sit down Taylor," Grayson admonished, "and I'll get the food out of the oven so we can eat." *I wish Taylor hadn't been quite so graphic. I'd like to have told Sarah what they were up to first. It's not that we let them do anything wrong, but she is so protective.* He put the casserole and plate of biscuits on the table. He sniffed appreciatively. "This smells terrific. Dig in hollow leg."

Taylor grinned and helped himself, then passed the dish to Sarah. Grayson reached to help her fill her plate and handed her a biscuit. Then he got his own plate ready and they ate in silence. When they had finished, Grayson told Taylor to clean up the table and he made a pot of coffee. *Sarah's been awfully quiet; I hope there isn't a storm brewing over this. Damn, I wish she'd found all this out in a different way, but Taylor was so thrilled there was no way to shut him up.*

He turned to find her watching him. "Do you want to get up? I can help you get organized in your chair again. She nodded and looked away. Grayson moved to her side to help her push her chair back and stand up.

"I'll go to the bathroom first," she said and turned away.

Grayson's heart took a dive. *I hope this doesn't move us two steps back. I don't like this dance.*

When she came out of the bathroom, he could see that her eyes were wet, but she walked to the big chair and waited for him to help her sit down. He took her hands and steadied her as she lowered herself into the chair.

"Thank you," she said softly.

He stood in front of her, looking down at her, but she refused to meet his eyes. Finally, he knelt by the chair. "You're upset with me? I'd sooner you tell me how you feel than bottle it up inside."

She picked at the arm of the chair, and then looked into his eyes. "I'm not mad at you. I'm just upset with everything. How I am, sitting around like a lump…"

He reached out and stroked her cheek. "I only see a beautiful woman. You look great. Frank obviously did what I couldn't do." He grinned as he cupped her chin and tilted it up so he could stare into her eyes, and whispered *"yet."*

Sarah flushed.

"When we are together as a couple, I'll shower you." He reached out and caressed her hair. "Until then I have to appreciate that she does it."

Sarah thought back to the afternoon and fought back a giggle. "It was some performance."

He smiled. "So are you alright with Taylor's try at rodeoing this afternoon?"

She shook her head as she took his hand and held it to her cheek. "No, not away down where I'm his protective mother, but he was so excited, so happy." She pushed her cheek into his hand and looked into his eyes. "I know I have to let him grow up, but it's so hard to let go and not try to protect him like I've always done. But I trust you and I trust Colt."

He leaned forward and kissed her forehead. "Thank you for telling me you trust me. I would protect that boy with my life because he feels like my son, and because I love you."

Sarah started to protest, but he laid a finger across her lips. "I know, you've told me you can't give me what I want. But I have nothing but time, Sarah, and I plan to court you after you're on your feet and I know that eventually you will give in to your desires, because I know you have feelings for me."

"That's not it," she protested.

He grinned. "I'll start packing a pistol on my hip and I'll target practice regularly. That big bad ghost from your past wouldn't have a chance against me." Tears brimmed in her eyes, so he changed the topic. "Frank told me she taped your ribs. Does it feel any better?"

She nodded. "They still hurt, but the whole area feels more secure. I just need to have patience and work this through."

"Patience is the big thing. Well, I could give you some homework to take up some of your time."

She looked at him puzzled.

"You could spend some time every day thinking about what it would be like to be Mrs. Grayson McNaughton; the wife of the man who loves you unconditionally, who loves your son and would dispose of all you fears and insecurities." He leaned forward and kissed her lightly on the lips. "Imagine us making passionate love," he whispered. "Even imagine us having a couple more kids. I know I'd like that and I'll bet Taylor would be thrilled too. And you would be a wonderful mother, and you could do it with peace and joy, without the fear that bastard forced on you when you cared for Taylor as a baby."

He smiled as he stepped back. He walked over to sit on the couch and surfed through the channels. "What do you like to watch, Sarah?"

"You choose. I've watched more TV in the past couple of days than I've watched in months."

"Shall we check the evening news?"

She nodded, thinking back to what life had been in her childhood home. *Dad just put the TV on the channel he wanted and that was it. He never considered what we might have wanted to watch. Everything but what he watched to watch was just foolishness, sure to corrupt our minds.*

Taylor came back to the living area and sat down next to Grayson. "News? Yuck."

Grayson put his arm around his shoulders and wrestled him down on the couch. "Look young man, you need to know what's going on around you. Life isn't all fun and games. It's about the country you live in too. The local news is only an hour long and it gives our weather forecast too. You need to pay attention to this stuff."

"Okay, okay," Taylor squirmed, trying to get out from under him. Grayson straightened up and helped him sit.

Sarah watched with a thoughtful expression. *I've always*

protected Taylor. I probably should have been stricter when he was younger, but I couldn't make myself do it. I guess I felt too guilty about the situation we were in. Anyway, Grayson disciplines him in a way that I can't and he's good for him.

After the news was over, the three of them decided on a program to watch and the evening slipped by in a comfortable, companionable way. It was over at nine o'clock and Grayson looked at his watch, then at Sarah. "Is it bedtime for hollow-leg, mom?"

When she nodded, Taylor protested, but Grayson stood up and sent him on his way to bed. Grayson smiled, listening to him grumble as he slouched down the hall to his room. He stretched, then looked at Sarah. "I think I'll have a night cap. Do you want to join me?"

She gave the invitation a moment's thought, then nodded with a smile. "I'll have a glass of wine. I think there is still some left."

Grayson poured the wine and took the glass to her. Then he went back and made himself a rye and coke. He snagged the chair at the end of the table and pulled it over beside the one she was sitting in. She looked at him with surprise. His eyes twinkled. "This is too good an opportunity miss. I'm going to sit close so I can hold your hand, and catch the scent of your perfume. I want to touch your hair and look into your eyes. I'm giving you notice, Sarah Brite. I'm starting to court you, right now."

Sarah blushed and she felt a surge of heat rise in her. "You're taking unfair advantage of me, you know."

He leaned over and put his head on her shoulder. "Not as much as I'd like to, but I'm determined to be a gentleman." He straightened up and looked into her eyes. "I'm beginning to think that idea is highly over rated through. Maybe I should just take you to bed and make love to you all night long—except I want you to be able to enjoy it and those damn ribs will make sure you can't."

Sarah's face was flushed. "You...."

"What shall we watch tonight, beautiful?"

"I...I don't know." Sarah stammered. The sudden heat of desire that settled in her groin threw her off track. *He has stirred me before, but this is almost overwhelming. If my ribs didn't hurt so badly, I'd be pulling him into the bedroom.*

"Sarah, are you alright?"

She didn't meet his eyes. "Yes, yes of course. I...I just..."

"Did you suddenly have an image of you and me together?

Don't be shocked. I have them all the time. That's what people, who love each other, do you know."

She groaned. "Please Grayson; just find something to watch. It will pass the time for the next hour or so."

He smiled happily as he surfed through the channels. He clicked on a comedy sitcom, then put down the remote and reached for her hand.

She didn't snatch it away, even though she thought it might have been the wise thing to do. He rubbed his thumb over the back of her hand, then turned it over and caressed the palm. She felt heat and moisture flood into her. She wanted to pull away, but he held her hand firm, lifting it to his lips so he could lick her palm.

She gasped and her eyes were heavy with desire. "Grayson...that isn't fair."

He smiled. "You don't think so? He pulled her hand forward and rested it against the zipper of his jeans. "See what you do to me? Not just now when we are sitting here like this, but every time I'm around you, every time I think of you?"

She felt the hardness that strained there and shuddered. "I...I think I should go to bed."

"Is that an invitation?"

"No, I need to think. I need some space so I can be rational about this."

"Do whatever you need to, Sarah. I'm just starting this pursuit." He kissed her hand. "I won't rush you, but I've loved you for so long you can't blame me for trying." He stood up. "Let me help you stand up."

Sarah didn't reply. After he helped her out of the chair, she went to the washroom and washed her face and hands. She couldn't ignore the feelings that still lingered. She crossed her legs, trying to push them away, but that didn't help. She uttered a soft moan when feelings she couldn't control flooded through her, as she thought about him. She leaned her head against the door. *What do I do?* she wondered.

When she came out of the bathroom, she walked to her bedroom door. Grayson had turned back the sheets and was waiting for her. He smiled and gestured for her to sit on the bed. Then he took off her slippers and swung her legs up. He pulled the sheets up over her and then looked into her eyes. They held the look for a few seconds. Then he leaned down and let his lips caress hers briefly. "Good night, beautiful lady." He turned off the light and left the room.

Grayson poured himself another drink and sat down on the couch. He stared blankly at the TV, not seeing what played across the screen, as he tried to push down his desire. He gulped down the drink, then pulled the quilt out from its place at the far end of the couch and made his bed. He stripped off his shirt and jeans, then turned off the TV and the lights and crawled into his cocoon. Sleep eluded him for over an hour, as he thought about Sarah. He was beginning to drift off when he became aware of somebody touching his face. He sat up quickly. "Taylor?" he whispered. "What's wrong son?"

Then his senses tingled. He could smell her. What would she be doing out of bed? "Sarah?" he whispered, reaching for her hand. "What's wrong?"

Pain knifed through her as she settled on the edge of the couch beside him. "I'm sorry," she gasped. "I...will you to come to bed with me and cuddle me. I can't get past how wonderful it felt to have you touch me tonight. I'm aching with need, Grayson. Is this too much to ask of you?"

"Sarah, I love you. I want to be with you, but I don't want to do anything that you'll regret tomorrow. No matter how much I want to be with you, I don't want to derail our fragile truce."

She leaned down and pressed her lips to his, hungrily devouring him. He heard her gasp and knew that her ribs were hurting, but her mouth persisted to search his, her tongue teasing until he greedily opened his lips and drew her in. The kiss was hot and filled with passion. Finally, he broke away. "Sarah, I'm only human," he whispered. "Is this what you want for the long term, not just because you are aroused at the moment?" He pushed his hands into her hair and held her back. "Look at me, Sarah." Her hungry gaze met his. "You have to understand this. Even though you aren't well enough to have sex right now, if I go to bed with you tonight, there's no going back for me. Do you feel the same way?"

She moaned as she stood up and tugged on his hand. He pushed himself off the couch, his erection forcing itself out against his shorts. She stroked him and pushed against him. "Are you sure, Sarah? You have been adamantly denying that you could love me. I'm not a whore, willing to use you for the night."

She moaned. "Will you just stop talking and come with me."

He followed her into the bedroom and turned on the bedside

light as she sat down on the bed. Her eyes were heavy with desire, her lips red and full from kissing. She tried to work the fingers of her left hand to undo the buttons of her pajamas, but it wasn't working very well. Hers eyes implored him and he stepped forward to help undress her. His fingers worked each button, softly caressing her skin as he undid them. He was agonizingly slow.

She kissed his fingers. "Hurry" she whispered.

"Patience," he said softly.

"Are you getting even with me?"

He grinned and kissed her lips. "I'm savoring what I've waited so long for."

As he undid the last button, he pushed the flannel top back and off her shoulders. He looked at her, taking in the fullness of her breasts, the nipples that stood erect. She gasped as he touched then lightly with his fingers, the bent down to flick his tongue around them. She pushed her left hand into his hair and pulled his head against her chest, wincing when the movement tweaked her ribs. She ran her hand over his back, feeling his muscles, pulling him to her. "Push off my bottoms," she whispered desperately.

Her hand ran down into his shorts, touching the hardness inside them. He bucked and gasped. "Sarah." Her pajama bottoms slid to the floor and he pulled her close to him. She gasped.

"Did I hurt you?" he asked anxiously.

"I hurt, but I want you more. Just shut up and take me."

He slipped his fingers into her hot moistness. She ground herself against his hand. "Ohhhh yes," she breathed.

"Let's get you into bed." She sat on the bed and he lifted her legs up onto the mattress. He leaned over and trailed kisses down her chest to the puff dark of curls that nestled over her entrance. She wiggled and pulled on him. He looked up and hesitated. "We have to shut the door. We don't want Taylor to discover us like this."

He shut the door and breathed a sigh of relief when he discovered it had a lock. Then he turned back to the bed. As he slid in beside her, his expression became serious. "Do you love me Sarah?"

"I...I care more for you than I've ever cared for anyone except my son. I guess that's love, Grayson. No one has ever touched me emotionally the way you do. I've never wanted to be with anyone else this way...even when I was eighteen years old; I don't remember feeling like this with Duncan."

"You won't be sorry about this tomorrow?"

"No. I've fought you so hard, but I promise I won't regret this."

He settled in beside her and turned on his side to face her. He threaded a curl of hair around his finger. "I've dreamed of this for so long Sarah; it's almost hard to believe we are here."

She reached up and touched his face with her right hand, wincing as she moved.

"That hurts you doesn't it?"

She nodded.

"How are we going to do this? I want to make love to you, but I don't want to hurt you. Maybe we should just cuddle and touch until you're better."

She groaned. "I want you now."

"You have me, love, but no matter how we try to do this, it's going to hurt your ribs."

He ran his hand lightly down her body, exploring her curves and finally stroking her moist warm entrance. She gasped. He kept moving his hands, working her until she was swollen and hot. Then he got on his knees and dropped kisses down her body until he reached the inviting heat. She gasped as he explored her with his mouth, stroking and thrusting with his tongue until she was crying and squirming. She moaned, begging him to stop, telling him it wasn't fair to him, yet forcing her hand into his hair and pushing him into her, seeking the explosive release she craved. He continued his quest until she finally cried out, shuddering and quivering as she climaxed. He withdrew and kissed his way up her body until he reached her lips. Then he kissed her deeply and slowly.

Tears were streaming down her cheeks. She pulled him close, sobbing.

"Shhh, don't cry."

"This is so unfair. What can I do for you?"

"Sweetheart, there are many ways of making love. This was just as passionate for me as it was for you. You will probably never be able to understand how I feel right now. I am reeling with the power of what we just shared. Yeah, I've still got a hard on, but I've had lots of those these past few months; they do go away. But tonight, I'm going snuggle up with you, cuddle your naked body and make the dreams and longings I've held all these months come true. There will be time later, when you are healed for us to make love the way we want to."

Sarah caressed his face, looking into his eyes. They were full of love and happiness. "You are the most selfless, patient and wonderful man I've ever met, Grayson McNaughton." Her voice was a husky whisper. "I can't believe you can do this. You have needs too."

"And right now some of my deepest needs are being met. In my heart, I've wandered alone ever since I hit Dillon Hixon. I haven't been able to forgive myself and I never imagined anyone else would either. I never thought of having a wife, a home, a child. Then you came here and Taylor just wormed his way into my heart. He wanted us to be together so bad, to be a family...I began to dream. And I thought maybe we were making headway until I told you what had happened."

"Grayson, I'm so sorry about that. I was so self-righteous and condemning."

"Shhh...you were afraid. You've been afraid ever since you escaped with Taylor. I don't know how you've managed to do what you have. But after that, I was certain that I would always be alone, even though I still loved Taylor and he still loved me. But then that night you came down to the bunkhouse and kissed me...*we* kissed so desperately. I began to hope again. And then, two days later, I thought I could lose you forever. I've never been so afraid or desperate; not even when I realized what I'd done to Dillon."

He stopped and looked around the room. "It's hard to believe that only happened a week ago."

She drew him down to her. "I do love you. I've been so driven by fear that I didn't think I could let you into my life. To be honest, I'm still afraid Duncan will find us. He'd delight in taking you out because he'd know I love you. I couldn't bear that, any more than I could bear losing Taylor."

"If he shows up we'll deal with him."

"I trust you. So now, how are we going to sleep together in this bed?"

"I'll come around to your side and help you slide over into the middle. I hope you can lie comfortably on your left side and I'll slip in behind you and cuddle you." After they had everything rearranged, Grayson slipped between the sheets and spooned with her. "I love the smell of your hair," he whispered as he pressed against her until they were skin to skin, all the way down to their feet. "I have to say, this beats sleeping on the couch," he whispered.

She giggled and squeezed the hand that rested on her thigh. They both luxuriated in the cocoon of warmth and intimacy that enveloped them and as relaxation calmed them, the shroud of sleep seduced them.

CHAPTER FOURTEEN

The nest morning, Grayson's internal alarm awakened him at five o'clock. The feel of Sarah's body, soft and warm against his, flooded him with joy. He nuzzled his face into her hair, inhaling the smell of it. Then he let his lips trail down to her shoulder and he kissed her softly. *Can this be real? Surely, she won't change her mind now.* He squeezed his eyes closed. *No. I have to believe in her. Last night she told me she loved me.* He reached for her hand and smiled as she murmured in her sleep and threaded her fingers through his. His body reacted in the usual way and he pushed himself against her, longing for the day that he could truly make her his own. But for now, he knew he would have to wait. He lay next to her for half an hour, swollen and throbbing with need, but enjoying the other aspects of his love for her.

Then he finally eased himself out of the bed and went to the bathroom. There he found release in the way he had many times since he'd fallen in love with Sarah. Several moments later, he went into the living area to put on the clothes he'd left there the night before. He folded the quilt and put it and the pillow back in its place at the end of the couch. He smiled as he looked around the room. *No one will ever know what happened here last night, except Sarah and me*. He was filled with happiness and love. He quietly set up the coffee pot, then pulled on his chore coat and boots and let himself out the door.

Grayson whistled a happy tune, as he made his way down to the barnyard. Colt was there ahead of him and poked his head out of the grain room. "Sleeping on that couch must agree with you," he said with a chuckle.

"You get used to anything. At first it was kind of awkward, but I had a good night last night."

"Sarah didn't chew you out about letting Taylor rodeo?"

"She wasn't thrilled but, Taylor was so excited about it, she handled it pretty well. She has protected him for so long, it has to be hard to let go and trust someone else."

"Frank said she and Sarah had a good afternoon together. She hoped taping her ribs will give that side more stability so she can get around a little better."

"She is so impatient. It kills her to sit and do nothing."

"Well, she's still in for a rough couple of weeks, but then it'll start getting better. Right now, her muscles are bruised and battered, and that's on top of the pain in her ribs."

Grayson bent to pick up two pails of grain and headed for the corrals. "The weather is starting to warm up. It won't be long until we'll be seeing leaves coming out on the trees."

Colt followed him with two more pails. "Yeah. Winter seems to drag on until we reach the middle of April and into May. Then Mother Nature goes full steam ahead and almost overnight, everything turns green. It's pretty amazing."

They finished the chores and headed to the house for breakfast. "I assume you're going to the apartment?"

"Yes. It's time to roust out Taylor and see how Sarah is doing."

The smell of coffee wafted on the air when Grayson opened the door. But something else was there too. He sniffed appreciatively as he took off his chore coat and boots. "Do I smell bacon?" he asked as he walked into the kitchen?

Taylor was grinning from ear to ear. "I've almost got breakfast ready. I've made toast and bacon. I'll let you fry the eggs."

Grayson's eyes slid to meet Sarah's. She was sitting on the chair by the table. "You're up already," he said softly.

She smiled, a twinkle in her eye. "I had the best sleep I've had in ages; possibly ever. Now I'm determined to get up and about, so my ribs don't hurt anymore and I'll have even better nights."

Tension whooshed out of Grayson. Her message was clear, and he hadn't realized how uncertain he'd been. "I'm glad to hear that, but you don't want to rush things." He walked over and kissed her cheek. "I don't want my excuse for being here to disappear," he whispered.

She blushed as she took his hand and squeezed it. "We'll make sure that doesn't happen," she said softly.

Taylor turned the last piece of bacon. "Hey Grayson, it's your turn now. I'll set the table. I'm hungry. Do you think Colt will let us rodeo again today?"

"You'll have to ask him."

Sarah's look was filled with misgiving, but she said nothing. Grayson fried the eggs and brought the plate to the table. He squeezed her shoulder as he sat down. "Try not to worry. He'll be okay. I'll watch out for him."

She nodded and sat back while Grayson served her an egg, then helped himself and passed them to Taylor. Taylor slid the three remaining ones on his plate, took six slices of bacon and two pieces of toast before he handed the plates across to Grayson.

"What's up this morning, hollow leg? Your plate looks like you're ready to feed an army."

Tyler shrugged his shoulders as he looked across the table at Grayson. "I'm going to get big and strong so I can rodeo. I need lots of protein and carbs."

Grayson looked at Sarah and noted that she was trying to stifle a grin. "Protein and carbs," he said with amusement. "Where did you get those big words?"

Taylor bristled. "Ellie taught us about them in school. They are the building blocks of our meta-blism."

Sarah chuckled. "Speaking of school, you'll be going back next week, right."

"Yeah." Taylor squinted, deep in thought. "I wonder if Ellie would let us rodeo instead of doing stretches and yoga and stuff like that in phys ed."

Grayson laughed. "Nice try, buddy."

Sarah's mobility improved every day. Each night she and Grayson shared her bed, but he was up early and went out to do chores by the time Taylor got up, so the boy had no idea what was happening.

Grayson took time off work to take Sarah to see the doctor for her two-week checkup. Frank offered, but he was insistent. The doctor said she was healing nicely and he didn't protest when he saw how Frank had taped her. After they came out of the clinic, Grayson looked at her with a sparkle in his eyes. "There are two things I want to do with you today. We never really get to be alone."

She blushed. "I still can't have sex in the truck," she said with a giggle. "What are you thinking?"

"Quiet, serious Sarah; who would have imagined you had such a one track mind." He kissed her hand. "But I like where it goes. I wish I could wave a wand and make those ribs heal, but I can't, so we have to be patient."

"So, what do you have in mind?"

"Both are surprises. Let me help you into the truck."

Once she was in her seat, with her seat belt fastened, he got behind the wheel. "Will you play along with me? No cheating? I want to take you somewhere, and I want it to be a surprise."

"No cheating?"

"No cheating. We don't have to go very far."

Her cheeks flushed, and her eyes were full of question. "Okay, no cheating. But don't take too long."

She closed her eyes and laid her head back against the headrest. He started the truck and drove a short distance. She could feel him making turns and stopping at stop signs, then traveling down the street. He reached across and took her hand. "We're almost there."

She felt the truck slow, then maneuver into a parking space. "Just wait until I help you out," he said. "But, don't peek until I say you can, please."

She nodded. Once out of the truck, they took a few steps and then he opened a door and led her into a building. Her curiosity was killing her. They walked a short distance, and then he helped her sit on a high stool. "What on earth are we doing Grayson?"

"You can open your eyes now," he said softly. He put his arm around her shoulders and held her against him.

She opened her eyes and stared at the counter in front of her. Confusions and then amazement flooded over her features. Then her eyes filled with tears as they met his. "Are you...?"

"I'm buying you a ring," he said softly.

"Oh, my, there are so many." She looked around. "What did you ha..ve in mi..nd?" she stammered.

"I've never done this before, so I thought we'd pick it out together."

She touched his cheek. "I'll love whatever you choose, but remember I'd prefer nothing big and blingy. Just decide on the one that speaks to you."

Grayson looked at the rings, the pointed to a solitaire with two baguette cut stones on each side. "What do you think of this?" he asked.

Sarah's eyes sparkled. "It's beautiful, but should we...should you spend so much?"

"I don't spend my money anywhere else, Sarah. You know, I seldom leave the ranch. It'll be different now because I'll have a family, but right now I can't think of a better place to use some of my savings." He motioned for the clerk to come over and take the ring out of the case. When she held it up for Sarah to look at, her eyes filled with tears again. "It's beautiful," she whispered.

Grayson took it and slid it on her finger. Sarah's face was aglow. She held her hand up and looked at it. Then she frowned. "I need a smaller size," she said with disappointment. The clerk assured them that it could be sized to fit and took the proper measurements of her finger.

"How long will it take?" Grayson queried.

"We'll have to send it out, but it should be back in a week."

"We could look at another one. What do you think?"

Sarah's gaze slid over the rings. In the top corner, she spied another one. "That one is very similar. Can we look at it?"

The clerk lifted the ring out of the case and let Grayson slip it on her finger. It fit perfectly and Sarah's eyes once again got moist. "What do you think?" she asked.

Grayson looked at it closely and then looked into her eyes. "I think this one was meant for you; its white gold and you usually wear silver jewelry."

She flushed. "I didn't know that you noticed." She spread her fingers to look at the ring. "I love this one."

He kissed her cheek, then slipped the ring off her finger and handed it to the clerk. "We might as well get our wedding bands now too."

Sarah's breath caught in her throat. *So soon? So final?* She stared into his eyes. They were filled with love and happiness. What was wrong with her? She swallowed hard. "I...yes, I guess we could."

He leaned down to whisper in her ear. "I'm not taking any chance that you will change your mind again. If I had my way, I'd rush you off to the courthouse right now and get married. But we can't do that without Taylor. It's not that he wouldn't be thrilled about us getting married, but I want him to be there when we do it."

Sarah blushed. "I'm not going to change my mind," she whispered back. "I was just getting used to being engaged and then you dropped the wedding rings on me."

He grinned happily. "I want to make an honest woman out of you as soon as possible. In fact, by the time your ribs are healed I want you to be my wife, so we'd better get with the program."

She giggled. "You already made love to me."

"Sweetheart that was just foreplay. When we make love, you'll definitely know the difference." His voice was just above a whisper, but full of promise.

Sarah's face flushed scarlet. The clerk had noticed the intimate by-play between them, so she cleared her throat when she approached with a tray of wedding bands. She made some suggestions as to what would fit with the engagement ring if they wanted matching bands. She also showed them the one that matched the ring they had chosen. Sarah said it was beautiful, but she'd rather they had matching white gold bands and Grayson agreed.

By the time they left the jewelry store, darkness was settling in. Grayson put his arm across her shoulders. "How are you doing? Do you need your pain meds?"

"I'm starting to feel sore, but this afternoon has been so exciting, I've just pushed it away."

"I didn't anticipate the time going by so fast. I wanted to take you out for dinner; that was going to be my second surprise, but Frank will have dinner ready for us now, so maybe we should just head home."

"When are you going to give me the ring?"

"Patience. You'll get it soon enough."

"I have no patience. I want it on my finger now," she declared impishly.

He looked at her and laughed. "I haven't seen this side of you before. I wonder what new aspects of the real Sarah will unfold as you let go of your fear! I can hardly wait, but like me, you, my dear are going to have patience."

She pouted. "Tonight?"

He started the truck. "There're a few ingredients missing, but it may happen tonight."

"What is missing? We're both here."

He touched the tip of her nose admonishingly. "I'm not going to give my bride-to-be her engagement ring in a truck. I have other plans."

Sarah smiled, wondering what he had in mind. Grayson turned on the radio and they sang with the music as they traveled back to the ranch. "You can sing," she said with surprise.

"I play guitar too. It's helped me through many lonely, dark hours in the bunk house."

She undid her seat belt and grimaced as she slid over beside him.

"No seat belt? That's illegal my dear," he chided.

She laid her head against his shoulder. "Is it possible that being this happy isn't illegal?"

When they reached the ranch, Frank had already delivered supper to the apartment. The smells from the oven filled the air when they stepped inside. Sarah noticed that her son had already set the table. He shoved himself off the couch and hurried to greet them. "Man, you guys are late."

Grayson ruffled his hair. "I had a few things I needed to do after your mom went to the doctor. I guess you're hungry. I see you've set the table. Good boy."

Praise from Grayson always made him feel ten feet tall and his eyes sparkled with happiness. "Yeah, I'm hungry. Are you ready to eat now?"

"I think we are, but there's one thing you forgot to do."

Taylor looked around, puzzled. "What did I forget?"

"You didn't ask your mom how she's doing. That's why we went to town, buddy."

Taylor looked embarrassed. "Sorry, Mom. I was so busy thinking about how hungry I was, that I forgot to ask."

Sarah shook her head and laughed. "I understand hon. Hollow legs demand more attention than moms."

"Not really. What did the doctor say?" Taylor asked, as he moved to hug her.

"Don't squeeze too hard. I'm coming along nicely, but I'm not totally ready for a big boy hug yet."

He slid his hand down to clasp hers. "I know you'll be okay mom because Grayson is taking care of you." He looked up at her, his eyes glistening in a moment of vulnerability. "Besides that, I need you." He cleared his throat and looked away.

Sarah's heart lurched. It wasn't often that Taylor expressed his feelings for her anymore. The days were long past when he looked into her eyes on a daily basis and said *I love you, mommy*. She fought emotion as she looked at Grayson. He smiled tenderly, sensing her mood. He moved to help her take off her coat, his fingers brushing her cheek softly as he eased it off. His hands lingered to squeeze her shoulder before he moved away.

"I think it's time we ate," he said as he laid her coat on the couch. Taylor pulled out a chair for her to sit down at the table while Grayson took the food out of the oven. As they ate, Taylor had them chuckling over stories about his day with Sam, Selena, and Miss Ellie. "Miss Ellie is a good teacher. She's strict, but she's fun too."

The biggest secret of the day lingered between Sarah and Grayson. She waited, wondering when he would mention *the* ring, but the conversation carried on until they were finished eating, and then Grayson and Taylor did dishes and cleaned up the kitchen. The three of them watched TV together until eight-thirty and then Grayson suggested that Taylor should probably get ready to go to bed.

Then he asked her if she wanted to get ready for bed. Frustration filled her, and she was sulky when she got up and went into the bathroom. *What is he waiting for?* After she'd washed her face and brushed her teeth, she stepped out into a room that was darkened, lit only by the flickering flames of many candles.

Grayson was standing in the hallway, waiting for her. As he reached to take her hand, her eyes filled with tears again. "How…where did you get all the candles?"

"I'm a resourceful man, my love." He tugged on her hand. "Come and sit. I want this moment to be perfect for us." She sat down. "We only need one more thing." She looked up at him, questioning. He leaned down and kissed her lips, then moved away and went down the hall. She heard him go into Taylor's room and then a murmur of voices reached her ears. Moments later the two men in her life came out to join her.

Taylor looked puzzled. "What's with all the candles?"

"I have something important that I want to talk to you about. Will you sit here on this chair by your mom?"

Sarah blinked hard, fighting back tears, as she realized what Grayson was going to do. Taylor sat down beside her and gazed around the room, looking puzzled. Grayson knelt in front of the two of them. Her reached out and took Sarah's hand, as he looked into Taylors's eyes.

"Taylor, I want to ask you if I can marry your mom."

Taylors's eyes widened. He sputtered and jumped to his feet. His face was split in a grin, radiant with joy. "Yes! Yes!" he yelled.

Grayson reached out and grabbed his hand. "There is something else I need to ask, Taylor."

Taylor was shaking with excitement. "Anything! Whatever!"

"Will you let me adopt you and legally make you my son?"

Taylor flew against him, throwing his arms around him. Tears streamed down his cheeks as he hugged Grayson. "That's what I've always wanted; for you to be my dad."

Sarah cleared her throat. "Where do I fit in this, you guys?"

Grayson smiled as he looked into her eyes. "I have something to ask you, too." He clasped both of her hands in his and pulled them to his lips. "Will you marry me and make my life complete, Sarah Brite?"

She looked at him coyly. "I think I might need some incentive."

"Mom! You have to say yes," Taylor cried.

Sarah smiled as her eyes met Grayson's. He leaned forward and kissed her deeply. "Is that enough?"

Her eyes shimmered. "It's a good start," she whispered, then took his face in her hands and pulled him close for another.

Taylor shifted uncomfortably. "Okay, you guys, all that mushy stuff creeps me out."

Grayson looked at him with a happy smile. "Get used to it, son. You're going to see a lot more of it."

"Yuck."

Taylor turned away.

"Just a minute, bud, I have one more thing to do here." He reached into his pocket and took out a small box.

Sarah's eyes sparkled. "Finally!" she said with a laugh.

"Does that mean yes?" Grayson asked with a happy grin.

"Yes, yes, yes. I'll marry you!"

Grayson flipped open the lid of the box, lifted out the ring and slid it down her finger.

"Holy Cow!" Taylor exclaimed. His eyes were as big as saucers.

Grayson and Sarah barely heard him. They were momentarily lost in their own world, until Taylor headed for the porch door. "I'm going to run to the house and tell them that you're going to be my dad."

Grayson lifted his head. "Not now, Taylor! We'll tell them that we're getting married sometime tomorrow. Then you can tell them the rest of the good news."

Taylor's face fell. "But I want to tell them…"

Grayson stood up, his eyes locking with the boys. "You will get to tell them," he said patiently. "But it's nine-thirty now. Your mom has had a long day, and she needs to go to bed. I have to go to work in the morning and you have to go to school. We'll visit them tomorrow night and tell them our news."

"I can't wait that long," Taylor protested.

Sarah reached out to him. "Yes, you can. You see, this doesn't just involve you and Grayson. They need to know that Grayson and I are getting married first. Then it's appropriate for him to be your dad."

Suddenly the significance of it dawned on Taylor. His face beamed. "Then we'll be a real family, just like the Thompsons, right?"

Sarah nodded. "Yes, we'll be a real family."

Taylor put his arms around her shoulders, then reached out and snagged his arm around Grayson's waist, pulling him into the embrace. "I've never been so happy. Thank you, mom, for finally seeing that Grayson is a nice guy. And thanks for not giving up on mom, Grayson!" He leaned back and grinned at the man. "I knew you liked her for a long time, but then she was so mean to you, I thought you'd give up. I was afraid you'd never be my dad."

"It may have seemed mean to us, but your mom was protecting you in the only way she knew how…just like she always has." Grayson looked into Sarah's eyes. "That is one of the things that made me love her. When your mother loves someone, I know she will be loyal and true and she will stand up for them and fight to protect them against all odds. That makes her a very strong and special person." He looked down at Taylor. "One day you'll understand how lucky you've been to have her for a mom."

Taylor was thoughtful for a moment. "You are like mom, too.

Look at how you look watch out for me when we're out doing chores, and when that crazy cow took her down, you were the first one there, trying to protect her and beat that cow off. You were crying, begging mom to be alright, even while you were hitting the cow with the fence post."

"I was scared to death, Taylor. I was so afraid she would be terribly hurt—even worse than what did happen." He shook his head slightly. "So now you see son, the three of us will watch out for each other and protect each other from anything and anybody." He made a fist and pumped Taylors in a silent pact. Taylor nodded. "It's time for you to go to bed now, bud."

"I'll never sleep. I'm too excited."

Sarah yawned. "I'm tired, even though I am excited." She stretched out her hand and looked at her ring in the flicker of the candle light. "It's been so long since I've dared to think about love and happiness." She smiled at Grayson. "It caught me unaware."

Grayson helped her out of the chair. "It's time to go to bed, love; you need your rest. I'm anxious for those ribs to heal." She blushed as she touched his face and laid her head against his shoulder.

"Yuck! Please, don't start all that mushy stuff again," Taylor protested. "I'm going to bed."

"'Night," Sarah said with a chuckle, as Grayson took her hand and walked with her to the bedroom. They grinned at each other when they heard his door close. "All that *yucky* stuff," she giggled.

Grayson shut the bedroom door behind them, and then pulled her into his arms. "I like that *yucky stuff*," he said softly as he kissed her forehead, then feathered a kiss on each eyelid and dropped his lips down to hers. She slipped her arms around his waist and carefully pulled him close, reveling in the strength of his muscles, the solidness of his legs against hers. He rocked his pelvis against hers and she moaned as she felt the hardness that strained against his jeans.

She nibbled at his lips. "I don't want to wait until my ribs are healed," she whispered. "Can't we make this work?"

He groaned. "I don't want to hurt you." His hand cupped the back of her head drawing her into him as their tongues mated, thrusting, entangling, dancing into each other mouths. Desire devoured them. Lips slid apart, searching hungrily, finding cheeks, necks, and then returning to meet urgently. Grayson swept her up in his arms and carried her to the bed. Pain slashed through her, but the fervor of desire pushed it into the background and she pulled him down onto it with her. Her hands began tearing at his shirt. She heard tiny moaning sounds, not knowing that they came from her own throat.

He took her hands, holding them, stilling them as he looked into her eyes. His breath shuttered. "I'm afraid I'll hurt you…let's do this slowly. I'll help you undress and then I'll finish what you've started." He rubbed the tip of his nose against hers. "I'll need the buttons on my shirt tomorrow," he teased gently. He leaned forward and kissed her hands before he let them go.

He sat up and got off the bed, then gently helped her sit up. "How are the ribs?"

Her face was flushed, her breathing rapid. "They're still there, but don't let that stop you. You're driving me crazy."

He took off her shirt, and then helped her stand so he could slide her slacks down over her hips. He hooked his fingers in her panties and slid them down, kneeling as they fell. He trailed his fingers back up, stopping at the tumble of curls at the apex of her legs. He felt her shiver as he stroked her gently.

"Oh Grayson," she moaned. He nestled his nose into the curls and slid his tongue out to caress her. Heat welcomed his invasion and moisture flooded onto his tongue. She was shaking as she shoved her hands into his hair. "Please don't do this," she whimpered as she squirmed. "Please…not without you this time." She tried to cross her legs, but he wouldn't let her. He stroked her again and again and she cried out each time. He finally felt her contract when she cried out a strangled "Oh, yes!"

He rose up quickly, taking off his shirt, while she pulled at his jeans. Then he leaned her back, swinging her legs up. He reached into his jean pocket as he pushed them off and extracted a package. In seconds, he had rolled on the condom and was on the bed, gently positioning himself between her opened legs.

"Are you sure this will be okay?" he asked with concern.

"Grayson, when I'm healed up I am going to torture you just like you're doing to me," she said with a half sob.

He braced himself on either side of her body and gently probed her. He closed his eyes savoring her heat; the welcoming twitches that he knew could quickly become contractions if he didn't move slowly. He fought the desire to plunge into her, taking everything at once. He wanted to make this act of passion last…he wanted it to carry them both to the highest heights, but he knew they were both so close already, that it might not be possible.

Sarah moved under him, bearing down, forcing him into confined places. *She's as tight as a virgin.* The thought was fleeting and then a cry, that was like a ragged growl in his chest, escaped as he felt himself losing control. "Oh my god, Sarah!" He gasped as he plunged into her and tumbled into the world of sensation that he hadn't experienced for many years.

Sarah's muffled cries joined his. He shuddered and slumped down beside her, careful to stay away from her damaged side. He slid his hand along her cheek and brushed away the tears that spilled over. She turned her mouth into the palm of his hand and licked it, tasting the salty moisture.

Grayson shivered, the sensuousness of her action teasing his senses. He ran his fingers over her lips and she caught one and gave it a light suck. He smiled. "My quiet Sarah; few would guess how passionate you are in bed."

She chuckled. "I didn't know myself. I can honestly say it's never been like this before."

He tweaked her nose. "Is that the line you gave all the other guys?"

She nipped his finger. "There was only one other and it was never like this. I was young and defiant. I was hungry to escape home and I thought I loved him, but it was never love." She squeezed her eyes tight and sighed. "It was never like this."

She ran her hand down over his chest. He grabbed it before she went too far. "I have to take this off before it breaks and defeats its purpose."

She smiled dreamily. "Hurry back."

He grabbed a handful of tissue and disposed of the condom, then slipped out to go to the bathroom. When he came back, he softly closed the door and walked to the bed. Sarah had rolled onto her side, making room for him to slide in behind her. He lowered himself onto the mattress and pressed himself against her back, enjoying the feel of her skin. He dropped a kiss on her shoulder. "You know, we are going to have to be more careful. If Taylor came out of his room and found me sneaking around in the buff, it wouldn't be a good thing."

She grasped his hand and pulled his thumb to her lips, where she nibbled on it. "You're right. I don't think he should know that we're sleeping together for a while."

"I agree, and I don't want to go back to the bunkhouse now. I'd like to get married right away. Couldn't we just go to the courthouse and quietly do it."

She chuckled. "We could try to, but do you remember what the 'family' did when Christina and Tim tried to do that?"

"Yeah, I remember."

CHAPTER FIFTEEN

The next morning Grayson made coffee and slipped out to do chores before everyone else was up. When he came back, he could smell breakfast cooking. He hung up his coat and walked into the kitchen to find Sarah and Taylor working together.
"Hey, what's going on here?"
"We're making breakfast," Taylor replied happily.
"I see that." He slid in between mother and son and dropped a kiss on Sarah's cheek as he gave her a hug. Then he ruffled Taylor's hair. "If you guys keep doing this, I'm not going to have a reason to stay here. I'll be banished back to the bunkhouse."
"Naw. We'll still need you here to reach the things on the top shelves in the cupboard," Taylor said with a grin. "And you gave mom a ring, so now you have to stay here so we can be a family."
Grayson pulled mother and son against his chest. "We're going to have to get married and make this all legitimate."
Taylor fidgeted as he ate breakfast. Sarah looked at him. "What's bothering you Taylor?"
"Nothing...." He ate his eggs and bacon and spread jam on a piece of toast, but it was clear to both Sarah and Grayson that he was distracted.

Grayson studied him for a moment, and then looked at Sarah. "Colt is in the house now—they're having breakfast. Maybe we should go and have coffee with them."

Taylor jumped up. "That's a great idea. Then you can tell them the news."

Grayson chuckled. "I figured that was what was eating at you." He looked at Sarah. "Is that okay with you? This kid will have a nervous breakdown if he has to wait all day to tell everyone."

Sarah smiled at her son. "Yes, we could go over for coffee, but I have to get dressed. I don't want to show them this gorgeous ring, looking like I just crawled out of bed."

Grayson nodded. "I'll help you get dressed." He grinned. "How are your ribs this morning?"

She blushed, her eyes sparkling as she met his look. "They're doing better than I imagined. Maybe all that activity, along with the rush of energy and quickening of circulation promotes healing."

Taylor groaned. "Don't get all mushy again. I hate that. I'll do the dishes and clean up so we can go to tell everybody the news."

Grayson laughed as he put his arm around Sarah and turned her to the bedroom. "Get used to it kid, that's how it's going to be around here from now on."

"Yuck," Taylor responded, making a face.

Grayson helped Sarah into her jeans and shirt, sneaking a kiss between buttons as he fastened them. She was flushed and reaching for him eagerly, but he captured her hands and held them now. "It's not a good idea to start something we can't finish now," he said softly. "Tonight," he promised, his voice husky and full of desire.

She nodded, knowing he was right, but struggling with the heat that coursed through her. She looked down at him. "You need to give that wonderful specimen a cold wash. He's very conspicuous."

Grayson shifted his jeans over the bulge that pushed against his zipper. "Don't laugh woman. You have no idea what it's like to deal with this guy. He just refuses to do as he's told when I'm around you. Go comb your hair and whatever else you do in the bathroom, while I talk some sense into him."

Sarah leaned forward and brushed him with her hand. "I could try to do that."

Grayson's eyes darkened and he groaned. "I don't think we have time," he said huskily. "Taylor will be knocking at the door any moment. He can't wait to tell everyone the news."

She smiled as she turned away. Taylor came sliding up to her bedroom door in his sock feet as she opened it.

"What's taking you guys so long?" He looked at the color in his mother's face. "Aw shucks, you guys were being all mushy again. Geeze! Do that stuff later. Right now, we have to get over to the house."

"I still have to brush my teeth and comb my hair. And remember, hot shot: the first news that we'll tell them is that Grayson and I are getting married. THEN you can tell them about him adopting you, so he'll be your dad for real."

"Okay, okay, just hurry up." He frowned. "What is Grayson doing?"

"He's making the bed for me. He'll be out pretty soon." Grayson grinned as Sarah shut the bedroom door behind her, giving him a chance to get his anatomy back in order. Taylor was young enough that he had no idea about sex between a man and a woman. He'd seen it in the barnyard amongst the animals often enough, but as it should be at his age, he never gave a thought to it otherwise. *I don't want to shatter his innocence*, Grayson thought with love.

He picked up Sarah's pillow and held it against his chest, inhaling her scent. *I'm caught in the middle here. I don't want to go back to the bunkhouse, even for a few weeks. I said I wouldn't. But how do we explain to Taylor that we're sleeping together? One of these days, he's going to discover that I'm not sleeping on the couch. I'm surprised that he hasn't already.* He sighed. *How will he react to that?*

Sarah opened the bedroom door. "Have you got everything under control," she asked with a twinkle in her eye.

Grayson put her pillow back and stood up. His look was serious when it met hers.

She looked at him, then stepped forward and stopped in front of him. "What are you thinking?"

"Nothing, we'll talk later."

She ran her hand up along his cheek and back to cup his head, pulling his lips down to meet hers. "Have I told you this morning how much I love you," she asked softly as she kissed him.

He pushed her back gently. "You're not playing fair." He looked over her shoulder to see Taylor standing there.

"Come on your guys," the boy burst out. "Quit all that yucky stuff and let's going before Colt leaves the house and we'll have to wait longer."

"We're coming," Grayson said, taking Sarah's hand and leading the way to the door. Taylor had swung it open and was running down the sidewalk.

Sarah and Grayson both yelled after him. "Don't go spilling the beans Taylor." They heard him laugh with delight as he turned the corner.

When they reached the house, Taylor was in the kitchen babbling non-stop about anything that came to his mind. Colt, Frank, Ollie, and Ellie were staring at him in surprise. Colt got up and walked over to him. "Hey man, what's got you so wound up?"

Grayson stepped forward and put his hand on Taylor's shoulder. "Relax son. Just take a deep breath and take my hand." Taylors's hand curled into Grayson's and he leaned against his hip. Grayson put his arm around Sarah's shoulder pulling her against him. "Sarah has something to show you."

Colts look narrowed slightly as it met Grayson's. "You old dog," he said softly, nodding with satisfaction

Sarah flushed as she held out her hand, showing them the ring on her finger.

Frank squealed with delight as she jumped up and flew to her side. "You two finally got your act together." She grasped the extended hand and looked at the ring. "Oh my god, that is beautiful." She hugged Sarah and then threw her arms around Grayson. "I am so happy for you!"

Taylor cleared his throat, and Grayson turned to him. "You guys, Taylor has something he wants to tell you."

Taylors's face was flushed with excitement. "Grayson's going to be my dad. He's going to adopt me and make me his son—like really his son." His eyes filled with tears. "I'm going to be Taylor McNaughton," he said with pride. He turned to Sarah and Sam. "I'm going to have a real dad, just like you guys."

The kids looked at him for a moment, then whooped with joy and flew to hug him. They wrestled down onto the floor, celebrating the way kids do.

Ellie smiled and shook her head. "I think school is dismissed for the day. Those kids will never settle down now." She smiled as she walked over to Grayson and Sarah. "Congratulations, both of you. I am so happy for all three of you. I'm sure you feel your world is complete, but that little boy..." Tears filled her eyes, and she gave her head a slight shake. "You have given Taylor everything he's dreamed about for months. You have just filled up all the empty spaces in his heart and while he's no wilting violet, he will just blossom from here on out. I am so happy for all of you."

"So have you set a date?" Colt asked.

Grayson chuckled. "As soon as possible; if that could be today, we'd go to the marriage commissioner and get married, but I think we have to get a license first."

"Slowdown, hot shot," Frank snorted. "You know this 'family' will never let you get away with that. You're going to have a wedding and we're going to celebrate with you. So head your tail back to the bunkhouse for the next few weeks while we plan it and get ready."

Colt looked at Grayson and chuckled. "Frank, I think that particular horse has probably broken out of the coral already." Sarah and Grayson's faces turned red.

Ollie snorted. "Look who's talking. It seems to me that people, who live in glass houses shouldn't cast stones. Don't you think, Ellie?"

Ellie giggled. "I'm not saying a word."

Grayson smirked. "Ellie and Ollie, what do we need to get a marriage license."

"Not much; just a birth certificate and a driver's license, or a passport and sixty bucks to lie down at the till."

Sarah looked crestfallen. "I don't have a driver's license or a passport. I have a bank account and a fake Social Insurance card and birth certificates from when Ryan and Charlie set us up. But neither one of them have picture identification." She shrugged. "I—we—have purposely lived an invisible life so long. Now, what do we do?"

"I know you can get a Personal Identity card through SGI. I've seen them," Ellie said thoughtfully." "They are a government issued picture ID."

Colt leaned back in his chair, his jean clad legs stretched out in front of him. "I think you two should give this a lot of thought, because down the road it will come back to bite you in the ass if you don't."

Sarah's hackles rose. "What do yo...."

Colt waved her protest aside. "To us you are Sarah Brite. And you can get married using your false ID, but the Canadian government has no idea who Sarah Brite is. The only record, they have, is a person who is registered on your real birth certificate and the person who is named on your original, legal, Social Insurance number. I assume you were that person when you gave birth to Taylor so that is how your son is registered too. For Grayson to truly adopt him, that is the record you'll need to use."

Sarah bristled, wanting to fight back, but she knew he was right. Tears filled her eyes as she turned into Grayson's chest. "Oh god, what a mess I've made of things."

Grayson held her close, cradling her head. "We'll work through all of this, Sarah; we'll do it together."

Colt stood up and walked over to put a hand on each of their shoulders. "I know you want to get married right away, probably as much for Taylor as anything.

Grayson nodded. "And I want to make things permanent between Sarah and me."

Colt grinned. "Man, a piece of paper doesn't make anything permanent. It sounds good, but if that worked, there wouldn't be so many divorces in this world. True marriage is based on commitment, and caring about the happiness of each other more, or at least as much, as you care for your own: it's about the willingness to respect and do your best to meet the needs of each other. Love is something that is up here," he touched Grayson's head "and lust is below your belt buckle. Both necessary and marriage would be a dismal affair without them."

Colt took Sarah's shoulder and turned her toward him. "You are through running Sarah. We're all family now and we'll all be there for you. I suggest getting a copy of your original birth certificate and social insurance number. Get a copy of Taylor's birth certificate and do this right. I'll put you in touch with our lawyer, to ensure everything is up to snuff."

"But how do I tell Taylor that Grayson can't be his father right away? He's so thrilled. I can't break his heart."

Grayson smoothed her hair. "Taylor is smart, hon. We'll sit down and explain everything to him and he'll get it." He cupped her face. "No piece of paper can make him any more my son than he already is, just like we don't need a piece of paper right now to make our commitment the real thing. Colt is right. We need to do this properly. No more running, no more fear of that animal finding you. We are committed to building *our* life now."

He turned to look at Frank. "Sorry Frank, but I'm not heading going back to the bunkhouse. I'm staying with my family. I might have done it for a night or two to satisfy convention, but I think this will take months and I'm not wasting any more time."

Colt turned to Grayson with a grin. "We could burn down the bunkhouse and you'd have no place to sleep, except where you belong at Sarah's, but it's a good building and who knows when we'll need it for another ranch hand."

"Well, you can do what you like with the bunkhouse Colt; you won't need another ranch hand because I'm not leaving."

Colt's eyes twinkled. "No, but you're a good vet, and my wife is a good vet; it's a shame to waste all that training and expertise."

Grayson looked stunned. "Jeez man…I can't even go there now. I'm just getting used to the idea of being a family man."

"We're not on any timetable, but now more than ever, because you are going to be a family man, you should think beyond being a ranch-hand. You are cut out for bigger things, and having a family costs money."

"You pay better than most."

Colt nodded. "But you have outstanding qualifications; you need to step up the ladder and see how high you can go."

"I like it here, Colt."

"I'm not kicking you out. I want you around here. Building a clinic here on the ranch has been in my plans for a while. I want Frank to be able to use her training, but since I realized that you are a vet also, another idea has been rolling around in the back of my mind. One day after everything else settles down, we'll sit down and discuss the possibilities."

Frank stepped to his side, her eyes shining. "Have you been holding out on me?"

Colt smiled as he looked into her eyes. "I might need you to support me when I'm old and gray and crippled up." He turned to Grayson and Sarah. "Take the rest of the day off, and take your son home and tell him the facts. He'll be okay with it if you are straight with him."

CHAPTER SIXTEEN

Grayson walked into the family room. "Taylor, you need to come home for an hour or so. Your mom and I have some things to talk to you about."

"Can't we do it later? We're having fun."

Sarah looked at Grayson hesitantly, and then stepped in front of him. "Taylor, this is important, so you have to come now. You can come back and play later."

Taylor recognized her no-nonsense tone of voice. His mom was back. "Okaaay," he said with a big sigh and pushed himself to his feet. "See you guys later."

When they reached the apartment, he kicked off his shoes and looked at them with frustration. "What's so important?" Then it was as if a light was dawning and he grinned. "You're getting married today?"

"That's what we have to talk to you about," Sarah said, her look sympathetic.

Taylors's face fell and he stared at her. "You changed your mind." His voice was full of accusation and pain. Sarah's eyes filled with tears. *Why does he immediately think it's me?* She shook her head and squeezed her eyes shut. *Because it is,* she thought. *Even this is my fault because of the choices I made.*

Grayson placed a hand on Taylor's shoulder and lead him to a chair at the table. They both sat down and Grayson reached out to Sarah, as his look held Taylors. "No one has changed their mind, Taylor. But there are some complications that we have to deal with. To get a marriage license, your mom would need something that has her picture on it, like a drivers license or passport. She doesn't have either. We could go to Regina and get her a Saskatchewan ID card, and we could get a license and get married. But as Colt pointed out, we want to do this right so there are no problems later. So we've decided to get your original birth certificate, as well as your mom's first."

"I've got my birth certificate," Taylor said proudly. "I needed it when we enrolled me in school because I was from Ontario. I'll get it." He started to get up off his chair, but Sarah caught his arm and pulled him back.

Grayson saw the agony in her face. He reached out to cover her hand. "Doesn't he know?" he asked softly

Tears streamed down her cheeks. "We've never really talked about that. He was too young to understand."

Taylor looked scared and angry. "What don't I know? What are you talking about? What have you done now, mom?"

Grayson looked at him sternly. "Don't you talk to her that way."

"Why is she crying?" Taylor's anger was giving way to fear and his eyes filled with tears.

"Taylor...you were so young when we left the resort and went back to Harahan's. There is a lot that you don't know. Ryan and Charlie—do you remember them?"

"Sort of. I liked them; the man and the lady. I didn't want to leave there."

"Do you remember me telling you that we had to and that things would be different this time?"

He shrugged. "Sort of."

"That was because Ryan and Charlie gave us new names. They gave us new birth certificates and Social Insurance Cards with our new names on them. Then we could travel and do things as Sarah and Taylor Brite and your dad wouldn't be looking for us. He'd be looking for people with our old names."

"So we are still us. What is the problem?"

Grayson put his hand over the boys. "You see Taylor.

Everybody here knows you as Taylor Brite and your mom as Sarah Brite, and we would love you if you were called Billy Boop and your mom could be Bonnie Boop. Your mom and I could get married using her present name, but legally the government wouldn't know that Grayson McNaughton had married Sarah Brite because they don't know her by that name. They have her registered in their official books under her old name. When I adopt you and make you my son legally, the same thing would happen. We don't want to make any mistakes because this is going to be forever. Colt has suggested that we find a lawyer and get everything done properly. But that is going to take time; maybe a few months, maybe longer."

"So you're not getting married now, and you can't adopt me?" Taylor got up and ran to his bedroom.

Sarah looked at Grayson, her misery plain on her face.

"Honey, it'll be alright."

Taylor came stomping back into the kitchen. "Who am I, mom? Who are you?"

Sarah looked shocked; dumfounded. She knew the question was fair. *Who are we?*

Grayson took Taylor's hand and pulled him against his chest. "You are you, Taylor. You are Taylor Brite and your mom is Sarah Brite. I'll do everything I can to make sure that these are your names until you change them to my last name. But remember this, I love you no matter what your name is, and I love your mom too."

Taylor dissolved in a flood of tears and Grayson held him until he gave the last hiccup.

"Are you staying here with us or are you going back to the bunkhouse?"

Grayson looked directly into the boy's eyes. "I'm not going anywhere. This is where I belong from now on: here with you and your mom." He hugged him. "So get used to it Taylor Brite."

"If I'm not really Taylor Brite, why can't I just call myself Taylor McNaughton?"

Grayson looked at Sarah. His demeanor became thoughtful, and then suddenly, he stood up. "There is something that I need to do. Give me about fifteen minutes and I'll be back."

Sarah's heart was torn. *When I left home, I made such a mess of things.* She looked at Taylor, who was leaning against a chair, his face the picture of resentment and frustration.

"Mom, why do you have to screw up everything?"

She looked into his eyes and sighed. "I guess it seems that way to you. I'm sorry about a lot of things, but I've never been sorry that I have you." She reached out to him, but he drew back from her touch. Her eyes filled with tears. "I hate that your father turned out to be the man he did, Taylor."

"Taylor!" He spit out the words. "Is that just another lie that you've made up to hide from your past?"

Tears slipped down her cheeks. "Taylor was your second name and I've always called you Taylor, right from birth."

"What was my first name?"

"Does it matter? I insisted on keeping your name as Taylor, so there would be something solid and real in your life."

"Mom, there's nothing that feels solid and real in my life except for Grayson; he's solid and real to me."

The words were like a knife in her heart, but Sarah's hackles rose. "Listen to me young man. I've done the best I could under the circumstances. I'll admit, most of it has been difficult; you not having a real father, us picking up and moving every time I felt we were threatened, but I wasn't just afraid for me. My love for you drove me. If I ended up dead, what would have happened to you? If Duncan had gotten a hold of you, what would he have done? He threatened to make me watch you die before he got rid of me. You were too young to know all this, to understand what it was like."

"Mom is that real or is it just like everything else?"

Sarah stood up and stared at him, defeat in her face. "If you really think that about me, I guess there's nothing I can say to convince you. I'm sorry you think so badly of me, but I gave *you* life. I could have found a better father, but then I wouldn't have had *you*. If our life hadn't taken so many turns, we wouldn't have eventually ended up here, where you have Grayson who loves you and wants to be your father so much it kills him." Tears were streaming down her cheeks as she walked to the bedroom. "I'm sorry I'm such a worthless, terrible person, and such a horrible mother. But I have loved you more than myself." She walked into the bedroom.

Taylor stared at the door she'd slammed behind her. He was quivering with frustration, resentment, and fear. He didn't even know who he really was. He fisted the tears from his eyes and stormed into his room to lie on the bed. *Where is Grayson,* he wondered anxiously. Then he could hear Grayson's voice in his head, reminding him of how much his mom had done for him and warning him not to forget it.

He sat up on the edge of the mattress remembering the hurt on Sarah's face. *I hurt her feelings,* he thought. He rubbed his eyes pushing back the tears that threatened to come. *I hurt her really bad.* His chest squeezed as he thought of her lying in the corral; when he'd thought she might be dead. He sobbed and ran to her bedroom door, pushing in as he cried, "I'm sorry mom. I was mean to you." He threw himself over her as she lay on the bed and hugged her.

She winced, but no hug had ever felt better to her. "I love you mom," he sobbed. "I really do love you. I shouldn't have said those nasty things."

She held him close, running her hand over his head as it rested against her chest. "It's okay, hon. I'll always love you, no matter what. I'm sorry our life has been so confusing. It was simpler when you were young and you didn't question me, but you're growing up and you are a smart kid. You're bound to have questions. You have always been my Taylor and I have always been your mom. I haven't been called Sarah for very long, but I think of myself as Sarah now. I don't want to be anyone else."

They heard the porch door open. Taylor kissed her and then sat up, brushing away his tears. "Grayson is back. He'll be mad at me."

Grayson stepped through the door and looked at them. "I'll be mad at you for what, son?"

"Oh, we just...."

"I wasn't very nice to mom while you were gone."

Sarah took his hand and held it tight, shaking her head, ever protective.

"Why weren't you nice to your mom, Taylor?"

Taylor shrugged. "I wanted to be your son right away and I said she always screwed things up."

Grayson's eyes darkened and he scowled, but before he could reprimand Taylor, the boy said, "I realized I was wrong and I said I was really sorry. I know you'll be mad at me."

Grayson studied the boy. "I understand how hard this is for you, Taylor. It's frustrating for your mom and me too, but in the end, any good thing is worth doing right. And I'm not mad at you, just a little disappointed."

"What were you doing? You were gone a lot more than fifteen minutes."

"I was talking to Colt's lawyer. While we are straightening everything out, we are going to apply for a legal change of name, so the two of you will keep the names you are familiar with; Sarah and Taylor."

Sarah let out a ragged breath. "Is that possible, Grayson?"

"The lawyer says it is. The only hitch could be Taylor's dad—I assume his name was on the birth certificate?"

Sarah shook her head. "No, Taylor's father is registered as unknown. Duncan wouldn't let his name be recorded as the father until after the paternity test, and then it just never happened."

"Thank God that asshole did one thing right!" Grayson said, pumping his fist. He hugged Taylor. "I need to talk to your mom for a few minutes. I want you to go to your room and clean up. Put on your best shirt and pants,"

Sarah looked at him with confusion. "What's going on?"

Grayson's eyes sparkled. "My dear, we are having a wedding and adoption tonight."

Sarah stared at him open mouthed. "How?"

"I'm not leaving this apartment—I'm going to live here with my wife and my son from this day on. The only people who will know if we are legally married or not, or if the adoption papers for my son have been legally processed, are the adults who live here. I went over to ask Colt if he would perform a ceremony. Ollie and Ellie will be there too, and Frank is making up a certificate that will declare that Taylor is my son. You'd be amazed what that woman can produce. Later, when we get all the paperwork cleared away, we'll make everything legal. But until we can do that, we'll have a paper that says we are Mr. and Mrs. McNaughton and one that says Taylor is Taylor McNaughton. It's just a piece of paper, but our parents will expect it and so will the neighbors."

"Parents?" Sarah looked shocked.

Grayson grinned. "Colt says we can take a couple of weeks off before haying. We have a few people to visit."

"Not my parents," Sarah fumed.

"Come on Sarah. Put a smile on your face and get dressed in your Sunday best for a wedding. Pastor Thompson is going to do the honors at four-thirty this afternoon."

Sarah's heart ached as they walked to the main house; part of her resisted, feeling that once again she was perpetuating a lie in her life. The only honest thing about it was that the three of them loved each other and wanted to be together. She understood that this was the best they could do for a while... possibly months and no one wanted to wait that long. She couldn't help but smile as she thought about Grayson's ingenuity. *Pastor Thompson.* She chuckled.

Frank had a twinkle in her eye when she came out of the office with a folder in her hand. "So I hear we are going to have a wedding here this afternoon."

Sarah's face flushed, but she giggled when Grayson enfolded her hand in his and said, "You are right, ma'am. We don't want to wait another day." He smiled. "That's a pretty nice dress you've got on."

"This is a big celebration. It isn't every day that Pastor Thompson officiates at a wedding for two of our best friends." Frank smiled, and then reached out and tousled Taylor's hair. "I hear you are getting a real dad at the same time, young man."

Taylors thrust his chest out and grinned from ear to ear. "From now on I'm Taylor McNaughton and I'll have a real dad that loves me as much as I love him." He grabbed Grayson's free hand and pulled himself up against the man's body. "I am the luckiest kid in the world. I have a great mom and dad!"

Sarah's faced flushed. "Thank you, Taylor," she said softly. Grayson hugged them both, as his eyes met Colts when he came into the room. He noted that he'd put on a suit for the occasion.

Ollie and Ellie arrived within minutes. They were dressed in their finest and carried two cakes that were still warm, just out of the oven. They set them on the island and Colt motioned for everyone to follow him into the classroom.

Sarah's heart flooded with gratitude when she saw the room. On such short notice, the people who were their supportive friends and 'family,' had done everything they could to make the occasion seem as real as possible. They had set up the bower they'd used on the lawn two years ago for Christina and Tim Bates wedding. They had placed the lattice structure into two large plant boxes, and flowers spilled out on either side. Chairs were set up on each side of an aisle, and a few streamers and balloons added to the festivities.

Frank smiled as she handed Sarah a bouquet of beautiful silk roses. "Flowers for the bride," she said, as she brushed her lips against Sarah's cheek. "They go nice with your dress. I'm surprised you found something white to wear."

"Julie Harahan gave it to me when we lived with them. I've

hardly ever worn it: I think I've kept it all those years because it was from her."

"It looks great on you. I'm sure she'd be pleased to know that you are wearing it for this occasion."

Sarah nodded, and then looked at the flowers. "Wh...where did you get these?"

"I took them out of the vase in our bedroom. I just added some lace and bound them together. They're perfect."

Sarah hugged Frank. "Thank you. You're always there for me and you always tell it like it is—even if I don't particularly like it. You are the best friend a girl could have."

"Hey, what are friends for?" Frank turned to Taylor. "Come here young man, you are going to walk your mom down the aisle and give her hand to Grayson. You two will wait outside the door until the music starts playing. Then you will *slowly* escort your mom to the front."

She motioned to the twins. "Sam and Selena, you sit in a chair on each side of the aisle. Ellie and Ollie are going to be the witnesses and I'm the photographer."

Taylor stood as tall as he could, pushing out his chest, and sticking out his elbow for Sarah to slip her hand into. Ellie and Ollie positioned themselves on either side in front of the bower and Grayson waited in the middle. Colt stood nearby.

Frank started the music and Sarah and Taylor came through the door. Grayson felt a lump rise in his throat when his look met Sarah's. Her eyes were glistening with tears, but her smile was radiant. His glance slid to Taylor and the lump doubled in size. He found it hard to swallow.

When they reached the front, Colt motioned for them to stop. He looked into Taylor's face, his expression serious. "Who gives this woman's hand in marriage?"

Taylor's eyes got big and he swallowed hard. "I...I d..do," he stammered.

Colt smiled encouragingly. "Thank you, son. You can sit down beside Sam now." He took Sarah's hand and led her forward to stand by Grayson, who folded her hands in his and smiled as he looked into her soul.

Pastor Thompson did a fine job of guiding them through the ceremony that his wife had found on the internet. When it came time for them to exchange rings, he reached into his pocket and brought out two, handing one to Grayson and one to Sarah. Her heart thudded as she looked at the ring, recognizing it as one of the wedding rings they'd bought when Grayson had purchased her engagement ring.

She didn't hear what Colt said, but her eyes welled with tears, as Grayson slipped the band on her finger. Seconds later, after speaking the words Colt prompted her to, she trembled as she placed the ring she held, on Grayson's finger. Then Colt pronounced them husband and wife and told Grayson to kiss the bride.

Frank had made up a marriage certificate for them, which they both signed and it bore the signature of Pastor Thompson.

Then Colt called Taylor to the front. I have a certificate for you too. This declares to anyone who cares to check it out, that you are now Taylor McNaughton.

Taylor's eyes glowed, his face split with a grin. He turned to Grayson. "It's official! Now you are my dad,"

Sarah watched as the two most important men in her life hugged. *But it's still not true,* she thought.

Frank grabbed her by the arm and walked her quickly out of the classroom. She pulled Sarah into the spare room and shut the door. "I know what you're thinking and I want you stop right now."

Sarah's eyes brimmed with tears. "You can't know what I'm thinking."

"I do…you think this is another lie."

Sarah started to cry. "How can you know that?"

"Because, I know you, Sarah—but this is the best it can be for now. Everything will work out in the end. We had a ceremony to celebrate the love you, Grayson, and Taylor have for each other. That was *real.*" She chuckled. "And Pastor Thompson filled the job very well!"

Sarah sniffed and grinned. "He did, didn't he?"

"Grayson is head over heels in love with you, and he loves Grayson so much. He *wants* to be married to you now…not six months or a year from now when the paperwork is done. He was so excited when he came over to talk to Colt."

"But it's not real; it's like the rest of my life."

"Will you quit beating yourself over the head? This is *freaking real.* The piece of paper you signed today is as much a symbol of the commitment between you two, as it would be if you'd gone to a marriage commissioner, or said your vows in a grand cathedral.

Believe me, we witnessed that ceremony and we'll be here to kick your ass if you ever start to lose sight of that. Do you have any idea how many couples who are not 'churched' live together, wear a beautiful set of rings, and call themselves Mr. & Mrs?"

Sarah shook her head.

"Tons of them and most of them do not have the reasons you do for not making it legit."

"Grayson said we were going to see our parents. My parents would have a cow if they knew. It would be just one more nail in my coffin."

"Well, your parents don't need to know anything about this. As far as they are concerned you are Sarah McNaughton."

"But I'm not Sarah to them."

"Oh…," Frank hesitated. "Then make sure Grayson doesn't call you by name. Honey, sweetheart—whatever will do. It's not likely you'll be there very long anyway."

"I'll be lucky if dad lets me in the door."

"Well, you will have tried, and that's all you can do. Now let's go and join everyone. This is our celebration of your commitment to each other. The rest of this stuff will work out in its own time." She put her hands on Sarahs's shoulders and pushed her out into the hallway to join the others.

Grayson moved to her side, concern in his eyes. "Are you alright? No regrets or second thoughts?"

"Not about you and me and Taylor. It's more about my past, and the thought of seeing my parents; I have lots of regrets and fears."

He hugged her. It's too late for regrets and we've gone a long way towards pushing all the fears of the past into the background. Frank and Ellie have gone out of their way to make a wedding dinner for us, so let's just enjoy the moment and look forward to tonight." He winked as his eyes held hers.

She felt heat rush through her. She reached for his hand and squeezed it.

Frank and Ellie had prepared a feast at a moment's notice. The reception held true to any other wedding, including toasts to the bride and groom. There were congratulations to Grayson and Taylor. Frank recorded the event with pictures.

By nine o'clock the party dispersed and the family returned to the apartment. Taylor was giddy with excitement. He looked at Grayson, his eyes dancing. "So if you are going to live here with us all the time, you can't sleep on the couch forever. I guess you'll have to sleep with me."

His face was full of confidence. Grayson and Sarah's eyes met over his head. Sarah had the look of a deer caught in the headlights.

Grayson reached out and took Taylor's hand. "There's something we need to talk about, son. I know you'd like me to sleep with you, but…"

"Where are you going to sleep if you don't sleep with me? We don't have an extra room. You told me you weren't used to sleeping with anyone else, but I'm small. We'll make it work."

"Taylor, husbands and wives sleep together. Your mom and I are married now and we are going to sleep together."

Taylor's eyes grew big. "You can't sleep together. She's a girl and you're a boy. Sam and Selena have their own rooms," he declared forcefully. "Mom never sleeps with anyone; well except when she did with me when I was younger."

"Do you think Frank and Colt sleep together? And what about Ollie and Ellie?"

"But that's different."

"How is it different? Your mom and I love each other and people in love sleep together."

"But I love you and you love me too, so why won't you sleep with me?"

"You know Taylor, I will happily crawl into bed and cuddle you for a while, but once you are asleep, I will go to your mom's bed. That's where I belong."

Taylor grinned. "Okay…I just won't go to sleep. Then you'll have to stay with me."

Grayson looked at the young boy in front of him. He knew Taylor would do his best to stay awake, but he'd had an emotional, tiring day and he knew he'd be out like a light in half an hour. He looked across at Sarah and smiled. "You've got a deal, Taylor. I'll cuddle you until you go to sleep tonight. After that, I'll sleep with your mom."

Taylor made a face. "You just want to do all that kissy, mushy stuff with her. Yuck!"

Grayson grinned. "That's part of it. I like all that mushy stuff that we do. That's all part of what happens when a man and woman are in love."

Taylor turned away. "Gross. I'm glad you don't want to do that with me. I love you lots, but that would make me want to puke."

"You're safe, Taylor. I promise I won't get mushy with you. Now go get into your pajamas and I'll come in and snuggle against your back until you fall asleep."

"I'm going to stay awake all night," Taylor promised as he ran to his room.

Grayson pulled Sarah into his arms, shaking his head. "That son of ours; he's got some adjusting to do."

"It's not really his fault. He's never seen me in a relationship with anyone. He doesn't have a clue about how these things work."

Grayson chuckled. "Well, he really doesn't like the *mushy* stuff, but he'll adjust to it all. I'm sure he won't last more than half an hour, maybe an hour at the most and then he'll crash. Will you wait that long for me?"

Sarah smiled as she touched his face. "I'll stay awake all night waiting for you to come to my bed."

"I like that answer, Sarah McNaughton." He kissed her deeply and she wrapped her arms around his neck as he gathered her against him, pulling her buttocks against the hardness in his groin.

Taylor came bounding out of the bedroom in his pajamas, sliding to a stop as he looked at them in disgust. "Yech! Mom! That is so disgusting. Why are you guys always kissing and doing that stuff? Grayson is coming to bed with me tonight. Leave him alone."

"I'm coming with you now, but one thing has to happen first, Taylor. I expect you to apologize to your mom."

Taylor glared at the floor. "But you're sleeping with me tonight," he said stubbornly.

"I'm going to snuggle with you until you fall asleep tonight, but you were disrespectful to your mom, and I expect you to say you're sorry. In the first place, we were kissing each other and I kissed her first. Get used to it because there is nothing disgusting about it."

Taylor scuffed his toe against the floor. "Frank and Colt don't do that *all* the time and neither do Ollie and Ellie."

"Taylor, one day when you grow up and fall in love, you'll understand all this. Now apologize to your mom."

Taylor grimaced. "I apologize, mom," he said ungraciously. Then he turned to Grayson. "Are you coming now?"

Grayson nodded, winked at Sarah and followed their son to the bedroom.

Grayson spooned the child, smiling as he felt Taylor's youthful body snuggle against his chest. He realized that the boy had never known a father figure, never had a man to cuddle him when he was an infant.

Taylor struggled to stay awake, talking to Grayson about everything that came into his mind as he fought to keep his eyes open. Grayson answered him softly and suddenly, in mid-sentence Taylor nodded off. Grayson hugged him, love for the boy filling his heart. He looked at the clock on the wall and noted that it had taken forty-five minutes for him to give in. Grayson lay beside him until he was certain that he was out for the night, then slipped out of bed and went to join Sarah.

Sarah smiled at him and patted the seat on the couch beside her. "Tonight Taylor said you told him that you weren't used to sleeping with anyone else."

Grayson slid his arm around her and pulled her against him. "That happened the first night I stayed here. He really wanted me to sleep in his bed, but I didn't know where our relationship was headed—or if we'd even have one. I knew what I wanted and I knew how badly he wanted us to be a family, but I couldn't do that to him. I knew he'd connect with me even more if I cuddled him and slept with him. I knew in my heart it wasn't fair, so I told him I wasn't used to sleeping with anyone else and we all needed to get a good sleep."

Sarah kissed his hand as it folded around over her shoulder. "You are such a thoughtful man. No wonder I love you so much."

He leaned his head against hers, nudging hers slightly so his lips could touch her neck. He nibbled down to her collarbone and she squirmed. "Let's go to bed," she whispered.

CHAPTER SEVENTEEN

Three weeks later Sarah's ribs caused her very little pain and she was working at the ranch house again. She was folding towels when Frank came into the house and peeked into the laundry room. "You're not overdoing things are you Sarah?"

Sarah waved her hand at her. "Pfft—this is far better than sitting in the apartment going stir crazy while everyone else is doing something worthwhile. I can't sit around doing nothing. I start thinking too much."

"What are you thinking about?"

She shook her head. "Grayson is so hyped about taking this trip. He's got it all planned out—maps in a pile and phone numbers in his little book."

"I'm glad that he wants to take you to meet his family. He's hidden away, shutting them out, nursing his guilt for too long. I know he feels that he disgraced the family name, but it wasn't like he intended to hurt the guy. It was a tragic accident." She picked up a pile of facecloths, ready to take them into the bathroom. "I'm sure there isn't a mean bone in Grayson's body."

"I agree with you; he is one of the most sensitive, kindest men I know. I want to go meet his family and I want to see him reconnect with them. He wants to go to Toronto and meet Julie and Ryan. I'm excited about that."

Frank looked quizzical. "So what's bothering you? Everything sounds great."

"He insists that we are going to go see my parents. When I left, my dad told me never to come back. I can't imagine going there now."

Frank put down the facecloths and cupped her friend's shoulders with both hands, looking intently into her eyes. "Talk about hiding…you're as guilty as anyone. You shut that door as firmly as your dad did and braced your foot against it to make sure it never opened again. You are one stubborn woman, Sarah. Your son should meet your family. Your mom must miss you terribly. Fourteen years is a long time. I think I'd die if one of the twins just disappeared out of our life."

"You don't know my dad."

"People do change, you know." She smiled and hugged her. "You've got Grayson to back you up now and he'd never let your daddy run over you…or your son. He'd stand toe to toe and stare him down. He'd go to fisticuffs if he had to."

Sarah looked horrified. "No, he can't ever do that. He could end up in jail this time."

"He'd do it if he had to for you, Sarah. He sure didn't hesitate to take that cow on." She stepped back and sniffed the air. "Whatever you've got cooking, it smells yummy."

"There's Beef Stew Bourbonnais in the slow cooker, salad, and fresh biscuits."

Frank picked up the facecloths and walked to the door. "That sounds wonderful. The guys will be coming in shortly."

"I'll set the table." Sarah smiled. "It feels so good to be a part of everything again!"

***

Activity on the ranch had been busy. The crew had been fixing fences and checking pastures in preparation for moving the cattle out to the lease. For them, the day never really ended until they went to bed. After supper, they sat around the table and discussed what would happen the next day.

Colt nursed his coffee mug with both hands. "Okay guys, will we be ready for the cattle liners to come at the end of the week?"

Ollie and Grayson looked at each other and nodded. "We're

pretty much done checking fences," Ollie replied.

"Frank and I went out to work on the corrals at the lease today. We might need to spend another half a day. I started up the wind generator at the waterhole too. It went like clockwork. That is one of the best investments we've made."

Ollie chuckled. "It sure beats that temperamental old pump you had out there for years. When it worked, it was great, but you never could be sure when it would decide to quit."

"Ollie, you and Grayson can take the salt and mineral blocks out tomorrow. Check the oilers, too. Best to make sure everything is in place before he leaves."

Grayson smiled as he captured Sarah's hand in his. "You got it man. I am looking forward to taking a holiday with my family."

"You've earned it. In all the years you've been here, you've taken hardly any time off."

Grayson stood up and pulled Sarah against him. "I've never had a reason to, until now."

Colt grinned. "Okay, I'll make arrangements with the truckers and invite the rest of the family out for the weekend. They'll be expecting the call."

Grayson pulled Sarah close as he ran his fingers up and down her torso, and she blushed.

Colt shook his head. "McNaughton, take your wife home before you embarrass us old guys." Then he chuckled. "I guess you have an idea of what you are in for when they find out you two got yourselves hitched." Colt winked at them. "We'll leave Pastor Thompson out of the picture though; don't want to tarnish my image."

Grayson laughed as he turned Sarah to the door. "We're warned. Maybe we should leave on Friday morning. You guys can move the cattle without us."

"Not a chance man. We're counting on Sarah's help with the cooking, and that young son of yours has gotten pretty good in the saddle. He'll never forgive you if Sam and Selena get to move cattle with the grown-ups and he doesn't."

Frank chuckled. "Besides that, he's going to want everyone to know that he finally has the dad he's wanted for so long. He'll be bursting at the seams, wanting brag about it. Sarah will have to fight for a chance to show off her ring!"

Early Friday afternoon Tim and Christina Bates arrived at the ranch. They went directly to Ollie and Ellie's place, and everyone else made their way down there to say hello and see how much the twins had grown.

The small old house was bubbling with activity when Frank and Sarah arrived. There was no point in knocking because no one would have heard anyway. Frank opened the porch door and they stepped inside, slipping off their shoes.

"I smell coffee and fresh baked cookies," Frank said, as they walked into the kitchen.

Sarah took in the scene with a sense of wonder. Ollie was sitting at the table in his faded cotton shirt and denim overalls, cradling his grandson in his arms. They all knew how much he loved Ellie, and his deep affection for Sam and Selena and Patch and LeAnne was genuine, but this was different. *Shay is an extension of him, something he never dreamed he'd have until he discovered Tim was his son.* She swallowed hard as her eyes sought out Grayson's. His arm was curved around Taylor, who was never far from him. Grayson smiled, and as their eyes connected, the love she saw there stilled her heart.

Frank had swept Zaira out of Ellie's arms and was talking to her in soft, loving tones. The five month old's hands were reaching out, touching her face as she cooed and smiled in response. As Sarah drew closer and peeked over her shoulder, Frank lifted her head and their eyes met.

"Do you want to hold her?" Frank winked as she offered the precious bundle to her. "It's a good chance to get some practice," she teased quietly.

As the implication of Frank's words registered, confusion flooded through her. *Practice?* Her eyes shifted to her son, and she felt a thrust of guilt. *Practice?* Sarah hesitated, realizing that she'd never held a baby, other than Taylor. She shifted the child in her arms, feeling awkward. Zaira's happy face looked up at her, little bubbles blowing from her tiny pink lips and drooling out of the corner of her mouth, as she made happy baby sounds. Sarah's heart warmed as she looked into the face of innocence. Within moments, she slipped into another world, that of nurturing and maternal longing.

Her eyes met Grayson's and she read a subtle change in his look; not just love, but longing, and she knew where his thoughts had gone. *A baby for us? Grayson's own flesh and blood.* Her eyes shifted to Taylor. *Would his love for Taylor change? Would it be like it is for Ollie with Shay? Would a new baby be just slightly more special?*

Taylor's expression was confused; Sarah saw a hint of jealousy as he watched his mother hold the infant. As if he'd read his thoughts, Grayson pulled Taylor closer against his side, almost protectively. The child leaned into him, soaking up the assurance his touch gave him.

Grayson patted the empty chair next to him, motioning for her to come and sit by them.

Sarah's look held Taylors as she moved around the table and slid into the chair. She held Zaira so that he could look into her face.

Taylor's eyes skittered away. *Babies! What's so wonderful about them? They cry and puke all over your clothes and poop their diapers.* He fidgeted, not knowing what to do. *Why is mom looking so...so happy?* He looked down at Grayson, who was leaning in front of him, looking at the baby. He watched him slide his finger along its cheek and smile as it made unintelligible noises. *Grayson's doing the same thing. It's like that mushy stuff that mom and him do all the time. Yuck!*

Sarah nudged her son in the thigh with her elbow to get his attention. "Do you want to hold her?"

"No!" he gasped.

Grayson smiled. "She won't bite, you know."

Taylor wrinkled his nose disdainfully. "She doesn't have any teeth, she can't bite."

Sarah's eyes met Grayson's. "Do you want to hold her?"

He smiled and reached for the tiny bundle. "I'm not very good at this, but I'll give it a try."

Sarah shifted the baby into his arms, and he adjusted her position until he was more at ease. Sarah pulled Taylor onto her lap, noticing how tall he'd grown right before her eyes. She threaded her arms around his thin waist and rested her chin on his shoulder. She kissed his cheek, noting the resistance in his body. "You used to be tiny, just like that," she whispered in his ear. "I'll never forget how wonderful it felt to hold you, knowing that you were mine."

Taylor's body softened slightly and he turned to look into her eyes. "I couldn't have been that small."

"You were. When you were her age, you'd coo and smile just like she does. Your little fists would wave around, and you'd pull at my cheeks and my lips and my nose. You were the most wonderful thing that had ever happened in my life; you still are."

"What about Grayson?"

"Honey, in a different way, he is the most wonderful thing that has ever happened in my life."

He frowned. "How can both of us be the most wonderful thing that has ever happened in your life?"

Sarah's heartfelt gaze held her sons. *How can I make him understand?* she wondered.

"Mom?" he asked impatiently.

"Taylor, love is kind of like having rooms in your heart or sharing a house. When you came into my life, a room was added to my heart, one that was filled love, just especially for you. Your room and that love will always be special, just for you. When I fell in love with Grayson, a new room was added to my heart, and it is full of love just for him."

"He doesn't have a special room, he sleeps with you."

"Taylor, I'm talking about how much I love both of you. Those rooms in my heart are both very special."

Taylor shifted uneasily. "Are you going to get a baby? Is that why you two are gooing all over her?" He nodded toward Zaira.

"Would it bother you if we did?"

Taylor hesitated, and then nodded.

"I'm glad you told me the truth. Why would it bother you?"

He chewed his fingernail. "I wouldn't be special anymore."

"You'll always be special, Taylor. We love you as much as Colt and Frank love Sam and Selena. Do you think Tim and Christina love Shay more than Zaira or Zaira more than Shay? Absolutely not! Love just expands to include everyone in the rooms in your heart. Grayson loves you as much as he does me."

"He doesn't sleep with me."

Sarah chuckled. "That really bothers you, eh?"

"Sort of. Does he love you more than me?"

"Not more, just differently; men and women, mommies and daddies, usually sleep together. Children usually have their own beds."

Grayson looked up at their son. "Why don't you sit in Mom's chair and hold Zaira for a moment. You have to be a little more careful, but she's like a puppy or a kitten, Taylor. She's still pretty helpless, but full of trust and happiness."

Taylor looked into Grayson's smiling eyes, then into the baby's face. He heaved a big sigh. "Oh, all right."

Sarah slid him off her lap and stood up, then took the baby out of Grayson's arms and positioned her in Taylors. "You have to watch because she is pretty strong. She could wiggle and slide out of your arms."

He was stiff as he held her carefully and talked to her awkwardly, not knowing what to say or do. Zaira's eyes met his and she cooed and babbled at him. In spite of himself, Taylor found himself responding and he was delighted when Zaira favored him with a laugh. His eyes widened, and he grinned. "She likes me! She didn't laugh at anyone else," he exclaimed. Grayson winked at Sarah as they watched their son open another room in his heart. He reluctantly gave Zaira back to his mother.

Sarah took her back to Christina and then claimed Shay from Frank. Her heart filled with warmth as she looked into his little face. She walked around the table and nudged Taylor out of the chair he'd been sitting in. He stood up and leaned against Grayson, watching as she sat down. Miraculously the tension had left him and he was full of curiosity. He studied the baby. "They look different, don't they mom?"

"Well, they are two different people."

"But they're twins aren't they? I thought they'd be exactly the same. He's bigger than her." He leaned down and touched the baby's hair. "His hair is light brown."

"Just like Tim's is," Sarah said softly.

Taylor looked at Tim. "It *is* like Tim's, and hers is like Christina's." He touched his hair. "I guess mine is like yours."

Sarah smiled. "It is, but your father had dark hair too."

"Oh." Taylor ran his hand through his hair and Sarah could see the wheels turning in his mind.

"You are nothing like him in any other way, hon." *Poor Taylor. What a thought, after all the years of running and hiding from his father.* "Do you want to hold Shay for a moment?"

Taylor's eyes were eager, but he lifted his shoulder nonchalantly. "Yeah, I could hold him for a moment if he's too heavy for you."

Sarah laughed. "He's really heavy. He's almost breaking my arm."

She stood to let Taylor sit down, and then placed the infant on his lap, showing him how to support its body with his hands. He was more at ease this time, and once again, as if the child recognized another child, Shay grabbed at the colors on Taylors shirt and smiled. Taylor leaned in close and spoke softly, mimicking the baby. Shay laughed, and Taylor smiled with delight. He let go of his hand and in an instant the tiny hand flew up and grabbed Taylor's nose. Everyone laughed when Taylor let out a small cry before he grasped the baby's hand.

Grayson ruffled his hair. "Do you want to share him with me now?"

"Yeah Dad," Taylor responded, marking his claim. He let Sarah take the baby out of his arms and hand it to Grayson.

Across the table, Christina's eyes opened wide. "Sarah! What do I see on your hand?"

Sarah beamed as she held up her right hand, pretending to be confused.

"Get out of here," she said as she reached out to slap the hand away. "I mean on your other hand."

Taylor's face split in a happy grin. "Mom and Grayson got married. And he's my real dad now."

Sarah blushed as she held out her left hand. Christina let out a whoop, and then glared at Frank. "Tell me, how did you let this happen without the rest of us being here? I thought nobody got married without the 'family' being involved. You literally hijacked Tim and me."

Colt laughed. "As I recall, you didn't have broken ribs, or a man who was afraid you'd kick him out when you got better. Grayson made his move while he had a chance. He was afraid he'd get relegated to the bunkhouse again if he didn't."

Taylor screwed up his face. "Now they do all that kissin' and mushy stuff. After they got married, I told Grayson he could sleep with me because we didn't have another bed and I'm small so I wouldn't take much room, but he sleeps with mom."

"Taylor! That's enough," Sarah exclaimed, her face scarlet.

Tim and Colt roared with laughter. Tim finally sobered enough to speak. "Taylor, I think most husbands and wives sleep together."

"But do they do all that mushy stuff too?"

Sarah's protest was strangled, but Tim chuckled again. "I'm afraid so. That's why they like to sleep together."

"Yuck."

Christina grabbed Sarah's hand. "Pretty nice," she said as she examined her rings. "So when did this happen?"

"Six weeks ago."

"Wow. That was a big leap. He's been in love with you for months, but what changed your mind, girl?"

"I finally woke up and realized what a fool I'd been."

Christina's eyes narrowed. "You did this for the right reasons."

Sarah blushed. "Most definitely!"

Christina pulled Sarah across the table and whispered in her ear. "That's good, because I think I'd have to kill you if you put that poor guy through any more misery. I felt so sorry for him. He was like a whipped puppy."

Christina felt a flush of guilt rise up her neck. "He's safe now. Unless I kill him with love, I promise you don't have to worry about him."

Early that evening the Johnsons arrived in time for supper. Tim, Grayson, and Colt helped them bring in their luggage and the dog carrier containing Karma.

Half an hour later, Tim filled everyone's wine glass while the food was put on the table. Once they were all sitting, Colt stood up and whistled to get everyone's attention. "I want to propose a toast before we start to eat." He raised his glass to acknowledge the new couple. "Here's to Grayson and Sarah McNaughton. Congratulations."

Shauna Lee looked stunned. "W.. w..hat?"

"Grayson and Sarah had a quiet ceremony here at the house six weeks ago."

Shauna Lee wheeled on Frank with indignation. "How could you let that happen? We all should have been here to celebrate with them."

Colt laughed and looked at Grayson. "Speak up man."

Grayson's happiness was obvious as he took Sarah's hand. "I should plead the fifth, but the fact is, I've loved this woman for months. Earlier I was pretty sure we had it made. Then everything fell apart, so this time when she gave me the slightest encouragement, I wasn't giving her a chance to change her mind." He leaned over and kissed her blushing cheek. "I admit, I took advantage of the situation, but I decided I wasn't going back to the bunkhouse. I bought her a ring and we *both* agreed to get married immediately. I wasn't leaving any room for another mishap, so it happened as quickly as possible."

He reached out and ruffled Taylor's hair affectionately. "And while we were at it, we made sure Taylor knew he really was my son; so guys meet Taylor McNaughton." He chuckled as he reached over and hugged Taylor, who was beaming. "Much too Taylor's disappointment, I'm not sharing his bed, but we are all one happy family."

The next morning Colt, Frank, Grayson, Tim Brad and Ollie gathered at the corral seven-thirty. Colt looked at his crew and grinned ruefully. "Ready guys?" he asked. "You know the program as well as I do by now. We'll separate the calves out of the first pen and put them into that one." He pointed toward an empty pen."

Ollie grinned. "I'll man the gate. You guys have longer and younger legs to chase those little buggers around."

Tim gave him a friendly punch on the shoulder. "You just don't want to run them through the shit and get splattered from one end to the other, Dad."

Ollie's chest expanded with pride. *Dad.* It still had a wonderful ring to him.

"You're dead-on son, and I've damn well earned the right to swing the gate, instead of plowing through the mud, trying to separate those little rascals from their mothers."

Colt grinned as he watched the newly united father and son affectionately.

Brad pulled his gloves on and turned toward the pen. Frank had already stepped up on the planks and swung up over the top, waiting for the men to come. She dropped down into the mass of cows and calves and Brad followed. Together they moved slowly, working as many calves to the side of the corral as possible without creating a surge of excitement among them.

"Get ready to work the gate Ollie," Brad called. "We've got half a dozen heading your way along the fence."

"I'm on it," Ollie yelled, as he hurried to the gate and unlatched it. He stepped into the pen so he could open it just wide enough to allow the calves through.

The first group moved through the gate easily and Tim moved them down the alleyway into the empty pen, where they stood desolate, separated from the familiarity of the herd, and calling for their mothers.

Panic accelerated in the bigger pen. Suddenly the bellow of

concerned cows searching for their calves filled the air and the animals started to mill around. Colt pushed a cow out of his way and waded in to help Frank and Brad. Gradually the number of calves dwindled as they successfully separated them from the herd, forming a human barrier to guide them along the corral fence and out the gate.

The last few calves were harder to separate. Patience wore thinner and profanity filled the air. Then a determined calf bolted, blindly charging into Frank and knocking her to the ground.

"Damnit," Colt yelled. He ran to her side. "Are you okay?"

She held out her hand. "Help me up, so I don't have to shove my hands into this muddy crap. I'm okay. My coat and jeans will be another matter." She stood up and Colt swiped at the back of her coat and jeans with his gloves. She looked over her shoulder. "Shit," she groaned.

Brad grinned sympathetically. "Yeah, it literally is, but it could have been worse. If you hadn't put your hair up, it could have been covered too."

Colt looked at Sam, Selena and Taylor, who were standing with the toes of their boots hooked on the second plank, leaning over the top one and watching eagerly, anxious to get into the fray. "Look you guys, get down from there. You saw what just happened. You can't come in here. You'll just get in the way and you could get trampled."

"But you said we could help this year," Sam protested.

"I said you could go riding with us when we move the cattle out of the corrals at the lease and onto the range, and you will, but right now I want you down off that fence. Go practice roping or something. Just don't get in the way here." When the trio hesitated, he glared at them. "Get moving…NOW," he roared. Colt seldom raised his voice at the children. Wide-eyed, they scrambled off the fence and headed to the barnyard.

Minutes later the last calf was pushed out the gate. Colt walked up to Frank and hooked his arm around her shoulders. "Did you get hurt?"

"Not really. I lost my balance, so he really only brushed me and I fell." She looked at her clothes ruefully. "They're washable, and so am I. It's too bad there wasn't an easier way of doing this. Every year it's the same thing."

"Well, the calves have to be able to nurse overnight, so we can't separate them earlier. As it is, some of those old girls will be dripping milk by the time we unload them and the calves get mothered up."

"I know." Frank conceded.

They walked to the loading chute where one of the two cattle vans, that had arrived twenty minutes earlier, had backed in.

"Are you guys ready to load?" the driver asked Colt. He nursed a cup of coffee in his clean hands and he smiled as he looked at their mud-splattered faces, dirty hands, and mud coated boots and jeans."

"Quit gloating, you dickhead. Your turn is coming."

The driver nodded. "Calves first?" he asked.

Colt nodded.

The driver threw out his coffee and walked to the cab of the truck. Within moments, a hydraulically activated ramp began to extend down from the top compartment toward the cattle chute. The driver jogged back and watched as it slid into place, making sure that it lined up properly. Then he returned to the cab and within seconds, they heard it lock into place.

When he returned, the driver had put on a pair of coveralls and gloves. "Okay guys, let's load them."

Ollie opened the gate and Colt and the rest of the crew herded the calves out into the alley, keeping the momentum until they were headed through the chute, up the ramp and into the truck. As the last calf charged into the van, they slammed the door behind them.

The driver nodded with satisfaction. "Smooth as clockwork guys. Now for the cows." He walked back to the truck, activated the hydraulic pump to retrieve the top ramp, and then eased out the shorter bottom one.

The crew drove the cows down the alley, through the chute and over the ramp into the belly of the big cattle van. The doors were shut and secured and the driver pulled away from the corral chute and turned it around to head up the driveway.

Colt swung up on the step by the driver's door and put his head into the window. "Do you want to stop for coffee at the house?"

The driver checked his watch. "I'd better hit the road. You still have to load the other truck. We're going to have to keep moving if we're going to finish up by tomorrow evening."

"Okay, Ollie will follow you and give you a hand unloading at the other end."

The crew went back to tackle the next pen of cows, sorting the calves and loading the second truck. When they were done, Colt lifted his battered cowboy hat and rubbed his shirt sleeve across his brow. "Well, that's done. We have a couple of hours before that first truck gets back. Let's go up to the house for coffee and a quick lunch and then we'll start sorting the next pen."

The second half of the day followed the same schedule as it had in the morning. In all, four truckloads were sent out to the corrals on the lease. By night, they were all exhausted and everyone headed to bed early. The next morning the procedure started all over again. By nightfall, the cattle vans headed down the road toward town and everyone else went for a shower and clean clothes. Afterward, they met at the ranch house for drinks and dinner.

When they sat down at the table, Colt looked across at Taylor. "Are you ready to ride with us tomorrow, Mr. McNaughton?"

Taylor's eyes brightened. "You mean we're *finally* going to get to do something?"

Colt met his look with amusement. "I promised you could ride with us, and we're going riding tomorrow.

"Okay." Taylor expelled his breath in a huff of frustration. "Yeah, I'm ready to go riding with you guys."

Colt loaded the horses in the big horse trailer, and the whole crew, including the twins, as well as Taylor and Shauna Lee, drove to the lease. When they got there, they saddled the horses and the cattle were pushed out of the pens in the corral. Then, everyone rode to move them, spreading them out into different areas of the lease. Sarah, Christina, and Ellie stayed home to watch the babies and cook supper for the tired crew that would return that evening.

The afternoon, when Patch and LeAnne were napping, Sarah picked up Zaira and cradled the baby in the crook of her arm as she sat down in the big rocking chair. Her eyes searched the baby's little face; her fingers explored the feel of her tiny finger and hands. She looked at Christina. "It's hard to remember that Taylor was so small." She smiled as she tickled the baby's chin, and it smiled up at her. "Is it hard…having twins, I mean?"

"I'm not going to lie; there are days when it's really tough. But I'm lucky to have so much support. Shauna Lee rescues me quite often, and Tim is great. We've talked about hiring a nanny. I think that will even things out and help a lot. It's not like you can put one of them on a shelf and ignore their needs when you are having a crappy day. And if you could how would you choose which one?

They are both precious and individual. They are so helpless and totally dependent on you." She smiled softly. "I wouldn't trade them for anything. I'll be forever grateful to Shauna Lee for making it possible for us to have them."

Sarah ran her hand over the baby's soft hair. "She is such a sweetie," she said softly.

"Do you and Grayson plan to have children?"

Sarah looked startled. "We haven't discussed it. I...when Taylor was little, things were...bad. His dad started abusing me. When I finally left, I was literally running scared...hiding. We had no money. It was awful. I feel like I've given Taylor's such terrible start in life in so many ways...I've never considered having another child..."

"But it would be different now."

Sarah frowned. "I don't know how Taylor would react to a new baby in the family. He's just gotten a dad; I wouldn't want him to feel pushed aside."

Christina smiled with understanding. "I think every kid feels pushed aside when a new baby comes into the house, but they adjust. It happens every day you know."

Sarah moved the baby into a sitting position on her knees, supporting it with her hands. Zaira's eyes sparkled. Her tiny mouth, a perfect cupid bow, turned up at the corners as she reached out to grab Sarah's hair. *She's so strong,* she marveled as she felt the muscles in the baby's body move. *And yet so helpless.* As she watched, a tiny flame stirred within, spreading warmth and a shaft of longing into her heart. She couldn't form the desire into thought, but the embers had been stirred.

Christina smiled as she watched. *There will be a baby or two,* she thought.

Suddenly Sarah looked at her. "Do you think Grayson would be able to love Taylor as much as he would his own child?" She hesitated. "I mean, if we had a baby?"

"Relax Sarah. He loves that kid. That isn't going to change." Christina sighed. Then her face brightened. "You should talk to Tim. When Mattie and Harry married, they adopted him. They had children, but he and his parents never lost that bond. Grayson and Taylor would be the same."

Zaira began to fuss and Sarah slipped the pacifier attached to the infant's shirt into its mouth, then lifted the child up to rest against her shoulder. She cuddled the tiny head into her neck and felt the baby relax. In moments, the sucking sounds became intermittent and the baby's weight settled against her like melting chocolate. Sarah closed her eyes and rocked slowly as she lost herself in the feeling.

That evening the whole crew was tired after spending a hard day in the saddle. Supper was ready and Sarah was holding Shay when Taylor came to stand by her chair. She smiled at him as he leaned his head against her shoulder. "Did you have fun?" she asked softly.

He nodded. She leaned her cheek into his. "Are you tired?"

He nodded again. "It was a blast though." He reached down and took the baby's hand. "He's kind of cute isn't he?"

Sarah smiled. "He is."

Grayson sauntered over and leaned down to drop a kiss on Sarah's cheek. Then he sat on a chair next to her and pulled Taylor against him. "You'd have been proud of our son today, mom."

Her heart filled with love. *Our son; it comes out so naturally,*

"He's turned into a good rider and he uses that noggin of his when we're moving cattle. He doesn't ride off helter-skelter in every direction; he watches what's happening and anticipates what the cattle will do."

He reached up and rubbed the boy's head. "I was darn proud of you today."

Sarah watched Taylor fill with pride at the praise, and her heart filled with love for Grayson. He leaned over and spoke to Shay. The baby responded to his gentle, deep voice immediately, its eyes sparkling and hands flailing with excitement as he smiled broadly at the man.

Grayson's eyes met Sarah's and a flare leaped between them. The look lingered. Then Grayson broke it and smiled at the baby. He pulled Taylor over onto his knee. "What do you think of the babies, son?"

Taylor shrugged. "They're pretty cute, but they still poop their diapers and puke all over. And they cry lots."

Grayson chuckled and squeezed him gently. "So did you when you were that age, but look at you now."

CHAPTER EIGHTEEN

Two weeks later, Grayson, Sarah, and Taylor hit the road in Grayson's extended cab F350 Ford at six o'clock in the morning. Country music played on the radio as the kilometers rolled by, and Grayson's heart was lighter than it had ever been, when he'd made this same journey. A few months ago, he'd gone home to lick his wounds after telling Sarah about his past. His parents had been supportive in their own way, but they too, were still dealing with the past that couldn't be erased, and he'd discovered that nothing about being in Eliott Lake had changed for him. His guilt and lack of self-worth had still overwhelmed him. *This time is different,* he thought smiling as he hummed along with the music. *This time I've moved on. Thanks to Sarah and Taylor, I can see a future.*

He looked across at Sarah, who was sitting with her hands folded in her lap. She was staring out the window, watching the gently undulating fields fly by as they traveled along the seemingly never-ending, ribbon of the Trans-Canada highway. Her look was brooding. *She's anxious about this trip. Mom and dad will love her. They'll love Taylor too.*

He reached across the console that was between them and touched her arm. "Earth to Sarah," he said softly.

She turned her head and looked into his eyes. "I'm here...just thinking."

He opened his hand for her to put hers into it. She smiled and complied. "Maybe you are over thinking all of this. My parents will love both of you. Julie and Ryan are excited to see you. I'm sure your mom and your brothers and sisters will be excited to see you." He squeezed her hand. "And your dad will be whoever he is now. Fourteen years have passed; maybe he's changed."

"You don't know my dad."

"Well, I know this; I won't let him put down my wife, so if he goes there, I'll meet him toe to toe."

Sarah sighed. "I know you'll stand up for me, but that's not what I really need."

"What do you need, hon?"

"I need him to accept me as I am."

Grayson sighed. "I understand that, but I'm sorry to say, that as much as I love you, I can't guarantee that. All I can guarantee is that you will never stand in front of him alone."

She lifted his hand and kissed it.

He glanced at the clock on the dash. "I didn't realize how long we'd been on the road. Whenever I've made this trip, I've just grabbed whatever I could eat when I fueled up and driven until I couldn't stay awake anymore. Then I'd pull over at a rest stop and snooze for a few hours, and hit the road again. But I'm hungry now. You must be hungry too."

Sarah nodded. "I hadn't really thought about it, but now that you mention it, I am too. I'm surprised Taylor isn't complaining."

"We'll stop at Indian Head for an early lunch."

"Indian Head?"

"It's just ahead. It has a lot of history that fascinates me."

Taylor was in the extended cab. Hypnotized by the constant movement and the unexciting scenery he had fallen asleep. As they approached the town, Sarah called him. "Taylor, wake up."

He sat up, rubbing his eyes. "Are we there yet?"

Grayson chuckled. "Not even close, son. We're going to stop for lunch at a little town just ahead."

"Where are we?"

"Indian Head. Hey, look!" Sarah pointed ahead. "See that big Indian Head up there?

Taylor's eyes widened. "Wow. Look at that." He was deep in

thought as Grayson turned left onto Highway 56, and drove across the railroad track, then turned onto the service road into town. "We'll look for a restaurant and eat. Then I'll go to a service station and fill up with diesel."

"Dad…Grayson, why did they call the town "Indian Head"?

"This small town has a lot of history, Taylor. In the early years, before the immigrants came to settle here, the fur traders came through. They brought diseases, like smallpox, to the First Nations people and a lot of them died." He pointed to the hills to the south. "The local Indians used those hills as a burial ground. It is said that they didn't even bury a lot of the bodies because they were so afraid of catching the sickness."

"You mean they just threw them out there?" Sarah asked.

"I can't say for sure, but I've heard that they did: and let's face it, if you were scared to death that you were going to get a horrible disease like small pox, you probably wouldn't want to handle the body any more than you had too. They didn't have an understanding of the disease like we have now. They must have been overwhelmed, watching their people die, with no way to fight it."

"Quite honestly, an outbreak of smallpox would be scary now. It's a horrible disease."

"Stories tell that they began to call the hills the Many Skull Hills. Apparently, when the new settlers came, they called them the Indian Head Hills. When the Canadian Pacific Railway came through the area, they needed a name for the railway station. Homesteaders had come into the area a few months before the railroad came through, so there was a settlement already." Grayson pulled to a stop in front of a restaurant that looked fairly new. As he turned the key, he looked back at Taylor. "The settlers wanted to call it Indian Head Hills. I've heard that they offered the First Nations people a camping ground near the town in exchange for the right to use the name." He grinned. "It probably became known as 'Indian Head' without the 'Hills' because there are no hills right here, just flat plains."

They got out of the truck and went into the restaurant. Lunch hour was over and the establishment was empty. It was clean, bright, and cheery. The three of them went to the bathroom first. When Sarah came out, Grayson and Taylor were looking at historic pictures on the wall.

"Look at this," Dad. "It's a round barn. Have you ever seen

anything like that?" Taylor asked.

Grayson shook his head. "No, I haven't." He reached out a hand to Sarah and drew her close. He read the information below the picture. "That wooden part on top is an eight-sided cupola that was the upper extension of the silo. It was used as a lookout." He rubbed his chin as he read. "It says the silo could hold four thousand bushels of oats and a hundred tons of hay, and the area around it could house thirty-six horses and an office."

Sarah moved on and looked at another picture. "This is interesting. This is a map of the town. The streets in Indian Head run at an angle, instead of on a grid, with streets running parallel to, and perpendicular to the railway line, the way most towns were built. Apparently, they did this to make it a shorter trip to the Bell Farm headquarters. And look at this; the streets are named after the first investors in the farm."

Taylor lost interest in the pictures. He patted his belly. "I'm hungry. Can we eat now?"

Grayson tousled his hair. "Grab a chair at one of the tables." He looked at his watch. "I'd like to make it to Kenora tonight. That'll put us at my folks place tomorrow afternoon. Are you guys good for the miles?"

Sarah nodded, and Taylor grinned. "I'll just go to sleep. I like traveling in your truck. There's lots of room in the back seat for me."

They placed their food order and chatted as they waited for it to arrive.

"It's funny there are no signs about the Bell Farm," Sarah said thoughtfully. "You'd think it would be a big tourist draw." When the waitress brought their food, she asked her about it.

The waitress, whose nametag identified her as 'Madry,' rested her hip against the next table. "Sadly but inevitably, life moves on and new priorities take over. The young guys are totally involved in the world they live in; everything is high tech and so fast moving, I'm sure they don't even see the parallels with the past." Her look was thoughtful. "People don't like it when big corporations suck up the old established farms, but all those years ago, when Major Bell came from Ontario to be the general manager of the Qu'Appelle Valley Farming Company, which later became known as the Bell Farm, they were way ahead of the times. It was really the first corporate farm in Western Canada."

Sarah smiled. "Ironic isn't it, how history cycles itself?"

Madry looked at Grayson and Taylor, who were both wolfing down their hamburgers. She stood up and nodded at them. "You'd better eat, or they'll be waiting for you."

When they left town, Grayson stopped at a service station and filled the truck with diesel. As they drove further east, the landscape changed. Taylor lay down in the extended cab and read the booklet that they'd picked up at the restaurant, and then fell asleep.

Grayson looked back over his shoulder. "He's slept half the trip."

"Travelling gets pretty boring for a ten-year-old. All they see is fields and more fields, then trees and more trees. He has no anxiety about tomorrow, only anticipation."

Grayson flipped up the console between them and patted the seat next to him. "Come and sit by me. I'll help you get over your anxiety."

Sarah hesitated, and then smiled as she unhooked her seat belt and slid across the space between them. He slowed down while she clasped the center seat belt. Then he rested his hand on the inside of her thigh, urging her closer against him.

"That's better," he said softly. "I like to feel you."

"I love it when you feel me too, but you have to keep your mind on the road."

His thumb caressed the fabric of her jeans. He grinned, knowing that desire flooded through her, as it did him. Traffic was light, but he kept his eyes on the road ahead. "So, why are you still anxious about meeting my parents?"

She thought for a few seconds before she answered. "It's probably habit. All my doubts and fears from the past. Why would they accept me?"

"Because I love you, that's reason enough, I'd say."

She squeezed his arm. "I'll try to remember that."

It was ten-thirty when Grayson stopped at a motel on the outskirts of Kenora, Ontario, that evening.

The next morning they were up by six o'clock, ready to hit the road again. Excitement thrummed through Grayson with the anticipation of introducing his new family to his mom and dad. Suddenly he could see beyond his terrible past. He wanted to show Sarah and Taylor around the town where he'd grown up.

Taylor was tired and grumpy, but he cheered up when they went to a nearby restaurant and had breakfast. Grayson was chuckling, when they got back into the truck. "Taylor, you slept so much yesterday, I can't believe you could pack away that big stack of pancakes this morning," he teased.

"They sure were good," the boy replied with a grin.

After they were on the road, Taylor asked, "So, are your mom and dad my grandpa and grandma now?"

Grayson's look met his in the rear-view mirror, as he nodded. "You're the only grandchild they have. I know they are going to be really proud of you, just like I am."

Sarah felt her stomach clench. *What if they didn't accept Taylor because he was another man's son?* She couldn't bear for him to be hurt.

Grayson reached out and touched her arm. "Stop that," he said softly. "They will love him because I do."

She snuck a look at him. "How did you know?"

"I sense everything about you."

Taylor was looking around with interest. "Will we be there pretty soon?"

"We've got a good ten-hour drive ahead of us. We should get there around four-thirty this afternoon."

"Oh...that long?" His disappointment was palatable.

Grayson and Sarah sipped their coffee as the miles slipped away; each lost in their own thoughts. Finally, Grayson reached out and touched her arm, smiling as he motioned for her to move next to him. She put her coffee in the cup holder, unclasped her seat belt and slid against him. She fastened the seat belt in the middle around her, after she got settled.

"That feels better," he said softly.

She smiled as she rested her head briefly against his shoulder. They drove in companionable silence, with the music from the radio flowing over them.

Taylor broke the silence. "Grayson, this is a pretty nice truck. What year is it?"

Grayson's eyes met the boy's in the rear view mirror. "It was new when I bought it in 2004."

"2004—it's as old as I am."

"I guess it is. I bought it before I finished vet school, because I was planning to work at the clinic with my dad. I knew I would need it to go out to farms."

"It's nice. I like the color. It's like a shiny cherry." He grinned.

"I love cherries." Taylor ran his hand along the dark gray leather seats. "I like these seats too. It looks brand new."

"It practically is. I didn't use it very much after I graduated. It sat at my mom and dad's place while I was…" Grayson swallowed hard. "While I was waiting for the trial to be over: then I'd know if I was going to jail or not."

Sarah squeezed his thigh sympathetically and he dropped his hand from the steering wheel to cover hers.

"Ohhh…" Taylor looked uncomfortable. "I didn't think about that." He was silent for a moment. "What was it like…I mean knowing you might go to jail?"

Sarah smothered a gasp. "Taylor!"

Taylor looked uncertain. "I…I just wondered."

Grayson's gaze met his in the rear-view mirror again. "It's alright for you to ask, son." He hesitated, and then continued. "I don't think anyone is prepared for what being in prison would be like. Aside from the fact that prisons can be really scary and dangerous places, you cannot imagine what it's like to have every little thing you do controlled by someone else.

"You are isolated from your family and friends and everything else you take for granted. I spent a few days in the local jail until the legal stuff was settled. It was a real eye opener for me. I realized that, if I was sent to prison, the little things I took for granted would be taken away. I wouldn't be able to get in my truck and run down to the grocery store. I wouldn't be able to go for a walk along the Wildlife Sanctuary trails and that was something I'd always done, even at your age. I knew I would miss the wildlife. I wouldn't be able to hear the birds in spring, the honk of a goose, the cry of a loon, or see a beaver or a deer or a moose in the wild. It hurt to imagine how much I would miss it all."

"Geeze," Taylor said softly. "That would really suck."

"You're right, son. I wouldn't have been able to go out on a date, take in a movie or go for a hamburger. I wouldn't have been able to go skiing at Mount Dufour or snowmobiling on the trails out of town. I wouldn't have been able to go fishing with dad or swimming in the lake.

"I worked with Dad, and I was still living at home. Those few days when I was locked up, I realized how much I would miss seeing mom and dad every day, hearing their voices, watching hockey with dad, listening to the news and hearing him rant about something that pissed him off. It had bugged me before, but when I was in jail, I would have given anything to hear him doing that and listen to mom trying to reason with him and make him see things from another point of view."

He sighed. "But, on the other hand, I felt I deserved that punishment. I'd ruined another man's life, destroyed another familie's dreams. Guilt is a very heavy burden, and I've had plenty of that. I'll always know what I did; I can't change that."

He looked away. "Working at the ranch has helped me get a different perspective. I've come to realize that I can move on and make something positive out of my life. You and your mom have helped me see that."

Sarah caressed his hand, knowing how hard it was for him to talk about that part of his past. Silence filled the truck cab.

Then Grayson spoke again. "Taylor, if there's anything I want you to learn from me, other than how much I love you, it's that there are consequences for your actions. I've learned that the hard way. A moment of anger and misplaced chivalry changed my life and that of another person.

"In my mind I was defending my girlfriend from his ignorant insults. I should have walked away and taken her with me, but instead I hit him. Now, he's in a wheelchair forever, his family are dealing with his brain damage and that result is like a..." He searched for words to explain how he felt. "It's like a minefield in my life." His look met Taylor's again. "And as soon the shit hit the fan, the girl that I was defending didn't want anything to do with me anymore."

Taylor looked away, uncertain how to respond.

Grayson let out a deep breath. "Sorry Taylor, maybe I unloaded too much on you. I just don't want you to make the same mistake I did." He shifted in his seat uncomfortably, suddenly feeling uncertain about going back to his old home. Remembering so honestly had hurt. He lifted his hand from Sarah's comforting hold and brushed it through his hair. *Can I do this?*

Sarah's hand squeezed his thigh. She leaned her head against his shoulder. "You have to forgive yourself," she whispered. "No one else can do that."

Grayson drove, with both hands gripping the steering wheel.

Taylor was silent for several miles. The he reached up and touched Grayson's shoulder. "I love you, Dad," he said earnestly.

Grayson's eyes blurred with instant tears. He pulled over on the side of the road and stopped, then leaned back against the headrest and struggled to keep them in check. One, then two slipped down his cheek.

Taylor stood up and wrapped his arms around Grayson's neck from the backseat, pressing his cheek against the man's cheek. "I don't care what you did before. You are the best dad I could ever have and I love you. I'm so glad you and mom got married." He brushed away Grayson's tears. "Mom loves you too, don't you mom?"

Sarah brushed away her own tears. "Of course I do."

They all shared an awkward family hug, straining against the pull of their seat belts and the confinement of the seats themselves. A few minutes later Grayson put the truck in gear and pulled out onto the highway.

The rest of the trip was made in silence, until they reached the outskirts of Eliott Lake.

Taylor sat up and looked around with wonder. "We're here!" he exclaimed. "Where is your mom and dad's house?"

"We're going to stop at the clinic first. Mom works as dad's receptionist, so they'll both be there."

Grayson drove down the street, made a couple of turns and then pulled up in front of a simple building. A big sign in front read *McNaughton Animal Clinic*. "Here we are." His eyes were shining when he looked through the window. "Mom is at the desk. Dad will be in the back. Let's go in."

When they came through the door, Ingrid McNaughton looked up, and then let out a yell. "Lee! Come here. Grayson and his family are here."

Sarah loved her immediately. *Grayson and his family.* The words filled her heart with warmth.

Lee McNaughton's greeting was just as warm and welcoming. There were hugs all around, and tears misted Sarah's eyes, when he drew her son against him and said, "I'm so happy to finally have a grandson."

They spent three days in Eliott Lake. Grayson took them to all the tourist spots; the Fire Tower Lookout and Heritage Centre, Elliot Lake Nuclear and Mining Museum and the Canadian Mining Hall of Fame in the Lester B. Pearson Civic Centre. He took them on walks through the Sheriff Creek Wildlife Sanctuary and showed them the places he'd loved to spend time when he was growing up.

On Saturday, Jon McNaughton came home to join the family. He was friendly, but not in the warm way that his parents had been. More than once Sarah caught him eyeing her or looking at Taylor.

That afternoon, Lee, Jon, and Grayson went golfing at Stone Ridge. Ingrid, Sarah, and Taylor went to Westview Park and sat at the tables in the Trans Canada Trail Pavilion.

Sarah relaxed as she watched Taylor skipping rocks on the lake. It was a beautiful sunny day and she'd finally shed the tension she'd felt about coming there.

Ingrid touched her arm lightly. "I'm so glad Grayson met you. I've worried about him these past few years. What happened when he hit the Hixon boy that night and…and going through the trial…all the anguish and uncertainty… that's been hard for Lee and me, too, but Grayson was so burdened by his guilt, I wondered if he'd ever be able to move past it."

"It's still hard for him, but being at the ranch is good for him. He has a strong support system and he's starting to open up."

"He loves you so much, it's good to see. And I can see that you love him too."

Sarah smiled. "I do. God knows I fought it, but he wouldn't give up. He gave me room and he respected my wishes, but as soon as he felt he could, he just swept my off my feet."

"And he worships Taylor."

"And Taylor worships him. They loved each other before Grayson and I did."

"Lee is so excited about having a ten-year-old grandson. He's already making plans to go fishing with him and doing all those grandpa things."

"I can't tell you how much it means to have you accept him the way you do. It would have been hard for some people to accept another man's child."

Ingrid clasped her hand in hers. "That isn't even a consideration. How could we not love him? He's such a sweetheart, and Grayson loves him. Grayson didn't elaborate, but he did tell us that Taylor's birth father was a pretty nasty guy and that you had done everything you could to protect yourself and Taylor, while you raised him by yourself. I'm happy that my son gets to be his dad now. He'll show him what the love of a father should be and he'll share his values with him, too. Together, you will be great parents. You remind me of

Lee and me when we were young."

"Thank you, Ingrid."

"Please call me Mom. I've never had a daughter to call me mom."

Sarah's eyes misted, but she smiled. "Thank you, Mom."

Ingrid gave her a sideways glance. "Speaking of Moms, do you and Grayson have plans to give us more grandchildren?"

Sarah blushed scarlet.

"I apologize for not being more discreet, but I've dreamed of having three or four grandchildren. I love Taylor, but I'd really love to hold a newborn and buy little things for it." She looked Sarah in the eye. "I'd be happy with another boy, but I'd love to have a granddaughter."

"To be honest, we haven't really talked about babies yet. Friends of ours have five-month-old twins and we were both admiring them on the May long weekend." She looked across at her son. "I don't want to make Taylor feel pushed aside, when he's just gotten a dad."

"I see your point, but if you include him as soon as you know, he'll look forward to a new family member too."

"We asked him what he thought of the babies. He said they were cute, but they cried and puked all over and pooped their diapers."

Ingrid threw back her head and laughed heartily. "That sounds like a boy."

Later they joined the men at Putters, the restaurant at the golf course. After they had eaten supper, and they were sitting around the table, enjoying their final drink of coffee, Sarah noticed a woman striding toward them. She had an indignant look on her face.

Sarah nudged Grayson's knee and nodded her head in the woman's direction. She felt him tense and heard him inhale raggedly. Ingrid noticed the interplay between then and looked up when the woman stopped behind Jon, glaring across the table at Grayson.

Ingrid scrambled to push back her chair and get to her feet. "Hello Mildred," she said firmly. "I didn't realize that you were here." She walked to her side and firmly took her arm, trying to turn her aside in the hope of defusing the situation.

But the indignant woman refused to be dissuaded. Her face was full of hate as she glared at Grayson. "I'm surprised you'd dare to show your face in a place like this. How can you live with yourself?

My son is in a wheelchair, thanks to you."

Grayson met her glare. "I live with that every day Mrs. Hixon. You could never know how hard it is to carry the guilt of what happened. But I'm still alive, so I have to move on."

"What should you hope to move on to? What future would you dare expect to have? Who would have anything to do with you, if they knew the truth about you? You should have gone to jail for life."

Anger flooded through Sarah and she was on her feet in an instant, tipping her chair over as she interrupted the woman's venomous spiel. "Stop it. I know Grayson for the wonderful man he is and I am proud to be his wife. I know about everything that happened. He made sure I did, even though he was afraid that I would leave him."

Mildred Hixon snorted with derision.

Sarah glared at her. "In hindsight he knows that he should have taken his date and walked away from the disgusting, degrading things your son said about her. But he didn't. Instead, he defended her honor. He did it, in the same way many young men have done. It usually ends with a few bruises and maybe a black eye. He threw one punch." She held up her index finger to emphasize her words. "One bloody punch and, unfortunately, that action had unexpected consequences. What happened was an accident. If you are honest with yourself, you know that.

"I understand your anger, your need to blame someone. Your son is in a wheelchair. He'll never be able to pursue the dreams you had for him. I am truly sorry for you and your family. Believe me Grayson is too. *You* can lay the entire blame on my husband, but doing that won't change the role that your son played in that tragic incident. It's time for you to face the facts and accept that Grayson wasn't the only guilty party that night."

Everyone around the table stared at Sarah in stunned silence. Grayson felt her body tremble as she glared fiercely at the woman whose red face had gone white.

Mildred Hixon was equally stunned; no one had stood up to her before. When she'd unleashed her anger on the McNaughton's, everyone else had simply made excuses for her or bowed in guilt.

Sarah's anger turned to compassion when she saw her combatants face turn white, but she held the look until the woman turned around and left.

Taylor was scrambling to set her chair up behind her and Grayson grabbed her arm, holding her steady until she sat down. Their eyes met and she saw the emotion in his. He leaned in and kissed her on the lips.

Taylor threaded his arms around her neck. "I'm so proud of you, mom," he whispered.

Everyone else shifted uneasily in their chairs, avoiding each other's eyes. Finally, Lee cleared his throat. "Sarah, you just did what I should have done long ago. There *are* two sides to what happened that night, but none of us had the courage to face her and say so. We bowed to the outrage of other people, because of her position in the town, as well as her grief and anger." He wiped a tear from the corner of his eye. "It isn't easy to see her push Dillon around town in his wheelchair, knowing what happened. But in truth, Dillon was always a spoilt boy and the whole town knew he'd been a loud mouthed bully."

His eyes met Grayson's. "We stayed silent and we failed to support you like we should have." His eyes were sad. "I'm sorry about that son."

"I understand what happened and I don't blame you. That's why I left. I couldn't live with it all. But now I'm making a new life." He slid one arm around Sarah and reached back, to pull Taylor against him. "I've found love and as you can see, I have staunch support."

Jon left for Toronto early the next morning. When he was ready to leave, Grayson walked out to the car with him. "Thanks for coming, Jon. It meant a lot to me."

"Oh yeah, it's good to see you again too; you and your happy little family." There was bitterness in his voice.

Grayson stepped back with a puzzled look on his face. "What's going on here, Jon?"

"Nothing new; I've worked my ass off to get where I am, but it means nothing to mom and dad. You screwed up your life and humiliated our family in this town. When the trial was over you ran off to some place where people didn't know what you'd done and left mom and dad to face everything on their own. Then you marry some woman who thinks you're a golden boy. You take on her bastard kid, who doesn't have an ounce of McNaughton blood in him and mom and dad are over the moon about their new grandkid. Jon slammed the car door shut. "And you come up smelling like a rose again." His face was flushed with anger. "The whole thing makes me want to puke." He started his sports car and squealed the wheels on the pavement as he roared away

Grayson's face was pale when he turned toward the house.

Lee stood at the porch door. "What was that about?"

Grayson shook his head in disbelief. "Not much."

Lee walked to meet him. He placed his hand on his son's arm. "Let's go for a walk. No one else needs to hear what we have to say: it would just upset the girls."

When they were out of sight of the house, Lee turned to Grayson. "What happened between you and Jon?"

Grayson frowned. "I....Dad maybe we should just let this go."

"No son. I love your brother, and I've tried to get close to him, but we never really seem to connect. I know he's resented the bond you and I share. He could have worked with me, but animals weren't his thing. You were always bringing home a stray or something else that needed fixing and the two of us working together was just natural."

"But he's done well, dad. He's got a successful career and runs his own business. My life has been a shambles. Why does he resent me now?"

Lee shrugged. "When you went to trial, there were times I felt, that deep down, he hoped you'd go to jail and we'd disown you. He felt you'd disgraced us."

"He reminded me of that this morning."

"What else did he say?"

"Enough to make it clear, he resents Sarah and Taylor being in my life."

"I'm sorry about that. You know your mom and I are thrilled for you, and we are happy we finally have a daughter-in-law and a grandson."

"Dad, why hasn't Jon married by now? He mentioned Taylor. He said he doesn't have a drop of McNaughton blood in him and you're over the moon about your new grandkid."

Lee shook his head. "Your mom and I have wondered when, or if, he'll ever find a wife. He's never talked about a girlfriend through the years. He lives in a condo with another architect, and all they seem to do is work. They've gone to Mexico a couple of times, but..." Lee's voice trailed off. "It seems odd sometimes."

They walked in silence for a while, enjoying the sunshine. Grayson stopped and looked at his Dad. "Do you think...how do I say this...."

"Could Jon be gay? I've wondered about that. It might explain some things. He seldom comes home. We've been at the condo a few times. The guy he shares it with usually goes somewhere else when we're there. There are three bedrooms and of course we've never looked in the third one, because we've assumed it was Teds."

"How would you and mom feel about that, Dad?"

"I think I'd be relieved if he came out and told us that was the case. It would be better than the distance that's between us now. But I can't very well go up to him and ask him."

"Maybe you and mom could invite him, and that Ted guy, home for a weekend. It might open the door for them to come out, if they are a couple. He's probably scared shitless about how you'll respond to it. Toronto is pretty anonymous, but he might be concerned about how people in Eliott Lake would react."

They turned around and walked back toward the house. Finally, Lee spoke again. "How would you feel about it if he was gay?"

Grayson responded without having to think. "Dad, people in glass houses shouldn't throw stones. Who would I be to judge him? I wish he'd get it out there if it would make our family closer. It's his life to live, not mine. He's my brother. I'd like to be closer. I'd like Taylor to know him."

Later that morning, Grayson, Taylor and Sarah went to church with Lee and Ingrid. The rest of the day was spent relaxing and enjoying each other as a family. Lee and Taylor had their heads together, planning a fishing trip for the next summer. Ingrid and Sarah were sitting at the kitchen table. He couldn't hear the words, only the soft murmur of their voices.

Grayson leaned back in the chair and smiled happily. *This is my family. I'd almost forgotten how wonderful it felt to be together like this.* His heart filled with gratitude as he watched them. *It's too bad Jon isn't here.*

The next morning they left for Toronto to visit Julie and Ryan Harahan. Sarah was proud to introduce Grayson to the people who had befriended her and been instrumental in saving her life. They spent Tuesday with them, and then set out for The Pas, Manitoba, at first light on Wednesday.

Taylor complained about being turfed out of his bed so early. "I'm still tired," he complained.

"You can curl up in the back and sleep, buddy. We've got a long haul ahead of us."

Sarah slid over beside him and buckled up. "How far is it?"

"Ryan and I looked it up on the 'net. It's a good two-day drive, if we drive hard."

Sarah groaned. "Let's just go home and forget about going there."

He grinned at her. "Where is my fearless wife? You took on Mrs. Hixon for me, but you're trying to jam out on seeing you dad. I know you've been dreading this visit to your family, but I already told you, I'll handle him. If the visit is a standoff, we won't go back, but we're going to give it a try."

She sighed heavily. "It's such a long drive."

"When we get your birth certificate and everything else sorted out, you're going to get your driver's license. Then we can share the driving on trips like this."

Sarah frowned. "I've never given it a thought. I don't know if I could get my license and drive in traffic the way you do."

"Sarah, there's nothing you can't do. You just have to decide you want to."

It was nine in the evening when they reached Dryden, Manitoba. Grayson yawned as he looked at the motels along the highway. "I'm beat guys. I think it's time to call it a day."

Sarah looked at her watch. "Please do. It's more than time to stop. You've been driving for almost thirteen hours. You have to be exhausted."

"It'll be another long drive tomorrow. I think we should get a motel in The Pas and get a good rest." He brushed her cheek. "What do you think? We can sleep in the next day. Then we'll go to your mom and dad's place."

"I'm all for that. Just traveling these long hours is tiring. Facing my dad…well let's put it this way. I think we'll need to be rested up. At least I will."

That night when they were in bed, Grayson held Sarah in his arms. "I think you should phone home tomorrow morning and let them know that we're coming," he said softly.

Sarah wrinkled her nose in the darkness.

"Sweetheart, you're not a little girl anymore and your dad has no control over you now." He ran a hand over her hair. "You know, a lot of things have probably changed since you left. There's a good chance your brothers don't live at home anymore. They could be married already and have kids of their own."

She nuzzled her face against his chest. "I hadn't even thought about that." Suddenly she pushed away and propped herself up on her elbow, so she could look down at him in the dim light. "My god—I left the house fourteen years ago. Brian is forty-seven now and Al is forty-four. And the younger kids...." She shook her head in disbelief. "Cripes, they're all grown up. Nathan was almost fifteen when I moved out—he's got to be twenty-nine or something like that. Justin must be twenty-four, Mary would be twenty-two and Anne—she's twenty already."

"They wouldn't have known how to contact you, would they?"

"No. When dad told me not to bother coming back, I was so mad and so hurt, I just walked away and never looked back." Tears suddenly filled her eyes and spilled over. "I shut out my whole family, Grayson. Poor mom; I don't know what I'd ever do if Taylor just disappeared out of my life. And the rest of the kids must feel as if I didn't care about them at all. That isn't true, but until just now, they've just stayed little kids in my mind. I was so busy with the mess I've made of my own life; I guess I thought Mom would always look after them."

"That's why you have to phone in the morning."

"They...they may not want to see me anymore."

"Well, you may not get welcomed like the prodigal son and I don't know that you can expect the fatted calf, but at least they'll know you're alive and that you have a son and a husband. Your dad may have mellowed by now. I'd be surprised if you were the only one who stood up to him and with the whole family growing up, changes probably have been made. If any of them are married, you can expect that he doesn't rule everyone with an iron hand anymore."

"I feel so guilty now."

"No guilt, sweetheart. You did the best you knew how, with the circumstances you found yourself in. We all make our own share of mistakes. Your dad wasn't perfect either."

The next morning Grayson hugged Sarah and tilted her face up so he could look in her eyes. "Would you be more comfortable if Taylor and I went to the restaurant next door while you call home? Or do you want us to stay here with you?"

Sarah smiled wanly. "Have I told you how much I love you today? Thanks for understanding. Please take Taylor and go. I have no idea how this will turn out. I don't want him to see me fall apart if that is what happens."

After the door closed behind them, Sarah sat down on the bed and lifted the phone from the cradle. Before she could chicken out, she dialed the number she had not forgotten over the fourteen years she'd been gone.

"Wasserman Logging." The answer was crisp and professional.

Tears flooded Sarah's eyes. "Mom?"

She heard a sharp intake of breath. "Honey, is that you? Oh, my god...can it really be you?" Love and anguish filled her voice."

"It.. it's me, mom. I can't believe you remembered my voice."

She could hear the tears in her mother's voice. "Honey, how could you think I'd forget?" Sobs rode down the line connecting them. "You're my daughter. I've been worried sick about you all these years. Are you okay? Where are you?"

"I...we're on our way to see you."

"Are you still with that...that same man you went to Montreal with?"

"No, Mom. Dad was right about him; he was a bad guy."

"Did he hurt you? Where have you been?"

"I'm with a wonderful man now mom. His name is Grayson McNaughton, and I have a son, Taylor."

"Where do you live?"

"Near Maple Creek, Saskatchewan."

"Honey, why didn't you come back home when you left that biker guy?"

"Mom, Dad told me not to come back if I went away with him."

"Pffft. He was just being your dad. He didn't really mean it."

"Well, he convinced me. Maybe I'm too much like him, but I couldn't bear to go crawling back and have him lord it over me again."

"You were both strong minded and you always did butt heads, but he cared about you."

Sarah blinked away her tears. "How is everyone else? In my mind, they've stayed kids. Then, last night when Grayson and I were talking, I suddenly I realized that they're all grown up. Have Brian and Al gotten married?"

"Oh Yes. They both have children. And Nathan got married last year too."

"Oh...I've missed all those things."

"We didn't know how to get a hold of you, hon." Selma Wasserman sobbed. "For the first five years we waited, hoping you'd call or send us a note. Then...well fourteen years is a long, long, time. Gradually we began to wonder...we didn't know if you were even...alive." The words ended on a painful note.

"Oh, Mom," she sobbed, tears running freely down her face. "I'm so sorry, but all I could remember was dad telling me to never come back."

"I would never have let him turn you away."

"But Mom, Dad always ruled the whole family, including you. You didn't say anything when he yelled at me that night."

"I was so shocked to see you getting ready to ride away with that...that man. You were so defiant. I guess I hoped your dad's threat would make you stop and think. I hoped you'd choose your family over that stranger and come back. I waited for your call every day for months; I looked for a letter in the mail, your knock on the door."

Sarah's voice was ragged with grief and emotion. "I'm so sorry, mom. If Taylor walked out of my life like that, I think I'd die. So would Grayson."

"I began to realize that it was mostly about you and your dad. I was really mad at him for a while. He and I had some tough years over it. Brian could see your point of view, but Al sided with your Dad."

Sarah nodded. "He would have. Does he boss his wife and family around like Dad did?"

Selma chuckled. "No, MaryAnn wouldn't put up with it!"

"And what kind of a girl did Brian marry?"

"Vivian is a school teacher here in The Pas. She is very organized, but a good balance for Brian, because he's so laid back. He's a great dad. They have two kids."

"Do the boys still work with Dad?"

"Yes, but there have been changes. Even your dad has slowed down some. He's enjoying being grandpa and he does a lot with the kids."

Sarah shook her head. "That amazes me. He never had time to do anything with us kids. Everything was work, work, work."

"He has mellowed. He takes them fishing and boating. He even went cross country skiing with Nathan and Audrey last winter."

Sarah chuckled. "Can we be talking about the same man that

was my father?"

"We are. Now tell me, when will you get here?"

"Sometime tomorrow."

"I can hardly wait to see you. How old is your son?"

"He's ten—he'll be eleven this month."

"I'm so excited. I'll let everyone know you're coming and I'll cook a turkey for supper. Justin just got back from his second year in vet school, so he'll be here too."

"Vet school? Really?"

"He's always loved to work with animals. He's got a few more years of schooling before he gets his degree, but then he wants to set up a vet clinic here in The Pas. He works in the bush with your dad and the boys, to make money to go back to school next term."

"Mom, Grayson is a vet, and so is the wife of the owner of the ranch where we both work."

"Justin will be thrilled to meet him."

"What about Mary and Anne? What are they doing?"

"Mary is a hairdresser. She loves that kind of stuff. She won't be able to come; she's working in Flin Flon. Anne's going to college here in The Pas. She's taking a secretarial/bookkeeping course. She just graduated from high school a year ago."

"All the kids have grown up. It's hard to imagine."

"Life carries on with or without us, hon."

Sarah wiped her eyes. "And I've missed all those years with you guys. I look forward to seeing you tomorrow."

"Drive carefully. We'll see you then."

Sarah could hear the happiness in her mother's voice. She placed the phone back in the cradle and stood up. As she reached for her jacket, she hesitated, then picked up the phone again and dialed.

"Wassermann Logging."

"Mom, it's me again. There's something I should tell you."

"What?"

"I've changed my name. I'm called Sarah now."

Shocked silence greeted her.

"Mom, are you there?"

"I'm here." She sighed heavily. "I'm... just trying to understand why you'd...."

Sarah interrupted her. "Mom, my life...Taylor and I have gone through some pretty scary and difficult times. Duncan Talbot...the guy I left with...is Taylors biological father. He didn't want a kid and he didn't want me after Taylor was born. He turned out to be a really bad guy. I learned he was a drug dealer and I heard him tell someone that he wanted to get rid of me. I took Taylor and ran.

"He didn't like that I'd gotten away and he threatened to kill us. He's tracked us down twice, but I've been fortunate to have people who helped me get away. I've lived in fear for the past nine and a half years; not just for myself and my son, but for the people who took us in."

She heard her mother's breath suck in. "Does your husband know all this?"

"Of course he does. At first, I refused to get involved with him, because I didn't want to put him or any of the people at the ranch at risk. I wanted to be able to pick up and run whenever I needed too. But Taylor's old enough that he didn't want to do that anymore. Grayson, and the rest of the people at the ranch convinced me that we're safer there with them, than being on the run."

Selma drew in a heavy breath. "So you want us to call you Sarah?"

"Mom, it's safer for everyone. Sarah McNaughton won't trigger any warning flags. Just tell everyone you have company from out of town and leave it at that. I don't want to risk anyone; not you and dad, not the boys and their families, or Mary and Anne. I know the rest will find it hard to understand, but who knows what feelers Duncan has out there."

"Alright, I'll figure it all out. See you tomorrow…Sarah."

"I love you, mom. Bye."

When she walked into the restaurant, Taylor had worked his way half through a big pile of pancakes and bacon and eggs. Grayson had finished his meal and was nursing a cup of coffee.

His face became concerned when he saw her tear reddened eyes. He reached out for her, indicating that she sit down in the chair beside him. "Is everything okay?" he asked softly.

"Yeah. As good as it can be. I have missed so much of my family's lives. The older boys are married and Justin is in vet school…"

"Vet school? That's interesting. Will he be there?"

"Yeah. He just came home. He'll spend the summer working in the bush to help pay for his tuition next year. Mary is a hairdresser and Anne is going to college. They've all grown up without me even knowing what happened."

"Was your mom happy to hear from you?"

"Yes. I told her we were married. That's another lie, but...."

"We are married in every way that matters. When we get all the paperwork straightened out, we'll quietly make it legal and no one will ever know the difference."

"I know. I just feel guilty, like I'm still living a lie."

He grabbed her hand and held it in his, offering her comfort.

"I told her I changed my name to Sarah and I wanted her to give the others the heads up."

"How did she react to that?"

"My poor mother, it was just one more shock. I told her about Duncan and explained that he'd tracked me down twice already and I didn't want to put any of them in danger."

"Does she still want us to come?"

She smiled at him. "She's not going to kill the fatted calf, but she's going to make a turkey dinner tomorrow night and she's asking everyone to come. That's everyone except Mary, because she works in Flin Flon."

He touched the tip of her nose as he smiled. "The prodigal wild chick returns."

"Yeah, the defiant, stubborn, wild chick who almost got her neck on the chopping block. Anyway, I'm glad mom and I got to talk. It sounds like dad has softened some, but I wonder if that will extend to me."

"First of all, don't go gunning for trouble. Second, let me handle your dad."

"You don't know what he can be like."

"I've dealt with some tough guys. Man to man, I'm confident I can talk to your dad and your brothers too, if need be."

She laid her head on his shoulder. "From your lips to God's ear, I hope."

He chuckled. "You'd better order breakfast."

They were on the road within an hour, and they pulled into The Pas after eight o'clock that evening. They stopped at a motel and got a room, then drove to a local restaurant and ate supper. Sarah was on pins and needles, worried that she might run into someone she knew. She was relieved when they'd finished eating and went back to the motel.

Her sleep was fitful, even though Grayson held her close in his arms, after assuring her that everything would be fine.

CHAPTER NINETEEN

The next morning Sarah's anxiety was palatable.

"Mom, why aren't you happy about going to see your mom and dad?"

"It's complicated, Taylor."

"Have we ever been there before...like, when I was a baby?"

"No."

He frowned and looked thoughtful. "Why? Grayson went to see his mom and dad before. They were really happy to see us."

"Things are different in my family. My dad and I didn't get along very good. When I left home, he told me I couldn't come back. That was fourteen years ago."

Taylor wrinkled his nose. "That's an awful long time to be mad at someone. He's probably got over it now."

Grayson smiled at him. "That's what I tell her. Things always seem worse when you worry about them. I promised your mom that I'll talk to her dad if he's still upset."

Taylor was silent, as he looked out the window, taking in the sights of the town. Finally, he spoke. "You'd never go away and not see me for fourteen years, would you?"

"Honey, I'd never do that to you."

Sarah directed Grayson to a driveway just north of town. Shock reverberated through her as she looked around. Logging equipment still filled the yard surrounding the shop. Five pickup trucks were parked in front of the open doors. Sarah drew in her breath. "Dad and the boys must be home. I thought they'd be working in the bush by now." She swallowed hard. "I'd hoped to spend some time with mom first."

Grayson stopped the pickup in front of the older sprawling rancher style house. He looked into Sarah's eyes. "Remember, you're not doing this alone anymore. Everything will be fine."

Grayson opened his door and slid out of the truck. Taylor bailed out behind him. His eyes were big when he looked toward the shop. "Dad, look at all those big machines. They make the tractors at the ranch look small."

Grayson smiled as he put a hand on Taylor's shoulder. "We'll look at them later, but first let's go to the house and meet your grandma." They walked around the front of the truck and Grayson opened the passenger door. His eyes met Sarah's. "Let's get this over with; you look petrified." He took her hand and tugged her off the seat. When her feet touched the ground, he pulled her into his arms and held her against him, kissing the top of her head. Then he released her and cradled her shoulders with his arm as they turned toward the house.

He looked up to see an older, grey-haired woman standing in the doorway. She had obviously observed the tender moment, and when they started to move toward her, she ran down the walkway, with her arms opened wide.

At that moment, she only had eyes for Sarah. When their eyes met, Sarah drew in a ragged breath. "Mom!" The word was strangled with emotion. She broke away to meet her in a tangle of arms, hugging as their tears intermingled. Sarah was sobbing. "Mom, oh..."

"Sweetheart, I've prayed for this day."

"Mom, I'm so sorry. I should have called you."

"You're here now, and that's what matters." Selma Wasserman looked past her daughter's shoulder. "And this is your husband? And your son? My grandson?"

Sarah stepped back and reached for the hands of the men in her life. She tugged Grayson to her side, then pulled Taylor in front of her and hugged him, with his back against her chest. "This is my son, Taylor McNaughton. She looked up at Grayson and smiled. "And this is my husband, Grayson McNaughton." Her eyes met her mother's again. "He is my rock; my valiant defender."

Grayson extended his hand, but Selma pushed it aside. "I'm not shaking your hand, son. I want to hug you and thank you for bringing my daughter home."

Then she turned to Taylor. "Now let me look at you young man." She looked into his eyes, and then hugged him. "Welcome home, grandson."

"Come in." She tugged Taylor's hand and turned toward the house. "I made fresh muffins and the coffee pot is on."

When they stepped inside, the wonderful aroma of home cooking, greeted them. Sarah sniffed appreciatively. "That wonderful smell of home!" She looked around the kitchen. "Nothing's changed…"

A rough voice shattered the moment. "Well, nothing except your name. What's this nonsense about you calling yourself Sarah now?" Ivan Wasserman filled the living room door, his eyes boring into her, in the way she remembered from days gone by. Sarah's heart pounded as she stared back at him, speechless.

Grayson stepped into the uncomfortable gap. "Mr. Wasserman," he said as he moved toward him, extending his hand. "I'm Grayson McNaughton; Sarah's husband." Grayson didn't flinch, his eyes didn't waver as he looked into the older man's.

Ivan Wasserman was the first to look away. He looked Grayson up and down, and then took his extended hand in a firm shake. "Well, at least you look like decent kind of man; a lot better than the degenerate she ran off with. I guess you must know how stubborn and bullheaded she is."

"Sir, I know that your daughter is a strong, loyal and determined woman. She told me about the way you two parted; that you told her she could never come back."

Ivan's face hardened at the implied criticism.

"But I know things that you don't know, sir. I know that your assessment of Duncan Talbot was correct, and so does she. I know that she had nowhere to go when she was desperate and afraid: she should have been able to come back home, but she knew she couldn't. I know how she fought to keep herself and Taylor safe from the man who threatened to kill them. I know she found work with a decent, caring couple, who grew to love them both. We visited that couple on this trip, and they still love her and Taylor: they are still concerned about their welfare.

"I know that when she'd worked for them for four years, the *degenerate* tracked her down. He threatened her and Taylor. The Harahan's didn't throw up their hands and tell her she was on her own. They protected her: they involved the law, and because the drug squad was already keeping tabs on Duncan Talbot, an undercover agent helped your daughter and her infant son, disappear. Three years later, when Talbot tracked them down again, the Harahan's and the undercover agent helped her disappear again. They provided her and Taylor with new identities, and she became Sarah Brite."

Ivan's demeanor didn't soften.

"She'd hate to hear me say this, but I'm beginning to realize that she's a lot like you; stubborn and bullheaded. That's why you two clashed."

Ivan scowled. "Are you telling me that I'm stubborn and bullheaded?"

Grayson looked him in the eye. "With all due respect sir, I believe you are."

The older man held his look. "Are you really willing to take on the responsibility for that degenerate's son?"

Anger flared in Grayson's eyes. "Sir, I'd do anything for that boy. I don't give a damn who donated the sperm, he is a wonderful kid and he is my son in every way that counts."

A twinkle sparked in the older man's eye, a twitch at the corners of his mouth. "I think I like you, Grayson McNaughton." He slapped him on the back. "Drop the Sir and call me Ivan. Now introduce me to my grandson."

"Maybe you should welcome Sarah home first."

Ivan's look was measured. Then Grayson saw him relent. "You're right." He stepped toward Sarah and held out his hand. "It's good to see you again."

The moment was painfully awkward. She hesitated, and then put her hand into his. "It's...it's nice to see you too, Dad."

He cleared his throat, to mask the obvious discomfort. "I like that husband of yours. You've got a good man there."

Sarah's eyes darted to meet Grayson's. He nodded with encouragement. "I'm glad you approve. I think he's pretty terrific too." She reached out to take Taylor's hand and pulled him close.

"This is my…our son."

"Grayson was telling me about him." He leaned forward and looked into Taylors's face. "Welcome, son. Your dad tells me you're a fine young man."

Taylor was suddenly shy, confused by the vibes in the room. It had been so different when they'd gone to meet Grayson's parents. They'd been so welcoming and affectionate. He looked at the man in front of him uncertainly. Sarah nudged him. He reached and put his hand in his. "Hi. Are you my Grandpa?"

The older man smiled. "Yes, I guess I'm your Grandpa, son."

He stood up and looked at Grayson. "Let's go to the shop so you can meet the rest of the boys. We've had a late spring and the bush is still too wet to go to work, so they're taking out their frustrations by tightening every nut and bolt, getting everything spit and polished."

Grayson nodded and then hooked his arm around Sarah's shoulders, pulling her against his side. "I'd say the worst part is over," he whispered. "Are you okay?"

She nodded. "Thank you," she whispered back.

He slid his fingers down her arm and grabbed her hand, pulling her in front of him, facing him. He brushed her hair away from her face and smiled as he looked into her eyes. "I love you," he said so softly it was only for her ears. "Everything will be fine."

He was rewarded with the first real smile he'd seen from her in the past two days. "I believe you," she whispered.

A couple of hours later Brian, Al, and Justin came to the house along with Grayson, Taylor, and Ivan.

Brian smiled as he enfolded Sarah in his arms. "It's great to see you again, sis. It's been way too long." He brushed her cheek softly as he released her. "By the way, that's a great kid you've got and Grayson is a real stand-up guy too. I'm happy for you."

"Thanks, big bro. You can't know how much that means to me. I'm looking forward to meeting Vivian and the girls."

"They'll be here this afternoon, after school is out."

"It's my turn now, bud." Sarah turned to meet Nathan's laughing eyes as he pushed Brian away. "It's so good to see you again, sis." Her youngest brother hugged her close.

She kissed his cheek and then tilted her head back so she could study his face. "You've grown up, but you haven't really changed that much." She pressed her face against his chest again. "It feels wonderful to be with you all again. I didn't realize how much I'd missed you." She stepped back. "Mom tells me you're going to be a vet."

"I am, and I love it. Grayson and I have already talked about that. It's a strange co-incidence that you'd marry a vet too, eh?"

She nodded. "And I hear you're married. I can't wait to meet your wife."

"Audrey; you'll love her. She'll be over in time for supper." He looked deep into her eyes. "I know what happened—you and dad. Things have changed for the better now."

"Mom says that too, but he didn't welcome me with open arms. Thank goodness he liked Grayson, or I probably wouldn't have stayed."

Nathen made a fist and rapped her on the head with his knuckles. "You are still too damn obstinate girl, and so is he. Mom gave him a lot of grief over what he did to you. It's hard for him to eat humble pie. You made a few mistakes too, so do the right thing and make it easier for him."

Sarah sighed. "I never thought of myself as being that stubborn. I just knew I didn't want to live under his thumb. He'd have tied me up here, working in the house and garden until I married some logger from around here."

"That was the old country way of doing things, sis. The family stayed together. The girls helped around the house and the boys worked with the dad."

"But I wanted to do my own thing. I wanted to experience life."

"Well, from what Grayson told us, you did that. It sounds like it was pretty difficult and scary for you."

Sarah looked shocked. "He told you what happened?"

Nathan's look was serious. "I hope you know how lucky you are, sis. That man would do almost anything to protect you. He more or less walked into a lion's den when he came out to the shop. We were all sort of pissed off—especially about you changing your name.

"Dad took Taylor out and showed him the equipment, while Grayson laid it all out for us. He explained how that Talbot guy tracked you down when you worked for that couple in Toronto, and how the man had called in an undercover friend who'd helped you get away and given you a new name. He told us about the second time Talbot found you. You've lived a nightmare girl." He cradled her face in his hands. "You made a really bad choice when you were a teenager, but I am so damn proud of how you fought to protect your son and survived. I only wish you'd have come home."

"How could I?" she whispered. "I'd been told I couldn't come back. Besides that, The Pas is probably the first place he'd have looked for me."

He looked across the room at Grayson, who was sitting down, talking with Ivan. Taylor was standing next to him, and Grayson had an arm snagged around the boy, pulling him to lean against him. "I don't think you have to worry about that anymore." He gave her a quick hug, then turned to their mother.

Sarah looked around the room. Al stood in the doorway, watching her. He gave her no welcoming smile, just stood there observing her, his gray eyes shuttered.

They should have named him after dad, she thought. *He's just like him.* She hesitated, and then walked up to him. "Hi there you big lug, I want a hug from you."

He was chewing on a toothpick as he studied her face. Then he sighed and reached out to her. "Damn you woman, how could you stay away so long, without even giving us a phone call or sending a letter. We had no idea if you were dead or alive. Do you have any idea what that did to us?"

Sarah opened her mouth to remind him again, of what had happened. Then she thought better of it and said softly, "I'm sorry."

He hugged her against his chest and rested his head against hers. "There's plenty of blame to go around and it's not just yours. I couldn't see things from your point of view when you left. I sided with Dad, but when Mom realized that you weren't coming back, she took it out on him. I thought she was unfair, but Brian said he had it coming.

"When Mary Ann and I talked about marriage, I got a real eye opener. She bluntly told me that she wouldn't tolerate an attitude like Dad's. Marriage needed to be a partnership, not a dictatorship." He chuckled. "I've had a lot of learning to do. I'm probably most like Dad, and you're a close second."

She pushed away from him. "I'm not."

He tipped her chin up and looked into her eyes. "Where do you think you got all that grit and determination from, sis?"

She frowned. "I'm not like him."

Al shook his head. "You are, more than you want to admit. He's not a bad man and I'd say you're lucky you have his genes. From what Grayson told us, you may not have survived without them. I'm proud of you."

The emotional moment was interrupted when the porch door pushed open and Anne flew in. Her gaze met Sarah's instantly. "Oh...you're really here," she screamed as she pushed past Al and threw her arms around Sarah. The two sisters hugged and their tears intermingled.

Sarah finally pushed her away so she could look into her face. "You're all grown up." She brushed away her tears and then touched her blonde curly hair. "You're so beautiful. You were only six when I left." Tears filled her eyes. "You were my baby sister."

"I still am. I missed you so much." She stifled a sob. "It was awful. You were just gone and I couldn't understand why."

"I'm sorry. I didn't think about that, I just wanted to get away."

"I understand, now that I'm older. But, Mom says the guy that you left with, was really bad."

"He was. At first, it was fun and glamorous. And he paid for me to go to university and get my teaching degree."

"You're a teacher?"

"I never got a chance to teach. When I got pregnant and had Taylor..." Sarah shook her head and took a deep breath. "I finally saw the real Duncan Talbot. I knew I couldn't stay with him."

"How devastating that had to have been for you!"

The porch door burst open again and a tall redhead accompanied by two children came in. "Here's Vivian and the kids."

Before all the introductions were made, two more women and three children came in. Anne bounced with enthusiasm. "Oh! Audrey and MaryAnn and the kids are here now."

The house was filled with the sound of voices. It was almost overwhelming for Sarah. She looked across the room to Grayson and found him watching her. He winked when she put her hands over her ears and squished her eyes closed momentarily.

He got up and walked over to her. "How are you doing, hon?"

"Much better than I'd hoped, but the family has almost tripled in size and I'd forgotten how boisterous it can get."

"In a good way though, right?"

She nodded as she leaned her head against his shoulder. "Where's Taylor?"

"With your dad."

"Dad?"

"He's quite taken with his new grandson."

An hour later, the table was set and everyone was getting ready to sit down when the porch door pushed open again. Anne looked up in surprise, and then gasped. "Mary! You came."

Selma almost dropped the bowl of mashed potatoes. "How did you…"

"I took time off. I wasn't going to miss seeing my big sis. Where is she?"

Mary flew into the room and made a beeline for Sarah. She wrapped her arms around her, tears rolling down her cheeks as she held her close. "I can't believe it's true. You're here. We've wondered so many times about you…where you were and if you were even alive."

"I'm sorry," Sarah murmured once again.

"Forget the past. This is wonderful." She stood back and looked around the room. Mom says you're married." She pointed at Grayson. "He's the only guy I don't know in here, so he has to be yours."

Sarah smiled. "Yes, that's Grayson."

"And your son, where is he?"

"Taylor's sitting next to Dad."

Mary smiled. "Hello, there handsome. I'm your auntie Mary."

With sudden shyness, Taylor mumbled, "Hi."

After dinner, the adults sat around the table and talked, while the children went into the TV room. Sarah was amazed to see her dad go to sit with them several times. *Some things do change,* she thought.

When they went to bed that night, Grayson took Sarah into his arms, pulling her against him with her cheek resting against his chest. "I enjoyed meeting your family today. You seemed to have a good time too."

"I did. I didn't realize how much I've missed them."

"Would you want to move back here? Nathan and I could open a vet clinic together."

"Not really. I like the ranch and our family there."

"So do I." He was silent for a moment, and then said, "One day I'd like to practice again, but I'm content at the ranch for now."

"Moving here is a possibility I guess, but if you were going to move to practice, wouldn't you want to go back to your dad's clinic?"

"I'm not sure. Dad's getting older. He'll probably retire in a few years and there are still a lot of painful memories for me there. It might be better to start in a neutral place."

She kissed his chest. "We've got time to work through that." She yawned. "Will we spend the day here tomorrow and leave Sunday morning?"

"I think so. We've got a long drive home."

She yawned again. "It's at least a couple days to the ranch, eh?"

"Yes, maybe two and a half."

"We'd better go to sleep. Tomorrow's going to be another full day."

Sunday morning the entire family gathered for breakfast. As the McNaughton's got ready to leave, there were lingering hugs and tears, promises to keep in touch, promises to visit.

Ivan pumped Grayson's hand and slapped him on the back. He bent down and spoke to Taylor, then came to Sarah's side and awkwardly extended his hand.

Sarah's gaze held his for a moment, and then she shook the hand. She quickly turned away, fighting the tears that shimmered in her eyes. Her heart ached. *Somethings never change*, she thought as she walked away.

When she opened the truck door and prepared to pull herself up into the cab, she felt a hand on her shoulder. As she turned, arms enveloped her. "I'm glad you came home, girl. We've missed you."

Sarah pushed her face into her father's shirt, tears spilling over as she slipped her arms around him.

"Thanks, Dad. I didn't realize how much I've missed my family either."

He tightened the hug. "I've always loved you. I've just never been good at sayin' it. And you and I...we clashed so much, I didn't know how to...."

Sarah uttered a muffled sob. "I know dad." She leaned back to look in his face. "Everyone tells me we're just too much alike. That's probably true."

Sarah's heart melted as he lifted his hand to cradle the back of her head and kiss her forehead. The unusual expression of affection was almost her undoing. She collected her wits, as she listened to his praise. "Sarah..." he hesitated as he tested the name on his tongue. "I'm proud of you. That young son of yours is a great kid, and your husband is a good man. He's strong and loyal. I know you'll be safe with him by your side."

"I know how lucky I am." She looked up at him. "And thank you for calling me Sarah. I haven't forgotten where I started, but this is where I need to be now."

He nodded. "I was upset at first, but I do understand now. I'd like to put a hit on that man...."

"No, dad. Just protect us all by making sure we stay under his radar."

Ten minutes later Grayson eased the truck out of the yard and they were on their way home. Taylor was thoughtful. "Mom, I don't know why you were so worried about going to see Grandpa and Grandma, they were really nice."

Grayson's eyes connected with his, through the rearview mirror. "They were nice to us. Grandpa has changed and so has mom. Going to visit them was a good thing. It gave the two of them a chance to make things right. I hope mom's family will come and visit us sometime, but I promise you, we will come back to see them again."

"I'd like that."

They arrived at the ranch late Tuesday afternoon. Frank insisted they have supper with them and Ellie and Ollie joined them. Everyone was eager to hear about the trip.

When they were discussing their visit in The Pas, Taylor broke into the conversation to make a proud announcement. "I have two grandpas of my very own now."

Colt leaned back in his chair. "You're a pretty lucky guy, eh?"

"Yeah! And they both like to go fishing. I told them they had to come here and go fishing in the river with Dad and me. And, Uncle Justin is going to be a vet, just like Dad."

Colt looked at Grayson. "A vet? Obviously you two had a lot in common."

"We did. It was interesting."

Sarah smiled. "Going home was a pleasant surprise for me too. My whole family has grown up, the older kids have gotten married, and I think that has sort of forced dad to change. He took a bit of a run at me at first; you know the "Sarah" thing. But Grayson stepped in and had a talk with dad and the boys. After that everything was fine." She smiled at her husband. "They all liked him and of course they couldn't resist Taylor."

"So where does your brother plan to practice when he gets his license?"

"He wants to set up a clinic in The Pas."

Colt regarded Grayson. "Did he ask you to be his partner?"

Grayson looked down and played with his fork. "He suggested it, but then there's my dad's clinic, too. I asked Sarah if she wanted to consider moving, but we're both happy here." He looked up at Colt. "I have to admit, I'd like to work in a clinic again. I have a family now...."

Frank smiled. "We should have a serious discussion about that. My kids are growing up and I'd enjoy using my training, too."

Colt leaned back in his chair. "That's been in the back of my mind. I put the windmills in the area next to the corals with the idea of building a clinic for Frank. We got busy and time just got away and it hasn't happened."

"That's an interesting idea. Could we draw enough people to make a clinic profitable?"

"We'd have to think about that. When I came up with the idea, I was thinking of Frank doing the vet work for the ranch work, and picking up a few tourists and locals on the side. But you would be looking for more than that."

"Yeah. My dad would love to have me come back, but I don't see myself going there. Anyway, I'm not pulling the pin right now: but you know how it is, I need to give more thought to the future now."

"How were your parents?"

"They're doing fine. They loved Sarah and Taylor. We had a great visit. My brother came home on Saturday and the three of us went golfing."

Taylor's head shot up. "Yeah, and you should have seen what happened. Some nasty lady came to our table in the restaurant and started saying bad things about Dad. Mom stood up and told her off. I was so proud of her."

"Taylor..." Sarah's face went red.

Grayson reached out and took her hand. "I was proud of her too... and grateful. It was Mrs. Hixon. She'll never forgive me for what happened and I can understand that."

Sarah's head shot up. "No. She knows there were two sides to what happened. She's just been able to push it all off onto you, and I couldn't listen to her do that. Other people know it too."

"My wife is a strong woman. Don't cross her."

Colt chuckled. "I've seen that side of her, but she can be reasoned with too."

The next day life settled into the regular routine at the ranch. Grayson and Frank, Sam, Selena and Taylor rode horseback to check the replacement heifers in the back fields.

On the way back, Taylor called out to Grayson. "Hey Dad, wait for me."

Grayson pulled up his horse and waited for him. "What's up?"

"Wouldn't it be fun to bring the grandpas out here and fish in the river with them?"

"I'm sure they'd enjoy it."

"Why don't we invite them for my birthday? It's next week."

"They are both busy men; I doubt if they could make it on such short notice."

Frank rode up beside him. "Besides we have a surprise planned for you."

"A surprise? For my birthday?"

She nodded.

"What is it?"

"If I told you it wouldn't be a surprise."

"Dad, do you know what it is."

"It's been planned for a while. I think you'll like it; a boy doesn't turn eleven years old every day."

"Does mom know?"

"Of course, but she's good at keeping a secret. She won't tell you either."

Taylor tried to find out what the surprise was all week, but no one would tell him.

Frank spent every afternoon with the twins and Taylor, helping them perfect the skills of team roping. Sarah often went down to watch them, and it helped to dispel her lingering fears that her son would get hurt.

Saturday morning, Grayson woke Taylor up early. "Come on Birthday Boy. It's time to hit the road."

Sarah smiled as she watched her son rub the sleep from his eyes.

"Where are we going?" he grumbled.

"You'll find out soon. This is your birthday surprise."

When they walked out to the truck, Colt was closing the back door of the ranch crew-cab. Ellie and Ollie were in the front and Frank had settled between Sam and Selena in the back.

"Happy Birthday, Taylor. Are you ready to find out what your surprise is?"

"Geeze, I didn't even get breakfast."

Sarah steered him toward the truck. "Get in; we don't want to be late." Sarah smiled as she handed him a gift bag. "I think you'll like to have these too. Happy Birthday, son."

Taylor was still frowning. "I'm hungry. When are we going to...holy cow! This is awesome." The frown was gone, and his faced flushed with happiness. "A cowboy hat." He plopped it on his head and looked into the rearview mirror in front of him. He was slapping Grayson's shoulder. "Look dad! It's just like yours."

"Did you dig deeper in that bag?"

Paper flew, and Taylor let out a squeal. "Cowboy boots! Oh man. I'm a real cowboy now." He threw his arms around Sarah's neck. "Thank you, Mom. This is the best birthday I've ever had."

Then he barreled across the seat to hug Grayson.

"Hey, be careful! I'm driving. You can hug me when we stop for breakfast. You'd better put on your seat belt now."

Taylor put on his boots, and then did up his seat belt. "Where are we stopping for breakfast?"

"Wherever Colt stops."

"I can hardly wait to show Sam and Selena." He took off his hat and looked at it thoughtfully. "Cowboys...are we going to a rodeo?"

"Would you like that?" Grayson asked.

"Can I go in the calf roping? We've been practicing all week."

"Slow down, Taylor, we're just going to watch today. You're not ready to ride yet."

"But I will when I'm older. Frank says I'm a natural."

"Maybe in five years," Sarah said.

"Mom, I'll be all grown up them. Colt says we can start when we're twelve. That's next year."

"We'll see."

That day at the rodeo was to become one of several days that the two families shared during the summer months. At the ranch, Taylor practiced roping with determination and by the time he had to go back to school in September, he and Frank were becoming a well-matched team.

CHAPTER TWENTY

At the end of September, Sarah received a large brown envelope in the mail. Grayson smiled as he handed it to her. "I think we've got the go-ahead to make everything legal now." She feverously ripped open the package. They looked the documents over and then high-fived each other. "Sarah Brite, it's time we went to the preacher man. I'll phone today and make arrangements. We'll have to get the marriage license and then the next day Frank and Colt and you and I will quietly go into town and we will tie the knot."

"Finally," she breathed as she leaned forward to kiss him.

Taylor came in half an hour later. He looked at the paperwork on the table. "What's that?" he asked as he went to fridge to get a juice box.

Sarah picked up the adoption certificate and handed it to Grayson, who was smiling proudly. He motioned for the boy to come and stand by him, then handed him the paper. "These are your final adoption papers, proof that you are legally my son."

Taylor's face beamed as he stared at it. "Can I hang this on my wall?"

"We'll make a copy of it and put it in a frame for you."

Grayson and Sarah went to the main house to make a copy of

the adoption certificate. They also asked Frank and Colt who they would recommend as a pastor. Grayson called the man they suggested and arranged for a wedding ceremony. The next day Sarah and Grayson went to Maple Creek to get their marriage license.

Three days, later the four of them met the minister at the quaint little church. Sarah wore the white dress she had worn when Pastor Thompson had performed a ceremony for them. She and Grayson held hands as they followed their witnesses up the steps. She hesitated and looked up at him. "The groom isn't supposed to see the bride until they meet at the altar."

He smiled and shook his head. "Well, if it makes you feel better, Colt and I can go in first and I'll wait for you at the altar." His smile turned into a chuckle. "Keep in mind, when you walk down the aisle, I'll be remembering you naked in our bed this morning."

Sarah blushed. "That's not very bridal!"

"You'll always be my bride, but we've been married for months now. This is just a legal formality." He opened the door. "Do you want me to go to the altar and wait for you?"

She leaned her head on his shoulder. "That would be kind of hypocritical wouldn't it? After all, I remember what happened in our bed this morning, too."

They were both smiling when they walked inside. The pastor greeted them and after introductions had been made, he performed a simple ceremony and pronounced them man and wife. Then they signed papers to make the marriage legal.

Colt smiled as he shook hands with them. "Mr. and Mrs. McNaughton: now it's signed, sealed and totally legit."

Sarah stretched on her tiptoes, to whisper in Colts ear. "I preferred Pastor Thompson's ceremony."

He chuckled, as he rested a hand on Grayson's shoulder. "We want to take you two out for supper. Ellie knows we'll be home later. She'll feed the kids."

Frank smiled happily. "The occasion needs to be celebrated, even if we are the only ones who know what happened here today."

"Just like only the four of us knew the first time—well that's not quite true. Ollie and Ellie were in on it too."

Frank shook her head and smiled. "Actually, we never told Ellie and Ollie that it wasn't legit. Colt and Grayson were in the office a long time. Grayson had talked to our lawyer and put the legal wheels put into motion, but he still felt bad about not being able to adopt

Taylor right away, because he knew how much to meant to the kid. Then, they came up with the idea of having a celebration ceremony for you and Grayson and presenting Taylor with a certificate that showed he was Taylor McNaughton. They figured no one would question it and Grayson wouldn't have to think twice about staying at the apartment: not that he would have anyway, but Taylor and both sets of parents would be satisfied!

"Grayson went home right away. Colt told us we were going to have a ceremony and made some comment that suggested that he'd gotten 'a hurry up consent' to marry you,--which he did from Grayson-- and left it at that. If Ollie and Ellie had really thought about it, they probably would have questioned the possibility of that happening. But, with technology the way it is today, almost anything is possible, and I'm sure they just accepted everything at face value."

Colt chuckled. "I just started telling everybody what had to be done, and everyone was too busy to even think about the unlikelihood of being able to get a legal okay to perform the marriage ceremony! Ellie and Fran started supper, while Ollie and I got the schoolroom ready. Then Ellie and Ollie went home and I hustled Fran into the office and told her what was going on. First, she told me it was a crazy idea, but the idea of me being Pastor Thompson made her smile. She went online and looked for marriage vows. Then she printed off something that could pass for a marriage certificate, and another certificate that she filled in for Taylor's adoption."

Frank chuckled. "Neither one would have passed close scrutiny, but who would look that close?"

Sarah reached out and hugged her. "You guys are the best! Being married never mattered before, but Taylor wanted to know that Grayson really was his dad and that pretend ceremony was a stroke of genius. It made him feel like his wish had been granted…"

"Which it had; in my heart he was my son," Grayson interrupted. "We just had to get all the paperwork done behind the scenes."

Sarah squeezed his hand. "I know, but I still felt guilty when we pretended it was real to the rest of our friends and worst of all our parents."

"Ah, my darling wife." Grayson hugged her against him, then dropped a kiss on her forehead, and smiled as he looked down into her eyes. "We've got it covered now and they'll never be any the wiser."

That night Sarah rested her cheek against Grayson's chest as he cradled her against him. "I'm so happy, what else could we ask for?"

"I've got an idea, for a few months down the road."

"Ummm...what's that?"

"I'd like to have more children."

She smiled sleepily. "Babies?"

He ran a hand down over her head, stopping to cup her cheek. "Not right now, but maybe in a few months. I've always dreamed of having a house full of children. Taylor will like them too."

She giggled. "He doesn't like babies. He says they poop and pee their pants and puke all over you."

He chuckled. "He's right about that, but he'll love them because they'll be his family too."

"I think we should consider that."

"We have a wonderful son. I'd like a little girl that looks like you."

Sarah closed her eyes. "She might look like you."

"I don't care who she looks like, she'll be yours."

***

Three months later Sarah snuggled up to Grayson when they went to bed. "Are you ready?"

"I'm always ready," he said with a sexy grin.

"That's not what I'm talking about."

"No? So what are you talking about?"

"Are you ready to be a daddy again?"

He pulled her against him. "Are you telling me...?"

She nodded. "I'm saying I'm pretty certain. I'm a couple of weeks late. I think we should pick up a pregnancy test the next time we're in town."

"We'll go tomorrow."

"It's not that urgent. If it's true, I'll still be pregnant in a few days."

"Are you kidding? I can't wait to know."

They cuddled as they whispered about the possibilities of having a new baby. Sleep was slow in coming.

The next morning, after the chores were done, Grayson told Colt that he needed to go to town. He and Sarah drove into Maple Creek and shopped. The first thing on their list was a pregnancy test kit. That evening the test proved that Sarah was right. In a few months, they would welcome a new baby into their family.

***

Christmas went by, and as winter slipped into spring, Colt, Frank and Grayson were busy with calving. Ollie filled in where he could, but the years were showing on him. He was complaining about stiffness and pains that he'd never mentioned before.

On the first of March, Lee McNaughton called. After greeting him, Sarah handed the phone to Grayson.

"Dad! How are you guys doing?"

"We're fine. The clinic stays busy, but the winter has seemed long. Mom's getting antsy. We thought we might drive out and have a visit with you guys."

"Hey, that would be great. When would you come?"

"We'll probably come for Easter. That's three weeks from now."

"That sounds wonderful. Taylor will be so excited. He'll drag you all over the ranch."

"How's Sarah feeling?"

"She's doing great. She hasn't had much morning sickness and she's just got a little bump—not much yet."

Lee laughed. "The bump will grow. I'm glad to hear that she's doing well."

"Dad, why don't you ask Jon to come along? Tell him to bring his roommate. Maybe he'd feel more comfortable."

"I guess we could. We haven't seen him since you were here. He was in Europe at Christmas time."

"What's his number?"

"Give me a moment. I'll have to look it up." Grayson could hear the rustle of paper as his dad thumbed through his address book. "Here it is." He gave Grayson the number and said, "I'll call him tonight, but it might help if you called him too."

"I will, and Dad…I'm glad you're coming. I have to warn you, long weekends are a big deal here at the ranch. Everyone comes out to visit."

"Oh, maybe it isn't a good time for us to come."

"It's a great time for you to come. You'll get to meet our friends. We're all like family. They'll be happy to have you with us. We'll have time to visit here in the apartment, but we'll all get together at Colt and Frank's for Easter dinner. It's a tradition around here. They put out Easter baskets for the kids and its fun. Well, usually it's fun." He stopped and swallowed hard, remembering the previous Easter. "Except for last year, when Sarah...that's when she got ran over by a cow."

"That had to have been frightening."

"It was worse than frightening. I thought I'd lost her before I really even had her."

"Well son, she's a very special woman and in the end it all worked out. You got the girl, a son and now there's a baby on the way. What more could you ask for?"

"Nothing! I really do have everything."

The two men said good night and Grayson shut off the phone. He looked across the room at Sarah. "That was Dad. They're coming for Easter."

Taylor perked up instantly. "Grandpa's coming?"

"Yes, and your Grandma. I told him you'd be excited about that."

"Will it be too early to go fishing at the river?"

"It's hard to say. It depends on the weather and if the ice is gone. But there are lots of other things for you to show him around here."

"Maybe Frank and I can team rope one day. Then he'll see how good I am at it."

Grayson grinned. "You'll have to give up your bedroom, so they have a place to sleep."

"That's okay. I'll sleep here on the couch. Then I'll have to stay up until all you guys go to bed."

Sarah chuckled. "You're always thinking, kid."

She looked at Grayson. "Did I hear you tell your dad to ask Jon and his roommate to come too?"

He nodded. "And he gave me his number. I'll phone him in a day or two. It'll give him a chance to think about dad's call. If things are different—I mean, if they are an item, then it may encourage him to open up and come. I'd like to reach out to him. He's the only brother I have."

"I agree. Where would we put them?"

"I'll talk to Colt tomorrow. Maybe they could stay in the bunkhouse. That would give them privacy and it wouldn't seem out of the ordinary to anyone else. There's a double bed and a couple of bunk beds in there. It would be perfect. A little rustic compared to their normal lifestyle, but they might enjoy it."

"That's a perfect solution. I can't see why Colt wouldn't agree. It's going to be fun having your family here. And it's great that they'll get to meet all of our friends."

The next day, Grayson was happy when he came in for lunch. "I talked to Colt when we were doing chores this morning. I told him Mom and Dad are coming for Easter and I wanted to ask Jon to come too. I explained that he might want to bring his roommate along. I didn't say anything about my suspicions; I just suggested that the bunkhouse would work for them since we don't have enough room."

"What did he say?"

"He didn't hesitate to say yes. So I'll phone Jon tonight."

"I hope he comes."

"So do I."

Grayson phoned Jon early in the evening. "Hi. Did Dad call you last night?"

"Yeah, he did."

"So he told you they are coming here for Easter?"

His voice was cool. "Yeah."

"Did he tell you we'd like you to come too?"

"He mentioned that."

"Sarah and I really want you to come. You can bring Ted along if you want. We only have one extra bedroom, but I lived in the bunkhouse before we got married and it's comfortable enough. You guys could stay there. What do you think?"

"I'd have to check my schedule and see how it works. Ted's too."

"Well, give it some thought. We'd really like to have you come."

"I'll get back to you."

Grayson stared at the phone, and then looked at Sarah. "Well, he didn't say no, but he just said he'd have to get back to me and hung up."

Sarah shook her head. "He is a different guy isn't he?"

Grayson shook his head. "He sure is."

Two weeks later Jon phoned. "Ted and I have talked this over. We don't want to drive that far for the weekend. The company has a small jet. If the pilot can come out with us for the weekend, he'd fly us to Swift Current and we could rent a car and drive to the ranch."

"That sounds great. There's no problem with one more person, but he'd have to share the bunk house with you guys. There's a double bed and set of bunk beds. I've never slept in the bunks, so I can't vouch for how comfortable they are."

To Grayson's surprise, Jon chuckled. "Ted and I go camping quite often. It can't be worse than a foam mattress and a sleeping bag."

"You'll do fine then. I'm glad you're coming."

"Will we get a chance to ride?"

"There are horses here on the ranch and lots of trails to ride. Do you ride?"

"Yes, we ride." His voice sobered. "There's a lot you don't know about me Gray."

Gray. Jon had just called him by his old childhood name. "It's time we fix that." He cleared his throat. "Jon…uh…are you and Ted more than friends. I mean…are you a couple?"

"Would that make a difference?"

"No. I've wondered for a while."

Jon sighed. "We are. I knew, early on, that I was…different. But I didn't know how to deal with it…or you guys."

"It doesn't matter to me or Sarah. I know Dad suspects it, but he doesn't know how to ask you. If he was wrong, it would be tough on everyone."

"You two discussed this?"

"I asked him when we were out there… after you left that morning. I don't remember you ever dating, yet I'm sure you'd have had lots of opportunity."

"I did. I still get approached by women, but I have no interest in them. Ted and I have been together for nine years." He was silent for a moment. "Gray…I'm glad you asked. Ted and I talked about this before we decided to come. He told me to go by myself, but I didn't want to. The bunkhouse made it simpler."

"It was the best solution here, but I also hoped it would make you feel more comfortable if…if you were a couple."

"Thanks, Gray. I appreciate that. I hope you truly understand that I'm still a man and I…we…Ted and I…probably enjoy a lot of the things that you do. We have a cabin in the country and we go there most weekends. We have a couple of horses that a neighbor looks after for us and we go riding, hiking, fishing and camping whenever we can."

"Taylor will love you guys! Jon, phone Dad and tell him the

truth. I'm not sure how much mom knows or what she thinks, but if you tell him, he'll work it out with her. The fact that you've been so distant has hurt them. It bothered me, but I thought it was because you were embarrassed by what I'd done and I carried so much guilt over that, I could understand."

"I was a real jerk about that. I didn't stand behind you; instead I distanced myself from it all and buried myself in my own world. I regret it now. It took Sarah to stand up and say what we all should have years ago."

Grayson smiled to himself. "She really is amazing. But tell me something; why did you tear into me before you left for home that day?"

Jon sighed. "To be honest, I was jealous. In some ways, I've resented you for years. You're so normal and you fit into dad's world, in a way that I never have. Then you came home with an acceptable spouse, and you had a kid. Mom and dad were thrilled and I felt even more alienated. I feel guilty now, but I took it out on you."

"Well, here's to new beginnings Jon. I'd like it if we acted like brothers again. Coming here for Easter is a good start for us."

"I'm glad we've talked candidly. I'm really looking forward to coming now."

"Jon, I need to tell you that Easter is a big deal here at the ranch. Sarah and I have live in an apartment and the main ranch house is just next door. A group of us, who work together on different levels, have become good friends; actually more like a family. Most long weekends, everyone gathers at the ranch. We all get together and visit, but everyone can do their own thing if they want to. If you want to go riding, you can. If you want to, you can go fishing in the Frenchman river. We all have a great time, and you guys will fit right in. And don't worry about anyone judging you; they won't even know that you are anything more than friends and co-workers, unless you want them too."

Jon was silent for a moment. "Are you sure it's not imposing on the others?"

"Not at all. This morning I mentioned that mom and dad were coming and I hoped you and your friend would come too. Colt and Frank basically said, the more the merrier. The girls are old pros at this stuff. They plan the meals in advance. Then everyone brings food and everyone pitches in. Us guys help cook too. You'll probably get assigned to flipping hamburgers or peeling potatoes, just like the rest of us."

"It sounds like fun."

"It is. I'm looking forward to having you here, but phone dad and tell him how things are between you and Ted. Or do you want me to give him a heads up first?"

"No, it's time I was honest. My relationship with Ted deserves that."

On Good Friday, Ingrid and Lee McNaughton arrived at the ranch just before lunch. They had called from Swift Current that morning to get directions to the ranch, so everyone had been anticipating their arrival. The men were working in the corrals when Taylor spotted their silver car slowly coming up the long driveway.

"Dad! Grandpa and Grandma are here!" He was running full tilt out of the corral before Grayson saw the car and sprinted after him. Colt and Ollie followed at a slower pace, both smiling as they watched Taylor's exuberance.

Taylor had reached the driveway seconds before the car stopped by him. Lee was opening his window as the boy reached the driver's door. "Grandpa! You're finally here. I have so much to show you."

Lee chuckled as he pushed the door open and stepped out. His heart flooded with warmth as he reached for the boy. "Give me a hug, son."

Taylor threw his arms around him, squeezing as tight as he could. Grayson had just reached the car and Lee's happy eyes met his, as he strode up beside him. As he hugged the boy with one arm, he reached out with the other to greet his smiling son. Father and son connected in an awkward embrace, sandwiching the boy between them.

Taylor sputtered and pushed himself free. Grayson stepped back. "You made it."

"GPS is a wonderful thing, and you gave us good directions."

Grayson turned to Colt and Ollie. "This is my dad; Lee McNaughton."

Colt extended his hand. "Pleased to meet you, I'm Colt Thompson." He nodded to Ollie. "This is Ollie Crampton. He's our old timer around here."

The men shook hands and then Grayson hurried around to hug his mother, who had gotten out of the car and was busily snapping pictures with her small camera.

"Mom, we're not ignoring you."

She smiled and kissed his cheek. "My ego isn't that fragile, son. I enjoyed watching you guys getting together again." She looked around. "This is quite a place. The setting is beautiful."

"It is. We're happy here. Come and let me introduce you to Colt and Ollie, and kick my son's butt for not remembering that his Grandma is here too."

"Don't be hard on him. Grandpas are special to little boys."

After Grayson had introduced his mother, he directed them up to the ranch house. Frank came out to meet them, and then he took them to the apartment.

Lee looked around. "This is nice, Grayson. The yard is big and from here the apartment looks to be a comfortable size for your family now."

"After the baby comes, we'll need more room. We haven't figured that out yet, but we have time. When Colt was building the house, he had it made for Ellie to live in. She was their nanny then. When she and Ollie got married, she moved down to the old ranch house, where he's lived since he came here. She still comes up here to home school the kids, including Taylor."

Sarah opened the door to welcome them in. "Ingrid! Lee! Come on in. You're just in time for lunch. I made soup and I just put on the coffee."

Ingrid laughed. "Lunch can wait. I want to hug my daughter-in-law first."

Sarah reveled in her warmth. "Ahh. That feels so good. I'm so happy you've come."

"Now, let me see..." Ingrid looked her over. "Not much of a tummy yet."

"It'll come. Just give it time!"

They stood around talking for a few moments. Then Grayson showed them the apartment, eventually taking them to the room they would be staying in. Sarah set the table and got everything ready for them to eat.

After lunch, Grayson and Taylor took Lee outside to tour the farm. Lee commented on Colt's forward thinking when he had installed the wind generators.

Grayson pointed to the generator on the other side of the corrals. "He installed the one down there with a clinic for Frank in mind. I told you she's a vet too didn't I?"

Ivan nodded. "Would she get enough business to make it worthwhile out here? It's a ways from anywhere, population wise."

"Well, he wanted her to be able to use her training. Even here on the ranch, it would be great to have better facilities for prolapses or cesareans, than crouching out in a corral. And we could do pregnancy tests and ultrasounds. He thought word of mouth would bring in clients from other ranches around the area. There are horse people and of course tourists that go through."

Lee was thoughtful. "They could diversify beyond the clinic. There is still room for a quality embryo transplant facility. They'd have room for a setup like that here, if they wanted to pursue the idea. It would take a while to get established though."

"I'd be happy if they got into something like that. I have a family now, so I need to think about the future. I enjoy working here, and we are all close friends; it would be hard to leave, but I've thought about practicing again."

Lee was quiet, lost in thought as they walked. A few minutes later, he stopped and looked at Grayson. "You know, the clinic in Maple Creek is for sale."

"Dad, I can't afford anything right now."

Taylor came running to meet them. "Hey, Grandpa! Come and watch me rope the cow horns."

Lee looked at Grayson. "Does he rope cows?"

Grayson chuckled. "Frank used to team rope years ago. She put a cow head on a stick and shoved it into a bale for the kids to practice roping the horns."

Lee chuckled. "He had me worried for a moment."

"When the ground has dried out, he and Frank practice team roping in the corral and he's pretty good at it. She ropes with Sam and Selena too, but she says Taylor has natural talent. He is crazy about it and can't wait to ride in a rodeo with her."

"He's lucky to be growing up here. He'll miss it if you move."

"I know that. I'm torn. That's why I haven't put much energy into thinking about making a change. This is a great place for the kids to grow up. I've got time to think about it. I certainly won't be making any moves until after the baby is born; probably not until next spring at the earliest."

Taylor demonstrated his roping skills on the skull, and then they moved on to look at the cattle. They did the evening chores earlier than usual, and then returned to the apartment to spend the rest of the day visiting.

Late that afternoon Brad and Shauna Lee Johnson arrived with their family. They got settled in the main ranch house with Colt and Frank and then after supper they all came to the apartment to meet Lee and Ingrid. Jon phoned at about eight o'clock that evening, to let them know that their plane had landed in Swift Current. They had rented a vehicle and were spending the night in a hotel. The three of them would drive to the ranch the next morning.

The evening passed quickly. When the others left to go back to the main house, Ingrid smiled at Grayson. "You have wonderful friends. I can see why you feel they are like family."

The next morning Grayson went out to do chores before breakfast. When he returned, Sarah had breakfast ready and the five of them sat down and enjoyed the waffles she had made. While they were drinking coffee, Grayson put down his cup and looked at his dad. "Did you and Jon have a talk?" he asked quietly.

Lee nodded.

"Did you talk to mom?"

"Everything is okay. She had begun to wonder about that herself, but didn't know how to say anything to me. I think she was relieved to have it out in the open. I know I am."

Grayson nodded in agreement.

Later that morning Christina and Tim Bates arrived with the twins. They went to Ollie and Ellie Crampton's house. Jon, Ted, and their pilot Peter, arrived shortly after. Lee and Grayson took them to the bunkhouse. They put their luggage inside and looked around.

"This looks great," Jon said with enthusiasm.

"I'm glad you're comfortable with it. If you want to look around the ranch now, feel free to do that. Or, we can go up to our place. Later we'll go to the main ranch house. By then everyone else will be there too, so you'll meet the whole gang. We're barbecuing hamburgers tonight. Don't be surprised if you get asked to help."

"We brought some chips and beer. Ted makes a good dip, and I'm fine with flipping burgers. Anyway, let's go to your place now. I'd like to say Hi to Mom and Sarah and introduce them to Ted and Peter. We can look around the ranch tomorrow."

The five men walked up the driveway to the ranch house, talking and laughing with comradely ease. When they reached the apartment, Ingrid greeted Jon with a hug and acknowledged Ted with warm affection. After Jon had introduced Peter, they sat around the table.

Sarah poured coffee for everyone and conversation flowed. Later she heated the remainder of the soup for lunch and they ate. Grayson sat back for a moment and watched them all. Gratitude filled his heart as he thought about how his family was getting a second chance.

After lunch, they went to the main house. Ollie, Ellie, Christina, Tim, and the twins were already there. After all of the introductions were made, Sarah picked up Shay and went to sit in the big rocking chair. He was content to sit on her lap for a few moments, babbling baby talk while he looked at her. "My, aren't you a big boy now?" He waved his hands around and pointed at something that caught his attention. "Have you any idea how heavy you've gotten?" He smiled and babbled as he pointed at the buttons on her shirt.

Suddenly he wanted to turn around so he could see what else was happening in the room. He squealed loudly and pointed when Taylor crouched down in front of him.

Taylor touched Shay's hand and smiled as the babies fingers closed around his. "He's cute. Will our baby be like him?"

"At first it will be very tiny, even smaller than Shay was when you held him at Easter time, last year. But babies grow quickly; Shay and Zaira are almost sixteen months old now. Pretty soon they'll be walking all over and talking like crazy."

Taylor's expression was thoughtful as he lingered for a few more seconds to watch, and he smiled when Shay wiggled to get off Sarah's lap. When his feet touched the floor, he took a few wobbly steps and then sat down and shrieked, as he pointed at Zaira, who was taking unsteady steps as she held on to the backs of the chairs that were pushed up to the kitchen table. Taylor covered his ears and laughed. "Wow, he's noisy!"

After breakfast at the main house on Sunday morning, the children and adults participated in the hunt for Easter baskets. At some point during that morning, each one remembered that the previous Easter hunt had almost ended in disaster, and expressed their gratitude that Sarah was there with them, healthy and carrying a new life.

Grayson, Taylor, and Lee drove down to the river during the afternoon and went fishing from the banks. Although they didn't catch anything, they had fun together. Jon and Ted went for a horseback ride with Colt and Brad. Tim, Ollie, and Peter visited at the old ranch house, and the girls stayed at the main house, visiting and catching up on their lives while they made dinner.

Monday morning, after breakfast, Jon, Ted, and Peter said goodbye to everyone before they left for Swift Current. They would be in Toronto by evening. The Johnsons and the Bates left after lunch, and Ellie and Ollie retired to their own house to rest. The McNaughtons sat around the table with Colt and Frank and visited.

Lee looked at Frank. "Grayson tells me you're a vet too."

"I am. I've kept my license up to date, but I haven't practiced since we got married. Babies and life kind of took over."

Colt chuckled. "She's been our in-house vet. She's still as good as anyone I've ever met in her field."

"Grayson tells me you've thought about building a clinic here."

"I have. I just haven't got around to doing it. She works with me on the ranch and she spends a lot of time with the kids."

"I know Kevin Marks. He owns the clinic in Maple Creek. I hadn't talked to him for years, but I called him the other day. He's thinking about retirement."

Colt's look narrowed. "That's interesting. I haven't been in there for years because I haven't needed too. I have no idea what kind of a setup he has."

"I've given some thought to selling. I'm not ready to hang up my hat, but I'd like to be closer to my grandkids. After spending the weekend here, I'm even more certain of that. I'd need to check it out and see what Marks has and what he'd want for the business. If Grayson and I invested in it, would you be interested in working with us, Frank?"

Frank didn't hide her surprise. "I'd love to practice again, but the ranch…"

"Hon, it would be a chance for you to do something you love. I can always hire more help on the ranch."

Lee held up his hand. "I understand how involved you are here. Your days at the clinic could be flexible. I haven't talked to Grayson about this yet, but he has said he'd like to practice again and he has a wife and kids to consider now. I see how intertwined your families are, and I know he'd like to stay close. I've given it more thought this weekend. Seeing you all together, like one big family, is something very special."

He looked at Grayson. "You and I have to discuss this, but I wanted to throw out the possibility. I'd like it if you chose to work with me, but that's up to you. As I see it, you could have the best of both worlds here; working as a vet and helping out at the ranch on occasion. And I wouldn't want to mess up Taylor's plans to rope with Frank at a rodeo."

They spent much of the afternoon discussing the idea. They decided that Lee should stop in and talk to Kevin Marks the next morning, when he and Ingrid started for home. He could tour the clinic and get a feel of what Marks was really thinking.

When they went to bed that night, Sarah and Grayson talked long into the night.

Sarah snuggled in his arms. "What do you think about all this?"

"It has possibilities. I'd love a chance to work with Dad again, and we wouldn't have to leave this area."

"We'd probably have to move into Maple Creek, and I wouldn't be able to work here, either."

"But then again, maybe you won't want to work when the baby comes, and we're going to need a bigger house soon. In time, you could be our receptionist and bring the little one to work with you. I'd guess my mom would love to babysit once in a while."

"What about Taylor? He's used to being homeschooled by Ellie."

"He could go to school in Maple Creek."

"He'd miss the ranch."

"He would, but it's not like we're moving far away. He'd still be able to come out here. I want him continue roping with Frank. I think it's good for him."

"And your mom and dad will play a bigger role in his life if we do this, which is great."

"That's true."

"But this is all speculation right now." He pulled her tight against him. "We'll know more after dad talks to Kevin."

The next morning the phone rang at a few minutes after nine o'clock. Grayson answered it.

"Good morning, Gray. I want to thank you for the weekend. We had a great time and you guys have a terrific bunch of friends. We'd like to come back."

"You're welcome anytime. Everybody liked you guys, too. I'm glad you came."

"Are mom and dad still there?"

"Yeah, they are, but they're leaving this morning. I'll let you talk to them." He passed the phone to his dad. "It's Jon."

An hour later, Lee and Ingrid were packed and ready to leave. Taylor clung to his grandfather's hand as they walked down the sidewalk to the car. Sarah and Grayson followed with Ingrid.

"I'll phone you in a few days, and let you know what I'm thinking about the clinic," Lee said, as he prepared to drive away. "Take care of that little one, Sarah. And thanks for everything, you two."

Two weeks later Lee phoned. He told Grayson he had approached a fellow veterinarian who he thought might be interested in his clinic. He and Kevin Marks were keeping in touch.

CHAPTER TWENTY ONE

Spring slipped into summer and when school was out, many of the weekends were spent at rodeos in Saskatchewan and Alberta. Sarah struggle during the hot days in July and August, feeling uncomfortable and awkward as her body expanded. She was grateful for the cooler days that came with September.

Anticipation was at a peak while everyone waited for the arrival of the baby. They knew it was a girl. Taylor was thrilled at the prospect of having a little sister, although he often said he hoped she wouldn't be as bossy as Selena.

In the early morning hours of September nineteenth, Sarah woke Grayson from his sleep. "Hon. I think it's time to go to Swift Current."

Grayson squinted, trying to get his bearings. "What...?" Then he bolted upright. "Did you say we have to go? To the hospital?"

She nodded and pointed to the small travel bag on the chair. "I'm ready. When I got up an hour ago, my membranes were leaking."

"Are you having contractions? How far apart are they?"

She smiled at his panic. "They're just starting, but I don't want to take any chances. This isn't my first baby, even if it's been years since I had Taylor."

"We'll have to tell Colt and Frank."

"I phoned them. Colt is starting the truck. He'll be here to take Taylor to their place in a moment."

Grayson was fumbling as he pulled on his jeans. "How can you be so damn calm and organized?"

"There's no need to panic. That's why we should leave now."

Colt knocked lightly and walked in. Grayson was stuffing his shirt into his pants when he appeared at the bedroom door. Colt smirked when he looked at him. He turned to Sarah. "How are you doing?"

"Okay. I'll wake Taylor. I want to let him know his baby sister is on her way and tell him I'll see him later."

Colt nodded and then picked up the packed bag. "Are you ready to go, Daddy?"

"Stop laughing at me you jerk," Grayson mumbled as he walked to the door to put his boots on.

"I promise you one thing; you'll be truly humbled after you watch that baby come into the world. It's an amazing experience. Our women put us to shame. I'd watched calves be born all my life and was pretty cavalier about it, but nothing prepared me for seeing my wife go through what she did to give birth to the twins."

Grayson nodded, and then looked past him to watch Sarah and Taylor walking down the hall. Taylor was sleepy, but excited too.

"The baby is coming!"

Grayson nodded. "She is. I'll call you as soon as she arrives."

When they walked to the truck, Grayson went to the passenger side and helped Sarah get in. When he walked around to the driver's side, Colt reached out and touched his arm. "Should I drive?"

Grayson smiled as he flipped him the middle finger."

Colt laughed and closed the door after Grayson slid behind the wheel. "Watch for deer on the road. We don't want to hear that you had to deliver that little princess at the Maple Creek hospital. They don't do that except in emergencies."

Two hours later Grayson drove into Swift Current. Sarah's head rested against his shoulder. She had slept off and on all the way, waking up to apologize for not staying awake with him, then slipping into sleep again. When he stopped on the side of the road, she sat up and looked around.

"We're here already?"

He nodded. "I didn't want to have to deliver her on the way, so I pushed it to the limit. How are you?"

"I'm fine." She sat up and stretched her back. "I've got mild discomfort, but the Braxton Hicks that I had earlier were worse."

"Well, she's due any day, so I'm glad we came now. I know Brad and Shauna Lee wanted us to stay at their place, but what do you think; should we go there or get a motel?"

"Let's get a motel. You need to sleep and it'll be more private. I don't want to set off alarms all over." She rubbed her distended belly. "This little girl might take her time coming."

"I agree with you. As far as the alarms being set off, you can be sure everyone else will know by seven this morning. Frank won't be able to contain herself any longer, and Shauna Lee will be phoning the hospital to see if we're there. Then she'll be prowling around town, looking for our truck."

Sarah chuckled. "I can see Shauna Lee and Christina getting together and hanging out in the waiting room at the hospital."

"I'll get a room now and catch some zees for a couple of hours. Then I'll phone the ranch and tell them we got a motel. We'll phone the others later and tell them that we'll let them know when things start happening."

She smiled. "Yes, we have to keep the 'family' happy."

"Speaking of family, I guess we should phone our parents and give them a heads up too."

"After we get some sleep. We've got time."

Four hours later, when they woke up, Sarah was feeling a higher level of discomfort, but nothing urgent. Grayson phoned the ranch and talked to Frank, then gave the phone to Sarah.

Taylor's voice was filled with excitement. "What's she like, mom?"

Sarah laughed. "Sweetheart, babies take their own time. It's going to be a few hours yet, maybe not even today. When she's ready, she'll come. Until then we all have to wait."

"Oh..." His voice was full of disappointment. "Frank called me to the phone, so I thought she was here."

"She just knew I wanted to talk to my son."

"Okay. Well, call as soon as she gets here." He hesitated for a second. "I love you mom."

"I love you too."

Sarah called her parents and talked to her mom. Then Grayson phoned his mom and dad. Excitement ran high and everyone was waiting with anticipation. Afterward, Sarah phoned Dr. Peale and told him what was happening.

When she turned off the phone, she smiled at Grayson and cradled her belly with her hands. "Well Daddy, the whole world is on high alert now, waiting for little Judith to make her entrance. Dr. Peale wants us to go to the hospital and get checked in, so when the action starts we're all on the same page."

"Can we have breakfast first?"

"I think so. I'm not really hungry, but I'm sure you are and this baby doesn't seem to be in any hurry."

Sarah picked at her toast and sipped a cup of coffee. Suddenly she grimaced and braced her hands against the edge of the table. She sucked in her breath, then seconds later let it ease out through pursed lips.

"Sarah, what just happened?" Grayson's eyes filled with concern. "Was that a contraction?"

She nodded. "A little harder than before, and nothing serious yet, but she's making her intentions known."

"Let's go." He stood up and helped her to her feet. He paid for breakfast, then walked her to the truck and drove to the hospital.

Sarah admitted herself at the reception area and then they went to the Women and Children's ward. When they arrived at the desk, a cheery nurse looked up.

"You must be Sarah and Grayson McNaughton. Dr. Peale phoned earlier and said to expect you. I'm Shelby Pearson." She reached out to touch Sarah's hand. "How are you doing? Doctor Peale said your membranes were leaking earlier."

Sarah nodded. "It started at around midnight. We left home shortly after one o'clock."

"Are you having contractions?"

"Mostly discomfort in my back, but it has been getting more intense."

"She had a stronger one about thirty minutes ago."

Sarah nodded. "It was, but it only lasted a few seconds."

The nurse picked up a file that was sitting on the counter. "Let's get you into a bed and check you out." She motioned for Sarah to follow her. "Dr. Peale is very thorough. I checked your file earlier. I see you have already been well briefed. She's made notes about your discussions and preferences for pain control, which is helpful to us."

Half an hour later Sarah was reclining in a hospital bed. Nurse Pearson winked at Grayson, as she pulled the curtain around the bed, shutting him out while Sarah undressed and put on a hospital gown." I know, it seems ridiculous, but its protocol."

Grayson nodded. "I understand."

Behind the curtain, she checked the position of the baby and then the dilation of the cervix. "Everything looks good. The head is down where it should be, but you've got a ways to go. You've dilated to about three centimeters right now. Your water has broken and since we're not busy in this department right now, I'll let you rest here until you're farther along." She smiled as she pulled the curtain open. "We'll let daddy in now, and I'll put the monitor on for half an hour, so we can measure the contractions, as well as baby's heartbeat and moms too."

After the monitor was removed, they walked the hallways and Grayson's company and reassurance helped pass the time. Sarah's contractions accelerated during the late afternoon. Nurse Peterson left for the day, and her replacement was Nurse Johnson.

At nine in the evening, they moved Sarah into the labor and delivery room, Nurse Johnson stayed by her side, continuously monitoring the contractions and the heartbeat of mother and baby.

Dr. Peale had checked in a couple of times during the day, offering encouragement to Sarah and Grayson. At two o'clock in the morning, he was called to the delivery room. An hour later, Sarah was cradling Judith Wasserman McNaughton against her breast. Grayson was gazing down at the two of them with complete awe.

A couple of hours later the three of them rested together in the maternity ward. Sarah caressed the baby's head, her expression one of adoration as she looked down at her. "Isn't she gorgeous?"

"She is." Grayson swallowed hard. "How can you do this? I could hardly bear watching your pain when she was coming, and now it's like you don't even remember it."

"Well, I'll be sore when the painkillers wear off, but the worst is over." She caressed the baby's tiny hand. "When I look at her now, it's almost as if it never really happened."

Grayson's heart filled with love and admiration. *Colt was right. Our women do put us to shame. Nothing prepared me for seeing her go through what she did to give birth to this precious bundle.*

A few minutes later Sarah nodded her head against the baby, as she fought sleep. Grayson stood up to lift it out of her arms. She smiled sleepily as she handed her to him. "We did it, didn't we?"

Grayson smiled as she closed her eyes. "We did, hon." He held the tiny bundle in his arms and marveled at her perfection. Her eyes moved under closed lids, as her lips made tiny sucking motions. Finally, he stood up and put her in the basket by the bed, caressing her cheek with his work-roughened finger. "Taylor will love you," he whispered softly. A soft smile curved his mouth. "Even though, you're sure to poop your diapers and puke all over."

He looked at his watch. Six o'clock. It was time to phone everyone and let them know the good news. He pushed the bell for the nurse's station and asked them to take the baby back to the nursery while he went to make his calls and get something to eat.

When he came back later, he brought a cup of coffee for Sarah.

A nurse was helping to get Judith latched onto her mother's nipple so she could suck, but the child fought her direction, her hungry little mouth searching her mother's breast for something else.

Grayson chuckled. "Stubborn like her mother eh?"

Sarah grinned. "Thanks for the coffee. I'm looking forward to it." She frowned as the nurse bunched the breast between her fingers and gently pushed the baby's mouth against it. The infant fought the pressure, but suddenly Sarah flinched when she fastened on and pulled a few swallows. Within half an hour, mother and child were worn out. Neither were totally satisfied, but some progress had been made.

The nurse fitted a pump to Sarah's breast and let it work to bring her milk in. When the second one was pumped, she left with a small amount of milk in a container.

"Does it hurt?"

Sarah wiped her nipples and applied a soft moisturizer. "I'd forgotten what this was all about, but it's coming back to me now. It's uncomfortable, but it'll be okay." She reached for her coffee.

"It'll be cold now."

"It'll be wonderful," she said as her fingers wrapped around it. She took a sip and then looked up at him. "I want to kiss daddy."

He smiled and leaned down to touch her lips.

"Did Dr. Peale come while I was gone?"

"No, she'll be here around ten o'clock. I heard someone say she was in the delivery room."

"Taylor wanted to know if we'd be home today."

"I think we might be able to go."

"I told him you were really tired, and I couldn't promise we'd make it."

"I want to go, unless Dr. Peale says we shouldn't."

"I don't want to see you get over tired. It might be better if you got a good sleep before we went home."

She stroked his cheek. "Honey, a full night of sleep is a thing of the past for the next few months. Babies don't sleep all night."

He cupped her face. "I guess I've got a lot to learn."

Christina and Tim arrived at the hospital to check out the baby. Shauna Lee and Brad were minutes behind them. Everyone exclaimed and oohed and awed about her and congratulated Sarah and Grayson.

When Dr. Peale said they could go home, Sarah was elated. Grayson felt happiness, tinged with a touch of feeling overwhelmed. He was delighted with their new baby, but he realized that life would never be quite the same.

When they reached the ranch, Ellie, Ollie, Colt, and Frank were waiting for them. Everyone vied for a chance to hold the baby, but Grayson insisted that Taylor should be first to have the honor.

Taylors's eyes were excited, but he frowned as he took her in his arms. "Why is she so little, mom? Your belly was so big."

Frank turned away to hide a smirk. Ellie bit her lip to hide her reaction. Ollie and Colt laughed outright. Grayson looked at Sarah, wanting to take his son's words back, but Sarah simply smiled. "You should have seen how big I was when I had you, Taylor. Babies need lots of protection. That's why mommies get big bellies."

Taylor studied the baby's features, and then suddenly he heard a squishy sound. He looked dismayed. "I think she pooped her pants."

Sarah smiled and reached to take the baby out of his arms. "She'll do that once in a while."

***

Two weeks later Ivan and Selma Wasserman arrived at the ranch.

Grayson and Colt had finished their morning chores and were walking up to the main house when they drove in.

Grayson stepped up to the passenger door and looked through the open window. "It's nice to see you, Selma." He looked across at Ivan. "Glad you made it alright, Ivan. Drive up to the house and I'll take you to our place."

When they stopped at the house, Ivan and Selma got out and

Grayson introduced Colt to them. Then he took them to the apartment.

Sarah met them at the door with the baby in her arms. "Mom and Dad! Come in." She hugged her mom and then her dad. "It's so good to see you. How was your trip?"

"The trip was uneventful. Roads were good. The weather was good."

"Ohhh," her mother interrupted. "Let's see this little one. Can I hold her?"

Sarah smiled as she handed the baby to her mom.

"Judith Wassermann McNaughton" she cooed as she touched the sleeping baby's face. She looked up at Sarah. "You gave her your name…your birth name."

Sarah nodded. "We both agreed that it seemed right."

Selma's eyes glistened. "We were happy when we heard that."

"I wanted to make up for some of the things I made a mess of." She caressed the baby's head. "We'll do our best to give her a good start."

"That's all you can do, Sarah. We thought we were doing that too, but we all make mistakes."

Sarah's parents stayed for three days, and then left for home. Life settled back into the normal routine for Sarah and Grayson and their family."

CHAPTER TWENTY TWO

Lee McNaughton called during the first week of November. Grayson answered the phone. "Good morning, Dad. How are you guys?"

"We're doing fine. How are you and Sarah and those two grandkids of ours?"

"Taylor's in love with his baby sister. He doesn't even have a conniption when she spits up or messes her diaper. Judi still has her schedules mixed up, so Sarah and I are short on sleep, but there's some comfort in knowing that it will work itself out in time. Sarah is a saint. She has so much patience."

"I called to tell you that I have a serious buyer for the clinic here in Elliott Lake. I think the sale will be completed by March."

"Good for you, Dad."

"I've been talking with Marks and we're working out a deal for the clinic at your end."

"Dad, are you sure you want to invest in it. You could just retire."

"Are you having second thoughts?"

"No. It would be my dream, but I have nothing to invest in it. I managed to save a bit during the past years, but I want to keep some of it as a cushion, now that I have responsibilities."

"You have your training and your youth. If you'd joined me after you got out of vet school, you wouldn't have had any money to put into it then. Consider this your inheritance."

"Dad, I can't do that. You and Mom have a lot of years to live. I don't want to risk you running short."

"Balderdash! We are looking forward to being near you and watching your family grow up. We hope to become part of your extended family too. We were impressed with them."

"They liked you guys too. But Dad what about Jon? How would he feel?"

"Don't worry about that; Jon will get his fair share. I think he might be happy for us, now that we've gotten past the other issues, and I'm excited about the move. It will open up a whole new chapter in our lives. I'll get to take my grandson fishing and hiking. Mom is thrilled about having a new baby in the family and a girl at that. You'll have to keep an eye on her, because she will spoil little Judi rotten."

Grayson chuckled. "She'll have to stand in line. She's the princess of Belanger Creek Ranch right now. Except when everyone else is getting a good night's sleep, and Sarah and I are awake, walking the floor with her. Then she seems like a little bit less of a princess and just a cranky baby."

"I'm looking at houses in Maple Creek, or possibly acreage to build on. I've talked to Marks about taking possession in July. That'll give mom and me a chance to get set up and maybe do a bit of traveling. That will allow you to stay at the ranch until after calving. Then you wouldn't be putting Colt in a bind. And Taylor will be finished school for this year by then too."

"You've thought of everything. How much is Kevin asking for the clinic?"

"He's being very reasonable. He doesn't have a big clientele and I want to install some newer equipment. There's some work to be done around the place and for the first few years we're going to have to hustle, but I'm confident we can make it work. I've got other ideas too. If Colt is interested, I think we could work out a partnership that will benefit the ranch, as well as the clinic."

"I guess I need to start looking at houses too. It's hard to make a break from the ranch, but this will make it easier. And by July, the little princess will need to be in a room of her own, so it's good timing."

"Don't get in too big a hurry. Maybe we can find acreage close to town. We could either build or if it had a newer house, you could live in it and mom and I could build an apartment on the same property. Something similar to what you have at the ranch. That would be the perfect size for us. We could share expenses on hydro installation, water, and yard work."

"Dad, I can't let you do that for me. It just doesn't sit well. I'd feel like a parasite, living off of you."

"That's just nonsense. Have you ever wondered how Jon got his start, how he opened his own firm so quickly?"

"He's a well-known architect, he makes good money."

"Architects don't usually become that successful overnight, son. Jon's got talent and he's done well, but there's more to that story. Your mother and I both received substantial inheritances from our families. We were already on our feet when that happened, so we invested the money. We've always intended to use it to help you and Jon get on your feet. When he set up his company, he received most of his share to build that fancy building in Toronto. He also used some of it to make a down payment on the condominium.

"Mom and I believed in giving it to you when you needed it, not when we died. We wanted to watch you succeed. You're not getting a free ride. Believe me, you are going to have to work, but it'll be a lot easier if you don't have to fight all the odds."

Grayson was silent; trying to digest everything he'd been told.

"Are you still there?"

"Yes. I just had no idea."

"We thought of telling you when you left Elliott Lake, but you were pretty mixed-up and we wanted you to get your feet firmly on the ground and have some idea where you were going before we put that much money in your hands. There's nothing wrong with being a ranch hand, but it would have been easy for you to let your inheritance slip away, a little at a time, in the frame of mind you were in, and we knew you had the potential to do so much more with it. Now, we know that you are settled and ready to make your way."

"Dad, would you be giving me the money now if I weren't going into business with you?"

Lee was silent.

"Dad?"

"Of course." He sounded crestfallen. "I should have been more diplomatic about this and asked you what you wanted before I just charged ahead. Do you want to take your inheritance and work on your own, Grayson?"

"No, Dad. You just caught me off guard."

"Sorry son. I'm so excited about this whole thing; I didn't think it might look as if I was just taking over and...."

"Dad, I know better than that. It's just that...suddenly the whole world looks different. It's hard to get my head around buying property and building on it. I'm kind of stunned. I mean, being broke has been the story of my life; well not really broke, but I certainly don't have enough saved to build a house. We have to get together and talk about this. Sarah will be thrilled."

"I hope so."

"She will. And Dad, I really am glad that we're going to be working together again."

Lee and Ingrid McNaughton came to the ranch for Christmas. Selma got to spoil the baby and Lee went snowmobiling with Taylor. He also spent several hours conferring with Colt, Frank and Grayson about his ideas for a bull test station at the ranch and the possibility of setting up an embryo transfer station that could be worked in conjunction with the clinic.

Lee and Grayson checked out the few houses that were for sale, as well as an acreage, but nothing really suited their needs, so they decided to keep looking throughout the coming months.

In mid-January, Colt and Frank drove to Swift Current to take the ranch tax information to *Swift Current Accounting and Bookkeeping Services*. When they came home, Colt went straight to the apartment to see Grayson.

"My banker and I have been friends since high school. Frank and I went to lunch with him today. We were discussing the idea of a bull test station here on the ranch and the embryo transfer business. I told him you were looking for a house or acreage close to Maple Creek. He said he thought he'd seen something about repossession, so he checked his phone and came up with the specs on a sixty-acre piece close to town. There's a house with a four-car garage on it, and hydro, water and sewer. The house is seven years old. They lived in it, but they never finished the inside and there is no landscaping. The paperwork is almost complete now, but if you approached the bank before it actually goes on the market, you might be able to make a deal and save yourself some money."

"Do you know where it is? Maybe we could run out and have a look at it tomorrow morning."

"He gave me a site online to check. The property is about fifteen minutes this side of town, but you can't see it from the main road."

"Let's go online and have a look. I hadn't thought of buying that big a piece of land, but it's worth checking out." An hour later, Grayson phoned his dad and told him about the acreage. They decided that Grayson and Sarah should look at it.

The next morning, after the chores were done, Colt went with them. When they found the driveway, they had to walk because the snow hadn't been plowed since the first fall. When they reached the yard, Sarah's eyes widened.

"Grayson...look at that house. We'd get lost in it."

Colt laughed. "You'll just have to fill it up with kids."

Grayson took her hand. "The attached garage makes it look bigger, but the house looks like it has lots of room too. The guy who built it aimed high."

Colt led the way, breaking trail. "We'll have to look through the windows to get an idea of what it's like inside."

There were many large windows and patio doors. Most of the furniture was gone, but they could see the kitchen and family room from different angles. They liked what they saw.

Colt looked at Grayson. "What do you think? I'd say it's worth a better look."

Sarah smiled and nodded as her eyes met Grayson's. He looked around the yard and then turned to Colt. "Let's go home and give your banker a call. We need to get inside and look around, but this has real possibilities."

Two weeks later Lee and Ingrid McNaughton flew to Swift Current. They rented a car and met with Jason Kallman to discuss the house and property. Then the two of them drove to Belanger Creek Ranch.

The next day Ingrid looked after Judi, while the others went to meet Jason at the house. When they arrived, they were happy to discover that he had arranged to have the driveway plowed so they could drive in. After they had taken a complete tour, they went back to the ranch and negotiated an agreement that Jason felt would be acceptable. Late in the afternoon, he left with the proposal and a check to secure the offer.

At the first of March, Lee closed the deal on the clinic in Eliott

Lake. A week later, their house sold. Jon and Ted came home to help them pack the few belongings they decided to take with them. The day they were leaving, Jason Kallman called to tell them the purchase of the property at Maple Creek had been approved.

Lee arranged to have the money transferred from the investment that contained Grayson's inheritance. Then he phoned Grayson and Sarah and gave them the good news.

Lee and Ingrid arrived at the ranch three days later. They stayed with Grayson and Sarah while they looked for a place to rent in Maple Creek until their apartment would be built on the acreage that fall. Colt suggested different contractors and in the end, they selected the same one he had used to build the main ranch house and the apartment at the ranch. The first priority was to finish the house so it would be ready for occupancy by July first. Then they would build the apartment and they estimated that it would take five months to complete it.

When the purchase of the clinic was complete, Lee and Grayson would start working on it. They discussed the new equipment that they planned to install, and which equipment needed replacing. The improvements would be made gradually, allowing the clinic to remain open.

The months slipped by quickly and before it seemed possible, Sarah and Grayson moved their family into their new home. Ingrid and Lee maintained their rental accommodations, but they were at the house every day, to help them settle in. Then the focus shifted to the building of the apartment and the renovations in the clinic.

Taylor spent a lot of time at the ranch, team roping with Frank and hanging out with the other kids. The new ranch hand that Colt had hired in June had a ten-year-old daughter. She and Selena became best friends quickly, and that strengthened the bond between Sam and Taylor. They practiced team roping in the corral, and by the end of the summer, they were performing very well.

Taylor enrolled in the school in Maple Creek in September. He quickly made new friends, two who came from a local ranch. The trio loved to ride horses and spent many hours together after school.

By Christmas, Lee and Ingrid were settled in their new apartment next door to Sarah and Grayson's house. It was a Christmas filled with celebrations, as a family, and with their friends from their Belanger Creek family.

CHAPTER TWENTY THREE

Two years later.
It was a warm, sunny day in June. The Thompson and McNaughton families had loaded two horses in the horse trailer and driven to Brooks, Alberta to spend the weekend at the rodeo. Sam and Taylor had been allowed to ride their horses around the grounds, mixing with some of the contestants, under the watchful eyes of their parents. Now they were getting ready to leave.

Sarah and Grayson walked hand in hand toward the truck. Judi rode on her dad's shoulders. Lee and Ingrid were a few steps ahead of them.

Grayson squeezed Sarah's hand. "How are you feeling, hon?"

Sarah caressed her belly. "Like a woman who is six months pregnant," she said with a smile. "It's been fun, but I'm ready to go home and put my feet up. And, it'll feel good to sleep in our own bed."

He let go of her hand and slid his arm around her shoulder. They walked together, absorbed in the moment.

Suddenly Ingrid turned and looked around. "Who was calling Judi?"

"I didn't hear anything." Sarah looked up at her husband. "Did you?"

"No." He turned to look behind. "Taylor and Sam are coming on the horses. Maybe Taylor called her."

Sarah looked back too, focusing on the boys. "It probably was him."

Ingrid frowned. "It didn't sound like him. He'd call her Judi, not her full name."

They walked a bit further. Then the four adults heard the voice again. This time someone was shouting, "Judith Wasserman McNaughton."

They all turned to look, just as Sam and Taylor rode alongside a heavy motorcycle that was idling along slowly behind them.

Taylor looked down at the fellow who was riding the machine. "Hey man, why are you calling my sister?"

The guy looked at him and grinned smugly. "I'm calling your mother, Taylor. I'm your dad."

Anger flushed Taylors's face. "I don't care who you are, the only real dad I have is Grayson McNaughton. And my mother's name is Sarah, not Judith."

The man's expression turned into a sneer. "She was Judith Wasserman when you were born. I've tracked you down, just like I told her I would, and now the game of cat and mouse will end." The words were a snarl.

Sarah heard his words and suddenly recognized the man on the bike. "No," she gasped. "Oh, no!" Her knees weakened for a moment and she felt faint. Then fear and anger galvanized her and she ran toward him. "You stay away from my family," she screamed.

The man on the motorcycle glared at Sarah. "You really thought you could escape me?"

Grayson slid Judi off his shoulders and shoved her toward Ingrid. "That bastard…," he bellowed as he ran after his wife. He grabbed Sarah and pushed her behind him. "Duncan Talbot." He spoke harshly, with no doubt.

The bearded, tattooed, man jumped off the motorcycle. "You got it man and you're Grayson McNaughton."

"If you're smart you'll get on that thing and ride away. You're messing with the wrong people here, Talbot."

"We'll see about that. I warned her…."

"A knife!" Sarah screamed when she seen Talbot make a quick move and a blade flash in his hand. "Grayson, he has a knife!"

Suddenly a rope snaked out and settled over the bikers shoulders, floating down over his chest. Taylor pulled it tight. "Shall I pull him down so you can hog tie him, Dad?"

"Keep that rope tight and I'll take care of him."

Taylor backed his horse up and pulled the rope tight as Duncan Talbot fought to free his arms. He yelled obscenities as he kicked at Grayson. Finally, a punch to the jaw staggered him and Grayson jumped on his back and pushed him to the ground.

Frank jumped into the fray with a pigging string that she'd snatched from one of the riders. Colt joined them, yelling that the cops were on their way, as he helped her tie Talbots feet together.

When he was certain that the man was secure, he made another call to his contact in the drug division. He told him that the Brooks police department was taking Duncan Talbot into custody and he should contact them, so they didn't let the man slip through the cracks and get away on a technicality.

A curious crowd had gathered and after the police had taken the biker away, everyone praised Taylor for saving the day. His quick thinking had been instrumental in the arrest of the man who had haunted his mother's life since his birth.

By the time the police had questioned them, took their statements, and corroborated Colt's story with the drug squad, Sarah was emotionally drained and physically exhausted. Grayson decided they would spend the night in a motel at Brooks, rather than make the long drive home.

Grayson tried to reassure her as she sobbed. "Everything will be okay now, hon. He'll be in jail for a long time."

"How can we be certain? He even knew who you were."

"Everything will be okay now," he reassured her.

***

Eighteen Months Later

It was a chilly September day. Sarah was working in the yard when a police cruiser pulled into the driveway. She gathered up Zaddie Marie and walked toward the officer when he got out of the car.

"Good afternoon. I'm looking for Sarah McNaughton."

Sarah felt her heart lurch. "I'm Sarah. Is there something wrong?"

He noticed how her face had paled. "No." He reached out to steady her. "I apologize. I didn't mean to alarm you. We received a package from the drug squad in Ontario. You knew an inmate." He stopped to reference a piece of paper that he held. "A Duncan Talbot?"

She sucked in her breath. "Has he escaped?"

He could hear the fear in her voice. "No, he hasn't escaped. He was killed in a prison brawl."

She sighed. "Thank god," she whispered.

"When they cleaned out his cell they found a package that he'd hidden. It contained pictures and a letter addressed to you. There was a knife in it too."

Sarah shrunk away from him. "I don't want to see it."

"Mam, I'm obligated to give it to you."

Sarah lifted the lid on the trashcan at the corner of the house. "Please, put it in there."

"I'll need you to sign for it," he said as he dropped the package in the container."

She slammed the lid on. "Let me sign for it and be done with this." Her hand shook as she wrote her name.

As the vehicle left the yard, she hurried inside and phoned the clinic. Zaddie squirmed in her arms, sensing her mother's tension. Sarah sat her on the floor, as she waited for Ingrid to answer. When she did, Sarah fought to keep her voice steady.

"What is Grayson doing, mom?"

"He and Lee are working in the back. It's been pretty slow here, so I was back there with them."

"Could he come home?" Now she couldn't control the tremor in her voice. "I...I need to talk to him."

"Sarah, what's wrong?"

"The police stopped by this afternoon. I just need him come home, please?"

Twenty minutes later Grayson strode into the house. His face was grave, filled with apprehension. "What's wrong, hon? Mom said the cops were here?"

"Duncan Talbot...." She ran into his arms, tears streaming down her face as she buried herself into his chest.

Grayson sucked in his breath and held her close. "Did he escape?"

"No, he's dead. He was killed in a prison brawl."

Grayson let out a sigh of relief, but Sarah still trembled as she leaned into him.

"Did the police come by to tell you that?"

She leaned back to look at him. Tears were still brimming in her eyes, but the torrent had stopped. She shook her head.

"Then why were they here this morning?"

"The officer—he brought a package for me. Apparently, they found a bundle of pictures and a letter addressed to me in his cell. He...he said there was a knife with it."

"A knife? How could he have had a knife in his cell?"

"He said everything was hidden."

"Where's the package?"

"I told him to put it in the garbage can. I didn't want to touch it."

"The one out front?"

She nodded. "Zaddie and I were cleaning up around the yard."

Grayson went out and retrieved the package. It was a white Xpress post envelope, addressed to the Maple Creek detachment.

He ripped it open and found a thin brown box. He opened the box and reached inside to take out a small package, which he laid on the counter. There were pictures of Sarah and Taylor, one of Sarah and Grayson, one of Sarah and Grayson walking downtown with Taylor and Judi, and a picture of the house where they now lived He shook his head. "That son of a bitch knew all about us. He stalked us."

Sarah's face went white. "How could we not have known?"

"And if he knew all about us, why did he decide to make a move at the rodeo when there were a lot of people around? He could have ambushed us anytime, right here."

Sarah shrugged. Suddenly her head shot up. "It was the weekend of Taylor's birthday!"

Grayson's look met hers. "You could be right."

He looked in the box again and pulled out a folded sheet of paper. He opened it and began to read silently. Then he looked up at her. "This is the letter. You should read it. It's not threatening."

Sarah hesitated, and then reached for it.

It was addressed to Judith Wassermann, aka Sarah McNaughton

You have done what few people have ever done, Judith. (I know you call yourself Sarah now, but you are still Judith as far as I'm concerned.)

I've kept you on my radar off and on for the past thirteen years, but you have been more elusive and creative than I believed possible. That damn Ryan Harahan threw a wrench in my plans. I didn't count on him being able to pull so many strings to help you. But he could and he did. After losing you in Nova Scotia, you managed to stay out of sight until you moved to Maple Creek. I could have finished the game of cat and mouse then, but I thought it was fitting to wait until the boy's birthday.

I underestimated all of you and that was my undoing. Now I'm stuck here in this hellhole. I thought about having someone else hunt you down, but having my own kid rope me, gave me a new respect for him and you. Even though I was as mad as hell when he did it, in a way, I'm proud of him. I've had a lot of time to think and I've come to realize that you haven't deserved what I've put you through. I've decided to drop this vendetta and set you and my son free. I'm sending you my broken knife, to assure you that I mean what I say.

I'll do everything I can to escape, but I know my chances aren't good. If I do manage to get out of here, I give you my word that I'll stay away. You have made a good family and your husband has accepted the child I didn't want. You have nothing to fear from me now. I wish you happiness, peace, and a long life.

Duncan Talbot

Sarah stared at the counter, her mind blank. Grayson held her for a few moments, until she relaxed. "He's dead. Now there's nothing to fear from him." Grayson reached over and picked up the broken knife. "Here's his promise. What do you want to do with it?"

"Throw it all in the garbage. Finally, we are free. We truly have a second chance."

***

Thank you for taking time to read *A Second Chance, Book Four of the Belanger Creek Ranch Series*

Few people realize how gratifying reviews are to an author and how important they are to the success of a book. Reviews are read by potential readers, who will value your opinion of a book and may decide to buy it (or not) based how on your experience with it.

Writing a review can seem intimidating, *but please do not feel that you can't do it.* Think about *how you felt* about the characters, *what you liked (or disliked) about the book,* and *how you connected with the story* when you were reading it. *Then write it down in simple words.* That is what really counts. Fancy words do not replace simple *honesty* and *enthusiasm*, which are the most compelling ingredients in a review.

Connecting with readers is a heartwarming experience, for an author. It reaffirms the value of what we spend hours doing in solitude. I would love to hear from you and learn a bit about your life.

If you enjoyed this book, I would be delighted if you could leave a review at any one of the following sites: Goodreads.com, ePrintedbooks.com, Amazon.com, Facebook, Twitter, or my website at http://www.gloriaantypowich.com

If you could post your review on several sites, I would be absolutely thrilled!

Facebook: Gloria Antypowich Author, (Please stop by and like my page!)
Twitter: @gantypowich
Website/Blog: Gloria Antypowich-Romance and Love Stories at **http://www.gloriaantypowich.com**
Email: gloria@heartsatrisk. com

I look forward to hearing from you!

Don't miss the other books in this series. For more information about them, check out my website at
http://www.gloriaantypowich.com

About The Author

Photograph by Suzanne Englund

Gloria Antypowich grew up on a farm and most of her married life has been lived on a ranch. Human relationships fascinate her. Ideas for stories can be found everywhere; overheard conversations in a public place, a couple fighting in a restaurant, a story in the news, even a chance remark in a conversation with a friend. She is enamored with the power of words and she loves to use them to paint images of characters that become so real, they feel like they could be your next door neighbor.

Gloria is an avid reader of several different genres and listens to a wide selection of music. A good game of cards, sharing a laugh with a friend over a glass of wine and spending time with her family are a few of her favorite things to do. She loves to write and says her husband was her inspiration for the heroes in this series of books. He was a cowboy, a rancher—and a lover. Gloria lives with her husband, in the central interior of British Columbia, Canada. They are retired now, but they still have "chemistry".

Made in the USA
Charleston, SC
09 October 2015